THIS IS
DOGERON KELLY TALKING:

"Why the hell couldn't they lay off me? I wasn't an unknown quantity they had to speculate about. They knew damn well what was going to happen if they pushed too far. When you make it through the hard way you aren't about to take any shit from anybody, anytime. A lot of tombstones spelled that out loud and clear."

And now Dogeron Kelly was out to cut a bunch of big bad boys down to size—the size of a six-foot hole in the ground. And on the way, he had his own ideas of what to do with the beautiful babes they threw out as bait— the kind of bait Kelly loved to gobble up.

Here is why Mickey Spillane is the greatest storyteller of our time—a novel so filled with blasting shock and nonstop action you won't be able to put it down. "There's a kind of power about Spillane that no other writer can imitate. . . . He's a master!"
—*The New York Times*

SIGNET Thrillers by Mickey Spillane

The Erection Set

by Mickey Spillane

A SIGNET BOOK from
NEW AMERICAN LIBRARY
TIMES MIRROR

SIXTH PRINTING

SIGNET TRADEMARK REG. U.S. PAT. OFF. AND FOREIGN COUNTRIES
REGISTERED TRADEMARK—MARCA REGISTRADA
HECHO EN CHICAGO, U.S.A.

SIGNET, SIGNET CLASSICS, SIGNETTE, MENTOR and PLUME BOOKS
are published by The New American Library, Inc., 1301 Avenue
of the Americas, New York, New York 10019

FIRST PRINTING, JULY, 1972

PRINTED IN THE UNITED STATES OF AMERICA

FOR SHERRI . . . whose part in this book
can hardly be denied. Elaborated on, certainly,
but a pleasure to research, peruse
and enjoy. Doll, you are magnificent!

I

By the time I had finished my two drinks at the bar, the tourist crowd that had packed the Lufthansa Flight 16 into Kennedy International had left the baggage area. The porters had parked my battered leather bag in the unclaimed area at the far end and I snaked it out from under a set of matched luggage and a pair of skis. The slalom slats looked a little out of place in June, but dedicated skiers could find snow anytime.

The lone cabbie at the curb glanced up from his paper, grinned and swung open the rear door. I flipped in my bag, handed him a ten-dollar bill through the Plexiglas partition separating us and sat down. He looked at the bill first, then me. "What's this for?"

"A slow ride in. I want to see what New York looks like now."

"How long you been away?"

"Pretty long."

"So they tore it all down and built it back up again. Nothing's new. It's still crowded."

I gave him the address I wanted. "Go the long way," I said.

And he was right. Nothing had changed. Like a farm, the ground was always there. The crops changed, the colors would be different, the stalks longer or the heads heavier, but when it was all cut down the ground line was still the same.

On the Triborough Bridge the driver waved a hand toward the skyline in an idle gesture. "Reminds me of Iwo Jima. All that fighting over a hill. Now all the guys are dead and the hill's still there. Who the hell ever wanted it anyway?"

"Maybe the people who lived there." He was thinking the same thing I was.

Outside Lee's apartment he took the meter fare and the other ten with a big smile, his eyes on mine in the rearview mirror. "Slow enough for you?"

I smiled back. "You were right. Nothing's changed."

"Y'know, you could take one of them bus tours and . . ."

"Hell, I was born here. Between then and now I've seen it all."

The driver nodded sagely and pocketed the dough. Then, slowly, and with that odd, direct curiosity only native New Yorkers seem to have, said, "Who's gonna catch all the heat, feller?"

I felt the grin twist the corner of my mouth. I had almost forgotten about the taxi psychologists. Next to bartenders they were the best. "Do I look like trouble?" I asked him.

"Shit, man," he said, "you're loaded for bear."

The doorman said Lee Shay had apartment 6D, didn't bother to announce a visitor and let me edge into the elevator with a mod couple whose offbeat clothes clashed with heavyweight jewelry in antique gold and diamonds. Lee had picked his quarters well. He still had a near-Greenwich Village outlook with an almost businesslike mind. One thing was certain. He was still having fun, so at least he had never changed.

I pushed his door buzzer, heard it hum against the stereo and high, tinkly laughter inside, then the door swung open and Lee stood there, tall and gangly, a highball in his hand, with a sudden grin that split his face from ear to ear. All he had on was a pair of red-striped jockey shorts with a *LOVE* button pinned to the side, but for him that was the uniform of the day until they posted further notice.

He said, "Dog, you dirty old son of a bitch, why the hell didn't you let me know what time you were landing?"

He yanked the bag out of my hand, gave me a hug and hauled me into the room.

"It was easier this way. Hell, we had to hold for an hour in the traffic pattern anyway."

"Damn, it's good to see you!" He half turned and shouted over his shoulder, "Hey, honey, come here, will you?"

Then the girl with the tinkly laughter came out, a big beautiful brunette who slithered over the carpet like opening the centerfold of *Risqué* magazine, and handed me a drink. She didn't have anything on except a black-satin sash

8

tied around her waist and for some screwy reason it was the only thing noticeable.

"Dog, this is Rose," he said.

"So *you're* the Dog?"

"*The* Dog?"

"From the stories I heard, I was beginning to think you were one of Lee's war stories. A myth."

"Rose is a whore," Lee laughed. "First-class and high-priced. We're friends."

I sipped at the drink. It was my usual. A good inexpensive whiskey blend and plenty of ginger ale. I looked at Rose and nodded. "Then we're friends too, kid. Am I interrupting anything?"

"Come off it, buddy. We've been waiting for you." He stepped back and took a good look at me. "Same damn disreputable Dog," he said. He glanced at Rose and shook his head. "Never did own a pressed uniform. The only reason the old man in the squadron didn't chew his ass was because he had more kills than anybody else. Besides, he never left the base anyway."

"I had more fun in the revetments with duty personnel while you were boozing it up in London," I reminded him.

Rose sidled up, took my arm to escort me into the living room, Lee behind us carrying my bag. "Like always," he said, "one lousy suitcase filled with trade goods for the natives, the only clothes the ones he wears on his back and he still needs a shave."

"I had a half-day layover in Shannon, kid. We got socked in right down the coast. Shannon was the only place open."

"So you grabbed a bottle and a broad and hit for the hills?"

"I grabbed a book and a beer and hit the lounge." I stopped at the end of the foyer and let my eyes sweep around his apartment. It was a wild place, this; big, bachelorized, with all the junk professional seducers could ask for and ready for takeoff at the first scramble horn. "Nice," I said. "Why the hell didn't you ever get married?"

Rose squeezed my arm and let out that laugh again. "Kids never get married. They just want to play."

"A pretty expensive playground." I looked at Lee. "What are you up to now?"

He picked an ice cube out of his drink and popped it into his mouth. "I'm an arranger, old buddy." He caught my frown and grinned even bigger. "Not *that* kind, you nut. I dumped advertising and busted into show biz. What I arrange is hard-to-get properties or people for the theatrical trade. It pays for the playground."

"Who pays for the playmates?"

Lee reached out and tugged the black satin cord at Rose's waist and it came loose in his fingers. Somehow it was like undraping a nude. Suddenly she was *really* naked and the effect was startling. I shook my head and took a sip of my drink.

"Friends are for fun," he said.

Rose tipped her head and her hair swirled down around her shoulders. "Dog," she said, "you should be staring. You're not. Why?"

"I wouldn't want to embarrass myself so early in our meeting. You won't be forgotten so easily, so don't worry." She finished her drink and put the empty glass down on the table. "Why don't I leave you two retreads to get your old-timer talk out of the way and when you both sober up I'll get another girl and we can plow this city up a little."

I said, "Look, Lee . . ."

But he stopped me right there with a wave of his hand and gave a handful of her hair an affectionate tug. "You get to be more of a woman every day, sugar. She's right, Dog. We got a lot of time to make up for in a hurry." He gave her fanny a tender pat. "Better not go out looking like that." He handed her the satin cord and she knotted it around her wrist. "That's more like it," Lee told her.

I shook my head and laughed. I thought a scene like this had died with the war. We both watched her deliberate burlesque-stage walk toward the bedroom with sheer appreciation, fascinated by the way the muscles of her thighs and back rippled in the light. At the door she turned and looked over her shoulder. "Dog," she said, "what's your right name?"

"Dogeron. It's an old Irish name."

"I like Dog better. Do you bite?"

"Only in the heat of passion," I said.

REFLECTIONS
ROSE PORTER, SINGLE, AGE 28.

Three years in whoredom and no married woman can match my knowledge. Except the answer to why to have a man. One push from a forty-five-year-old fat grocer and my virginity became history with two boxes of Shredded Wheat and a candy bar for silence.

Linebacker for Bailey High thinks he's a rape artist specializing in virgins and, because I was tight, figures up another notch on his scorecard. For a while, I was real popular with the team. Maybe I should have looked in the mirror. I was one of the lucky ones. No acne, big tits and sour-apple fresh with a pussy aching to be filled.

Hal said I was a bitch in heat . . . but he was a crazy, comic-book artist and the first tender man I had met. Wild, but soft and sweet and tender. He liked to kiss before screwing and laughed when the excitement got me wet. Some nights he didn't even bother screwing. He laughed and kissed and . . . then one night he told me how very much he loved me, but he had leukemia and wanted to die somewhere on the slopes of the Florida Keys. He gave me twelve thousand dollars in treasury bonds, told me to take the pill, not get the clap and to have fun.

I bought a college education and became a whore. No man could fool me, trap me or fake me out. That's what I thought. Two years ago I lost count of all the lays. Anyway, all johns look alike. No scars, either. A few bite marks, maybe, but no scars, no needles and I'm top cat in the trade. The blow-job pro, that's me. Anal intercourse? A pleasure, mister. Simple screwing? Must be an odd nut to pay for the unfancy.

But they all respond. They dig the long hair, the smooth, long legs.

Oh, they love it, all right, all but this big slob of a Dog. He looks at me naked and says hello. He appreciates, nods his approval, shakes my hand and couldn't care less. Shekky Monroe gave me five hundred just to run his fingers across my snatch one night. This dirty Dog says hello and smiles.

That's the bad part. He really smiled. The bastard is for real. They're all going to take him wrong and somebody will hurt.

Me, I'm lucky. I can't be hurt anymore. Now I'm curious. Especially about that smile. The louse knew me inside and out like he knew everybody else.

Okay, Dog, now let me read you. Clothes good, but old. Perhaps fifty bucks in your jeans. I made more between cocktails and dinner last night. I had felt his arm and it scared me a little bit because I knew about how old he was and the arm was a little too big and too hard. Poseur? Some do it. A cheap barber had chopped his hair, but it was all there and would be grown back in another week. Gray spotted it and a little white streak tufted up in front. He looked heavy, but there was no fat and he walked funny, one hand always hanging loose, and whatever those green eyes looked at, they saw and understood.

I wanted to screw him, only it wouldn't be any use trying. Tomcats pick their own time and place.

11

Time. The clock said three minutes after five. I had known the Dog exactly eight minutes.

The empty Pabst beer cans made odd splotches of color around the room, their big blue ribbon seals decorating every piece of furniture in the bedroom, including two that I had balanced delicately on the headboard of the bed directly over my face. A couple of soggy towels lay on the floor, sopping up the beer that Lee had spilled and I lay there listening to him sound off just like he used to. Only in those days he didn't wear a LOVE button on his shorts.

"Just quit being a silly bastard," he said. "And don't tell me staying here is an imposition. Shit, man, why spend loot on a hotel room? You can't even *find* a decent apartment in this town anymore unless you're loaded with cash or have a couple months to poke around in."

I popped open another beer. "Can it, Lee. You lover types need privacy."

"Balls. I got two bedrooms right now. If it gets crowded, so we have an audience. I lost all my modesty twenty years ago."

"Look . . ."

"Forget it," Lee said. "You're staying here. We shared everything during the war, we do it again. Besides, you're going to need more than a pad, buddy. I'm damn glad we're both the same size. I got three closets full of clothes and we're both about the same height. You take your pick of the rack, I'll get them let out a little in the chest and shoulders and you can look like nowadays."

I went to say something and he shut me up again. "I get them wholesale, Dog. I do big favors for a guy who heads up a chain and he pays off in threads. What the hell do I need? I change twice a day and it would take me a month to repeat a suit. Nice, hey? I'm not rich, I'm not poor, I get along pretty well and, by damn, you're my buddy and you're going to share it with me. I'll give you a week to get stretched out, find your way around, then we'll hunt up something with scratch behind it so you can get on your feet."

The beer stopped halfway to my mouth. "Lee . . ."

"Don't crap me out, Dog. I got plenty of contacts and it won't be all that hard. Who has to know you stuck yourself in Europe all this time because a bunch of half-assed relatives kicked you out? Man, you have too much false pride. You were a fucking war hero, man. You could have shoved

12

it up their tails. Why the hell did you try to bury yourself for?"

I tried to answer him, but he wouldn't let me.

"Oh, sure, there's always a dame. But you're still not married, are you?" I shook my head. "See, so you blew it, you didn't even nail a broad. You still look like you always did, a raggedy-tail flyboy who'd sooner scream around the wild blue yonder than screw a dame."

"I got my share."

"You could have gotten more."

"I was too busy flying," I said.

"And you came up with zilch. Plenty of kills, lots of ribbons and you weren't even smart enough to get bullet creased a little so you could get a partial pension. No, you have to come home anyway." He yanked a cold beer out of the bucket of ice water and looked at me with funny Pabst-colored eyes. "Why did you come back?"

"The old man died and left me an inheritance. I've been trying to tell you."

He paused, his finger hooked into the circle of the pop top. "Old Cameron Barrin?"

I nodded. "My maternal grandfather. I guess he figured he owed me something, my being a sort of blood relation. If I can establish myself as having a good, clean . . . or, let's say, totally pure . . . moral record since leaving his household, I can claim the munificent reward of ten thousand dollars."

"Cash?"

"Uh-huh."

Lee finished opening the can and let a grin twitch at the corners of his mouth. "How much chance have you got?"

"Not a smidgen," I told him.

"Then why come back?"

"Hell, maybe I can lie a little," I said.

For a good ten seconds, he looked at me, then took a long pull of the beer and shook his head. "Damn, it's the same old Dog. Still as naïve as they come. You never did learn, did you? Ten grand and you come all the way back for something that can be eaten up in a matter of months. Buddy, the world has changed. The war's over. This isn't Europe. The old days are gone. If we were kids all we might ask for is a bike, sleeping bag and an occasional remittance from home to buy some pot or a little snatch and maybe a side trip into a little bistro on the Left Bank for some gourmet spaghetti, but we're big kids now and we can't go that route."

I shrugged and drank my beer.

"Brother," Lee said. "Am I glad you checked in with me. I guess I got a father image. I got to take care of you, Doggie boy."

My teeth showed in a grin when I looked at him.

Lee grinned back and nodded. "Sure, I remember you pulling those ME109s off my tail. I got a good picture of you squiring me through the skies like a Dutch uncle and keeping my ass intact. You got one lousy year on me, nursed me through the whole damn war and made sure I came out with all my skin and now it's my turn. I play big daddy. From here on in until you're on your own two pedals again I'm *going* to be big daddy and take care of *you*." He finished the beer off in a single long pull. "You are now my responsibility and the first thing I'm going to do is dump your past into the incinerator, dress you like a living New Yorker and put you back into the world again."

He flipped the empty can against the wall, yanked a dressing robe from a hook behind the door and wrapped it around him. With a faked gesture of distaste he picked up the battered suitcase with all the pasted-on stickers that were loose around the edges and said, "Anything in here of sentimental value?"

I took another taste of the beer. It was cold, refreshing and lighter than all that other stuff. "A few things," I said. "You can tell which ones."

Lee tossed the old bag on the bed, undid the straps, fingered the clasps open and threw the lid back. His expression was very funny. He took his two forefingers and poked around in there and didn't quite know what to say.

It wasn't often that a guy saw a couple of million bucks in ten-thousand-dollar bills.

He looked up. "No underwear?"

"No underwear," I said.

14

II

The law offices of Leyland Ross Hunter occupied an entire floor of the Empire State Building, a private world hundreds of feet above the concrete and asphalt surface of the city, existing in the almost-stunned hush of a library where even the whisper of feet shrouded in thick pile carpets was a minor commotion. Supposedly silent typewriters were touched with timid apprehension as though the operators were waiting to be castigated for every tiny click. It should have smelled of old leather and old people, but modern air conditioning and artificial atmosphere gave it the lewd tang of incense inhaled.

Behind the antique desk the maiden secretary peered at me over her gold-rimmed, flat-plate glasses, thought she bought me with an invisible peripheral glance and said, "Yes, Mr. Kelly, do you have an appointment?"

I said, "No, ma'am."

"You'll really have to call for an appointment."

"Why?"

Her smile was very condescending. "Mr. Kelly, please, Mr. Hunter is . . ."

"A very busy man," I interrupted.

"Quite."

"What do you bet he sees me?" I lit a cigarette and grinned a little bit.

The vox populi had to be kept in its place. She took off the glasses with a ladylike gesture and smiled back indulgently. "Mr. Kelly . . ."

"When I was ten I took a picture of him skinny-dipping with Miss Erticia Dubro, who, at that time, was common nanny to our clan." I took another drag on the butt and

15

blew the smoke over her head. "Miss Dubro was forty-some and fat and was the first broad I had ever seen with hair on her chest. I think old Hunter had a thing for hairy-chested ladies because he let me drive his car that weekend around the estate in exchange for the film."

"Mr. Kelly!"

"Just tell him Dog is here and mention Miss Dubro. Please?"

She was funny. The indignation was real, but so was the curiosity, and with me standing there speaking too quietly to be anything but real too, she flushed, turned a pair of toggle switches off on her intercom and sniffed up out of her chair into the office behind her.

And when I heard the high cackle of laughter come through the locked doors I was ready for her red face and wide eyes, with that total expression of disbelief that comes from living too long in a commercial nunnery.

"Mr. Hunter will see you now," she said.

I stuffed the butt out in her paper clip bowl and nodded. "I figured he would."

"Twenty years," the old man said.

"Thirty." I sat down. "You were a horny old bastard even then."

"I wish you worked for me so I could fire you."

"Balls."

"You're right. I'd give you a raise for reminding me I used to be a real he-goat. Now word'll go around I'm an old roué and maybe some of those young squirts will give me a little respect. Good to see you, Dog."

"Same here, old man."

"You got a copy of that picture of me and Dubro?"

"Hell no. You got the film before I even developed it."

"Shit, I wish I had a copy. I'd have it enlarged and hung over the front entrance. I could use a taste of those days."

"Don't tell me you had your prostitute gland removed."

"Only massaged, Dog. That's not even fun when a doctor does it."

"Why not try a lady doctor?"

"Who the hell you think I went to?" He sat back and roared, a wizened old guy with a face like a shaved pixie in a leprechaun body. You could see why he could still make it in a courtroom against the young ones and when the chips were down you'd have to guess where he got the single cauliflower ear that looked so ridiculous stuck there on the side of his head.

"I should have gotten that film developed," he said.

16

"Look, if it worries you, I'll set you up for another one. I know some dolls . . ."

"Ah, me. It sounds so good, but let me live with my memories. I'm too old to be embittered or flattered. It's just nice to be reminded." He handed me a silver and walnut humidor. "Cigar?"

I shook my head.

"You got my letter, naturally. I had a dickens of a time locating you."

"No sweat. I jump around a lot."

For a few seconds he looked at me, then sat back and folded his arms across his chest. "There's something peculiar about you, Dog."

"I'm older."

"Not that."

"Wiser?"

"Don't we all get that way?"

This time it was my turn to wait. "Not everybody."

His smile was impish, his eyes twinkling. "Too bad the old man didn't like you."

"Why should he? All he wanted was a legitimate heir. My mother got knocked up by an itinerant bartender and I was locked in under the bar sinister to preserve family pride."

"Did you ever know your mother married your father?"

"Sure. I still got a copy of the wedding certificate. She made sure I knew about it."

"Why didn't she mention it?"

"Maybe she had her pride too."

Leyland Hunter unlocked his arms and leaned on the desk. "If the old man had known, things would have been different."

I tapped another cigarette out of the pack and lit it. "Who gives a damn? All I want is my ten grand. It was standard practice in the family ever since they had slaves and servant girls. They buy you off, kick you out and the foul deed is forgotten."

"Speculate further," Hunter said.

"Why not? If the perpetuator was a male, it was laughed off as a boyish prank. If the recipient of the seed was a female claimant to the family name, she was buried under the cloak of shame."

"You should have been a lawyer."

I grinned at him again. "Let's say I'm a philosopher."

"No hard feelings?"

"What for?"

"All the others take ownership of Barrin Industries.

17

Cousins Alfred and Dennison are president and chairman of the board, respectively, Veda, Pam and Lucella own a majority of the stock, your uncles and aunts sit back and direct operations from the big houses at Mondo Beach and Grand Sita, arranging debutante balls and marriages that highlight all the celebrity columns."

"Sounds pretty dull."

"And now you're back."

"I promise not to spoil their fun. All I want is my ten grand."

"The will was very specific. If there's one hint of immorality in your past . . ."

"I killed a few people, remember."

"That was wartime. You were decorated for it."

"So I've had a few dames in the hay too."

"Even that was anticipated. Boys are prone to experiment."

"I'm not a boy."

"Exactly."

"Then get to the point."

"Is there any possibility that any, er, woman, could ever substantiate that you and she . . . er, had . . . let's say, an illicit relationship?"

"Now I know *you're* a lawyer."

"You didn't answer the question."

I sucked in on the butt and leaned back, grinning. "Old friend, I'm not exactly abnormal. I've had me broads and I'm damn glad to admit it. In fact, I'm damn glad to hear *them* admit it. I come with a pretty good set of references."

The laugh lines creased his face and he snuggled back in his chair again. "Dog, you're still a puppy. Talk like that and you'll wipe out that inheritance sure as hell. Why can't you fib a little?"

"I'm not an expert at it like the family is. I always get caught. Hell, even when I told the truth I got nailed for lying, so where's the percentage? All I want is my ten grand."

On the wall, the old-fashioned windup clock ticked ominously. I looked at the family solicitor sitting there, knowing he was feeling for words he didn't want to say, and just waited. It was an old story; I just wanted to hear it again to make sure nothing had changed.

Finally: "Nobody even wants to let you have that."

"A small price to pay out of all those millions. Why rattle skeletons in the closet?"

"You ever read stock market reports, Dog?"

I shrugged again. "Sometimes. They fluctuate. I hate to gamble."

"Barrin Industries is shaky."

"Ten thousand bucks can break them?"

"Not exactly. The old man's will had to conform to his father's will and if you have a copy of your mother's original wedding certificate you can take over as the first male heir."

"It's only a photographic copy made a long time ago. I guess you know the courthouse it was filed in burned down and the preacher and the witnesses are dead?"

"Yes, I know that. How did you find out?"

"I wanted to make sure." I squeezed out the hot tip of the cigarette and dropped it in the ashtray on the desk. "No ten grand, then, I suppose?"

"No nothing, Dog. I'm sorry."

I stood up and stretched. Outside it was a nice day and despite the smog I was going to enjoy myself. "Want to bet?" I asked him.

"Not with you," he said. "Of all the family, you got your grandfather's mouth, his hair, even the way he held his jaw."

"Look at my eyes," I said. "Whose are they?"

"I don't know, Dog. They aren't your mother's."

"They were my dad's. That guy must have been a terror. Let's go have a beer. You probably haven't been in a saloon for ten years."

"Make it fifteen and I'll go with you," Hunter told me.

She said her name was Charmaine, but only a Polack knows how to smell a kielbasa to make sure it's real and slip it inside a hunk of doughbread she whipped up out of natural ingredients from a delicatessen at one o'clock in the morning, and when she came out of the bedroom wrapped in a bath towel, all peasant legs and cow-busted with a lovely people grin showing through teeth that tore the sandwich apart, I laughed and turned the Beethoven down on the record player and poured the rest of my beer in the glass.

"That old man's pretty hot stuff," Charmaine told me.

"Big?"

"Nope, just talented. Kind of like surprised me." She tore the sandwich in half and paused a moment. "Hey, Dog, he ain't . . ."

"No relation," I said. "It would be a hell of a thing for a kid to buy his old man a piece, wouldn't it?"

"Guess so. Didn't they used to do it the other way around?"

19

"That's what I heard. They gave him a year to get some hair around his gizmo and the kid got treated to a whorehouse job on his birthday. Poor slob, he probably sweated, couldn't get it up, tipped the dame a bundle to lie to his old man and went home bragging about the experience."

"You do it that way?" she asked me.

"Sugar, I was an old pro by the time I was twenty."

"How about twelve?"

"I was an old amateur," I said. "Hunter treat you kindly?"

"A dream. I think maybe I'll specialize in old men." She bit into the sandwich and sat down opposite me, the towel falling open before she rearranged it. Then she leaned back and propped her feet on the glass-topped coffee table.

"Will you cross your legs or something," I said.

"Uh-huh." She finished the sandwich and licked her fingers. "Do I embarrass you?"

"No, but you get me horny and I'm tired."

"You got Marcia all pooped out. You like my roommate?"

"Good kid."

"A crazy kook. She was an acid head until I straightened her out. Always giving it away. Now she meets the right people. She thinks you're out of sight. What'd you do to her?"

"She needed loving. Incidentally, I'm sending her to an old buddy of mine tomorrow. She's going to get a job."

"She told me. One-fifty a week taking dictation. What a way to ruin a good hooker."

"Sorry about that."

"I'm not. She graduated from Pembroke, y'know. Me, I barely made Erasmus High in Brooklyn. I wish somebody had done that for me."

"Come on, Charmaine, you like it this way."

"Only because I'm a nympho. I only know two other girls who really get their rocks off when they're making it for pay with a guy. Maybe I'm the total professional. How'd you ever find me anyway?"

"Joe Allen in Belgium. Remember?"

"Ho, old Joe. He wanted me to get tattooed." She smiled at me and looked for more crumbs on her palm to lick. "He told me about you too. I didn't believe it." Her eyes flicked toward the other closed door. "Marcia says old Joe was not lying, repeat, not lying."

"I try harder," I said.

"That's what Marcia says. Why ring the old man in too?"

"Just to make sure he doesn't have to lie when he kills me."

"That's about that ten grand, isn't it?"

"Even great lawyers will tell a prostie anything, won't they?"

"Look at Mata Hari," she said.

"And look what happened to her. She got banged the real hard way."

"You guys are nuts," Charmaine said.

"All nuts," I repeated.

"Balls," she laughed.

"That's what I said."

We sat in the Chock Full o' Nuts mopping up the plate of eggs with crisp toast, two guys watching the early shift of New York go to work before seven in the morning. Leyland Hunter's cauliflower ear was redder than the day he got it and his suit was a mess, but there was a James Cagney twitch in his shoulders that was a suppressed laugh at himself and me at the same time.

"You're dead now, Dog. You proved your point," he said.

"I just wanted you to be sure."

He tucked the last piece of toast in his mouth and sat back, happy and satisfied. "I never thought an old fart like me could get laid anymore."

"When was the last time?"

"I forget."

"Charmaine thought you were pretty damn good."

"Lovely of her. She'll never be forgotten. Ah, the feel of silky flesh unmarred by wrinkles is something to be remembered. What annoys me is that I never thought of the alternative. Never again will I be so devoted to my work. By the way, I understand you footed the bill. What do I owe you?"

"My treat. I always felt guilty about spying on you and old Dubro." I laughed again. "How did you make out in the end?"

"A brush-off. I understand she married the gardener a year later. In those days a skinny-dip was a real orgy."

"Man, have you got a lot to learn."

"Unfortunately, no. I'll get all my kicks from pornography collected during the censorship trials or wait for those rare, exotic visits from distant friends. Now let's get back to you. I'm not quite stupid, you know."

"I didn't want *you* to have to lie, friend."

21

"There are some lengths you don't have to go to."

"Why not?" I asked him.

"Because I could have told. You're not the same Dog they used to kick around."

I finished my coffee and picked up the bill. "Isn't it going to be a ball when everybody finds that out?" I said.

This time Leyland Hunter wasn't smiling. With a studied, serious look, he scanned my face and nodded solemnly. "I'm going to be afraid to look," he said. "Do you hold still for advice these days?"

"Depends on the source. From you, yes. What pearls of wisdom have you got for me?"

Hunter took out a gold ball-point pen and fiddled idly with the calibrated rings that made it a slide rule. "Remember, Dog, I've been close to the Barrin family all my life. It was your great-grandfather that made sure my education was attended to and who established a business for me. All that because he and my father were friends, old prospecting buddies, and my father was killed before he ever saw me. Like it or not, I have a moral obligation to be of service."

"You paid off any debt a long time ago, Counselor. It was your business acumen that saved the Barrin corporation during the Depression, your foresight that built them into millionaire war profiteers and your ingenuity that kept them rolling ever since."

His fingers kept working at the dials, arranging them into precise figures. "That was while your grandfather was alive and active. Unfortunately, the generation gap isn't a new thing at all. When Cameron Barrin began to decline, the family was quick to introduce a new regime . . . their own. I was one of the old guard and my opinions were merely tolerated, not accepted."

"Then why sweat it, mighty Hunter? You've made it big on your own. Today you're handling conglomerates that make Barrin Industries look like a toy. Oh, a damn big toy, but that's all."

"I told you," he said. "I feel the obligation."

"Good for you, but I'm still waiting for the advice." I signaled the waitress for some more coffee. It looked like it was going to be a long lecture.

"Remember when your cousin Alfred had that accident with his new roadster?"

I let the sugar lumps drop in my coffee with soft plops. Somehow they had the faraway sounds of bones breaking. I said, "There was no accident. The little bastard ran me down deliberately. He got a roadster and I got a used bi-

22

cycle. He went off the road to get me and if I hadn't jumped for it there would have been more than a broken leg."

"He said he lost control in the gravel drive."

"Balls. You know better." I stirred the coffee and tasted it. Now it was too sweet. "Funny, but I was more pissed off about my first bike being wrecked than getting the leg busted."

"Remember what you did to Alfred when you got out of the hospital?"

My mouth was working to suppress a laugh. I had swiped a short-fused aerial bomb from the July Fourth fireworks display in town and rigged it under his car. It blew right through the seat of Alfred's roadster and they picked stardust out of his ass for a month. "How did you know about that?"

"Being of a legal, inquisitive mind, I surmised it, then made inquiries until I located a few witnesses. Tying in a boy with missing pyrotechnics wasn't too difficult."

"You could have burned my hide, buddy."

"Why?" His eyes twinkled. "Frankly, I thought Alfred deserved it and it was an original form of revenge. I don't think he ever molested you again, did he?"

"Not physically. There were other ways."

"Except they never really bothered you."

"What I didn't have, he couldn't steal. Alf had more to lose than I did."

"That brings us up to Dennison."

"He's a prick," I grinned. "I suppose you're referring to the time that little town twist said she was knocked up and the old man paid off for an abortion?"

Hunter nodded and waited.

"She was an uninvited guest at the picnic. We were all playing in the same area out of sight. I never touched the dame. It was Dennie who took her into the bushes, but he blamed me for it and paid her a hundred bucks to point the finger my way."

"I understand you were rather severely reprimanded, weren't you?"

The laugh came out and I nodded. "With a stick. I was in bed for a week, all privileges revoked and before I was on my feet they had even disposed of the dog I had adopted." I laughed again and sipped at my coffee.

Leyland Hunter frowned again, watching me curiously. "Was it all that funny?"

"In a way," I told him. "Now it seems even funnier. You see, I was the only one who ever really knew the kid, being

23

the only one who ever managed to slip out into town. She was a smart little slob, a whore at fifteen who used to make it on pay nights with the factory crowd. She was no more knocked up than you were, but she saw money in the deal and pulled the act on Dennie. It scared him shitless, especially since it was his first piece. The old lady everybody thought was her mother actually was Lucy Longstreet who ran a sleazy bordello on Third Street."

"I still don't see the humor in it, Dog."

"Ah," I said. "It's there. Dennie boy got the damndest dose of gonorrhea you ever saw. I used to enjoy watching him hang from the overhead pipes in the garage toilet and scream while he tried to piss. His treatment was a closely guarded family secret. I used to take great pleasure in hiding his medication."

Hunter's slow smile turned into a silent guffaw. "You know, I wondered what that was all about. There were some dealings with the public health service when the doctor turned in his report. It took some doing to keep it quiet. Small Connecticut towns can make a big to-do about the scion of its leading family getting a dose from a local wench. I don't suppose there was any attempt to mollify your indignity at having been made a patsy?"

"You're slipping, Counselor. That's when the old man made me a present of a new car and told me I could pick my own college. That trust fund didn't come from the goodness of his heart."

He picked up his coffee cup and held it in front of his mouth. Over the rim his eyes were birdlike, with a strange intensity. "I think maybe it did, now that I know the whole story. Your grandfather had his own peculiar code. You were the sucker, you could have blown the whistle on his scurrilous nephew and made the family a laughingstock and have been justified in doing so. On your own volition you chose not to. That was when he began to like you. I think it was a great misfortune that you saw little of him from that time on. Does anyone else know about this?"

"Sure. My mother before she died. She thought it was kind of funny. And there was the gardener your skinny-dipping Dubro finally married. You see, he knew me better. The real funny part was that at that time when Dennie was ripping off his first piece, I had been through a dozen women. I was far from a virgin. There wasn't even a chance of me hitting that little twist because I knew damn well she had the clap. All I did was stand back, take my lumps and wait for the pee pains to hit Dennie. It was worth the wait."

I waited while Leyland Hunter finished his coffee and

24

set the cup down. Finally he said, "Then I take it that going back is not a personal vendetta?"

"All I want is my ten grand," I told him. "That is, if I can get past the morals clause."

"By your own admission, an impossibility."

"Yeah, but if there's one for me, there must be one for the others too, isn't there?"

"An astute observation. However, their lives have always been under careful and constant scrutiny. They have a proven, up-to-date record that will stand the cold light of investigation."

I laid a five-dollar bill down on top of the check and stood up. "Hunter, my friend, you are old enough to be my grandfather, but there are still some things you have to learn. Everybody's got something to hide."

"Even you, Dog?"

"When I bury my bone," I said, "I bury it deep."

"Nobody can dig it up?"

"They have to fight me first."

"All this for ten thousand dollars?"

I shrugged and lit a butt.

We walked across town and back to Hunter's office in the tower on Thirty-fourth Street. From the elevator starter to the receptionist on his floor, we got the same looks, some bemused, some incredulous. Leyland Hunter never wore the same suit twice in any month, and here he was showing up disheveled and happy along with another randy mutt and there wasn't any doubt about where we had been or what we had done. The maiden lady behind her desk whipped off her glasses, dropped them in her confusion, tried to hide her embarrassment in a stuttering "good morning" and when we were inside the old man said in a low growl, "She don't know it, but what I got is just what she needs."

"Hell, friend, I didn't mean to turn you into a lecher type."

"You didn't. I'm beginning to think I always was. I just never had time to perfect the art."

"Never too late," I said.

His eyes twinkled as he eased into his big chair behind the desk. "Well spoken, Dog. Now I'll quit giving to those damn high-handed charities and put my excess money into hands that can truly justify their existence. Incidentally . . . what was her name?"

"Charmaine."

"Lovely creature. Would I need your, er—endorsement for another engagement?"

25

I grinned at him and he grinned back. "Now, what's on your mind, Counselor?"

Leyland Hunter leaned back in his chair, tugged his tie open a little bit farther and let the air of his profession seep back into his face. "Do you know how often I tried to locate you, Dog?"

"Nope."

"At least every year," he said.

"Why bother?"

"Because certain business matters were entrusted to me and I intend to fulfill my obligations. You didn't make it easy for me at all. You took your Army discharge in Europe and promptly dropped out of sight. I went to every extent possible to find you, ran down every lead, none of which ever panned out, and frankly, Dog, I was beginning to believe you were dead. It wouldn't have been unusual at all. Army Intelligence, Interpol and the police departments of every country had all too many cases of ex-soldiers heavy with discharge pay suddenly being found dead or not found at all."

"I had no trouble."

"Why, Dog?"

"Counselor," I said, "there was nothing for me back here except aggravation. I was twenty when I left and twenty-four when I got out. I wanted to see things and do things without the entire Barrin family breathing down my neck. And don't tell me they weren't happy about my decision. I was their skeleton in the closet, but I rattled a little too loudly when I was home and they didn't like to be reminded of my mother's indiscretion that brought everlasting shame upon the great family standards. The entire clan was a pain in the ass and I was glad to be rid of them. When my mother died there were no ties left, so this Dog snapped his leash." I stopped and tapped another cigarette from my pack and lit it. "Funny, but I sort of miss the old gent. Gramps was just at the age where I could get him all shook up with my oddball behavior. I used to play games with him and he took the bait every time."

"Maybe you weren't really fooling him," Leyland said. "He was pretty cagey."

"Ever hear him fart he got so mad?" I let out a little laugh, remembering. "The day I beat hell out of that snotty Webster kid and his old man wouldn't sell the acreage Gramps wanted on the south side of Mondo Beach, the old boy almost blew the seat out of his pants yelling at me."

"I know." Leyland smiled. "And you told him to go to hell and joined the Air Force the next day."

26

"I was going to anyway. I had my two years of college and wanted to fly."

"You made quite a record. Old Cameron was rather proud of you."

"Balls," I said.

"True, however. It was something he only mentioned to me. In a way you reminded him of his own youth. Your main fault was never aspiring to greatness. You know how he was about wanting a direct male heir."

"Come off it, Hunter buddy. As far as he was concerned I was a plain old bastard in the true sense. Even when my mother married my father, it was too late to lift the stigma. At least his brother's one kid left enough progeny around before he kicked off so he had plenty of blood relatives to leave his money to. Barrin Industries fell into well-trained hands. My ten-grand inheritance was only a token gesture, but I want it."

"Oh, it's there all right. Cameron's instructions were to deliver to you stocks whose total worth was ten thousand dollars within a certain period after I contacted you. Provided you met the requirements, of course. Had you returned home in forty-six, you would have received five thousand shares. They had quite a market value in those days. However, the situation has changed. Wall Street is wallowing in an all-time low. Ten thousands dollars now represents twenty thousand shares. The remaining five will be split equally between Alfred and Dennison. It was a rather strange provision in Cameron's will and he certainly didn't foresee the drop in the economy or the current inflation. The only reason he held back those shares of stock from Alfred and Dennison was to let them mature further before handling a greater interest in the business."

"But it's still only ten grand," I said.

"There's a little more."

"Oh?"

Hunter spun around in his chair, pulled a file drawer open and extracted a stiff yellow folder. He handed the contents across the desk to me. "Nothing much, but part of my obligation. Your grandfather once purchased a large tract of land in New Mexico, speculating that a government irrigation project would be instituted in the area. The bill never passed Congress and the land is still there . . . beautiful, rocky and arid. It's a snake collector's paradise and tourists take pictures of it. He left it to your mother and now it's yours." He tapped the paper in front of me and handed me a pen. "If you can find a sucker you might get him to take it off your hands at a quarter an acre. That

27

would net you an even thousand dollars. At least it's something. Taxes are negligible and paid to date."

I scratched my name on the papers and shoved them back to him. "Thanks a lot," I said. "Now how about my ten grand?"

"You just signed a notification of availability for it. Delivery *may* take place to you, Alfred and Dennison simultaneously at a formal meeting at Grand Sita, your former palatial residence. Let's say day after tomorrow?"

I scowled in disgust. "Do I have to?"

Leyland nodded. "I'm afraid so. Besides, think of the reunion you'll have."

"Like meeting a pack of cobras," I said.

A ghost of a smile crossed the old man's face, but I didn't catch what he said. I asked, "What?"

He shook his head and smiled. "The day after tomorrow. We'll leave from here. Four P.M."

REFLECTIONS: LEYLAND HUNTER

"Like meeting a pack of cobras," Dog had said, and didn't hear me when I answered, "But who's the mongoose?"

Dogeron Kelly, the kid they could never figure out or pin down. He didn't give a damn for anything then and he sure doesn't now. Anybody else would take him for just another big guy who had been around the world and had seen and done as he damn well pleased, a guy who wasn't anything and didn't want anything.

But me, I'm old in the trade. Too damn many courtrooms. Too damn many times looking through wire screens at clients and watching their minds work. There are types and types, but they all fall either on one side of the fence or the other. Dogeron Kelly was walking around behind a disguise. He was a predator in camouflage, always stalking, but so much at home in whatever world he lived in he was completely at ease.

Idly, I wondered how many men he had killed. The ones he didn't get medals for killing. Once Interpol had queried me about a possible identification of a man whose description answered his, a man who had hijacked a shipment of stolen Nazi gold destined for Moscow. The picture was indistinct, Moscow denied the incident, and, upon further investigation, the man was reported supposedly dead or missing. I still had the photo in my desk drawer. I took it out and looked at it for the hundredth time. It was still indistinct. It could and could not be Dogeron Kelly. Or anybody else for that matter.

28

Who are you really, Dog? That look that comes from the back of your eyes isn't new to me at all. It has violence in it and something I can't pin down at all, something that doesn't belong there.

I glanced at the calendar and wondered how much longer it would be before the explosion went off.

You're a bomb, Dog, a damned walking bomb, but I like you anyway. You bring excitement into an old man's life.

III

LEE SHAY . . . REFLECTIONS

Oh, boy, when I buy trouble I buy it in big, fat bundles wrapped in FBI WANTED posters smelling of cordite and burning rubber. Already I could hear the hum of the spectators as the jury filed in and the rap of the judge's gavel and the clanging of steel bars. How the hell does it feel to have your hands braceleted behind your back with nickel-chrome cuffs? The only guy I ever knew who spent time in the pen said the food was lousy, the guards sadistic and the queers a menace.

And here I sit like a big idiot in front of an old open suitcase carefully counting out the bills. It wouldn't have been so bad if they had been all old or all new, but they were mixed, and by the time I reached two million five I was in a sweat, my hands shaking and the pain in my gut wasn't to be believed. The crazy green stuff was all over like grass thrown from a mower and more was still in the bag.

Where did it come from?

How the hell did he get it through Customs?

Whose was it?

That wild loon of a Dog didn't even give a shit about leaving it here, and me with a single lock on the door and not a gun in the place. I kept looking around wondering where I could stash the stuff, but modern apartments didn't come with hidden panels and there wasn't enough room in the closets to take care of an extra shoebox.

Damn it, Dog, we're buddies. You saved my tail and I owe you, but how much, buddy, how much? We were full of piss and vinegar during the war, but for me the vinegar is all gone and all I have left is the piss and the way I've been leaking over your pile, there won't even be much of that left.

You were such a nice guy at one time. No trouble. Always doing somebody a favor, flying extra missions when a pal wanted to get laid in London; dumping yourself in front of a junior birdman to get a Jerry off his tail; taking care of the dame who got stood up. Man, you were a fooler. I don't know what happened or why, but you changed. You wouldn't come back after it was all over . . . no, you take a European discharge and disappear into the back alleys of the world and except for a few postcards from screwball places like Algiers and Budapest, nobody knows anything about you. Ernie Kirrel thought he saw you in Marseilles, but he couldn't be sure.

Then I remembered yesterday's News, the item about the new controls to be exercised in narcotics production. Turkey was cutting back on her licensed poppy fields; France was going against the illegal processors; the U.S. was funding for an all-out war against the distributors. I started to sweat all over again. The origin of the postcards made sense now. So did the money. Dog was in the racket and was cutting out before they had him over a barrel. Damn it, Dog, are you nuts? You went and heisted somebody's bundle and they weren't law-conscious, good-guy police types. They'd track you down, cut your nuts off and let you bleed to death while you were holding them in your hand.

And me. I was in it now too. I was his protector. I couldn't give the stuff away . . . I couldn't take a chance dumping it somewhere without leaving tracks. I just didn't think that way at all. All they had to find was the money or the bag and I'd be holding my own balls too. There was no way out, none at all.

But there was. I had almost done it the first time. I picked up every bill lying around, repacked it, closed the lid of the suitcase and buckled the straps.

The whole thing would just about fit into the hall incinerator.

I was sweaty and grimy and looked forward to a cool shower when I stuck the key in the lock and walked into Lee's apartment. He was standing in the middle of the living room pulling on his pants with nervous hands, his face white and puckered looking. He jammed his feet into a pair of loafers and never saw me until he picked up my suitcase and started toward the door and when he caught my eyes across the distance he nearly lost his grip on it.

"Going somewhere?" I shouldn't have let my teeth show through the grin like that. Hell, I could have *told* him where he was going. His face was like the proverbial open book. He was scared halfway out of his mind, but he was still the same old Lee and going through no matter what happened.

"Don't stop me, Dog."

I shrugged, stepped aside and pulled a cigarette from my pack. "That leather's tough. It won't burn so easily. And besides, supposing some of that money starts drifting up the flue and lands in the street?"

The simple idea of it shook him and this time his fingers did let go. The bag slammed to the floor and rocked over slowly to lie on its side.

"You always could think things through, you bastard." His face was mad now, more at himself for being stupid, then his anger turned back to me again. "Okay, where *can* I dump it?" He was ready to come through me again.

"Why not try the bank? There's one across the street." I looked at my watch. "We still have an hour until closing."

"Don't try bluffing me out, Dog."

"You can always call, kid."

"Okay, I'm calling," he said.

I went over, picked up the bag and he followed me out, pulling on a tattered sport jacket over his T-shirt.

The teller called the manager and the manager called the president. Lee waited in the reception room while the president took me into his office. Two bank guards stood by watching Lee, and his lips were dry and cracked. When I came out, the bank was closed for the day, but we got a grand escort to the front door and a fine shaking of hands.

Outside, I handed Lee an envelope with the two passbooks, so he could look at them and he still didn't have enough spit in him to wet his lips. All he could say was, "What took so long?"

"They had to count it," I said.

"You're crazy, Dog, absolutely crazy. You're going to get nailed sure as hell. Right now they're on somebody's hot line and we'll have visitors before we ever get home."

"What makes you say that?"

He shook his head, astounded at my lack of interest. "Buddy, unless that was tax-paid, clean money with verified sources of ownership, your ass is in one hell of a sling."

I grinned at him. "How about that? Now can I get my shower?" I asked.

I said, "Rose?"

"Yeah, Dog." She sounded sleepy, but she knew my voice.

"I need you."

"Sure. I knew you would. I've been waiting."

"Sorry to be so long."

"It's only a day. Forget it." I heard her yawn elaborately and let her get it out.

"You're going to get a kick in the twat, honey. Money you can grab, but take that from the slobbies, okay?" I said.

"Come on, Dog . . ."

"If you really want me to wake you up . . ."

"Try getting past the doorman." She hung up with total, flat finality and I went up and got past her doorman. The fifth pick opened the lock and I kicked her out of bed and watched her lie there, eyes wide open for a good five seconds, wondering if she was going to be raped or robbed and when she finally recognized me all she could say was, "What happened to the doorman?"

"I gave him a hundred bucks," I told her.

"He can't be bought."

"If he didn't take it I'd of killed him," I said.

"He's a retired cop. An honest one."

"So I lied. I said I was your lover . . ."

"He believed it?"

"Shit. He said you deserved the likes of me," I grinned at her. "He thought I was a cop too."

"He would have asked for your badge."

"Come on, I showed it to him."

"Dog . . . all that for a piece of ass? You could have had it for free if you wanted."

"Then . . ."

"Shut up and get dressed."

Rose said, "Tell me . . ."

"No," I told her, "Lee doesn't know. Only you know. Amateurs are out and that's for sure."

"I want my due. Something's on your mind and if I have to go along I want my due."

"That's old-timey talk, sweetie."

"So give me my due."

"Like what?"

"A piece of ass," she laughed.

"Supposing it hurts?"

"Use some baby oil. It won't hurt. I can control my sphincter muscle."

"Oh, you dirty girl."

33

"But don't you love me?"

"Naturally."

"So? Don't tell me it's your first time?"

"It isn't."

"I didn't think so. You probably come equipped with your own lubricant," she said.

"Not now."

"At least I did," she told me.

"So break out the baby oil," I said. I smirked at her and stepped out of my pants. "Stop watching," I told her.

"I just wanted to see if you were equipped," she said.

"Hell, doll, I only want to satisfy you without hurting your little teeny tiny body."

Her laugh was loud and clear. She flipped the covers off, switched onto her spread legs in such a classic position with her head buried in her folded arm that she damn near forgot what I came for. "Go, man," she said.

I lit a cigarette and said, "Sorry about that, kid."

Rose looked around, all expecting to see the weirdo, the incapable, the all talk, but I was big and able and ready to go, only I wanted a smoke first.

"Dog, you're a dirty slob."

"I could have told you that."

"Why?"

So at last the lovely whore turned over and let me look at all that naked garishness, big tits tightened into hips and legs that were all so damned luscious, especially with that gorgeous snatch peering it's lonely eye into mine. . . .

I got up and got a hairbrush. There's one hell of a way to talk to a broad when you want to think. So I began brushing her hair.

She talked.

Nice and easy, but there were a few things I had to learn. The dolls overseas were all different. Their wants were specific, every undulation pointing to the specific, but at last here was a pure American whore, specific only in her attitude toward money, and I said, "Oh, you capitalist, you," just as the hairbrush gave her an orgasm.

"Son of a bitch," Rose breathed.

"Compliment or criticism?"

"Nobody should know that much about a woman. What will happen to the girl you marry?"

"At least she'll lead a sexy life," I said.

"Somebody better believe that."

"Oh, they will."

"I'll give you references."

"For a hairbrush?"

"Damn, Dog, if you can do it with a hairbrush, what can you do with the rest of the goodies?"

"Just try me," I said. "Roll over."

"You bastard. You know you only wanted to talk to me."

"I was softening you up."

"Like I needed it. You're the one who needs softening."

"How do you feel?"

"Can you give me a little more than the hairbrush?" Rose asked.

I said uh-huh and gave her a little more and when she got her breath back she looked up at me with a terrible smile and said, "Maybe Lee will kill you."

"He already tried."

"Really?"

"Certainly. That's why we're friends."

"You guys are all nuts."

"That's why we're winners," I said. "You want to be with us?"

Rose took a long look at me. Very deliberately she licked her forefinger and ran it up through her slit. "Pornographic?"

"Damn," I said, "you sure know how to build a man."

And for the first time I knew she was like me. "Who the hell you kidding?" Rose said.

"Not me, that's for sure."

"Dog . . . you ever been shot?"

"Young lady, I went into World War Two at the early age of twenty. I was a flier and my personal history before then belongs only in the unwritten biography, but four years of garbage got me nothing, then four years of civilian life got me shot four times. There's only one way you can see the scars."

"I was hoping you'd say that. Now let's get laid."

"Only if you'll tell me what I have to know."

"You're asking for a lot."

"Not really that much."

"Truly, Dog?"

"You know I'm a mean son of a bitch."

"I know."

"Still want me?"

"After that last episode . . . damn!"

"Okay, roll over."

"But where away, buddy?"

"Were you in the Army?"

"No."

"So why the army talk . . . or was it navy?"

"Aw, shaddup and just screw."

"Not without your consent," I said.

"So pick a hole," Rose told me.

"Now who's the nut?"

"You, if you don't start screwing somewhere."

"I guess you did know I had something to do when I came here."

"Certainly."

"Why the hell do you keep distracting me?"

"Shut up and keep screwing. Think about it later."

"You dames are all alike," I said.

"We are not," Rose told me. She did what I wanted her to do, rolled over, swore at me and clamped her legs together. "You got a death wish, man?" she asked.

"Naturally," I said.

I soaked up the eggs with the last piece of toast and looked at her across my coffee cup. She had thrown on a necklace and a wide leather belt and the effect was a little startling. "Do you always dress like that?"

Rose snapped the belt against her bare flesh and smiled. "It's only a little shorter than my minis. Anyway, do you always have to gorge yourself after you've had a woman?"

I nodded. "Always. It has an immediate regenerative effect."

"Well save it. I'm beat." Her eyes danced a little solo. "You're pretty good. I liked it. It was one of those rare occasions when I'd be willing to pay the tab myself."

"You already did, Rose. That was a good conversation. Time and distance change things. You caught me up in a hurry."

Rose nodded sagely, her eyes still on mine. She sipped at her coffee, thought a moment, then said, "You want more than that, though, don't you?"

"Smart."

"I've been around some. Maybe not like you, but enough to read the signs."

"What do you read?" I asked her.

She finished the coffee, set the cup in the saucer, then began turning the cup in lazy circles with her forefinger. "You meet me once, you set me up so I can hardly refuse you, now I'm waiting to swing at your pitch. There are a lot of pretty women in New York, Dog. Why me?"

"Because I lucked in the first time at bat. I know Lee . . . he won't mess with a phony. You can be trusted."

Rose made a moue and shrugged. "One of my few virtues. I'm glad you noticed. It makes me feel that I haven't wasted everything. Now what's on your mind?"

"I'm going to use you."

"Yes, I know. Am I to be a goodie or a baddie?"

"Either way, you won't be hurt," I said. "You'll come out of it a little richer than when you went in."

Her teeth bit into her lower lip very gently, then she raised her eyes and looked at me. "And you, Dog, how will you come out of it?"

"Let's say satisfied. There are things that need doing that have been left undone too long."

"But *somebody* will get hurt."

"That they will, pretty girl," I told her. "You can damn well bet on it. They deserve it and they'll get it."

"Are you sure you know what you're doing?" Rose asked me.

I sat back, let my thoughts drift back across time a few seconds, then said, "Maybe I don't look the type, kid, but I did my homework pretty well."

"Revenge, Dog?"

"Nope. Simply a necessity."

"I don't think I believe you."

"Maybe I don't want to believe it myself." I paused and watched her a moment. "No, it isn't revenge. It just has to be done."

The cup spun under her fingers for a full minute before she looked up again and nodded. "All right, Dog. There's something funny about you and I have to find out just what it is. I sleep with men for money and nearly everyone wants to know why I got into the business. Oh, I tell them something and rarely ever the same story twice. But I'm always curious why they bother being serviced by a call girl. They fall in love, they marry, then start knocking around with whores."

"It's the animal instinct," I said.

"They're crazy," Rose told me. "If they like specialties, teach their women to perform. Hell, you'd be surprised how happy a woman is to go along with their games. They even have some of their own and when two people perfect the art of turning a bed into a happy workbench you couldn't pry either one of them away from the other with a crowbar. Damn, I know an old fat couple who haven't missed a two-a-day turn in forty years and they have eleven kids."

"Who?"

"My folks. They used to embarrass hell out of me. If they knew what I was they'd feel genuine pity for me. To them marriage is one big happy ball. Me, I'm missing something."

"How about Lee?"

"We're good friends, Dog. Screwing buddies, sort of. He's a big, friendly puppy type who hasn't grown up yet. I don't think he ever will."

"And if he does?"

"What would he want me for? He could grab any woman then."

"I doubt it. Not after he's been trained by you."

"Thank you, my friend. It's nice to contemplate, but a little on the improbable side."

"You hedged," I said.

"What?"

"You didn't say *impossible*."

"Female vanity, big Dog. I'm curious about him, too, but you the most. I wonder what you *really* want."

"I've pondered that too."

"And when you find out?"

"I'll take it."

"No matter who's got it?"

"Roger, pussycat. No matter who's got it."

"Okay, Dog. At least you got me. Now I have to stay in the game just to see how it turns out. Are you going to kiss me good night now?"

"In my own inimitable fashion," I told her.

IV

New York was getting its midweek bath under a slashing northeast rain that churned up ripples in the street and blew waves of spray across the sidewalks. Empty cabs cruised by, but the shoppers had stayed home and it was too early for the office crowd to be leaving the grotesque sepulchers that contained them.

Lee's voice was a muttered undertone of total futility. Weller-Fabray, Tailors, his pants legs and shoes soggy under the hem of his black raincoat. I paid off the driver and climbed out of the taxi, letting the rain tear at me, then walked past him and into the store.

Lee's voice was a muttered undertone of total futility. "A whole year before this class joint would even *sell* me a suit, now you blow it in one bounce."

"Down, boy," I said.

The British gentleman with the sweeping moustache and formal tails nodded politely to Lee, studied me a second and nodded with an almost imperceptible bow. Somehow he seemed to wear the cloak of royalty around his shoulders, his eyes observant and capable of instant analysis. For that scant moment we just looked at each other, then, in perfect French, he said, "Yes, m'sieu, how may we help you?"

There was no trace of accent in my French, either. I said, "I would like a complete wardrobe for every occasion. I haven't the time to stand for fittings and need two suits immediately. There are certain alterations of design that are somewhat unusual, but necessary, as you will see. My measurements are on file at Betterton and Strauss in London, and Mr. Betterton will be happy to give them to you at any hour, so please call him immediately and bill me for any charges. Choice of material and styling will be at your discretion. Please include shirts, ties, underwear, socks and whatever you consider pertinent." I wrote out a check, handed it to him along with Lee's address and added, "Only the finest, if you don't mind, and this should cover the preliminary expenses. When may I expect delivery of the two suits?"

He never even glanced at the check. Completely unperturbed he told me, "Tomorrow, sir. About noon?"

"Fine," I said. There was that slight bow again and I walked Lee back outside into the rain.

We were halfway down the block before my friend could find the right words. I knew his smattering of French had let him in on the conversation, and the look he gave me was almost one of awe. "How the hell do you do it, Dog? Nobody gets a suit out of Weller-Fabray under four weeks. It takes a dozen fittings and ten character references to even get a shirt there!"

"It's all a game, pal, and I haven't got time to play games."

"Baloney. You know they wouldn't make a suit for the mayor? They refused that polo-playing millionaire and Count Stazow because they thought they were boorish. Ha!"

"You got in, didn't you?"

"With a knockdown from two bankers who owed me a favor and an abject air of proper humility for great craftsmen. I'm not listed in their golden file case, but I get my picture in the papers on all the right occasions and don't demean their product. But you . . . you walk in like a slob, all soaking wet, and they lay out the red carpet."

"They know class, kid."

"Shit." He ducked his head against a blast of rain. "Now where're we going?"

"Downtown to Barney's. I'm going to pull a couple things off the racks for tonight. Might even get a raincoat if this weather gets any worse."

"I wish I could figure you out, Dog." Lee gave me a nervous, sidewise glance. "Frankly, I still think you're crazy. You're trouble on the hoof."

"Don't let your imagination run away with you."

"Then why lay a trail as broad as the Hudson River behind you?"

"Why not?"

"Because you have too much to hide," he said. "Like that money." Lee paused a moment, then pushed me into the

40

alcove of an office building. "Your French is perfect, buddy. How many other languages do you speak?"

I shrugged and looked at him curiously. "A few."

"Turkish?"

I nodded.

"Any Arabic?"

I nodded again. "Why?"

"Some interesting items have been showing in the newspapers lately. You know anything about narcotics, Dog?"

My face was cold and hard when I looked at him and he pulled back instinctively. "Never touch the stuff," I said.

Lee squeezed his mouth shut until his lips were a thin line, but he wouldn't let go of it. "There has to be a reason for somebody dropping out of sight like you did. For showing up the way you did too. I thought I knew you, and maybe I did back there during the war, but I sure as hell don't know you now at all. Talk about enigmas, you're the perfect example. What happened, Dog?"

"We all get a little older, kid."

"Okay, let it go at that. You're still the guy who saved my ass too many times, so I'm sticking with it. You got me shook, but the ride is wild. Maybe I'm as sappy as you are. Only don't blame me if I get the shakes and suddenly cut out. I'm just not geared to this kind of living. Goose bumps come awfully easy and last a long time. You got me so I'm looking over my shoulder half the time. I'm beginning to think I'm back in the blue in a P-51D peering into the sun for bogeys."

"Good thinking, then. Keep your head out of the cockpit and you won't get it shot off."

"That was the first thing you ever told me," Lee said. "I get the chills hearing it said again. At least the last time you were talking about the war."

"Everything's a war," I told him.

He looked into my eyes, shivered involuntarily, then turned his raincoat collar up around his neck. "Okay, buddy, so be it. I kind of have the feeling you really don't need me bird-dogging you around, so I'm going to peel off and get back to work. The date still on for tonight?"

"Sure. I want to meet all your beautiful people."

"Look a little decent, will you? They're kind of important. You really going to get clothes off the rack at Barney's?"

"Doesn't everybody?"

He grinned at me, spotted a cab coming and ran out to the curb to flag it down, then held the door open for me

41

so I wouldn't get any wetter. He stood there shaking his head in annoyance when I told the driver to take me to Barney's.

They built New York's first skyscraper downtown at Twenty-third Street and called it the Flatiron Building, an ornate, old-fashioned triangular antique that rose on the south side of Twenty-third at the juncture of Fifth Avenue and Broadway where it stared out majestically on a city about to explode into growth, and remained a couple of generations later, still staring, but with windowed eyes a little sad and clouded with the dirt the new age had thrown up. It was a wistful building, its orginal name and history almost forgotten now, but a building that had lived through many years and a multitude of experiences, yet still stood like a miniature fortress planted in the middle of an anthill.

On the seventeenth floor, in the pointed nose of the structure, Al DeVecchio had his office. The door had triple locks and the gold-leaf sign simply read L.D.V., Inc., beautifully ambiguous, not at all encouraging to solicitors, yet in certain areas well known and caustically respected.

Two secretaries and an old man wearing outdated sleeve garters and an archaic green eyeshade worked in compartments lined with modern business equipment, but Al's private quarters were in the front end of the triangle where he could look out over his city like the master of a ship conning his vessel from the bridge. His coffee maker was still in the perpetual state of percolation, his small freezer still full of imported salamis and cheeses, one wall still full of books on mathematical formulas it took an Einstein to understand, and the same pair of rocking chairs he had had in the operations shack in England during the war. The arms were polished from use and the hardwood sweeps a little thinner now from the years of oscillating, but their gentle roll was still as damnably mesmerizing as ever. A lot of generals had cooled off in those chairs and a lot of command decisions arrived at in their easy motions.

"Nostalgic, isn't it?" Al asked me.

"You were born too late, buddy."

"I'll buy that," he grinned. "Coffee?"

"No, thanks."

"Hunk of Genoa? Came in last week. Spicy as hell. You could stink up a place for hours with it."

"Unh-uh. I can still remember the last one we split."

"Tasted lousy when you burped into an oxygen mask, didn't it?"

"Fierce. I don't know how you guineas can eat all that stuff."

"So you Irish live on corned beef and cabbage draped around a melted potato. Peasant food."

"Only when we're affluent."

"You must be gorged by now," Al said.

"Glad you did your research, Captain."

"Oh, you were always a pet project of mine." He held a cup under the coffee spigot, filled and sweetened it, then got back in his rocking chair. "You know, little Italiano from the poor end of Hell's Kitchen wondering what made the rich kid from the big estate tick. We all looked alike in uniform, but the difference was still there."

"Keep talking," I said. "How does a prejudiced slob from an uptown penthouse feel going back to the old turf?"

"Great," he told me. "I keep rubbing it in to any of the old gang who are still around. I like the envious look. They all think I belong to the Mafia."

"Tell 'em any different?"

"Nope. It gets respect, especially from the young punks I use occasionally."

"Let the mob get wise and you'll be holding your head."

"They already tried. Just once. I get respect from them too."

"How?"

"Easy," he said. "I used your name."

"That must have gone over big."

Al grinned slowly, mulling over the memory. "You'd be surprised, Dog. They sent their three best hatchet men out to chop you down and none were ever heard from again. They simply disappeared. No bodies. No rumors. Just sudden and total disappearance like they never even existed, and within three days after each one vanished somebody's grand villa burned down or their seagoing yacht mysteriously blew up. Oh, and I almost forgot the one in Naples those old French Resistance boys nailed with new and damning evidence of being a Nazi collaborator and hung from the bell tower in the church he had financed."

"You're talking over my head, buddy," I said.

"Sure I am." His tone held mock sarcasm. "Let's just say I'm a good guesser. Aren't you taking a chance exposing yourself away from your own field of operations?"

"Al, you got one hell of an imagination."

He nodded, looking at me squarely. "I hope you have too. Somebody with all your earmarks left one hell of a mark on things over there. Here too. You echo, Dog, big and loud. Why didn't you come home with the rest of us?"

"Social football isn't my cup of tea, kid."

"Man," he said, "you could have taken over all of Barrin Industries with your smarts. The old man could have used you."

"All I want is my ten grand," I told him.

Al sliced another chunk off the salami, skinned it and pulled two cold beers out of his freezer. He popped them open and handed one to me. "Sure you don't want some Genoa?"

I shook my head and took the beer. It was tangy and tasted good going down. "Just your report, old buddy."

"You know, I think I liked you better in the old days. You're a mean bastard now," he said. Al didn't have to look at any files. They were all carefully stored away in his mind, detail by detail, and when he finished his salami he stared out the window a moment, then looked back at me. "You want it all broken down?"

"Just your summation."

"Uh-huh. Okay, Barrin Industries is still very much blue chip unless some shrewdie from SEC really digs into it. They're turning out products with the help of government contracts and old-line investors who thought your grandfather was the greatest guy alive. Their operation is marginal as hell. Equipment is out of date, standing up only because the old man insisted on the best original installations. Two of the original employees got Barrin off the hook by developing a by-product when pollution control went in and the by-product was worth more than the product itself. Your cousins conned them out of their rights just when both those men came up with something really tremendous and they got so damned pissed off they retired, died within the year and took their big secret with them."

"What was it?"

"If I told you, you'd never believe me."

"Try me."

"Okay, an antigravity device."

"Come on, Al, knock off the crap."

"I told you." He leaned back in his chair, smiling. "I saw it, Dog. A little steel-looking marble that would stay anywhere you put it. On the ground, ten feet up . . . anywhere. Throw it, it would keep on going. Rest it, the ball stayed there."

"Really?"

"Damn, you're an emotionless slob. You know what that could mean?"

"Sure I do."

"Then say something."

"I'm glad they didn't let anybody take it away from them."

"It was a billion-dollar invention, Dog."

"Shit. The government would have confiscated it. Or somebody would have squeezed them for it. They were smarter doing what they did."

"You don't really believe me about the gimmick, do you?"

"Why not?"

"Because you're not excited."

"Al, I got enough trouble *with* gravity without worrying about the anti garbage." I felt a tug at the corners of my mouth. "Damn interesting idea, though. You could take a broad and . . ."

"There you go again!"

"So get back to Barrin Industries," I said.

Al looked at me, shook his head in disgust and smiled crookedly. "Barrin is busted. They've borrowed all they can on the sheer weight of the physical properties they own, but they're at the end. All they can do is deal in odd bits and pieces, but the big contracts will go right past them. The more sophisticated products are beyond their reach and they couldn't possibly stay inside the time elements on the new contracts being let out. Your cousins committed Barrin to a contract that is absolutely going to slay them, then the vultures are going to move in and take over, as they say, lock, stock and barrel."

"What vultures, Al?"

"You ever hear of Cross McMillan?"

I let out a low laugh and picked a cigarette out of the open pack on the table and lit it. "Sure. His old man and my grandfather were mortal enemies. He was born when his father was sixty-some and grew up to be the meanest kid in the area. That son of a bitch knocked me for a loop one day when I helped some doll carry packages into her car. He was eight years older than me and was after her hide and didn't want anybody cutting in. What a cocksman he thought he was."

"So you put a firecracker under his car?"

"Nope. I hit him in the head with a rock one day and ran like hell. He never did catch me."

"Well, friend, he caught your cousins. He's the big vulture. Right now he's got millions going to waste and all he wants is to get hold of Barrin Industries."

"So let him."

"He'll get your ten grand too."

45

"Like hell," I said.

"Don't believe me, then." Al reached over and cut himself another slice of Genoa salami and nipped an end off it with evident pleasure. "Just watch," he told me.

"Where did it go, Al?"

"The money?"

I nodded.

"You don't know your cousins."

"Tell me. That's what I'm here for."

"And a paid-up customer at that." He swallowed the chunk of meat, burped and took a sip of beer. It's what you call letting skeletons out of the closet."

"Like you said, I'm the customer."

"Okay, Dog." Al told me. "Your funeral."

"No flowers, please."

"Sure. Well, if you remember, all that Barrin stock was left to the family . . . at least the controlling majority."

"Fifty-seven percent," I reminded him.

"Exactly. And according to the terms of the will, neither your cousin Alfred nor Dennison could sell."

"True."

"They owned fifteen percent apiece, with the rest going to Veda, Pam and Lucella. The old man figured the girls needed something to attract a husband."

"Yeah," I said sourly, "I know. They got them too. All except Veda."

"Remember them?"

"Only too well, buddy."

"So you could have forgotten. They were all older than you. Anyway, remember Veda's vice?"

"The cubes?"

"Oh, Dog, she's got more class than that. Your cousin Veda discovered Las Vegas. She got with the wild bunch from New York and some of the sharpies who used to be based in Havana. Man, did she go down, and I don't mean sexually. That crazy broad went through everything she had and hocked everything she didn't have. Right now she's living off the income from a small block of securities she won when she was having an early streak of luck. If it weren't for that, Cousin Veda would be humping for a living."

"Stupid dame," I muttered. "She wouldn't make a nickel being a whore."

"You haven't seen her for a while. I kind of think she did take some of it out in trade. Morrie Shapiro wiped out her chits and so did Hamilton from that theater chain. She's a real swinger, that one. Built like a brick outhouse now.

46

No mind, but built. Talented, too, I hear. A real sex machine . . . something like having a new antique car. Style, performance, color, but a little aged."

"That leaves Pam and Lucella," I said.

"Same old story. Pam's husband Marvin Gates got himself caught in one hell of a gigantic swindle when he tried to finance a cute little operation and Pam had to bail him out. It was either pay up or visit him in jail. Pam paid up and now Marv's her own personal little ass kisser who had better not ever open his mouth again except when she says when, where or how. And I think you know what I mean."

"Remembering Pam's sexual preferences, I sure do," I said. "And Lucella?"

"Too many luxuries. She woke up one day and it had all dribbled away. The Riviera, Paris and Rome were memories. That guy she married . . . what was his name?"

"Simon."

"Yes, Simon . . . she sold his polo ponies, his race cars. Simon got a divorce in Mexico, married some old dame and Lucella keeps looking at her pictures of the Riviera, Paris and Rome."

"Sad."

"Isn't it?" Al said. "But typical. Who was it said three generations from shirt sleeves to shirt sleeves?"

"Some wise-ass," I told him.

"The rough part is this," Al said. "Alfred and Dennison don't know about all this machinery. They're trying to operate on the assumption that the gal cousins have all their stocks and are bugging them to turn over control to them. None of them will buy the attitude . . . not that they wouldn't if they could . . . it's just that they can't. It just ain't there to sell anymore. Al and Dennie own thirty percent of nothing with old Cross McMillan ready to reach in and snatch it all away. He already owns one hell of a block he picked up when the original investors died and if it ever comes to a proxy fight, he can pick up all the marbles."

"Maybe not."

"Come on, Dog. The dame cousins of yours dumped everything. Whoever picked it up bought a sucker deal and it's got to be spread out all over the place. It's only junk, and who would bother with it anyhow?"

"Oh, you never could tell."

For a long time, Al looked at me, his eyes tight little beads trying to see inside my mind, and finally they did. "You got it," Al stated.

"Why not?" I asked him. "Like you said, it was only junk."

47

He let me have that long look again. "McMillan is going to kill you."

I grinned at him.

"He wants everything . . . Barrin Industries, the Mondo Beach property . . . the works. He's going to get even with your grandfather."

"Fuck McMillan."

"Not him, Dog. I told you, he's a vulture. He's got the money and the power. To him Barrin Industries is only a toy to be played with. That guy plays in international finance. He can buy anything he wants to."

I took a long drag on the cigarette and snuffed it out in the empty beer can. "Almost everything, Al. Or do you know about that too?"

"You even look at his wife sidewise and you'll be dead, buddy. Like D-E-A-D."

"I wasn't intending to. I just said there were some things you just can't buy."

"Dog, you're nuts. Those two are crazy in love. They always have been."

"Yeah, I know."

"Maybe there's an age differential. Not much, but they're sure as hell in love."

"I wasn't talking about that," I said.

"What them?"

"Nothing that makes any difference right now."

We sat there rocking a few minutes, looking up Broadway. North of Thirty-fourth Street a gray cloud was beginning to encompass the Empire State Building.

"It's going to rain." I said.

For the first time, old Al DeVecchio's face was a study in consternation. I never had seen him like that before. It was like he had stumbled into somebody else's foxhole and found it full of shit.

"I never should have answered your letter," he said.

REFLECTIONS: AL DEVECCHIO

Who the hell is he now? You think you get to know somebody under four long years of war and gunfire and he zeroes out like a pissed-on cigar butt and the guy you knew isn't there anymore.

"Say, mate, you wanted Spit time, didn't you?"

"Now?"

"Really, Major, if it wasn't for this girl . . . daughter of one of your senators, y'know . . . sort of asked for me and it's hands across the ocean and all that sort of crap, y'know?

48

Now, she's a new Mark Thirteen and never been scratched. Only two milk runs on photo across to the sub pens . . ."

"She armored?"

"Full up, Major."

"If I get my ass snarled on this one . . ."

"Blimey, Major, I got them all prepped. No sorting out to do at all. Beansey, Jerry and Tag are off your wings. Good chaps, those. Twelve kills among them. Relatively new and not like you at all, but remember, dear boy, you wanted to fly the Spit . . ."

"No time goes on my record?"

" 'Pon my word, Major. I wouldn't want to go before Old Snarly for anything. Realize you and the flight surgeon are having it out over those missing missions, but don't forget, it was that little niece of mine who lifted your records. Good job, what?"

"Yeah, lovely."

"Too bad you chaps get rotated so soon. It's really a gorgeous war," he said. "Tell me, Major, why don't you want to go home?"

"Long story, my friend. And like you said, it's a gorgeous war. I always did want Spit time. That crate handle well?"

"You should know, Major. Much better than the Nines. Just remember to find me an empty Mustang on the next Nuremberg run. There's a farmhouse there occupied by a particularly nasty character who stuck a pitchfork in my buttock when I bailed out on his property. Damned near didn't escape. If it weren't for the little beauty across the river who always had been partial to the sons of John Bull I never would have made it. Quite an interesting stay, that was."

"You Limeys are nuts," Dog said.

"Determined, you must admit."

"Sure, to lay an American senator's daughter."

"Oh, just trying to improve our relationship with the colonials, Major. Enjoy the Spit, old boy. My batman has everything arranged. Would appreciate it if you could bring her back more or less unscathed. Old Snarly has an eye for details like bullet holes and he knows my new buggy is still a virgin. Unpenetrated, y'know?"

"Yeah."

"Well, cheerio."

"Dog," I asked him, "why the hell do you squeeze in extra missions? You coulda been out long ago. You like all this crazy fighting?"

"Something to be learned," he told me. "You survive or

you don't. Get the worst of it in now and all the rest will look easy."

He survived, all right. I wish I could confirm all those rumors that had been seeping out of Europe the past twenty years. But no matter what I heard, they didn't jell with the Dogeron Kelly I knew. Nice guys just don't change. And the rumors were all screwed up too. One told of a darkly lethal character who blew the whole postwar black market business to hell and gone when he creamed out the hard operators, using Stateside mob money to disrupt the economy. Nobody wanted to talk about what happened after that. Then there was the other "El Lobo" . . . the Wolf . . . who tangled with the international financiers and took them for all they were worth. The Dog and The Wolf. There was a sameness there. The difference was that Dog could hardly handle simple mathematics. He never could solve a navigation problem when he had to use a Weems Computer or triangulate a course. If he hadn't had a pigeon's instinctive memory for time, distance and direction, he couldn't have hit the floor with his hat. But he had, and he was always on target and always back again, sometimes leading strays and once a squadron whose numbers failed them. When it came to finance, he couldn't even make sense out of British money, far less a French franc. If it wasn't the American dollar it was all play money. The only other rate of exchange he understood was cigarettes and candy bars.

Yet, there was that change. Those damn eyes of his. They watched everything. He moved funny too, always knowing who was behind him and on either side, an odd awareness of where everyone else was and, when they were out of position, he knew and was ready to pounce.

Two Dogs? Three? It was possible. He was here now and I'd see him again. Digging into the dark corners was my game and now I'd really get to the answers. I had to. I was curious. I hoped I'd like what I'd find.

I was afraid I wouldn't.

V

I never could figure out why people didn't like the rain. A dull day, a little wet and it was growl time. Women brooded in tight little apartments tying up the telephones; husbands fidgeted on barstools, dragging out lunch hours into early hangovers; the few on the streets fought for taxicabs whose drivers seemed to take a sadistic satisfaction out of their predicament. Hell, the rain was nice. It cleaned things out. A good rain in New York was the city's only mouthwash and it gargled happily and rumbled with pleasure as the garbage got spewed out down the drain.

At Park Avenue I turned north and walked a dozen blocks to the old Tritchett Building, found Chet Linden's office number on the directory and took the elevator up to the sixth floor. He grinned when I walked in, waved me toward a chair, finished his phone conversation and swung around toward me. "Having trouble adjusting, Dog?"

"Catching up fast. The town sure has changed."

"Not for the better."

"That's for sure," I said. "When did you get in?"

"A week ago today. I miss London already. Get your ten grand yet?"

I pulled out my last cigarette and lit it. "There's a morals clause attached to it."

A slow laugh spread across his face. "And you can't beat the rap?"

"Hardly."

"That's no statement for a quick thinker like you to make," he said. "Besides, I still figure you for a nut to even bother with the deal."

"Let's say it's a matter of principle."

"Sure. You toss over the whole European operation to play games. Oh, not that we're not properly appreciative, buddy. You handed us quite a nut, but I'm not so sure we like you entirely out of the picture. You were the iron fist in the velvet glove that kept everything greased. So far we haven't found anybody who's up to your ability."

"How about Purcell?"

"Still got too many rough edges. Give him a year and he may mellow."

"Montgomery?"

"We're considering him. If he makes it on the new assignment he may get the spot. Incidentally, we picked up that other block of stock in Barrin from the Woodring kid. He was glad to dump it at the price. We made you a present of it, and as far as I know it's the last of the stuff floating around. You know a Cross McMillan?"

"Uh-huh."

"He had tracked it down too, but our price was higher and the kid sold before McMillan could raise the ante." He stopped a moment, then stared at me, frowning. "You onto something, Dog?"

"Just my ten grand."

"Somehow I get the feeling you're holding a fungo bat with the bases loaded."

"Let me have my fun, Chet."

"Okay, clam. Just keep the repercussions down. Right now we don't need any static. We got things fairly quiet on the Continent, John Bull has retired back into politics and you're nothing but a legend now. That Mafia bunch had a housecleaning, a few mass funerals and even Interpol is sitting back smugly enjoying the scene no matter how it came off. If they only knew."

"And we're not telling, are we?" I asked him.

"Indeedy no, my crazy friend. The other side carries too much heavy artillery." He rocked forward and leaned on his desk. "You going to be needing any of the contacts?"

"Unlikely, but keep them open for me."

"That fungo bat's getting longer."

"No sweat, kid, it's just that I'm used to thinking that way. Besides, you never know what's going to turn up."

"Yeah," he growled sarcastically. "So what's on the agenda?"

I looked at my watch and stretched out of my seat. "Little party tonight. Should be fun."

"Your buddy Shay showing you the town?"

"He thinks I need reorienting."

"Do you?"

"It's not like the Old Country, Chet. They've screwed everything up back here. The broads . . ."

"All broads are alike, Dog."

"The kind you pick are."

"Lucky Linden, they call me. My little beauties never give me any trouble. Very clean, very quiet and very commercial. Now take you, what those classy dolls ever saw in you I just can't figure. I'd think you'd scare them to death."

"I got class."

"You got more than that, but it's something only the dames can smell."

I grinned at him and snuffed the cigarette out. "Where's that paper you want signed?"

He slid open the desk drawer, drew out three sheets of printed copy and pushed them toward me. "The dotted line, Dog. Three autographs and you're on your own. If you do use any of the contacts, make damn sure it's an emergency and one foul-up will leave you wide open. From here on in you're out of the picture. Completely. This office is closing down today; the others have already moved. The old numbers and exchanges have been switched and our people have been informed that you're nothing more than another Johnny-on-the-street."

"The picture's clear, Chet. I know the rules."

"Maybe you forgot one, Dog."

"What's that?"

"They wanted you hit. The board was one vote shy of having you knocked off."

"Yours, Chet?"

"Mine, Dog."

"Why? I didn't know you were that sentimental."

"I'm not. I just didn't want to see a lot of our good people go down before they finally tagged you. It was a case of choosing the lesser of two evils."

I slapped my hat on and grinned at him, reaching for the door.

"Dog," he said.

"Yeah?"

"I though about it a long time before I cast that vote," he told me.

Lee had a pair of TV dinners staying warm in the oven when I finally reached his apartment. A couple of drinks had obviously taken off his jumpy edge and he gave me that old half-silly grin I remembered so well. He took one look at me and shook his head. "They got cabs and subways in this town, buddy. Did you forget how to hustle one?"

"I walked."

"No kidding. A new suit and you walked. I hope the raincoat worked."

"Good enough. I'll press the pants dry later."

"Where were you?"

"Taking care of some business details."

His grin faded and he held up his hands. "Don't tell me about them, Dog. Whatever they are, I don't want to know."

"Hell, you wouldn't believe it anyhow."

"The hell I wouldn't." He grabbed my arm and led me over to the bar. When he mixed a drink and handed it to me he said, "Look, Dog, about tonight . . ."

"Relax. I won't embarrass you. Besides, I told you I had met Walt Gentry."

"It's not you I'm worried about. They're a pretty hairy bunch, Dog. Me, I know them. We speak the same language. It's when somebody new they can't cross-index comes on the scene that you see the fangs come out. They're nosy as hell and know how to dig things out and I'm just scared they'll latch onto you."

"So what's there to find out?" I tasted the drink, nodded and put half of it down.

"About all that money, for one thing."

"Let them call the bank."

"Dog—I'm not kidding. That Merriman chick who writes the gossip column will be there, Dick Lagen who handles the political stuff from Washington . . ."

"For Pete's sake, Lee, I'm not big news."

"Not news . . . just new. And you got that *look.*"

"What look?"

"Like you *could* be news. Listen, I know these people . . ."

"I'm glad you do. How's the female situation?"

"Don't you ever think of anything besides women? It used to be flying . . . now all of a sudden you're dame happy."

I finished the rest of the drink. "They're kind of nice to have around."

"Pardon me for sounding redundant again, but you're absolutely nuts. Absolutely."

"That didn't answer my question."

Lee gave a hopeless shrug and a short pull right out of the Scotch bottle. "Every damn she-wolf in New York will be there—and don't say it."

"Say what?"

"Good company for an old dog like you."

I laughed at him and let him make me a refill.

VI

Originally, Sharon had planned to forego the cocktail bash at Walt Gentry's penthouse. It would be the same old crowd; a few live celebrities who owed a favor to the host, a half-dozen oldies still recognizable from their reruns on the late late movies and a host of hangers-on who lived in the fringe areas of show business. A handful of new ones would make an appearance, mainly recently imports from Europe or the West Coast, and a handful of regulars would be missing, either bored with the routine or having shipped out to some remote corner with a stock show or picking up a bit part "on location."

Sharon had expected to see a special screening of the new Cable Howard production, but S. C. Cable, who long ago had assumed that employees worked for him twenty-four hours a day every day, made a special request that she handle the social action, since it was rumored that Walt Gentry was thinking of dropping a few millions into a co-production venture on some property he had discovered . . . if he could find the right partners. And if Cable Howard Productions managed a deal with Walt Gentry, there would be a nice bonus, or perhaps even a small running percentage for Sharon Cass.

Nice, she thought. I have become an economic seductress. I am expected to give my all for Cable Howard. And they call the streetwalkers names and arrest them. Beautiful, modern morality.

She looked at herself framed in the six lights that encircled the vanity mirror, concentrated on getting the left false eyelash properly fixed, then steadied her hand to apply the black eyeliner that gave her the final naïve touch and sat back, satisfied.

Pretty, she mused. I'm all sleekly feminine, grossly beautiful and the perfect target of attack. Bait. A lousy piece of bait. Fifteen thousand a year and expenses to draw the suckers into the net. A bonus when S.C. thought the job was worth it. What happened, Sharon? You used to be a little country girl smothered in ideals, with starry eyes. You liked the smell of cut grass and the wind coming off the ocean. You collected seashells and bugs, then one day you grew up and the bull dike editor from *Future* called you in to do some more teen-age modeling, saw the change and did the spread that got Cable Howard Productions to pick you up for that sun-fun picture. Oh, you were great, little sexpot, only you didn't like to have to walk the plank of assistant directors and fat-lipped agents who had been mail room clerks the year before. Your Coke bottle made old S.C.'s ears ring and he thought you were cute enough to work out your option on his staff . . . except that you did your work a little too well and here you were.

She got up, posed in front of the full-length mirror, a naked, overgrown pixie. "I still like me," she whispered. "At least there's still one thing left."

The lovely, tanned image stared back at her, its eyes traversing the curves of her body, then meeting her eyes with a direct, peculiar stare. "I have a funny feeling," she said.

The image looked back without saying anything. Then, slowly, it smiled.

The invitation had said six thirty, and Sharon was fashionably late, two propositions and a champagne cocktail down, a roomful of people to say hello to still and a conversation with Raul Fucia to contend with. Somehow she couldn't remember how it started, but she pulled herself back from thoughts that were too many years old into the near-mesmerizing voice of the sensually lean man beside her.

"But, my dear, women are the *true* predators. They are the ones who do the . . . how do you say it? . . . the prowling. The men simply make themselves available when they desire to."

"Your attitude is a little too European, Mr. Fucia."

"Please, call me Raul . . . and my attitude is only universal. The masculine viewpoint, and especially true here in New York."

"We New Yorkers pride ourselves on being rather sophisticated. I don't think it's true at all."

"Oh? Then look around you. See the men? They stand and let themselves be surrounded. They listen to the overtures, gauge the quality of the bodies and select the one they believe will be most appreciative of their favors. Already there has been some discreet pairing off."

"Regular cocktail party routine, Raul. Same people, just a different time and place."

"No, my dear, not routine at all. The women *vie*. Yes, they vie. They beg, they implore, they demand. Unlike the animal world, it is the women who compete in style and showy displays of flesh to entice the opposite sex into accepting their advances. For instance, look at yourself."

Sharon turned and looked at him, smiling wryly. "I seem to be on the conservative side, don't I?"

The smile he returned was deliberate, eyes dropping beneath the level of her own. "Not really," he said. "Assuming that professional women are all properly coiffed and made up, carefully tailored and impeccably mannered, can you explain why you are not wearing a brassiere, nor why neither seam nor hem of undergarment shows beneath that silken Pucci minisheath you're wearing? Except for your dress and shoes, you are completely naked, and when you stand erect certain basic hirsute attributes are proudly evident despite the outer covering."

"I didn't think it showed," Sharon said. She knew the red was showing on her shoulders, but the blush wasn't in the casual tone of her voice.

"Perhaps I have a more experienced eye than most. And perhaps I think you are lying. You *do* know it shows."

"Then you shouldn't be looking in that direction."

"Why not? It is the reason for your . . . undressed appearance. Flaunting the female plumage, no? An admirable approach. I am thoroughly enchanted. And why not? Your skin is flawless, your physique perfect. Of all the women in the room, your breasts are by far most suited for their purpose. Large enough to be the objects of attention, to sustain themselves without implementation, yet not so large as to interfere with more important actions."

"Is sex all that you have on your mind?" she asked him. His half-shaded eyes unveiled themselves momentarily in surprise and she was pleased that her voice had held no expression of excitement he had deliberately tried to implant in her.

"That is generally true," he told her. "Can you suggest something that should take precedence?" He sipped his drink and waited for her answer.

"Try gainful employment."

57

Raul shrugged and smiled again. "Hardly necessary. I am quite wealthy. Working for more would only be a pretense. I would rather spend my time and energy working on you, my dear. You interest me immensely."

"For what purpose?"

"The ultimate purpose," he said, "of taking you to bed with me, totally naked and ready for the unlimited capacity of Raul Fucia. Your enjoyment of my efforts would be profuse."

Sharon let her eyes range over him, then her teeth glinted in a small grin. "I'm afraid I'd be a disappointment to you, Raul. You see, I'm quite virginal."

"Lovely," he said. "A woman virginal in spirit is a wonder to behold."

"In body, my friend. I'm a complete maidenheaded virgin. How about that?"

There was no denying the tone of her voice at all this time. She had calculated it to perfection without any effort at all and for a moment nearly enjoyed the consternation that showed in his face.

"Impossible!"

"Not so impossible. I've just never been laid, that's all. I never met a man I wanted to get that close to. Simple, when you consider it."

He put the drink down, pulled up the ottoman beside her and sat down quickly, his hand reaching for hers. She let him take it without resisting. "Then, by all means, you must have me. I insist, you must!"

"Why?"

"Because the initial experience has to be a momentous occasion. Only a man of experience can . . ."

"Raul . . . balls. When I want to, I'll go. Not before. You're not the man either."

"But you have not seen me."

"You're beginning to show, Raul. The thought of a possible virgin in your life was a little too much. Was that why you sat down?"

"My dear Sharon . . ."

"I've been around, my fine foreign friend. I've necked, petted and experienced orgasm. I've engaged in a few sexual episodes that produced the proper physical pleasures and enjoyed it and I'll probably do more of the same again when I want to. I know all the tricks, positions and erogenous zones and I'll be a real terror when the time comes. Only right now I still have the little goodie that makes me an unpenetrated virgin and I'm going to keep it that way."

58

She felt his hand slip away from hers slowly, his eyes uncertain. "You are a . . . a . . ."

"Lesbian?"

He nodded.

"No, though I allowed myself the pleasure of experimenting in that direction several times. Does that startle you?"

Apparently it did. The bewilderment touched his mouth and he reached for his drink again. "But . . . when you could have had a man . . ."

"I have," she said firmly, "but not in the primary circumstance. I have felt and tasted several men. There was great mutual enjoyment. Have I been explicit enough? There has even been penetration of another nature I found extremely satisfactory. So no, I am not a Lesbian, I am not frigid, I am not sexually abnormal. I am simply hanging on to an asset a man might consider quite valuable someday."

Raul finished the drink, found an empty spot on the end table beside him and put the glass down. "American women," he said. "You are quite shocking."

"At my age I can afford to be," Sharon told him. She deliberately leaned forward, knowing he was able to see the full sweep of her breasts beneath her dress in the movement. The slippery feel of the fabric made her nipples thrust forward prominently. "Now, why don't you practice your erection on someone more appreciative."

Somehow he managed to contain his frustration and rose to bow in a continental manner. She took his fingers in a gentle handshake. "I feel sorry for you, Sharon Cass," he said.

She smiled again, a flash of amusement in her eyes. "I feel sorry for you, Raul. You know what you are missing and there is no possible chance of getting it at all."

"Not quite true, my dear."

"*Quite* true, Raul. I would deball you before you could rape me. My thirty-two years have been very athletic and, like I said, I know all the tricks . . . even those."

His exit was graceful, she thought, for someone who had to revise all his thinking. Tonight he'd have some woman tucked under silken sheets next to him, wondering if somewhere along the primrose path he had lost his touch. His performance wouldn't be up to par at all and tomorrow he'd begin to worry. So he'd try for her again and lose the battle again and the decline would begin. Like the gross income chart on S. C. Cable's wall behind his desk.

"Would you really deball him?"

It was a funny voice, oddly scratchy with a strange accent she couldn't quite place, a Brooklyn voice with the New Yorkese deliberately rubbed out. She half turned and looked at him, then smiled because he was out of place somehow and she couldn't tell why either. She let all the reasons compute in her analytical mind and decided that he was too big in the shoulders and chest for one thing, and his hair too short for another. It was what they used to call a crew cut. His black suit was new, but molded from a different era, as if he were conscious of only one style and couldn't care less for what the "in" crowd had adopted. He looks like an eagle, she thought.

Suddenly she was back in front of the mirror again. She felt the tiny blonde hairs rise on the backs of her forearms and a prickle go across her shoulders. It was like dropping into an abstract vortex of time and sound and colors she couldn't understand at all. Her stomach muscles seemed to tighten until juices were being squeezed right out of her. Inside her mind a faraway voice said, "I have a funny, funny feeling." And she answered back, "No. It's silly and childish. It never will really happen."

"Well?" he asked.

"It wouldn't have been very difficult."

"Your destruction of the boy was a little more practical," he said.

"I didn't think there was an eavesdropper."

"Hell, kid, I wouldn't miss a scene like that for the world. I was envying his approach until you dropped him. You really mean all that stuff?"

A curious laugh escaped Sharon's lips. "Yes. It was all true."

"Even about being a virgin?"

"Does it sound odd?"

This time he grinned and shrugged, toasting her with his drink. "Sounds crazy, kid, but it's your game."

She wondered where he had found a beer in Walt Gentry's supply. It was something Walt only brought in for his slumming parties. "What's *your* game, Mr. . . ."

"Kelly. My first name's a beaut. It's D-O-G-E-R-O-N, but people call me Dog. I don't take offense."

But it *did* happen. It was too quick, too fast and she wasn't prepare for it. It was the bomb blowing up in your face before you even had the time set for it. It was the world rocking to a standstill when a second before it was serene and placid. It was a chasm opening under your feet while you were walking up a beautiful path lined with flowers and happiness and the sense of accomplishment.

Discipline and self-denial reacted before she was aware of it . . . ages of fighting the battle of the sexes brought out the instinctive armor of words and demeanor. And always that little thought . . . she could be wrong. The chances were that she was.

Forget it, little blonde girl. Coincidences do happen and it's hard to remember anymore. That was all a long time ago and you've romanticized the image. You've held on to a stupid dream too long and now it's starting to show. Like the time two years ago when he turned out to be a Brazilian engineer with ten kids. And the seaman on the Esso tanker with the same name. Only he was sixty-three and a grandfather. There is no real Dogeron Kelly. You left him there at the train station and now he's dead. The whole family says so.

"So Dog's your name, but what's your game, Mr. Kelly? You look like a cop. Are you?"

He shook his head. "Hardly. I'm an individual entreprenuer. I do whatever is profitable and comes to hand. I'm a specialist in generalities and it would have been fun to watch you deball your friend."

"You think I couldn't?"

He gave a tight-lipped shrug and then grinned at her. "It's not very hard. I've ticked off a few knotheads that way in my time too. It's just that it's an extreme penalty to pay."

"For rape?" she asked quietly.

"Come on, nobody would have to rape you."

"Now you're on a sex kick too."

"Kid, *you* brought the subject up. I wouldn't bother raping you."

"Oh? What would you do?"

He let out another strange, raspy laugh. "Hell, I like it better the other way around. I'm the lazy type myself. Prolific, imaginative, but lazy. Half the time the only thing I get into is a conversation."

"And the other half?"

"That's another story not fit for virginal ears," he said.

She almost had an answer for him, but he winked and walked off, sipping at his beer. For some reason she felt annoyed. Raul Fucia had been right, of course. She *had* known what she was doing when she dressed for the party, instinctively aware of her potential, but it was not more than any of the others had known. No one was needed to tell her that she was beautiful and well constructed. They had, but the mirror was enough. Raul's reaction was enough to satisfy her judgment, but then that damned Dog had to come along and shatter her illusions. He couldn't have cared less.

She picked up her drink and tasted it, swirling the ice around in the glass, feeling a little smile pulling at the corners of her mouth. Hell, the dog, yes, small "d" dog, did it to her. He couldn't have cared less. And she wasn't too old, either. She was just right, absolutely prime, beautiful, knowledgeable, apt and exactly right.

The smile widened when she realized she had put her finger on it. She had been around just a little too long in the fast-moving world of show business where judgment had to be quick and correct if you wanted to survive not to miss it. She had put him in the forty-plus class, but the full head of short hair and only light touch of gray had fooled her. That and the strange lack of aging and the musculature. Heredity. Dog Kelly was a real, total predator.

And now he was stalking. She watched him across the room, his complete unconsciousness of what he was doing. The women's eyes would drift and follow him, return blankly a moment to what they had been doing, then drift again. In the small groups he would join there was an uncomfortableness among the men, barely discernible because they were aware and the act they chose as a facade would cover them. Sharon knew they felt the same way she did. They wondered what he was doing there.

For some obscure reason a funny thought ran through her mind. She wondered if he were carrying a gun.

It was Darcy Taylor who took the initiative as always. A sweet thing on the screen, but a wild one when a man passed she wanted. She left Raul in midsentence and had her arm through Dog's, taking the glass out of his hand to taste his drink with a mock shudder and steering him out of sight to the bar beyond the French windows. It just wasn't Raul's day at all. Sharon felt sorry for whoever he managed to go home with this night.

"Enjoying yourself, Sharon?"

She looked up, smiling, knowing the voice. "Hello Walt."

Walter Gentry III was the prototype of any and every bachelor who ran his own private world with inherited millions that Hollywood had attempted to emulate. The major difference was that this, the last of the fabulous Gentry clan, had, by shrewd business acumen, more than doubled his inheritance, another factor he had inherited along with a natural aristocratic appearance and charming manner. He had been the target of women from monied families for the past twenty years, but somehow never bothered to become permanently attached to any of them.

"I see you met Dog," Walt said.

"Yes, who is he?"

He tapped a long cigarette from a gold case and lit it, letting the stream of smoke drift from his lips. "We met in the Army. Quite a guy. He was one of the natural-born killers. He make an impression?"

"Unusual type," Sharon told him noncommittally. "What's he do?"

Walt smiled and shrugged. "I often wondered but never bothered to ask. One day he took me to a fraternal club in London and I saw a picture of him in a football uniform. Seems like he was an All American in college."

"He looks like a cop."

"I kind of think he dabbled in that business too. He's got some odd friends." He picked a drink from the tray of a passing waiter and tasted it. "Good to see you again, Sharon. It's been quite awhile. How come old S.C. let you out?"

She looked up into his knowing grin and smiled back. "My boss is dangling me like bait on a hook for his enterprises, as if you didn't know."

"Lovely bait. How could any fish resist it?"

"You're not supposed to. I was critically inspected for capture appeal by the great one himself before being turned loose in your pond."

"And what sort of catch are you supposed to land this time?"

He signaled the waiter over, took another glass from the tray and handed it to her. "Thank you," she said. "S. C. Cable wants you for a coproduction deal. He figures you for at least a five-million-dollar bite."

"Nice, he laughed. "And you're the bait. I imagine you are expected to give your all."

"That's what I've been told. You'll never miss a slice off a cut loaf, and all that sort of thing."

"Except that your boss doesn't know . . . or believe . . . that this particular loaf has never been sliced."

"He's been told, but he doesn't believe," she said.

"Ah, you demi-vierges must have a rough time. You're too much for me, young lady."

"I thought you enjoyed the last time."

"Oh, I did. And thoroughly too. A little nerve-racking, but absolutely enjoyable. You're quite a performer. If you must know, I never had a more pleasant night and day after, but it was a real cliff-hanger with that attitude of yours. Not that I don't appreciate it. All I can think of is how awful it would be if you ever had an accident, like slipping on a bicycle pedal or something. All your efforts would have been wasted."

"I could still take a lie detector test," she said.

"Sharon, I'd sure like to be the lucky man. Want to make a trade?"

"For what?"

"Your virginity against the five million?"

"Walt, you're a wonderful man, but I think I'll hold out awhile longer."

"Old S.C. is going to be pretty mad when he hears about the terms you're turning down."

She smiled at him, a laugh in her voice. "He'll never believe it," she said. "The bonus factor alone is worth five percent."

Gentry had to laugh back at her. "You know, sugar, I usually can get anything I want with a nice sidewise glance of my gorgeous blue eyes, and if that doesn't work a cheap diamond compact will do the trick. Except with you. Honey, you're impossible, but to get you off the hook and let you enjoy your own personal hang-up a few months longer, you can tell S. C. Cable that the deal is on. If you even like me a little bit, tell him you gave me some of that precious stuff just to preserve my reputation."

"Any options?"

"Sharon . . . I'm too lazy to fight for it. Or over it." He looked across the room to where Dogeron Kelly was standing, leaning against the doorjamb of the French windows, looking out into the misty night with Mona Merriman nuzzling his shoulder. "Watch out for him, Sharon," he said.

"Why, Walt?"

Gentry took another sip of his drink and idly flipped open a gold cigarette case. "He reminds me of a title of a book. Not the book, just the title."

"Oh?"

"Call of the Wild," he told her.

She could feel the heat in her and he was a full room away. When she looked down, her fingers were twisting the ring around . . . third finger . . . left hand. It was made of brass and she had to wash the verdigris off every night. The stone was glass, green and chipped, something they laughed at but she excused as her good-luck charm when everyone knew she was neither sentimental nor superstitious. Her virgin stone one had named it, still green, not yet ripe, and when it changed color, ready for picking. She had culled out all the answers when they queried her and the answer were enough to stuff up the mouths of the smart

64

ones. She had been around too long and too well. The diamond's cutting edges were just a little too sharp to touch. Nobody ever mentioned the ring anymore.

Across the room Mona Merriman had taken him outside the French doors. The rain had stopped and a gentle fog turned the windows across the avenue into soft orange ovals. Sharon got up and walked up to Raul Fucia, holding her glass in front of her.

"I need a drink," she said.

VII

"Mona Merriman," I said, "you're a scratchy woman. Why don't you go get yourself a celebrity?"

"I've done them all, dear. You look like better copy."

"Except that I'm a nonentity."

"Not quite, Dogeron. I've already spoken to your friend Lee Shay. You see, he doesn't dare hold things back from me. Your being an heir of Barrin Industries makes you an item."

"Mona, an heir I am, but an inheritor I'm not. I told you I was the family bastard."

"Even *that* is news," she smiled sweetly. "After all, mine is a gossip column."

I ran my fingers down the side of her face and pinched the skin under her chin. "Baby," I said, "you wouldn't want me to chew you up, would you?"

"That sounds like fun."

"I didn't mean that way."

"There's another way?" She was laughing at me now.

"Suppose I told everybody how old you are."

Her laugh didn't fade a bit. "Impossible!"

"Want to bet?" I asked her.

Then the smile started to ease off.

I said, "Give me one hour on the telephone and I'll give you the place, date and time."

She cocked her head and looked at me, not quite sure of herself. "I don't believe it."

"Look at my eyes, Mona," I said.

"I see them."

"Now you know. It's a game I can play better than anybody you ever saw. Just nip me and I'll bite your head off."

"You really *are* a bastard, aren't you?"

"Everybody keeps telling me so," I said.

"Would you really tell how old I am . . . *if* you found out?"

"Just try nipping me, kid."

"You're interesting, Dog. How old am I?"

"Wild guess?"

"Sure."

I let my fingers travel over her face again and felt the tiny lines. "Twenty-one," I grinned.

"Do it again, but for real this time."

"Sixty-two," I said.

"You overaged me by a year, you bastard. If you tell anybody I'll kill you."

"If they ask you're under thirty."

"Shit. I love you, you crazy creep. Now I'm going and find out all about you, then *you'll* be sorry."

"Come on," I said, "why work for it. Anything you want to know, I'll tell you."

Mona Merriman looked into her near-empty glass, swirled the contents around a few times, then met my eyes. "Have you ever killed anybody?"

I nodded.

"Want to speak about it?"

"Not necessarily."

"Guess I got me a live one. You know what I'd like to do to you?"

"Naturally. I always have trouble with you young broads. Pick on somebody your own age."

"Okay, killer. Now one little kiss and let's go back inside."

Her lips barely brushed mine, but I could feel the tiger behind them and all the real want that was there. The little pubic touch, the outthrust chest that tried so hard to initiate the nipples into a semiorgasm behind the engineering of elastic and fabric. Twenty years ago she could have been fun.

So I grabbed her arm, kissed her right, just once, and she went all tight at first, then to pieces, and I got that funny little-girl look and said, "No more, Mona. You and I have a generation gap."

"I'd like to gap you."

"But you won't. Now behave."

"Bastards I have to run into," she smiled. "I'm going to take you apart, Mr. Kelly."

"It's been tried before."

"By experts?"

67

"By experts," I said.

"You only think so, Mr. Kelly." Her hand dropped from my shoulder, reached down and felt me, then went back to my shoulder again. "My, you *are* impervious."

"Not really, doll. I just pick my own time and place."

"Let's go back. I want some friends of mine to meet you."

Walt Gentry saw us step across the sill of the French doors into the alcoholic hubbub of the room, waved and excused himself from the couple he had been talking to and ambled over in that loose-limbed stride of his. He gripped my hand and shook it with a grin and a wink toward Mona. "Good to see you again, Dog. It's been awhile."

"Same here, Walt."

"Mona got her hooks into you already?"

She gave his arm a pinch and faked a pout. "You could have prepared me for this beast, Walter. He's a refreshing change from the usual group."

"That's because I'm a commoner," I said.

"You back to stay?" Walt asked me.

"Could be."

"Things get a little dull on the Continent?"

I shrugged, trying to remember the last twenty-some years. "What's excitement one time gets to be pretty routine the next. Maybe I'm like the salmon coming back to spawn where it was born."

"And die," Mona added. "They always die after they spawn. Is that why you came back, Dog?"

"Dying isn't my bag, lady. At least not yet."

"Ah, an item. You've come home to spawn. And who will be your spawnee?"

Walt laughed and patted her shoulder. "Mona, my girl, must you always look at the sexual side of things?"

"It's the interesting-item side, dear boy. My readers eat it up. We have an extremely provocative and eligible bachelor in our midst, so naturally I'm curious." She looked at me, still smiling. "You haven't answered my question, Mr. Kelly."

"I haven't given it any thought, either."

"No lonely heart waiting for your return?"

"Can't remember any. Most people were glad to see me go."

Walt waved a miniskirted waitress over with the drink tray, and when we picked up our glasses said, "Don't let all that Barrin Industries background fool you, Mona. Dog here was born a hundred years too late. There aren't many places for a real live charger anymore. He was glad to be booted out."

"And who is getting the boot?" a quiet voice asked.

We all turned and nodded at the weathered face of the heavy-set man behind us. "Mona, Walt . . ." he said. "Dick Lagen, Dog Kelly. I don't think you've met."

I held out my hand and he took it politely for a second. "I'm a regular reader of yours, Mr. Lagen."

"Ah, at last someone interested in news with an international flavor."

"That's more than he said of my literary gems," Mona told him.

Lagen smiled and ran a forefinger across his hairline moustache. "Mona, dear, we are hardly competitors. It is he with a bent for finance that is interested in the news I report. Is that not true, Mr. Kelly?"

There was an odd note to his tone and his eyes were watching me carefully. "Pursuit of the buck is a necessary evil. I'm always glad to break even," I said.

"I understand you've come back to claim an inheritance."

I let out a laugh. "Ten big G's. How did you know about that?"

Dick Lagen tasted his drink, made a satisfied pat at his mouth and said, "My earliest researches were made during the height of the Barrin regime. You'd be surprised how much I know about your family fortunes."

"Well, as long as I get my ten grand, I'm happy. I never was much of a family man."

"So I understand. However, ten thousand dollars isn't much of a nest egg these days. Plan to invest it?"

"Hell, no," I told him. "I plan to blow it. Money is no good unless you convert it into something useful or pleasurable, anyway."

"That's a rich man's attitude, Mr. Kelly." That odd note was back in his voice again.

"You'd be surprised how rich a guy with ten grand can be." I grinned at him and he smiled back.

"By the way, Mr. Kelly. Your name is Dogeron . . . D-O-G-E-R-O-N," he spelled it, "isn't it?"

"Yeah, why?"

"Unusual."

"Old-fashioned. Not many of us left."

"True. I've heard it mentioned several times however. Istanbul, Paris . . . you have been there, haven't you?"

"Sure," I agreed.

"Could it possibly be that it was the same Dogeron?"

Mona gave us both a quick, sharp glance. "Now see here, Dick, if you have something about my friend, don't go wasting it in your portentous columns . . ."

I stopped her with a laugh. "If Mr. Lagen ran across me in those places you could use the items, Mona. I'm a grade-A student of those belly dances and cancan joints. You hit those places, Mr. Lagen, and it's a real good chance my name came up. I have a reputation of sorts too. You like the fleshpots?"

His hand touched the moustache again to cover up the flesh on his face. Mona laughed and pulled at his sleeve. "Why, Dick, you old roué, you. And here I thought you were always the proper one. Dog, dear, you're a darling. At last I have something to hold over his head."

Lagen let out his suppressed laugh and made a faint grimace of embarrassment. "You have caught me red-handed, Mr. Kelly. Now my secret is out. I'm a rather shy voyeur. My opportunities to indulge myself are rare and discreet."

"Don't worry," I told him, "your secret's safe. I've already threatened Mona with exposure on one account. I'll add this in."

"Remarkable guest you have here, Walt," Lagen said. "Not at all continental. Good to see you, Mr. Kelly."

When he left, Walt said, "I hope you didn't pinch a nerve, buddy."

Mona tossed her hair and chuckled. "Don't be silly. He was pleased as punch. And here we all thought he was stuffy. Dog . . . what else do you do? You seem to have an odd insight into people."

"Comes with age, lady. Besides, aren't all men supposed to be alike?"

"If they were, you wouldn't be with one of *my* age. As you told me, why don't you pick on somebody your own size? I see any number of covetous female eyes turned in this direction. Take him around, Walt. I'm anxious to see how he can deal with all those professional little things flaunting their wares. Ah, me, for the days of firm tits and thighs again."

"Quit kidding, Mona," I said. "Experience more than makes up for it."

"Get him out of here before I attack him, Walt."

When she walked off squealing at the two current TV stars, Walt said, "Some woman."

"Yeah."

"Just don't let her fool you. She'd blow the whistle on her own grandmother if there was any gossip in it. No social

70

conscience. Same thing with Lagen. He considers himself the great crusader these days. Some senator tagged him the fiscal watchdog of unscrupulous industry and he's trying to live up to the name."

"What's he doing at a bash like this?" I looked around the room. "They're hardly his type of people."

"As you so ruthlessly uncovered, Dick's a girl watcher. He still gets a kick out of the show business crowd. You meet everyone?"

"Pretty much."

"You got all the guys jumpy. They have their territory all staked out and now they're waiting to see which one is going to get his claim snaked out from under his nose."

"Where's Lee?"

"Out at the bar lining up a couple of in-town celebrities to do guest shots on TV commercials. What's he so rattled about?"

"Beats me."

"He acted like he was afraid to leave you alone. I thought you were the big brother type in the old days."

I grinned at him. "Lee worries too much. He ought to get married."

"Look who's talking," Walt said. "Incidentally, who *are* you going to lay your paws on tonight. Even I'm interested. They're all available, you know. Well, almost all."

"Oh?"

Walt inclined his head to the corner of the room where the blonde I had met on the way in was perched on the arm of a chair, talking to the pumpkin of a man who was one of the bigger paperback book publishers. "That one. Little iron pants. A sexual Molotov cocktail and nobody can get a match to her fuse."

"Sounds interesting."

"Tiring is the word. Even the experts gave up on her. One was a psychiatrist and even he couldn't reach a conclusion. Right now she has Raul flipping his lid. Until he tangled with her he thought he was the epitome in conquering maleness."

"I heard her take him down. Everything she tell him true?"

"Everything. I can vouch for it. She left me hanging on the ropes too. Come on over and say hello. Let's see what kind of impression you can make."

"Let's not. She's a little young for this dog."

"Consider it a change of pace."

"Suit yourself."

The pumpkin publisher acknowledged our introduction

71

and left to chase down his newest acquisition who had come in like a summer storm surrounded by effete young men.

Walt said, "Sharon Cass, Dog Kelly. I'm making it formal." He smiled in my direction. "Sharon objects to casual associations."

Those big, brown eyes looked into mine with a twinkle and she held out her hand. "Walt's always running me down, Mr. Kelly."

"Call me Dog. It's easier."

"He tell you about my iron pants yet, Dog?"

"Why sure."

"He's a real squealer. It's better when they find out for themselves."

"Watch it," Walt said. "One day somebody's going to carry a can opener."

She took her hand away gently and tilted her head at me. "Someday."

Sharon Cass was beautiful. She was different. The beauty was as much internal as physical, but the one inside her seemed to be carefully repressed. Her hair was a tinted blonde that shimmered in soft waves around her shoulders, accentuating the full maturity of a lithe, sensual body. The miniskirt over her crossed legs ended at midthigh, lush offerings shaped to perfection, unashamedly exposed. She was frank and direct, not coming at you like most women would, and I had to laugh at her. "Walt said you'd be a change of pace."

"Not very flattering of him."

"Why don't you guys talk," Walt broke in. "I have to go play host."

We watched him leave, then Sharon toasted us with her cocktail and said, "I think Walt deliberately sicced you on me, Dog."

I looked at her, puzzled.

"Earlier I conned him out of five million dollars for a co-production movie deal with Cable Howard Productions."

"Just like that?"

"Like a lamb to the slaughter. My boss expected it to be a matter of intrigue, with the deal to be consummated in Walt's silken-sheeted bedchamber." She let out a little-girl giggle. "Instead, he was very nice about it. Now I think he's avenging his actions."

"What the hell kind of business are you in?" I asked her.

"Skin and celluloid. Cable Howard makes movies. Good ones, bad ones, but all money-makers. Walt knows he'll double his investment."

"And you have to put out to con in the investors?"

"It's not a new game, Dog. Anyway, I play it by my own rules."

"Damn!"

"Don't tell me you're a moralist," she said softly.

"I don't buy into anything under those conditions."

"And how *do* you buy in?"

Her expression was one of open curiosity.

I felt my teeth showing in a tight grimace. "Forget it. Maybe I *am* a moralist. I have my own rules too."

"Will they work?"

"What?"

"I understand you're one of the Barrins."

"Word sure does get around," I said.

"Secrets don't last long in this place," Sharon told me. "By tomorrow you'll be exaggerated into a mythical European multimillionaire financier come to capture Barrin Industries for yourself. The stock market will reel under the impact of the news."

"Bullshit," I said.

"Why, Mr. Kelly."

"I have ten grand coming, that's all."

"So Lee mentioned, but it's more fun making it millions. When do you collect?"

"I won't. They'll beat me out of it. My maternal grandfather left that money subject to certain conditions that make it almost impossible."

"I like that word 'almost,' " she said. "Can you make it?"

"Nothing much else to do."

"Your smile is too gruesome, Dog. What's up your sleeve?"

"A long arm that would like to carry you out of here."

She put her glass down and stood up. The top of her head came up to my mouth and when she tilted her face up her eyes were shining and her lips were wet.

"All you have to do is ask," she said.

"I'm asking."

"Then let's go."

The rain had turned her into a spring blooming flower, dewy with glistening droplets of moisture. She wore no hat and let her hair tangle in the wind, not caring when she sloshed through puddles at the curb. She laughed at the night, her arm linked into mine, and the few people who passed huddling under umbrellas looked at us strangely and smiled.

We ate in an offbeat Italian restaurant, walked another

six blocks to a bar where the only occupant was a bored bartender, but we ordered our drinks, excluded him politely to go back to his television and sat at the end, watching the city bathe.

"It's fun, Dog. I haven't done it in a long time."

"Tell me about it tomorrow when you have pneumonia," I said.

"Will there be tomorrow?"

"Sure. You're giving me a sense of responsibility."

"Like taking in a stray bird?"

"Something like that."

"Okay, I'll call you. Full of health and vigor and youth . . ." She stopped and the humor left her face. "I . . . didn't mean it that way . . "

"Kitten," I reminded her, "I ain't no stripling. I look in the mirror every day when I shave. The gray is there and the lines are beginning to show. It happens to everybody."

"I like you that way."

"Good, since I don't have a choice. Besides, kicking around with you is a little rejuvenating. It brings me back to the old days."

"Mondo Beach?"

The glass stopped halfway to my mouth. "How'd you know about that?"

Her eyes danced a little bit. "Because I'm originally from the same neck of the woods as you. About six miles away. When I was little we used to go to the north end of the strip . . . the part the Barrins didn't have fenced off for their estate. Sometimes we'd swim around the jetty and picnic on their property, pretending we were rich."

"How about that."

"Did you ever go there, Dog?"

"A few times. I was pretty much of a loner."

"Tell you something else," Sharon added. "My father worked for Barrin Industries . . . oh, about fifteen years. I was even inside the big house once when Dad had to deliver some reports from the factory."

"Small world. You never should have left the countryside. What the hell you see in the city is beyond me."

"Commerce, big Dog. One has to clothe and feed oneself. I'm not exactly the factory type and there was nothing left for me in the old hometown once Dad died. You ought to know the feeling."

I pulled over the peanut bowl and stuck it between us. "My leaving wasn't entirely voluntary. I was encouraged. Hell, if you haven't heard the old stories you're missing a lot of scoop."

"Oh, we heard things, but mostly it was overhearing what the grown-ups were talking about. It didn't make much of an impression. Just before I left, there was a lot of hoopla going on about those girl cousins of yours. I never paid much attention to it. You're going to be quite a shock to them, aren't you?"

"My lawyer is preparing them for the strain," I glanced at her. "Why are you so curious about the Barrins?"

"I guess I'm still hungry for any news from home. I haven't been back since I left."

"Good. Let's take a crack at it together."

She looked at me a few seconds, smiled and nodded. "Okay. When?"

"Tomorrow . . . if you can get off."

"Mr. S. C. Cable is damn well indebted to me, Kelly boy. My time is my own for a while."

I looked at my watch. It was after one in the morning. "Then let me get you home. It's going to be a short night. Where do you live?"

"Not far. We can walk."

I shook my head and laughed, threw some money on the bar, grabbed a handful of peanuts and held out her raincoat. "Come on, seal," I said.

Her apartment was a high rise on the East Side, a modern slab of polished concrete and glass that towered next to its twin, presided over by uniformed doormen with calculating eyes that could read through any pretense but couldn't quite accept reality.

Sharon's offer of a nightcap was warm and for real and she let me open the door of her apartment, entered ahead of me switching on the lights, then hung our coats in the foyer closet. "You make the drinks," she said. "The bar's over there and I'm going to change, as they say, into something more comfortable. At least dry." She let out another tinkly laugh. "You'll just have to suffer. I don't think you'd look very good in one of my housecoats."

"I'll live."

I made the drinks, then toured the room, wondering how the hell anybody could stand the cold efficiency of modern living. Everything was functional American, conscientiously decorated according to the rulebook of Manhattan. It took a few minutes before I recognized what was wrong. There was nothing personal about the place at all. It was just that . . . a place. Like hotel suites that came out of their own rulebooks.

Her voice came from the darkened corner of the room

75

and I could feel her eyes watching me. "What are you thinking, Dog?"

"How long have you been here?"

"Four years. Why?"

"This isn't a girl's place at all." I turned around and she walked into the light, a picture of loveliness in a sheer blouse knotted under her breasts and a gamin skirt that swirled around those lovely legs. Her hair was up under a turban that made her look like something from the Arabian Nights and I felt a thump in my stomach before I got hold of myself.

"Strange observation. Most men would never notice it. But you're right." She took the drink I held out and folded up on the plastic couch with her legs tucked under her, then settled back, smiling. "I can't call an apartment in Manhattan home. I just live here. I don't even want to fake it with all the nice little goodies women usually enjoy playing with. I'd rather wait."

"For what?"

"The real home I'm going to have."

I rattled the ice in my glass and tried the drink again. "Positive little gal, aren't you? Who you got picked out?"

An impish grin tugged at her mouth. "Oh, I'm already engaged, so I can afford to be positive."

"He's going to have his hands full with you, kitten."

"Yes, I know." She put her drink down and uncurled from the chair, then walked slowly across to me. Her arms went up and encircled my neck, her mouth moist and open. "Wouldn't you like to have your hands filled with me, Dog?"

It was a strange kiss, slow, easy, then like magnets pulling together hard and frenzied with her body melting into mine, fusing with heat and crazy wanting. The knot of the blouse became undone and her warmth was pressed against me, a low moan deep in her throat.

When I held her away my breath was coming too damn fast and I had trouble keeping my voice under control. "You're an engaged woman, Sharon. Remember?"

"There are times when I could forget very easily."

I tied the knot back under her breasts. "Quit making me pant. I'm beginning to feel like one of the toadies at Walt's party. I have to go."

"You can stay if you want to."

"No I can't."

"Why not?" Her tone was teasing and that impish grin was playing around her mouth again.

76

"I didn't bring my can opener," I said.

"I can lend you one."

Then we both laughed and she got my coat. At the door I kissed her good night, a small, brushing kiss with my hand under her chin. I looked at those big eyes again and took a deep breath. "Any trouble from you, kitten, and you're going to get bounced."

"Wonderful!"

"I didn't mean it that way," I laughed.

"Tomorrow?" she said.

"Tomorrow."

A war movie from the late forties was thundering through the apartment when I walked in. Lee was sprawled on the floor, a soft cushion under his head and a drink in his hand, staring glassy-eyed at the TV screen, an overflowing ashtray beside him. He jerked around, startled, when I touched him with my toe, taking a full second to recognize me and relax.

"Buddy, do you cut a path when you move."

I walked over to the bar and poured myself a ginger ale. "Now what?"

"Oh, nothing, nothing at all. Nobody can get near that Cass doll without it being plotted like the D-day invasion and you walk out with her on your arm in five minutes. Just how do you pull it off, Dog?"

"I'm polite."

"Balls. I don't know what you're after, but you got everybody watching you like a hawk. From now on, a nonentity you ain't." He burped and finished his beer, tossing the empty can at a wastebasket and missing. He pushed himself to his feet and stood there, swaying. "Dick Lagen made a phone call."

"Good for him."

"It was about you."

"Great," I said.

Lee made a disgusted face and weaved over to a chair. "Look, Dog, when that guy starts a project, he just doesn't let up. I didn't get most of the conversation, but he's doing a rundown on you and Barrin Industries."

"So?"

"If you have anything to do, get it done fast."

I finished the ginger ale and started taking off my clothes. "Why should I?"

"Because if you have anything to hide, forget it. That newspaper syndicate of his lets him go all the way out. They've got contacts all over the world and . . ."

"Lee," I cut in, "knock it off. If he wants a biography, I'll give it to him personally."

"Sure you will. How much of it will be true?"

"None of it," I said.

"That's what I thought." He stared into his hands a second, then wiped them across his face. "Dog . . . no shit now, you in some kind of trouble?"

"Just staying alive is trouble," I told him. I folded my coat across a chair and stripped off my shirt. His eyes saw the scars and went wide, his tongue flicking out nervously to lick his lips.

"Dog," he said, "you know this apartment is being watched?"

"Who says?"

"The doorman, Danny . . . he's a retired cop. He spotted them this afternoon. I heard him telling Clarence when they changed shifts. Look, nobody ever cased this building before, even when the whores had an operation going in the penthouse. These guys aren't cops, either."

I walked over to the phone, picked up the receiver and dialed a number. When a voice I recognized answered, I said in Spanish, "Chet, you have a tail on me?"

Chet Linden had just awakened, but was totally alert. "Uh-huh," he said. "We decided to keep you under surveillance until we're sure. Have a good time with that pretty blonde, Dog? If you want any information on her I can give it to you."

"Friend, you wouldn't want to aggravate me, would you?" I asked him.

"Certainly not, Dog."

"Then cancel the tails. The next time out I'll simply lose them. If I pick them up the second time I'll lean on them a little. If it happens for the third time I'll hurt them good and come after you."

"You change colors fast, Dog."

"Let's keep it pleasant, Chet. This isn't amateur night. You should know better. Now, do you lift the tails?"

After a moment he said, "What's your itinerary?"

"Tomorrow a meeting with the family. Then back here, I suppose. I'll be glad to let you know if you don't deactivate this number."

"You wouldn't screw me, would you, Dog?"

"Chet, if I did you'd never know it."

"Okay. We'll keep this line monitored."

"Chet . . ."

"Yes, Dog?"

"What are you leaving out?"

78

He chuckled, and I could picture his face wrinkled in a grin. "Still the shrewdie, aren't you?"

"Let's have it, kid."

"There's a rumble on in the Paris area. Some of your former associates are trying to locate you. Pretty soon they'll tumble and pick up your trail."

"Hell, I'm not hard to find. I used my own passport and came back the way I went out."

I heard that same laugh again. "That's what fooled them. They never figured that angle. It looked like a beautiful decoy."

"So tell them where I am."

"Yeah, sure. Take it easy, Dog. You know conditions in this racket."

I grunted and hung up. Lee had an uneasy expression on his face, not able to tell what it was all about. Finally he said, "Just answer me one thing, Dog. Do I have anything to worry about?"

It was too good a question to resist. "Hardly a thing," I told him.

He looked a little pale around the mouth, swallowed hard and shuffled off to his bedroom. "Hardly," he said. "Oh, boy!"

VIII

The three of us sat in the back compartment of the limousine. Not the back seat. The compartment. When it came to practical luxuries, Leyland Hunter hadn't been niggardly with himself. He perched in his own specially made swivel chair, idly rocking, grinning at Sharon and me like a kid showing off a new toy.

"Like it?"

"I've misjudged you, mighty Hunter," I said.

He tapped the back of the partition beside him. "Color TV. The bar comes out of the wall on your side. Well stocked, I might add. Radio, freezer compartment for ice . . ."

"If this back seat makes up into a bed you'd have a nice rolling bordello, friend." Sharon's elbow gave me a nudge and I knew she was trying to suppress a smile. "Don't laugh, kid," I told her. "The old goat can still deliver. In fact, he's thinking of taking up the sport seriously."

Sharon said generously, "I believe it."

Leyland's eyes twinkled. "He's right, you know. Of course, it will be on a carefully calculated . . . and timed basis. My age doesn't allow for too much exuberance these days."

"Men," she laughed.

"And now," Leyland answered her, "let's talk about women. Specifically you. Dog here has told me about your forays onto Mondo Beach. Is it possible I knew your father? Was he Larry Cass?"

Sharon's forehead wrinkled into a puzzled frown. "Why . . . yes."

"Ah, then I did know him. Quite well, in fact. At one

80

time he was in charge of new projects at Barrin. A valuable man. Too bad they lost him."

"He couldn't stand the new management," Sharon told him bluntly.

"And I can't blame him," Leyland said. "The era of big business came to a standstill when the giants died off. Industry has succumbed to the computer age. The incompetents move in and make up for their inadequacies by the sheer weight of numbers, college degrees and inherited wealth. Nobody pounds a table anymore or walks down in shirt sleeves for a head-on clash with a foreman who screwed things up. Cameron Barrin was a giant. It was a shame to see him go too." The faraway look left his eyes and he glanced at Sharon with a little smile. "I remember Larry having a daughter. She went fishing with us one day."

"In a boat?"

"Yes, a rowboat. We caught flounders. You didn't want to put live minnows on the hook . . ."

"And cried! Yes, I remember that. But you were so . . . I'm sorry."

"Don't be. It was many years ago. From the way it looks I'll be having more fun now than I did when I was young. Incidentally, pretty little lady, I hope you have no designs on my unscrupulous friend here. There are better prospects in the world, I'm sure."

"I'm engaged, Mr. Hunter."

"That is no excuse. Would your fiancé approve of your being on a junket with someone like him . . . even for a day?"

"I doubt if he'd object. He's very broad-minded."

"So is Dog. That's what I had reference to."

"Aren't you an acceptable chaperon?"

"Not anymore, little one. Dog has seen to that. I've become quite lecherous."

"In that case, he'll just have to protect me."

"In that case, the cure will be worse than the disease," Leyland said.

"Well, like the man said, 'When rape is inevitable, lie back and enjoy it.' "

I let out a low growl and said, "You know, I really don't have to ride back here with you two sex maniacs. There's an empty seat beside the driver."

Hunter gave me that funny look again. "I wish I were young enough to take you up on that, Dog."

"Someday you might try," I told him. "Then I'm going to ask how you got that cauliflower ear."

"It's quite a story," he said.

81

Three generations ago Grand Sita had been a distant retreat, a manufactured barony hand tailored to Cameron Barrin's personal preferences. The rolling hills that covered six hundred acres surrounded a mansion that reflected the tastes of the era, a walled area with private roads and every accommodation money and talent could buy. The original structure with its simple design had long ago been obscured by new additions that social position demanded, and Cameron's Castle had ceased to become a joking venture into the country, but a place where only the fashionable were invited.

That was three generations ago.

Now it wasn't a six-hour carriage drive any longer. A superhighway sliced through a corner of the estate, making one-third of it unusable. Public utilities won condemnation proceedings and stretched a row of ugly latticework pylons hung with high-voltage cables from east to west. New York City was an hour and fifteen minutes away and obscured by fog, but Grand Sita was worth ten times more than it cost if the land developers could force it onto the market.

Due northeast, two miles away, the vast complex of buildings that housed the machinery of Barrin Industries nestled in the archaic splendor of ivy-covered red brick on the edge of Linton, a city built, structured and occupied by people working for Barrin or servicing its employees. At one time, Linton was only the name of the millowner who had his establishment on the bank of the river. With the advent of the first Barrin factory it became a city without government. Time had changed that, though. They had a mayor now, a city council and all the trappings of modern society. They had murders, fires, a small race riot and a welfare program.

From the crest of the bridge over the railroad tracks you could see the curve of the road that turned east midway between the estate and Linton, boring through the seven miles of countryside to the summer domain of the Barrin family old Cameron had named Mondo Beach, a vast crescent of sand and surf that looked out on a still unpolluted section of water.

We turned at the fieldstone columns where the ornate wrought-iron gates were rusted into the open position. The roof of the old gatehouse had collapsed and the building was unoccupied, but an old dungaree-clad gardener riding a motorized lawn mower looked up curiously, waved and motioned for us to go on in.

Leyland Hunter said, "Most of the staff have died or retired. They never replaced them."

"It's still beautiful," Sharon told him. She was peering out the window, a strange expression on her face. "I never came in this way."

"I thought you were only here once," I said.

"In the house. Many a time I sneaked onto the grounds."

"Hell, I used to sneak out. It's hard to picture somebody wanting to sneak in."

"This was the house on the hill, Dog. Every kid I knew used to envy the ones who came here."

"I had more fun in town."

Hunter chuckled again, his eyes moving between us both. "I'm afraid you were to the manor born, but not bred, Dog. Whatever genes your father carried sure took hold in you."

"Bastards have more fun, buddy," I assured him.

"And coming home doesn't raise any nostalgia at all in you?"

"Not a damned bit. This place doesn't represent opulence for me at all."

"What does, Dog?" He had stopped smiling and was watching me with a lawyer's eyes now.

"I've seen better and worse."

"You've played a lot of poker, too, haven't you?"

He didn't have to tell me what my face looked like. I said, "I hardly ever bother to bluff, Hunter boy."

"Again, that qualification. *Hardly*. Very improper. I think you mean rarely."

"So I'm stupid," I said.

The gravel drive gave way to old-fashioned Belgian paving blocks as we pulled into the area in front of the house. I let my eyes drift out the side window and took in the towering three-story mansion with its imposing Doric columns flanking the broad staircase, and for a single second I could see the old man standing there, hands on his hips, the cane in his hand, lips twisted in a snarl as he waited for me to walk up to where he could take a cut at my rear end, a sample of what was waiting for me inside. My mother's face would be a pale white oval in the upper window, suddenly covered by her hands, and the grinning faces of Alfred and Dennison would be hidden behind the great oak door, unseen, but their muffled laughs of anticipated pleasure ringing in my ears. Somewhere the girls would be cleverly out of sight, but not out of earshot of that cane landing on my hide.

But he never made me yell and he couldn't make me

cry. I did that later when I was alone, not from the pain, but the damn humiliation of having to take Alfred's lumps for him. Or Dennie's. Or one of the girls'.

It passed in a second. The old man was out in the family plot now, my mother discreetly buried in another cemetery, and the others probably above such trivia by now.

The only one there was a middle-aged butler obviously awaiting our arrival. I didn't recognize him. "Fine reception," I said.

Hunter nodded and hefted his attaché case. "You aren't exactly a *cause célèbre* and I am simply a family retainer, I'm afraid. And, of course, Miss Cass here is an outsider. Nothing to require a formal reception."

"Just tell me one thing, Counselor. Am I expected?"

"Of course not," he told me. "Do you think I want to spoil all the fun?"

I grinned at him, then the grin broke into a taut laugh. I said, "I have the feeling you're going to drag this out as long as possible."

"You feel right, Dog. Until now, my relationship with the Barrin family has never been what you'd call fun. I think it's about time I had a little."

Sharon shook her head and stared at both of us. "Look, maybe it would be better if I waited in the car."

"Kitten," I said. "after all the trouble of sneaking onto Grand Sita. I think you deserve seeing what the Barrin clan is *really* like."

The butler's name was Harvey, and he took our hats, ushered us to the polished walnut doors of the library, slid them open ceremoniously and stepped forward to announce us.

Somehow the years fell away again for another brief instant and it was like peeking into the same room when something of momentous portent was being acted upon. There were other people then and Cameron Barrin would be seated behind the hand-carved desk. Now there were seven faces, five oddly familiar, and one was behind the desk. The butler's voice had the same intonation old Charles's had had and there was that same casual, almost disdainful turning of the heads as we were announced.

Harvey said, "Mr. Leyland Hunter, Miss Sharon Cass and Mr. Dogeron Kelly."

It was funny. No . . . it was damned well hilarious. Oh, they saw us all at once and were willing to grant Hunter a degree of recognition with supercilious smiles, then offer Sharon an expression of semipolite curiosity, but when my

84

name sank in there were five people there who damn near shit in their pants.

Dennison stared at me from behind the desk, his beady little eyes almost popping out. Alfred stiffened in his chair and knocked over an ashtray. Veda had a drink halfway to her mouth, didn't know what to do with it and set it on the floor like some harridan in a Bowery barroom Pam and Lucella just gave each other open-mouthed expressions before they looked at me again.

Only Marvin Gates, the husband Pam kept on the marital leash, was able to smile. He was half drunk, impeccably dressed like an outdated Hollywood director and he raised his drink in my direction. "Ah," he said, "the family skeleton has come out of the closet. Welcome home."

Pam snapped out of her shock as though she were being awakened from a bad dream. The voice that used to be shrill was coarse now and she snapped, "Marvin!"

"Sorry about that, dear," he told her. "Thought it was the proper thing to do, y'know?" He took another pull at his drink and grinned again.

"Don't bother getting up," I said to the room in general. I took Sharon by the arm, led her to a leather wing-back chair and sat her down. Behind me, I knew Leyland Hunter was watching the entire tableau with satisfaction, so I put on the rest of the show.

Somehow Dennison had struggled to his feet and was standing there, still glassy-eyed, and reluctantly held out his hand. "Dogeron . . . I thought . . ."

I squeezed his hand and saw him wince. "No, I'm very much alive, Dennie." I ran my eyes over his pudgy body. "You've gotten fat, kiddo." I dropped his hand, looking down at the remains of the slob who had made my life so miserable those long years ago. He was four inches shorter than me, weighed just as much, but it was all in front and back of him, bulging through his clothes. I said, "How's your pecker these days, Dennie?" Behind me I heard a couple of sharp gasps and Hunter covered his laugh with a cough.

Cousin Alfred didn't bother offering his hand. That snaky face of his glared pure hatred at me, but he didn't chance staying seated and having me yank him out of his chair. He stood up, a lanky caricature of a ferret with the same expression he had the day he clipped me with his new roadster. He said, "Dogeron," with a voice veiled in sarcasm, wishing I'd drop dead on the spot.

"Still got a sore ass, Alfie?" I asked him.

"That broken arm ever give you trouble?" he said with quiet venom.

I grinned at him, a nice, slow, easy grin that was all teeth and half-lidded eyes. "Not a bit, Alfie." I bent down, picked up the brass ashtray he had flipped over and squashed it double in my fist. "See?"

Not a muscle moved in his face. "Good. I often worried about it."

"I thought you would," I said deliberately. "It makes me feel better to know you were so concerned."

My hellos to my three female cousins were polite and brief. They couldn't get the horror out of their eyes so I gave them time to adjust, letting them sit there wondering what the hell was going on. Marvin Gates still wore his silly smile, busying himself making drinks for us without asking what we wanted, his eyes touching Pam's with wry humor all the while. Somehow he was enjoying the show too and I couldn't help liking his attitude. He was an incompetent jerk who had gotten his balls in the wringer from a sour swindle and had been paying for it a long time. Pam had laid the clout on him pretty heavy and now he was getting his turn to watch the squirming.

Behind me, the metallic snap of Hunter's attaché case reminded me we had come for other things and I pulled up an ottoman and sat down beside Sharon. Unconsciously, her hand reached out and touched my shoulder. I could feel her fingers stiff with tension, trembling slightly at the hostility in the air.

It was Hunter's scene now and he played it well. He had held the stage too many times in this same room and he knew all the lines and all the tricks. He knew the audience too and how to play to them.

For a moment he looked at each one individually, then: "Ordinarily, this would have been a routine meeting. However, with Mr. Kelly's return we can enter a new dimension that has been necessarily delayed by his absence. Now . . ." he looked around once more, "I take it you are all quite satisfied with his identity?"

It was Alfred who said, "Shouldn't we be?"

Hunter smiled indulgently. "After all, twenty-some years is a long time. If you prefer further documentation . . ."

Alfred said, "It won't be necessary."

"Very good." He picked several printed sheets from his case and spread them open on his lap. "Most of the details of your grandfather's will are well known to you. However, there are certain provisos that were to be explained only when all of you were present. Each of you who shared in the estate was given his inheritance immediately after the death of Cameron Barrin. It was only Mr. Kelly's share that was not awarded. As you are aware, it was to be ten thousand dollars in Barrin Industries stock at the time of Mr. Barrin s death As you well know, the number of shares representing ten thousand dollars now are quite disproportionate from the date of Mr Barrin's death. I am now prepared to deliver those shares to Mr. Kelly."

I could feel Alfred's snide smile from where I was sitting. "Wasn't there a provision attached to that award, Mr. Hunter?'

"You are referring to the morality clause, I believe?"

"That's right."

"Do you intend to investigate Mr. Kelly's background for a possible breach of that clause?"

"You're right again."

Hunter looked at Dennison and he stared a smirking smile too. "I agree completely," old Dennie said.

I was about to get up, slap them both on their ass and get out of there, but saw the motion of Hunter's hand and sat down again.

The lawyer said, "In that case, I have been instructed to enforce another proviso which was not known to you." He paused for a second, his face bland, but his eyes were twinkling. "Before the remainder of the estate can be awarded, Mr. Kelly has the option of conducting a full investigation of *your* background for a breach of the morality clause. The time limit on such investigation will be limited to three months."

Dennis and Alfred were on their feet instantly, Dennie's face flushed and Al's livid with anger. "That is ridiculous," Dennie stated.

Hunter shook his head and cut him off. "I'm sorry. It was your grandfather's request. You both have stated your intentions, I now state his. Had you not bothered, this matter could have been settled immediately." Hunter turned slowly and looked at me. "It still may be if Mr. Kelly does not care to exercise his prerogative. If he refuses, the bequest will be made as stipulated."

Alfred stood there, his fists clenched at his sides. Dennie was leaning on the desktop, his face still flushed with the indignity of it all. The three girls hardly breathed and Marvin grinned over the top of his drink.

"A question, Counselor," I said. "Supposing they get something on me *and* I get something on them?"

The introspective stare Hunter held on me told me more than he realized. He was evaluating me again and his estimate was going up. I was reading back into a dead mind and reading it right.

Leyland Hunter nodded sagely and said, "In that case, the entire remainder of the estate goes to you."

Inside my head my mind was laughing because the old boy was paying off for all the times I had gotten the dirty end of the stick. He was saying, "Go get 'em. It isn't much, but you never wanted much anyway. If they deserve it, stick it up and break it off."

"Well," Hunter asked me, "do you choose to exercise your prerogative?"

I didn't bother to smile. I simply looked at Dennison, then at Alfred and let a few seconds go by. "You're damned well told I do," I said.

We drove into Linton and had supper in the log and fieldstone restaurant that used to be a gristmill. The decorations were from another era, flintlock pistols, spinning wheels, strange household utensils and relics from the time when America was vibrant with potential energy and every man an individual who knew how to determine his own destiny. The food was simple and magnificent, the wine a tasty local product, and we finally sat back, filled and ready to talk.

With our glasses filled from a fresh bottle, Hunter toasted us all. "To a successful day," he said. "It was a pleasure to see the Barrins outraged at the mere suggestion that they might have a moral flaw."

"You're a crafty bastard, Counselor. The old man was a shrewdie too."

"Indeed he was. I hope you think more of him now."

"Not more, just better." I sipped my drink and put the glass down. "One thing went over my head, friend. You could have laid me out on that morals clause right then. Why didn't you?"

Hunter finished half his glass before he answered me. "Had they not demanded the investigation of you, I would have. You see, that was another proviso of Cameron's. I imagine he figured you wouldn't have stood a chance otherwise, so he gave you one at their expense. If they wanted to be nasty about it, they had to put up with some discomfort at least. If they weren't so simon-pure, they'd pay for their attempt to discredit you."

I nodded and made wet circles with my finger on the tabletop. "Think much of my chances, buddy?"

"Frankly, I think it's a lost cause. I told you, I have already made inquiries and your cousins are quite respectacle."

"You're too orderly, Hunter," I said. "You didn't get your nails dirty. If you want dirt, you dig where the dirt is. Something always turns up."

"You think you have more experience at that sort of thing than I have?"

"I wouldn't be surprised, mighty Hunter."

"No," he said. He finished the rest of his drink. "Nor would I." He snapped his fingers for the check, put it on his credit card and stood up. "Now," he said, "I hate to be party to a possible immoral act, but tomorrow I have a session with the accountants at the factory. I have arranged to stay at the Gramercy Inn for the night, with separate accommodations already made for you two. In the meantime, you may have the use of the limousine, with or without the driver. I rather suspect Willis would be happy to be relieved. He has a room reserved for him too. If you wish, you can drive back to the city if you can pick me up again tomorrow. It's your choice."

Sharon started to laugh and gave him a look of faked anguish. "Mr. Hunter, you *really* are something. How can you even suggest a thing like that? Don't you know anything about women at all? I have no change of clothes, no nightgown . . ."

"Hell, sleep in your drawers," I said.

"Why, you . . ." She punched me in the arm and hurt her hand.

Hunter was watching us impishly. "I've provided for such a contingency," he said. "The necessary apparel was purchased earlier by phone and has already been delivered to your room. I trust you'll find my selections satisfactory. My legal mind also encompasses a fairly accurate estimate of female sizes and delicate necessities."

"You know, Counselor," I said, "I'm beginning to wonder if there aren't a few things you could teach me."

"In some areas only, Dog," he replied.

For an hour after we dropped Hunter and Willis off at the hotel, we cruised around Linton. By full moonlight the town was a prettier place, the grime hidden, the gradual decay of the buildings unseen. No longer was there a night shift at the factory, so the streets were quiet, most of the windows in the residential area dark. A patrol car was parked outside an all-night diner and another drifted by idly with barely a glance at us.

The memories came back again, but with little impact . . . the old sandlot where I played softball with the Polacks was still there, littered with garbage now, but the wire backstop was still in place, rusted and sagging, a collection area for windblown papers.

We drove down Third Street and I said, "See that old building on the corner?"

Sharon nodded. "Looks like a haunted house."

"Belonged to Lucy Longstreet. She was Madam Lucy then. Only whorehouse in town. That used to be a swinging joint on Saturday nights."

"How would you know?"

I let out a laugh, remembering. "Hell, girl, kids know everything. There was a tree in the back we used to climb so we could watch the action. I'll never forget that black-haired girl from Pittsburgh. One day she and Mel Puttichi were inside on that big brass bed sexing up a storm and got little Stash so damn excited he let go of his limb and fell down on top of me and knocked us both out of the tree. I felt like whamming him. Things were just getting good."

"Dog!"

"So what's wrong with watching? All kids are curious. It was first-class sex education."

"And I suppose you were a steady customer at the place from then on?" she pouted.

"Hell no. Ran plenty of errands for Lucy, though. Always a buck tip and a chance to see one of the dames bare-ass when we brought in the package . . . if we were lucky. That black-haired dame never used to wear clothes ever. Quite a sight."

"You're terrible."

"They had a double murder in there one night. That ended things for Lucy. It was never the same again. I think she took her suitcases of money and moved out to the coast."

"What happened to the girls?"

"Probably all respectable married by now. You'd be surprised how much in demand they are."

"After working . . ."

"Well, who wants a virgin anyway? Like the man said, if they're not good enough for somebody else, they're not good enough for me either."

"Two words to you, Dog, and they're not good night."

"You *really* a virgin?" I asked her.

"If you promise to be gentle I could prove it to you."

"That's taking quite a chance."

"Maybe."

"Never mind, I'll take your word for it."

We drove past the outskirts of Linton and Sharon told me to take a left on a country road, then another left into a

90

lane that ended a hundred yards away. I turned around the rutted dirt oval wondering what she wanted to see here, then the lights of the car swept over the remains of a small frame cottage set back in the trees. The windows were gone and a large oak had collapsed on top of the porch, one of the limbs taking out an attic dormer. A rubble of red bricks from the chimney made a mound at its base, nearly hidden by weeds and grass.

Very softly, Sharon said, "That's where I used to live. I was back here once before. My old bicycle is still out in back. It's all rusted to pieces now."

"Who owns it?"

I felt her shrug. "The bank, I guess. There used to be a For Sale sign in the front, but nobody ever wanted the place. I had a lot of good times here, Dog. Dad and me. It wasn't much, but he was happy. Neither one of us ever cared for pretentious living."

"Then why sneak into Grand Sita?"

"Little girls are curious too. About different things, that is. You know what puzzled me about that big house you lived in?"

I shook my head.

"How you didn't get lost in it. I used to try to figure out how you could find your way between ends. I could picture myself running upstairs and down and into all sorts of crazy empty rooms, yelling and screaming and never anybody to come get me out. I was always glad to get back home."

"You're silly," I told her. I nodded toward the cottage. "Want to go in?"

"No. It would be too depressing. Don't let's spoil the evening."

"We're not going to find any night life in Linton, kid."

"You know what I'd really like to do?"

"Just name it."

"Drive out to Mondo Beach. For once I'd like to go through the main gate as a genuine guest."

"You know, Sharon," I said, "I think you're a snob."

"That's me," she said.

I found a hammer and screwdriver in the trunk of the car and knocked the lock off the hasp that held the gates shut. Wind-driven sand had piled up two feet deep along the bottom edge and we shoveled it away with our hands. When it was cleared I forced one section open, heard a hinge pry loose from the top, then I was inside. The road-way was too drifted over to try to get the car through, so

91

Sharon took a blanket from the back seat and we started to walk toward the ocean.

After a dozen steps she stopped and said, "This ain't no place for city clothes, buster," then kicked off her shoes, stripped her stockings off, tucked everything under her arm and waited. I grinned, did the same thing, rolled my pants legs up halfway and held out my hand.

You could smell the salt air and hear the gentle rumble of the surf long before we came out of the near-jungle of trees and undergrowth. Once all this had been neatly planted and tended, a showplace for the elite who came in horse-drawn carriages, and later in thundering, brass-shiny automobiles. Vegetation had overrun the picnic areas, the cabañas were flattened somewhere under the sand and only the foundation ruins of the old icehouse were visible. At the south end, ghosting against the sky, you could see the turreted outlines of the twenty room summer house. My grandfather had built that out of quality materials and the sea storms still had a lot of years to go before they nibbled it to pieces.

"Funny, isn't it," I said.

"What?"

"It used to be such a great place. Now it's almost back to where it was before the old man built it up. You know, I think I like it better this way."

"So do I."

We were silent for a while, just looking around in the pale moonlight. Then I took her hand, tugging her up and over the rolling dunes, the foot-high strands of grass brushing against our bare legs. We came to the last mound, and there was the gentle slope of packed sand and the water in front of us.

She spread the blanket out and curled up cross-legged on one side. "It's beautiful, Dog."

I sprawled out next to her. "It's about the only thing the old man owned that I used to want. I figured I could put up a shack made of driftwood and pull a Robinson Crusoe bit." I rolled on my side and looked up at her. "One year I did just that. They sent Al and Dennie to some fancy camp while the rest went to Newport for the social season and my mother and I camped out here for six days. That was when she told me about marrying my father."

"You never knew him, did you?"

"Only through her. He was some hell raiser. She sure loved him though."

"Why wouldn't they accept him?"

"Come off it, baby. You know the drill on that bit. If

there was no money there was no position, ergo, no marriage into the Barrin family. They never thought my old lady would tell them to go toss it and get herself knocked up outside the family circle. Trouble was, when my father died she lost all the spunk she had. They squeezed her until there was nothing left. The old man had her yanked out of the apartment they were living in while she was alone and dragged her back to Grand Sita. She didn't even know she was pregnant then. He hired guards to keep my father away, got him fired from his job, had him rousted out of the state and kept my mother incommunicado until after I was born. One day the old man showed up, beat the hell out of four of the guards and took off with my mother and married her. A week later he was dead and she was back in exile again in the old man's little Siberia. I don't think she ever left it except to come here on rare occasions. When she did I was just a kid and it was all over so fast I can hardly remember it. She was dead in the morning, in the coffin by noon and buried before nightfall. I threw some rocks through the old man's greenhouse, spit in his decanter of fine booze and opened the sluicegate on the pond behind the house and drained his imported goldfish into the creek. I think the gardener covered for me and he never noticed anything wrong with his booze. The next day Alfie and Dennie knocked the shit out of me for something or other and I hit Dennie over the head with a rake. For that I got a week alone in my room and had time to think." I stopped for a minute and looked at the ocean. "They never should have left me in that room," I said.

"Why?"

"I thought too much," I told her.

Down the beach something disturbed the gulls and they set up a screeching racket for a minute. A wisp of cloud ran across the moon and snaked away, letting the brightness come back again. The wind was soft and warm, a tail end of summer feel to it, just strong enough to stir the soft sand into easy motion.

Sharon's hand ran over the back of mine and she tossed her head so her hair made ripples in the yellow light. "Dog . . . it's a shame to waste this whole ocean."

"Who's wasting it?"

"We are. We should go use it."

"Now?"

"Uh-huh. Right now." She uncurled from the blanket, stood up and stretched luxuriously against the sky. Then her hands came down and did something at the back of her dress. Soundlessly, it slithered to a heap at her feet. She

93

found the hooks of her bra and undid them, tossed that beside her, then with a single, fluid movement seemed to slide out of the tiny flowered bikini pants that were left. She turned and looked at me, the night shadows flowing around tanned shoulders, reflecting off the silken whiteness of magnificent breasts that swept up and out in a daring gesture before molding into the tanned flatness of a stomach that was navel dimpled before contrasting with the bathing-suit whiteness around her hips. In the moonlight the hair of her loins was a tantalizing vee of auburn, her legs firm and softly muscular. She let me look at her a long minute, standing there with her hands on her hips, pelvis pushed forward provocatively.

Finally she said, "Coming?"

"If you don't get the hell out of here I will," I told her.

She laughed, turned and ran toward the surf, her stride loose and boyish. I heard her laugh again and her body splash into the water. Then I got up and took off my own clothes. I was going to leave my shorts on but that wouldn't help matters at all, so I shrugged, took them off too and walked down to where she was waiting.

We were pleasantly exhausted when we got back to the blanket. The wind smiled and let its warm breath dry us off, and we lay on our backs staring up at the cloudless sky. I closed my eyes, wondering just how the hell this ever happened, feeling like some kind of an idiot for messing around with a nonprofessional kid. Then my eyes snapped open because the gentle touch of her fingers were on my stomach, moving slowly downward until they held me, and Sharon was leaning over me, her mouth inches from mine.

"You are beautiful, Dog," she said.

Her mouth came closer and closer until it was a soft, warmly moist thing tasting mine with the strangest kind of touch I had ever known. My own hands ran down her naked back over the rise of her buttocks, pushed her away so I could cradle the firm thrust of her breasts, then began to explore all those lovely parts of her.

Sharon's breath caught in her throat sharply. She smiled, kissed me again, then let her smile widen when she felt the pressure of my palms holding her away from me. "I told you I really was a virgin."

"Damn, kid," was all I could say.

"Does it make a difference, Dog?"

I turned on my side and let the heat ease out of me slowly. It was easier now and I felt like an even bigger idiot. "Look you," I said, "you're an engaged girl."

94

"Woman," she corrected.

"Okay, a woman. You got yourself a guy and you think enough of that thing to save it for him, so don't go tossing it away."

"Isn't the choice mine?"

"Not with me, kid. This time it's my choice. Just keep it safe between your legs until he gets it, hear?"

"You're mean."

"Just sometimes. Right now I feel damn moral. Old Hunter should be here to see this performance. He'd never believe it."

"I'll tease you."

"Try it, Sharon, and you'll be an unsatisfied, neurotic wreck in one hour. I'm too damn old not to know every gimmick there is to turn you women-children inside out."

Her laugh tinkled in my ears and she tossed her hair again. "All right. I've managed this long, so I guess I can hang on a little while longer."

"Who is he, Sharon?"

"A very nice guy. We grew up together."

"Would he appreciate this little picture?"

"I don't think he'd mind at all. Not really."

"You don't know men very well."

"But I do. I truly do."

She touched the side of my face, leaned down again and kissed me lightly, the tip of her tongue barely brushing my lips. My arms went around her and I laid her down beside me. Around our heads the grass rustled in the wind. I reached over her and pulled the blanket over us both. Beside me her body was snuggled into the curve of mine, warm and naked. The moon watched us and another wisp of cloud passing its face made it seem like it winked at me.

Then the early sun woke us both and we looked at each other and kissed. Her hair was tousled and full of sand, but she didn't care at all. We brushed each other off, got dressed, folded up the blanket and walked back to where we had left the car.

And this time we had company.

The black sedan and the patrol car flanked the limousine and the uniformed cop was peering through the window at the interior. The big beefy guy in the sports shirt and slacks was inspecting the wreckage of the padlock on the gate and neither of them heard us coming.

I said, "You fellows want something?"

The heavy-set guy turned and looked at me, his face set in a nasty scowl. "You do this?"

"That's right."

He dropped the lock and started toward me, but I was coming to meet him too and he didn't like what he saw. The cop edged between us watching me, another hard-looking character with a broken nose and cold, flat eyes that come with too many years on the force. He didn't like what he saw either.

The cop said, "Who are you, mister?"

"I asked the first question."

"Don't get smart, buster. I can handle you real easy."

I looked at him with that old smile starting to come out. I couldn't stop it because it always happened that way. "Don't you wish you could," I told him.

The two looked at each other, but by the time they looked back to me again I had taken two easy steps in the right direction and I wasn't bracketed any more. The civilian wiped his hand across his partially bald head and curled his lips again. "You know this is private property?"

"Sure. It always has been. That's why I want to know what you're doing prowling around."

The question came at him too fast and the sneer went back into a puzzled frown. I flipped a cigarette in my mouth and lit it. The cop was changing his original attitude now. Maybe it was because the limousine was bigger than the black sedan and I wasn't the type he could shake up with a badge and a gun.

"I asked you your name, feller," he said again.

"Kelly," I told him. "Dogeron Kelly. My grandfather was Cameron Barrin and this area is still part of his estate." I blew out a cloud of smoke and flipped the butt at the feet of the beefy guy. I said, "What difference does it make to you what I do here?"

His face was tight with anger, but the limousine was backing me up and he couldn't quite figure the play. Finally he said, "This place won't belong to the Barrins much longer, that's for sure." He looked at the cop, the cop shrugged, then they both turned and went back to their cars. Both of them kicked up sand getting out of there and the radio antenna on the black sedan snapped off when it cut too far under an underslung limb of an oak tree on the bend.

When they were out of sight Sharon came up and slipped her hand into mine. "You know who that was, Dog?"

"Sure, Cross McMillan. He still has that scar on his skull where I beaned him with a brick."

"You love trouble, don't you?"

"Not exactly, honey. It just seems to find me. It's always been that way."

96

IX

We met Leyland Hunter in the coffee shop of the inn, both of us looking a little silly like kids caught playing doctor behind the barn. He noticed, but outside a small smile, said nothing. When we finished eating, he said, "I understand you met another old acquaintance."

"Cross McMillan. The CIA should have this town's grapevine."

"Not really. It just happens that he is negotiating for the Mondo Beach property. His lawyer has to deal with me. Mr. McMillan wants the situation expedited."

"How does it stand, Counselor?"

"McMillan has first option to buy outside the family. It was put on the market last year by your cousins. It has rarely been used, the buildings are destroyed and pretty well depreciated and they don't see any reason for keeping it."

"In other words," I said, "they need the money."

Hunter nodded. "Frankly, yes. They intend to put it into renovations in the factory."

"It's prime property, buddy. Why haven't they sold for a year?"

"Guess."

"Waiting for further development of the area," I said.

"True. There have been rumors of a new highway and some of the bigger land speculators have been probing around."

"Only there were no highway appropriations and the land boys are holding off."

"And now Alf and Dennie are really in a bind. What's the asking price?"

"One quarter of a million dollars."

97

"Come on, Counselor, that's a steal."

The lawyer looked at me and shrugged. "For McMillan it is. He has the property boxed in right now. If he got that he'd have the nicest chunk of valuable property in the state."

"How long before he picks up the option?"

"Another week."

"He the only bidder?"

"Sure," Hunter told me. "The way his land surrounds Mondo Beach nobody wants to be bothered with development. The *really* valuable acreage would be his for commercial development and he won't sell. Right now the beach and the right-of-way belong to the Barrin estate. He wants it all."

"Let's screw him, Hunter boy."

The lawyer's eyes tightened a moment and he watched me carefully. I grinned and took out my brand-new checkbook, wrote in it and tore out the page. I handed it to him. "This ought to take care of sales, fees, taxes and insurance," I said.

His forefinger ran up and down the edges of the check, then his eyes ran up to mine again. "Sometimes I can go along with a joke, Dog. Sometimes I can't. Will you excuse me a moment?"

I nodded and he pushed back his chair and left.

Sharon was looking at me with an expression of puzzled humor, like she had heard a funny story she didn't quite understand. "Where did he go?"

"To make a phone call," I told her.

When Hunter came back he slipped into his chair with his mouth set in an odd grimace.

I said, "Well?"

"You astonish me, Mr. Kelly."

"What happened to our pet names, Counselor?"

"Anyone who hands me a check for over a quarter million is automatically a 'mister.' " He ran his fingers across his head with a nervous chuckle and stared at me again. "You are now sole owner of Mondo Beach, my young friend. You'll have the papers shortly, the undying hatred of Cross McMillan and the everlasting animosity of the Barrins for having underrated you."

"You *bought* the beach?" Sharon asked incredulously.

"He did," Hunter informed her.

"Just like *that*?" She snapped her fingers to emphasize the point.

"Just like that," Hunter repeated.

"But . . . why?"

98

I said, "They never let me play Robinson Crusoe before, kitten. Remember?" I squeezed her hand and my fingers played with the ring she wore. I glanced at the green mark on her skin and she pulled her hand away gently. "Counselor . . ."

"Yes?"

"Don't bother mentioning who bought the place. Okay?"

"The deed will specify . . ."

I cut him off. "It'll be a corporate setup. All in the family. I'm the sole stockholder. If there are any complaints you can bust the story, but sit on it if you can. Incidentally, what was the option price?"

"McMillan put down fifty thousand."

"My cutie cousins are going to hate to give it back."

"I wish I knew what this was all about," Sharon said.

The lawyer let out another sigh. "So do I, my dear, so do I. Now, shall we go?"

Habit kept me sitting so I could see the side mirror on the limousine, and the white car that had dogged our trail since we left Linton was still there. It would lie back, then catch up whenever we ran a close traffic signal, and now it was three cars back, but staying to one side so it could keep us in sight.

I opened the sliding glass panel and tapped Willis on the shoulder. "How about pulling over at the next station for gas?"

"Oh, we have plenty, sir."

"So fake it. I want to use the john."

"Certainty, sir."

A quarter mile up a flashy new service area beamed its neons at us and Willis pulled into the driveway and stopped beside the pump. The white car went by, slowing down, and rounded a turn out of sight. I jumped out, went inside to the pay phone, got the operator and gave her my number.

A voice I didn't recognize said, "Yes?"

I recited the recognition sentence and said, "Did Chet pull that tail off me?"

"One moment, sir." I heard him patch into another line, then Chet came on himself.

"I thought you were going to cool it, Dog."

"Cut the comedy, Chet. Am I being tailed?"

"Not by us."

"Somebody's on me."

"Tough, kiddo. You expect anything else?"

I let out a hard laugh. "I'm not yelling for help, pal."

"The best help you could get would be to be dead, then nobody could squeeze anything out of you. They got some pretty tricky gimmicks today to make a guy talk. I never should have voted down that hit."

"Who are they, Chet?"

"My bet is they belong to The Turk. Three of them came in yesterday. We figured them for that new expansion operation in Jersey, but it could be anybody's guess. We're laying off them until they make a move."

"The Turk ought to know better."

"He carries a big grudge," Chet said. "Anything else?"

"Nope. See you."

"The hell you will," he told me and hung up.

Hunter was busy with his paperwork and Sharon was sitting there with her head back and eyes closed when I got in the car. We eased back into traffic and a half mile down I saw the white car half backed into a driveway. It gave us a hundred yard lead, then got behind us again. I felt my mouth pulling into a grin, then I leaned back beside Sharon and took her hand. My fingers found the ring again and rubbed against the little stone. I held up her hand and looked at it. "That thing is going to poison you," I said.

"I think it already has."

"Why don't you throw it away?"

She gave me an annoyed poke and took her hand back. "It has sentimental value."

"Worth the poisoning?"

"I think so."

Hunter shuffled his papers, his eyes smiling at us over the top of his glasses. "Must be nice to be young."

"I wouldn't know. Besides you had your chance with old Dubro and blew it."

"I didn't blow it."

"Okay, horny. I didn't mean it that way."

"Who's old Dubro?" Sharon asked sleepily.

"Some dame he went skinny-dipping with when he still was a charger."

"And what's skinny-dipping?"

"Honey . . . bare-ass swimming is what it is. Like last night, remember?"

"He sleep with her too?"

"Mighty Hunter didn't have the nerve," I grinned. "Maybe she was lucky. Counselor here has got himself a reputation."

I saw him flush and make a negative motion with his head, his eyes darting sidewise at Sharon.

"Can you imagine being married to that old doll, buddy?"

The stern grimace twisted into a grin. "Yes, I can. Maybe that's why I've stayed happily unmarried."

"Nothing like being wedded to a job, kid. Now you can screw a tort instead of a tart."

Sharon's elbow jabbed into my ribs and Hunter let out a grunt, then went back to his papers.

Behind us the white car had closed up until only a station wagon separated us. Ahead was the madman maze of concrete that led into the city of fun and when we stopped at the tollbooth it pulled into the adjoining aisle and I had a look at the driver and the guy alongside him.

The Turk was stupid. He should have used somebody else. Markham, who drove the car, was an on-the-toes shooter, but he was to damn direct. He laid everything on a moustache and goatee hiding the snap in his nose and Bridey-the-Greek who rode the jump seat beside him had the idea that all his kills had gone unnoticed. A little nothing of a guy who could be buried in a crowd of two thought he was still one of the grand gang of anonymous killers. A first-class ice-pick man who could cripple or murder on order. It couldn't be murder, or The Turk never would have sent Bridey-the-Greek along. I was to be an example. Markham would hold me under the gun and Bridey would do the job.

Right side paralyzed, Turk? Or maybe from the waist down? You want, I can make it so that only his head swivels around. He can't even pee without somebody holds his dick and somebody else squeezes his bladder. Like that sex operation, a vase-something, you know? All the way it can go with one slice and not only babies don't he get, but no fun either.

Shit. The Turk was laying on a twenty-five-grand job split two ways and all I could think about was why my price went down. Last year Kurt Schmidt had me on open season for a half million. The two Frenchmen tried me and after that he had no takers at all. Marco could have had me in the pub outside of London, if he had really gone for it, but what good is a half million if you're dead? I had the .45 in my hand under the table and the sound of that hammer going back was like the crack of thunder, even if the girls didn't hear it. But he heard it. He smiled a little bit, kissed Lisa's hand without taking his eyes off mine and told all the others that I couldn't be made unless it was in the back.

But The Turk was no Kurt Schmidt. He couldn't get over his kid days of haggling for fake rugs with the tourists and would try for a fistful of cheapies before he went the big route. Or he got scared out of the marketplace.

Leyland Hunter rattled his papers back into their folders and stuffed them into his briefcase. He popped open the bar, poured himself a short brandy and downed it. "That one was for you, Dog."

"Thanks."

"Help yourself if you want to."

Sharon and I shook our heads. I said, "What's next on the agenda, pal?"

The old lawyer gave me a wry look and folded his hands in his lap. "I am empowered to conduct an investigation into your moral character. Needless to say, after our, er, recent episode that is hardly necessary."

I had to laugh. "Old buddy, a lawyer you may be, but a psych pro you're not. The little laughing ladies you are referring to wouldn't cop out for all the cash in the world. You'd have to admit your own pariticpation in the group therapy and I can see the boys at the club giving you the heave-ho already."

"You do have a point there, Doggie boy."

"What are you two talking about?" Sharon demanded. She was giving each one of us funny looks, waiting for an answer. I spelled it out for her in a couple of succinct sentences and she glanced at me wide-eyed and started to giggle.

"Maybe I can help, Mr. Hunter. We slept together last night, all naked and warm playing tickle finger all over until we fell asleep."

"I would hardly enjoy involving you, my dear," Hunter told her.

"It probably wouldn't do any good anyway," she said. "The big lunk refused to violate me. I could even have a doctor verify it."

"And ruin his reputation?" Hunter smiled.

"Well, it could *prove* how high his moral standards are."

"My cousins wouldn't like that," I said. "Why don't I just give you an affidavit to the effect that I have been a little promiscuous at times?"

"Don't make it easy for them. Besides, I'd rather enjoy the investigation. My reading matter has been rather dull lately."

I grinned back and glanced at the mirror. The white car was still there, tucked behind two others. It squeezed through a yellow signal light, closed up some so we

102

wouldn't separate at the next traffic light and followed us up the avenue to the spire of Hunter's office building.

Hunter said, "Can I drop you two somewhere?"

I glanced at Sharon. "Home for me," she said. "I'm on East Fifty-fifth."

"That puts me two blocks away, Counselor. We'll go back in style."

"Good. The garage is right in the same area. I won't be needing the car again today." He picked up his briefcase and checked the clasp. "Do you, er, have any specific plans, Dog?"

I squeezed Sharon's hand. "I'm contemplating a few."

He caught the action and smiled. "I mean in reference to your family."

I nodded and shook a butt out of my pack. "Don't sweat it, friend. I have three months to think about it."

"And it's a frightening thought. Are you sure it's worth the now-paltry sum involved?"

I watched him, my lips tight across my teeth. "You bet your sweet ass it is," I said.

We let him off in front of his building, went crosstown to First Avenue and turned north. For a minute I thought we had lost the white car in the tangle of traffic at the intersection, then I caught a flash of it crowding the opposite side of the one-way street and settled back against the cushions.

Things were going just right. I slid open the glass partition and told Willis we'd drop Sharon off first, but she bounced up with a hard negative and said I was going to walk her back from the garage and things weren't going so right after all. The time and the place to intercept the two goons in the white car had to be mine or I'd be hurting. I was betting they were being paid for a smash job, but if it was necessary a direct hit would be acceptable. For the first time I missed the comfortable feel of the iron that used to hang on my belt and the way the spring-loaded holster would throw it into my palm at the right touch. There were other ways to do things, but it was nice knowing the advantage of a standard Army .45 automatic with alternating rounds of armor piercing and lead nestling in the clip.

The garage was midway up the street and the driver nosed down the ramp into the bowels of the building above it, swept around the fender-scarred concrete columns with skilled ease and stopped. I hopped out in front of the ticket booth, gave Sharon a hand through the door and watched the car pull up to the open elevator at the far end. A Volkswagen came down next, scraped one of the pillars, then

103

pulled into an open slot on one side evidently reserved for it. Then I looked around the curve and saw the white reflection of the next one in line and knew it was time.

I told Sharon I'd be right back, asked the guy behind the window of the ticket counter where the men's room was and walked off in that direction.

The flat windshield of an older car made a good mirror. Bridey-the-Greek and Markham had left their car and were right behind me, Markham splitting up to take an angled course through the parked vehicles. I spotted them again in the plate glass of a framed ad for a Broadway show just before I turned the corner of the alcove that led to the toilet.

I had my belt off and wrapped around my hand, feeling that funny expression I always got cutting creases into my face. Maybe the slobs thought I had been away long enough to forget the tricks. Or that being out of the game would spook me. Hell, it was spicing up the day for me.

I pushed open the door and went inside. There were two urinal bowls and three unoccupied toilet booths and I knew I had lucked in. I picked the one to the right, took my shoes off, placed them so anybody looking down would figure I was squatting there nice and helpless on the pot. I closed the door, locked it, hopped over the top and got behind the entrance door and waited for Markham.

He came in right on schedule with a snub-nosed .38 in his hand, saw the single closed toilet door and my shoes in position and walked right past where I was behind the opened door and never even looked when it snicked shut. He never heard me come up behind him in my stocking feet and was just raising his foot to kick the toilet door when I smashed him in the skull behind his ear and sent him splintering through the wooden partition so hard his knees broke the seat right off the bowl. Before he could yell I had his head in my hands, slamming his face against the two-inch dirty ceramic and his teeth broke like dry matzos in a splatter of blood that speckled the stagnant water like obscene curds.

Markham was totally unconscious and never felt what happened to him. He never heard me break the bones in both his hands and never even moaned when I cupped my palms and clapped his eardrums into split pieces of delicate flesh. But in a few hours and for a month later he'd be one hellish piece of agony and his days of usefulness to The Turk would be over.

I picked up his gun and put on my shoes.

Outside the door Bridey-the-Greek would have heard the

noises and be anticipating the finish. It was a pleasure to oblige him. All I did was open the door and say, "Come on," and by the time he realized it wasn't Markham's voice he was already inside looking up at me with eyes gone suddenly wide with fear.

He tried one lunge with the ice pick and I broke his wrist with the barrel of the .38 then laid it across the side of his head before he could let out a scream. He went down in a heap like dropping an old laundry bag, the pick rolling from his fingers. It was a nice new sliver of steel, that pick. You could buy them in any dime store and when you loosened the handle and sunk it into somebody you pulled back all your fingerprints and only left pain and slow death behind. Voorhies and Brown had gone that way. Bridey had given it to Bud Healey in the spine and Bud had been a paralytic from the waist down ever since, vegetating in that cottage outside of Brussels.

So I broke every finger on Bridey's hands too, then stitched him up the side of each cheek so he'd never be invisible in a crowd again. I opened his belt, pulled his pants and shorts down and waited the two minutes until he started to wake up, holding the point of the pick right over the two goodie sacs, and just as a groan wheezed through his lips and his eyes opened and rolled toward mine I drove the ice pick through those lumps of tissue into the rubber-tiled floor and the frenzied yell of horror he started never got past the sharp hiss of his sucked-in breath before he fainted.

The next person to go in that bathroom would do more than relieve his bladder or bowels.

Sharon watched me walk toward her, her face expressionless. Then she frowned momentarily and teased her lower lip with her teeth. I took her arm and walked up the ramp to the street. Her apartment was only five minutes away and she didn't speak until we turned at her corner.

Then she said, "There's blood all over your shirt."

"I'm a messy dresser."

"Two men followed you in there."

I nodded.

"They didn't come out."

I nodded again.

"Did you know them?"

"Yes."

We reached the canopy that strung out over the sidewalk in front of her building and stopped.

"They were in that white car that followed us all the way home, weren't they?"

105

"How did you know that?"

"Because I was watching you. I saw them in the rearview mirror."

"They were from another time, kitten. Forget it."

"What did you do to them?"

"Jogged their memories a little so they'd either be more careful the next time or never do it again at all.'

"Which one will it be?" she asked me.

"I don't think they'll try to renew our old acquaintance, sugar."

"Can you tell me why it happened?"

I lit a cigarette and stared down the street. "No "

"I see."

"Want to see me again?" I asked her.

There was something solemn in her face. Her eyes went to mine, looking deeply into each one Finally she said, "Yes."

I tilted her chin up and kissed her gently. "You're going to be sorry."

She nodded. "Yes, I know."

"And don't care?"

"No."

Lee had left a note on the dresser that my suits had arrived from Weller-Fabray and were hanging in the closet. There had been a call from Al DeVecchio and I was to call back at my own convenience. A secretary from Dick Lagen's office had called, but had left no message. He ended the note with an invitation to join him for supper at a new place called Oliver's Lodge if I had the time.

Not that my old buddy wanted my company that much. He was chewing his nails to know what the gig was with Sharon. I tossed the note back on the dresser top and thought about Sharon again. Crazy broad. Professional virgin. I wondered what the action would be at the final second if I had taken up her offer of deflowering her. You might think you could avoid a knee in the balls, but them damn dames could bite too and even a small bite in the neck or shoulder could pretty well discourage the hardest ardor. Crazy, but nice. Like having a lion cub. Soft, cuddly and fun, but watch it when they grow up.

I walked to the closet and took a look at my new threads. I had forgotten to tell them to take in the extra fullness that usually covered the outline of a rod, now I was glad I hadn't. Times and conditions weren't getting any better. If anything, they were worse and promising to get even more tangled.

106

The note from Betterton and Strauss in London was coded on W-F stationery, a seemingly innocuous letter thanking me for my patronage and suggesting certain other additions to my wardrobe. What it really meant was that Garfield and Greco the Spaniard had gone headfirst into the last trap I had set for them and were completely out of the action now. Simon Corner who operated out of a bookshop in London's Soho district was trying to take advantage of my absence, but was moving cautiously until he knew which way the wind was blowing.

Things were working out nicely, I thought. When nobody knew anything they suspected everything. In those circles, no news was bad news. It represented superefficiency. Right now they'd be counting noses every day to see who was missing or who was sweating too hard. Waiting for the ax to fall was the hardest part of the game.

I climbed out of my clothes, showered and shaved, put on my new outfit and dialed Al's number. When he answered I said, "Hi, *paisan*."

"You've been getting around, soldier. That damn number of yours never answers."

"You know how it is."

"How are American broads shaping up?"

"Not bad. They have a few raunchy ideas, but this women's lib bit doesn't seem to affect most of them. What's up?"

"A few pieces of information. You're still my client."

"Shoot."

"You familiar with Farnsworth Aviation?" Al asked me.

"Didn't they just relocate somewhere out in the desert? There was something in the paper about that."

"Correct. They were major pollutants in the Los Angeles area and the ecology groups came down on their necks. Trouble is, their product is essential to the government and they made some kind of a deal."

"Pity the poor Indians."

"No redskins where they are. Anyway, they have a little gadget they want to subcontract to Barrin Industries. It seems that they have the only facilities to handle the job immediately."

"Nice. Where did you pick up this tidbit?"

"Casual conversation with an old friend who works for Farnsworth. There's a catch to it though."

"Oh?"

"Barrin will have to do some revamping. It's going to cost more than they can afford if my information is correct."

"How much more?"

"Roughly, two million. So don't be surprised to see something go on the block."

"What have they got outside the physical properties of the corporation?"

"A few patents, pal. It seems like some of the old technicians were ahead of their time. If it weren't for a couple of cagy codgers who had lifetime contracts with your grandfather, they would still be in the vaults. Anyway, they'll be losing one hell of a potential if they let them go."

"Those cousins of mine are bird-in-the-hand types," I said. "They'll sell."

"Yeah. Do you know they sold Mondo Beach?"

"Sure. I bought it."

There was silence for a few seconds, then: "How much?"

"Two fifty G's."

Al said, "Uh-huh," and the tone meant he was wrapping up all the pieces into a rubber body bag so the sight or smell wouldn't make anybody sick.

I deliberately let him hear my soft chuckle. "Clean, you computer-head," I told him. "I earned it and I got it. Plenty more, too."

"Dog," he said quietly, "you were never smart enough to grab that kind of cash."

"Let's say there are some people more stupid than I am then."

"What kind of people?"

"There are all kinds of stupid people."

"Yes." His tone was far away again and I could see him toying with a beer can, reading the fine print on the label. "There's another thing. Cross McMillan is setting up for a proxy fight. Most of the old stockholders are dead and their heirs hold the shares. They don't feel any old-line loyalty, so the company's just liable to change hands in the management department. That wouldn't be so bad, but McMillan is strictly a raider. He'll take Barrin Industries apart block by block, pocket the proceeds and thumb his nose at the stockholders."

"He ever make an offer to buy?"

"I understand he did some years ago but was turned down flat. Now he'll get it without paying for it."

"Maybe, Al."

"He's head of one of the biggest conglomerates already. But he hasn't got Barrin and that's the one he wants most. It's the one he'll fight hardest to get, too," Al reminded me.

Too bad Al couldn't see me grinning. "He wanted Mondo Beach."

"I know. Guys like McMillan don't like to be undercut in anything. Now he'll be mad as hell."

"And whom the gods would destroy," I quoted, "they first make mad."

"I wish I knew you better," Al told me.

"So do I," I said, and hung up.

I waited a few seconds with my finger on the cutoff button, then let it up and dialed Leyland Hunter. The old man said, "And how are you going to brighten the rest of the day, Mr. Kelly? You couldn't have caused panic in the few hours since I've seen you."

"Strictly business, Counselor. On the Mondo Beach property . . . there's a company called Ave Higgings, Incorporated. I'm the sole owner. It doesn't do anything, but it's in existence."

"Right-o."

"My grandfather had a second cousin a lot younger than him who wound up being a recluse in Canada. Word had it that he was gold-wealthy, but nobody knew for sure. At least he used to send some pretty damn expensive presents out. He even sent old Cameron a racehorse once. Now, if it isn't against your principles to lie a little, just mention the money was a certified check, the letter postmarked from Canada and Cousins Alf and Dennie will do the rest. They'll remember the old relative and think he's just coming through with a helping hand like he did a couple of times before when old Cameron was in a spot."

"Lying isn't one of my foremost capabilities. I do represent Barrin interests, you know."

"You're doing your job, buddy. They put the beach up for sale, set the price, now the terms of the will are being fulfilled . . . first crack at the property goes to a family member. If it soothes your conscience any, tell the slobs who's buying. If they need the money they'll have to sell anyway."

"Why not tell them?"

"Let's save it for a surprise. That way McMillan will be squirming too. He'll be all shook to know there's money hidden on one of the relatives. Just consign the property to Ave Higgins, Inc. and I'll get all the papers in your hands within two days. Can do?"

"You're more fun than defending on a rape case. Yes, can do if I compromise my principles a little. By the way, who handles all your business affairs?"

"From now on you do, great Hunter. Look for a big package in the mail."

When he said "so long" I called Western Union, sent

the wire that would get his big package delivered into his hands, made one last call to Dick Lagen's office whose secretary told me he was out at the moment, but could be reached in an hour, then left for the two-room office in the dilapidated building across town where a stringy guy in a greasy leather apron was very happy to sell me a clean .45 automatic, belt holster, a pair of extra clips and two boxes of standard Army cap and ball ammo. I checked out the action of the piece, loaded the clips, slammed one into the gun and jacked a shell into the chamber with the hammer on half cock. The stringy guy pocketed my money, nodded once and went back to his bench and began filing down the sear on a dissembled foreign weapon.

Outside there was a muted kettledrum roll of thunder and I knew it was going to rain again. I was glad I had brought my trench coat.

X

Lee and Rose were on their second round of Martinis when I walked into the Spindletop restaurant on West Forty-seventh Street. They were upstairs in the rear scratching names on the back of an envelope, arguing about one of them and crossing it off.

I pulled out a chair and said, "Cozy."

Rose gave me a silly grin and raised her glass. "Hello, big man."

"Nice to see you with your clothes on," I told her.

"She's better bare-ass," Lee grunted. He folded the envelope and stuck it in his jacket pocket. I signaled for a drink, and when it came Lee leaned back in his seat and leered at me. "Cradle robber."

"Eat your heart out," I said.

"Well, let's have it, Dog. The way the rumors are flying, you're liable to be up for statutory rape."

"Not him," Rose said lightly. "Seduction, yes. Rape, no. He makes a girl beg for it."

I gave her a quick look and Lee grinned. "Don't sweat it, kid. Share the wealth, that's my motto. Rose tells me you're quite a card. It's good to know you square types have rounded corners, at least."

"Hell, are *you* a kiss and tell doll," I said to Rose.

"Tell? Man I was bragging on you. It's a goal for these puppies to shoot at."

"Things sure have changed," I said.

"Shee-it," Lee laughed. "You haven't forgotten those leaves in London, have you? There was you in one sack with that tall Wren and me in the other with the cute little

WAAC dispatcher from squadron five, switching beds every time the air raid siren went off. Why, man . . ."

"I *had* forgotten it until now."

Rose giggled over her glass. "She leave a painful memory, Dog?"

"No, but we both had to chip in on an abortion fee for the Wren. Neither one knew who did it."

"Forgot about that," Lee muttered. He took a quick sip of his drink to try to erase the look of worried concern that began to cloud his eyes. When he put the glass down he nodded to me approvingly. "Nice threads, kiddo. I'm still impressed."

"He's got that *in* style," Rose said. "Welcome to the now generation."

"I've never been away."

Once again, I got that funny glance from Lee.

I said, "What have you been up to?"

"A bash," Lee told me, "a first-class, Sunday-supplement-making, swinging bash. I'm trying to work up a list of guests."

"What's the occasion?"

"Didn't Sharon tell you? Hell, she pried loose a few million from Walt Gentry for big daddy S. C. Cable. They're going into a coproduction deal with Cable Howard pictures. Old S.C. optioned the current best seller and is going all out to change his sex-exploitation image into that of artist-genius public-entertainment benefactor."

"What's the book?"

"Fruits of Labor."

I let out a grunt and lit a cigarette. "That title and no sex?"

"Where've you been, kid? Everything's sex. It's just how you handle it. S.C.'s giving this the modern treatment, as they say, telling it like it is."

"How is it?" I grinned.

Lee looked at Rose and laughed. "He's asking *me*," he said. "Good, man. I haven't found anything to take its place so far."

"Maybe you just haven't looked."

"Baloney. Name me one thing that's better."

I shrugged and took another drag of the butt. "Not better, but the kicks are there. At least for some."

"So name it."

Both of them were looking at me interestedly now.

"Remember your first kill, Lee? It was a Heinkel bomber over the Channel. You watched two guys tumble out of it and never get their chutes open. How did you feel?"

One of his shoulders twitched and he made a wry face. "Sick," he said.

I had to grin again. "Like the first time you got laid, remember? You told me about it. They initiated you into the gang by making you screw a two-buck whore on a torn-up sofa in the back of a garage. You, a nice moral-conscious kid from a good family. You got sick then, too."

"All right, I was fourteen years old."

"You could still get it up, buddy," I reminded him. "Now, how about that second kill? I was right off your wing when you got that ME 109 and followed him all the way down watching him burn. You threw a party that night and got bombed."

"After all, Dog . . ."

"The point isn't made yet, pal. After that you started hunting. You went looking for the kill. You fought the competition off to cut out your target, engaged in the fight and climaxed with the kill. After that it was barroom smugness and a little braggadocio until your juices settled down and then back to the hunt again. After enough of it the whole thing became a routine game."

"Knock it off, Dog, killing and sex aren't the same!"

"They call an orgasm 'the little death,' don't they?"

Rose had her chin propped in her hands and was watching us oddly. "You know, he may be right, Lee." Her eyes dug into mine then. "Tell me, Dog, did you get your kicks from killing?"

"After the first one I understood the similarity."

"I didn't ask you that."

I snuffed the cigarette out. "Probably, but I didn't give it much thought until it was all over. War really isn't a natural state of affairs."

"Dog . . ."

His face was tight and his tone searching.

"What?"

"And now that the subject has been researched, how do you feel about it?"

"Most people never know what killing is like."

"I didn't ask about most people. I'm relating to you and killing and sex."

"They both become subjects at which you pass or fail, enjoy or despise. If you're a winner, it's good. If you flunk, it's misery time."

"How do *you* feel, Dog?"

"I'm still alive and happy, buddy."

"You scare me," he said.

I frowned at the seriousness in his face. "Keep thinking

113

about it the next time you straddle a broad. You really might be an incipient homicidal maniac."

"Quit lousing up his screwing," Rose said. "These deep-thinking types take this kind of conversation to heart and I don't want any Jack the Rippers in my bedroom."

Lee's face came unstuck from the frozen grimace and he broke out into a fooling smile. "Damn, you sure can put a guy on. You and your way with words . . ."

". . . And words are what make the world go 'round," a voice said. We all looked around and saw Dick Lagen watching us, a half-empty highball glass in his hand. "Mind if I join you? After all, I was invited."

I pushed out a chair and waved toward it. "Sit down."

"You people eat yet?"

"Just about to," Lee told him.

"Fine, then I'll join you and let you pick up the check. A typical columnist's attitude I'm sure you all deplore."

"Forget it," Lee told him. "You have just made this meal tax deductible."

We went through the soups and steaks, had coffee and while Lee and Rose were going over their invitation list again, Lagen fired up a thin cigar and leaned back in his chair. "My staff have been digging up a few facts on you, Mr. Kelly."

"They have any luck?"

"Enough to intrigue me."

"Oh?" I popped a cigarette out of my pack and let him light it.

"You accepted your Army discharge in Europe in 1945."

"Public information."

"And being a resident you were subject to the tax laws of the resident country," he continued.

"Isn't everybody?"

"Quite. The exception is that your taxes reached a considerable proportion, so that in computing your income we arrive at a very substantial sum."

"Proving that I am an honest man who pays his taxes," I said.

"In that regard, yes. It's the accumulation of that money that interested me."

"You're a nosy bastard."

"So I have been told. At any rate, my researchers went at it a little harder and came up with some interesting information."

"Like what?"

"Like lack of information," he said. "Your income was declared, but, except for 'investments,' not the source of

114

it. Furthermore, there was nothing in your background to indicate you had any particular ability or desire to achieve success with, eh . . . *investments*. In fact, all indications are quite the contrary."

"So?"

"Would you care to clarify the matter?"

"Not especially."

"Then perhaps I might speculate on the matter."

"Be my guest," I said.

"Fine. Income is derived from one or both of two sources, legal or illegal. Since there was no proof positive of legal source, we investigated the possibility of illegality."

I said, "You know, for a guy who only met me a couple of days ago, you've gone to a hell of a lot of trouble."

"The affairs of the Barrin family makes interesting subject matter."

"I hope you have competent personnel."

"Oh, I have. The very best. Former FBI men, retired police officers, top newspapermen who know all the tricks and angles. What information they can't dig out they can buy. Funds for that purpose are unlimited. Therefore, whatever we want to know, we find out, as my numerous exposés have no doubt proven to you . . . and the fact that my information is so accurate that even congressional committees have used my records to restrict certain business operations or convict well-known persons of working criminally against the public interests."

"Good work, sport. And what did you find out about me?"

Dick Lagen smiled gently and puffed on his cigar. "Absolutely nothing. That's what makes it so intriguing. In certain areas, my people were rebuffed at every attempt at inquiry. One was even roughed up a little. Attempts to buy information got a blank stare or implied threats. The name of Dog, or in some places *El Lobo,* got such a reaction as to scare off my own people. It was the first time that ever happened."

"What's in a name, pal? You know what the poet said about the rose."

"Except that you don't smell so sweet, Mr. Dogeron Kelly. When you mention the name of Dog, you aren't mentioning a popular figure. In certain quarters, that is."

"You have any enemies, Dick?"

"Certainly, and justifiably so. I deliberately try to cultivate them. It's part of my business."

"Know anybody without enemies?" I asked him.

He thought a moment and shook his head. "No."

"I do."

Lagen looked at me with a small, superior smile. "Really? Who?"

"They're all dead," I said quietly.

For a good ten seconds he sat there staring at me, then he took a long pull on the cigar and watched the smoke drift toward the ceiling. "Who are dead, Mr. Kelly, the persons . . . or the enemies?"

"Take your choice, Mr. Lagen," I said.

Across the table Lee and Rose had stopped talking and were looking at us both. Lee's face had that tight expression again and his eyes were worried things, like those of a guy crossing the street and seeing a truck bearing down on him, not knowing whether to jump back or make a dash out of the way.

We dropped Rose off at a beauty parlor uptown, then cut back toward Lee's office. Outside, the walkers huddled close to the sides of the buildings, away from the blast of the rain, or fought umbrella duels going down the middle of the sidewalks. In the front of the cab the wipers kept up their clocklike ticktock above the humming of the tires.

Finally Lee said, "Lagen's got an unhealthy interest in you, Dog."

"Ah, he's always had a thing for the Barrins."

"It's you, not the Barrin family."

"Balls."

Lee turned his head, his expression questioning. "Why, buddy?"

"Why what?"

"Come on, Dog. I know how he operates. He never comes up without any answers. He won't let it go until he gets one, either."

"I still believe in personal privacy. I wish him luck."

Lee nodded and looked straight ahead again. "The way you say that makes it look like he isn't going to have any."

"Could be."

"Most people aren't that sharp at hiding things."

"Most people," I agreed.

"I've been wondering too."

"All you have to do is ask, Lee."

"Yeah, that's what you told me before."

"Then ask."

"I'm afraid of what you might tell me."

"So don't ask."

"I don't think I will," he said.

When Lee went to make arrangements for his bash, I

116

told him I'd pick him up about five, then had the cabbie take me down to the elite establishment of Weller-Fabray, Tailors. Two gentlemen who ran an oil company and a newspaper syndicate were being serviced by a pair of immaculate young men in formal morning wear, showing shirts and cravats whose label and style were their own price tags.

In the back, the manager saw me enter, gave me a businesslike smile of recognition and left his account book to say hello. This time he spoke Spanish without realizing it and took my hand. "Nice to see you again, Mr. Kelly. I trust the suits were satisfactory."

"Perfect. Sorry I didn't let you know I was coming the last time."

"I understand."

"My buddy was a little upset."

"He *didn't* understand."

"Your merchandising attitude is a little rough, my friend."

"It's an attitude that affords me the pleasure of doing what I do. Now, let's back to you."

He took my arm and we drifted back toward the fitting rooms. I said, "Something's getting scratchy on the Continent."

His shrug was eloquent. "One leaves, another one comes in."

"Somebody wants me tapped out. They tried through The Turk."

"Tried," he repeated. "A word that says everything. I'm surprised that it would be The Turk. One would think he'd be glad to leave well enough alone."

"That's what I figured. He could be fronting for somebody."

"Likely, but he is crass enough to try something on his own. The last episode was quite detrimental to his stature ... and his little empire. Don't forget, it was The Turk who personally wiped out Louis Albo and took over his operation."

"He was a younger gun then. He didn't have anything to lose."

"Does he have now?"

"I'm retired, my friend. The event sent shock waves throughout the troops."

"But you're alive," he said. "Speculation persists that you have something that can guarantee your living."

"Maybe."

"Then you'd better decide which way you'll go."

117

"Sure. Meanwhile, send out a probe and see who's doing the pushing. If there's going to be an advantage, I want it on my end."

"Very well, I'll try." He held out his hand and I took it. "I hope I don't open up old sores."

"Don't sweat it."

I went to leave and he stopped me with a hand on my arm. "Mr. Kelly . . ."

"Yes?"

"Just why did you . . discontinue your activities? You knew what would happen."

"Yeah, but I hoped it wouldn't. Just let's say I got tired of the whole fucking shooting match."

Lee had made a pair of drinks and brought one into the bedroom for me. I had my coat off and was hanging it up when he said, "What's that for?" He was looking at the gun on my belt.

The weight of the .45 was so natural I had forgotten about it. "You counted the money," I said. "Millions make for targets."

His voice was shaky. "It's all in the bank."

"Only you know that."

"Dog . . ." Before he could finish the buzzer went off, a long, insistent growl from the other room. Lee put his glass down and went to answer the door. I took the gun off my belt, stuck it on the closet shelf along with the box of shells and went out to join him.

This time he was pasty white, his eyes wide, darting back and forth between the two standing there before reaching out to me. One was in his middle forties, built like a heavyweight fighter, the other a few years younger, slim and angular, but with all the earmarks of a terrier. They didn't have to flash their ID's; the cop sign was all over them. No matter where you are, that look never changes.

"Evening, gentlemen," I said.

The older one stared, frowned a second, then asked, "Mr. Kelly?"

Lee stepped between us, the old wingman moving up to cover his partner. "Listen, they haven't got a search warrant . . ."

"At ease, kid. They were invited in." I looked at the cop. "Weren't you?"

"After a fashion."

I tasted my drink, liked it and took another pull. "What can I do for you?"

It threw them a little off base. That and something else

118

they hadn't put their finger on yet. The one who identified himself as Sergeant Tobano said, "Can you account for your whereabouts today?"

"Every minute."

"Witnesses?"

"All the way. Why?"

He held out his hand and the other one handed him a manila envelope. He tapped the package against his thigh and watched me. "How about, let's say, eleven thirty this morning."

"We had just gotten back into the city."

"We?"

"Two friends of mine and the driver of the car."

"Go on."

I took another pull of the drink and put the glass down so I could get a cigarette out. "We dropped my lawyer friend off . . . his name is Leyland Hunter, by the way, then my other friend, female Caucasian named Sharon Cass, and I got out at the garage and I walked her home."

"What garage?"

"Beats me. It's in the East Fifties."

"Denier Garage?"

"Now that you mention it, yes."

He opened the envelope and drew out two eight by ten photos and handed them to me. I held them out in front of me and looked at them. Beside me Lee's breath gagged in his throat. Bridey-the-Greek and Markham were enough to make anybody gag. They both looked dead as hell with all the blood around Markham's face and the ice pick still stuck through the Greek's balls.

"Messy," I said.

"Recognize them?" the cop asked me.

"Am I supposed to?"

"That's not the question, Mr. Kelly. Look at them again."

"So it's two guys laid out in a public john."

"How do you know it's a public john?"

"Who has urinals in their house anymore?" I said without taking my eyes off the photos. I was beginning to enjoy myself. "Where do I fit in?"

"That's the toilet in the Denier Garage. You were in that toilet when you were there."

"That's right. I asked the attendant for directions, had my friend wait for me and went to take a leak. I finished, buttoned up my fly and left."

"Did you see these two?"

"Not when I went in." I handed the photos back and he stuck them in the envelope. "How did I come into this?"

"The attendant remembered the limousine you came in. We checked the license out, contacted your friend Leyland Hunter and he gave us you."

"I can give you my other friend's address too if you want."

"Never mind. We have that."

"So?"

The two cops glanced at each other, not quite decided whether to be puzzled or aggravated. The younger one said, "We thought you might have seen something. They came in right after you. One wanted to know if that alcove went out to the street. The attendant said it went to the john and they headed in that direction."

"There wasn't anybody around when I came out," I told him. "There were plenty of parked cars, though. Somebody could have been behind them."

Sergeant Tobano's mouth was in a taut smile. "You didn't seem very shook up over those pictures. Not like your friend here."

"I've seen dead men before, Sergeant."

"These aren't dead, Mr. Kelly."

Lee breathed a quiet *Damn!*

They both moved toward the door. "Okay, thanks. We may check back."

Tobano was reaching for the doorknob when I asked him, "Who took those pictures, Sergeant?"

"A free-lance photographer who happened on the scene right after you left. He ought to make himself a buck from them."

"He a suspect?"

"Nope. One of the boys who parked cars happened to go in with him at the same time. The other guy fainted."

"Queasy stomach," I said, and picked up my drink.

"Some people are like that," the sergeant told me.

When they left, Lee half ran to the bar and poured himself another drink. He finished that one and made another before he turned around. A shudder ran across his shoulders and he swirled the ice around in his glass. Finally he raised his head and stared at me. "You lied to them, Dog, didn't you?"

I finished my drink too and joined him at the bar for another.

"Yes."

"You actually saw them there . . . that guy with his face all mashed in and the other one . . ."

I raised my glass in a silent toast. "Hell, buddy, I *did* it to them."

XI

I knew the call would come so I sat up and waited for it. At ten minutes past three the phone rang and I told Chet Linden to meet me at the Automat on Sixth Avenue. There was a deadly evenness to the tone of his voice and I could feel the mad seeping up my arms into my shoulders.

Why the hell couldn't they lay off me? I wasn't an unknown quantity they had to speculate about. They knew damn well what was going to happen if they pushed too far. When you make it through the hard way you aren't about to take any shit from anybody anytime. A lot of tombstones spelled that out loud and clear.

They were waiting at a table in the back for me, Chet and Blackie Saunders, the wipe-out boy from Trenton, sipping coffee like a couple of night owls on the way home. I faked sneezing into a handkerchief and had my face hidden when I went past their backup man who made like he was looking in a storefront window next to the Automat. I turned the corner, cut back and had the nose of the .45 in his ribs without him spotting me and said, "Lets join the others, buddy."

His reaction was real pro. Just a simple shrug of the shoulders and he headed toward the door. There might have been others, but with three under my gun, nobody was going to make any trouble at all.

When they saw us coming the picture was all there. Blackie started to rise, but Chet waved him down and nodded to me like nothing had happened at all. I took a seat with my back against the pillar, told the outside man to join me and looked at all three unpleasant faces.

"Coffee?" Chet asked.

I ignored him. "Why the kid games?" I nodded at the guy beside me.

"Blackie a habit too?"

The rangy killer from Jersey stared at me, aching for a chance to cut loose. I was hoping he would. Chet said, "He's on something else."

"He'd better be, Chet. Or didn't you tell him about me?"

"Blackie knows."

"Then he isn't very impressed."

Saunders let a snarl slip into low gear. "I'm never impressed, hotshot."

"There's always a first time, Blackie. It's generally the last time, too."

"He's got a gun in his hand," the guy beside me said.

Chet gave him a disgusted grimace and looked back at me. "Cool it, Dog. I just want to talk."

"Your party, kid."

"We saw Markham and Bridey."

"How about that?"

"You like to add all the fancy frills, don't you?"

I grinned at him. "Why not? I don't have a murder one going against me. As soon as the cops check those hoods' records they aren't going to be too interested in running me down. They like intramural rivalry. It keeps the economy active in floral shops and funeral parlors and makes their job that much easier."

"A nice clean kill might, but this looks like an invitation to war."

"You nailed it, Chet. That's what it is. Unless The Turk takes it gracefully and figures it's a warning to lay off."

"The Turk never takes anything gracefully."

"So I'll put some machinery in motion."

"In a pig's ass you will! This kind of crap is what we were afraid of."

"Don't bug me, buddy," I said. "I didn't instigate it. Anybody who rides my tail is going to hurt and that goes for The Turk too." I paused and looked at him. "That's what surprises me. That little fat turd isn't big enough to go for this kind of heavy work."

"Ever figure somebody's behind him pushing hard?"

"I thought of it."

"Why, Dog?"

I didn't answer him.

"Nobody retires from this business," he stated flatly.

"Me," I said. "I did."

"You only thought you did. When you retire, you're dead."

"So I hear. I've decided to be the exception."

Chet tasted his coffee again, then handed it to Blackie and told him to get a fresh hot one. He told the other guy to join him and when they both left he said, "I made a lot of phone calls, Dog. Right now I'm beginning to get some strange notions."

"Like what?"

"Like why are three different international syndicates sweating like hell because you left the scene."

"Because I know too much."

"Everybody knows too much," he told me. "They don't give a damn about *knowing*."

"Knock off the games, Chet."

"Being able to *prove* too much is something else again."

"Ah, hell," I grunted. "You mean the old dodge about tangible facts that would come out if I got knocked off?"

"Something like that."

"Then why send Bridey and Markham after me?"

Blackie and the other one came back with coffee and set the cups down on the table. When they sat down Chet stirred in his sugar and milk, then pushed the cup away from him. "Maybe it wasn't supposed to be a hit. Maybe they were going to just take you and put the squeeze on. That pair knows all the tricks and when they want somebody to talk that somebody talks."

"Those jokers got the wrong somebody this time."

"And next time?"

"Get to the point, Chet. This shit is beginning to bore me."

"We're involved in this too, Dog. If you talk you throw all of us out into the open and let me tell you something, kid, we mean more to us than you do."

"That why you brought your bit hit man along?"

"We have plenty of hit men, Dog. You don't know all of them."

"But they all smell alike."

"I'm real sorry now that I kept the others off your back," he said viciously. His voice was barely a whisper, but he meant every word of it.

My teeth were showing when I said, "You can always change your mind, pal. Like starting right now. I'll take all three of you out and be gone before the noise dies down."

Chet's eyes narrowed and the skin pulled tight around his mouth. He knew I wasn't fooling either and it showed in his face. "You wouldn't get away with it."

"Want to try?" I sat back and they could see the nozzle

123

of the .45 staring at them from the crook of my crossed arms.

All three of them sat absolutely still. "Never mind," Chet said.

I nodded slowly, watching them. "Then you call the plays, Chet. Just remember . . . I don't play a defensive game. It's only the guys on the offense who win. Any more tries come my way and I won't worry about where they come from. Everybody is going to be a target, so if you're on the ball you cool it, and get the word out to the others to cool it, otherwise it's just all one big package as far as I'm concerned."

I got up and stuck on my hat. The gun was back in the holster, but my hand was right where I could get to it faster than they could theirs. Chet picked up his coffee, his eyes still slitted above his cheekbones.

"Were they right, Dog? You protecting yourself with something that could blow the whole schmear?"

"You'll never know, kid," I said. I waited until a couple started to pass me and stepped in front of them, heading for the door, letting them cover me in case anybody decided to start blasting. When I was outside I looked back and they were still sitting there, Blackie and the other one listening to Chet. Blackie's hands were clenched into tight fists and he slammed one against the table. I could almost hear what he was saying.

I looked at my watch. It was a quarter past four.

Sharon finished putting her makeup on, snapped the compact shut and let it drop back into her pocketbook. "You sure get a girl up at ungodly hours. You know we're almost in Linton and it's only ten o'clock?"

"Kids are supposed to get up early," I said.

Her eyebrows raised and she gave me another of those oddball expressions I couldn't quite decipher. "Kid?" You wouldn't know one if it hit you."

"How old are you, sugar?"

"Old enough to know better than play gal Friday for you."

"You didn't *have* to come."

"Mr. Kelly, I wouldn't miss being with you for the world. You know what the rumormongers are putting out in our sewing circle?"

I turned my head and looked at her. "Tell me."

"There's something deep and dark about you. Dick Lagen has hinted at the worst sort of things and Mona Merriman

124

seems to think you were the consort of a certain young lady who's father was the deputy dictator of one of those new countries . . . who was shot to death shortly thereafter."

"Ah, fame," I said.

"Are those things true?" She was staring straight ahead through the windshield, her hands clasped in her lap.

"If they are, you'll read about it in their papers soon enough."

"You don't seem very concerned."

"I quit worrying a long time ago, doll."

For a mile or so she didn't speak, then she squirmed in her seat and I could feel her eyes on me. "What's the matter with Lee then?"

I shrugged my shoulders and took the turnoff going east. "Nothing."

"Dog . . . he's scared to death. He looks at you like . . . like you're going to explode or something."

"You know Lee."

"Not that well, but enough to know he's never been like that before." She stopped a moment, then: "It has to do with the other day, doesn't it? I mean, about those two men. There was a piece in the *News* . . ."

"Coincidence."

"It was on television, too. They said they were attacked and . . . mutilated. The police were following up leads."

"I know. They contacted me."

"And?"

"I couldn't help them out. So they left."

"Dog . . . they contacted me, too. I . . . told them we were there . . ."

I reached over and squeezed her knee. "You did right, honey. What's there to hide? New York's a big town. Anything can happen. We just happened to be there when it did."

"Dog . . ."

"Look, you know how long I was gone . . . about a minute and a half. You think I could attack and mutilate two big guys and come out of it without a scratch?"

Her answer was a long time coming. She was remembering the blood on my shirt. "I don't know," she said softly.

I let out a laugh. "You flatter me, baby." Sharon grinned back and flopped back against the cushions.

Up ahead the outline of Linton showed above the treeline, and the quadruple smokestacks that marked the Barrin factory reared their fingers toward the sky. Three of them were dormant. The fourth was gasping out a thin wisp of gray pollutant. If Linton reflected the economy of the Barrin Industries, it wasn't a very thriving town.

We cut through the center of the city and took the road that circled the vast factory site. The old-fashioned brick, the archaic tower and the climbing vines made the place look more like a college than a commercial complex The one-hundred-fifty-year-old clock still kept the right time and the acres of land inside the low wall were well trimmed, but empty of the stacked materials that used to clutter the place. A steady throbbing came from inside the place and occasionally a figure would cross behind one of the win· dows, otherwise activity was at a minimum About fifty cars were aligned in the parking spaces. One was directly in front of the main office entrance, even with the *No Parking* sign. The make and color were familiar and I looked at it again, but the question was answered when Cross McMillan stepped out of the doors, two others trailing him, and glanced around with the air of a person about to take possession.

"Your friend," Sharon said. "I wonder what he's doing there."

"He thinks he's going to take over the joint." I laid on the gas and pulled out of sight of the entrance. "He'd better not get too smug about it."

"Maybe he has reason to be. The McMillan family never was known for their humility. They always were pirates."

"They never went up against big guns before."

Again, a furrow appeared between her eyes and she took the edge of her lower lip between her teeth. "What's happening, Dog?"

"The bastard wants it all. He's always wanted Barrin ever since the run-in with the old man."

"He's forced out everybody else around here."

"Not everybody, kid," I told her quietly.

"You think he can't get"—she swept her hand toward the factory site— ". . . all this?"

"Not without one hell of a fight."

"Your cousins aren't capable . . .?"

"I'm not talking about my cousins."

"Who are you, Dog?" Her voice had a quiver to it.

"Just a guy who wants to come home."

"Is that all?"

"Nobody wants to let me," I said.

"But they can't keep you out."

"Not anymore, kitten."

I turned onto the intersection that angled back into town and crisscrossed the area until I came to the corner of

126

Bergan and High streets. Time had washed over the section leaving the scars of fading paint and crumbling bricks, but Tod's Club still stood defiantly, one of the earlier buildings structured with materials and skill old-fashioned enough to withstand the deteriorating effects of season after season and almost total neglect.

Once it had been the hub of nearly all the poltical and social activity that went on and twice the site where heavyweight contenders trained for the big bout. One of them even won the crown. Now, half the ground floor frontage was occupied by neighborhood stores to pay the upkeep and a shoddy frame warehouse took up the space where the half-acre picnic grounds used to be.

We parked outside the entrance and I helped Sharon out of the car. She looked around, glanced up at the grimy windows and the dirt-streaked brick. "What's this place?"

"Don't you remember?"

She squinted at the building again and nodded. "My father used to come here, I think. Some kind of a club, isn't it?"

"More or less."

"The name sounds familiar. Tod's. Yes, Dad even brought us here one time. There were games and barrels of beer and they had a sprinkler going for the kids someplace."

"In the back."

"That's right."

"What's here now?"

"I don't know," I told her, "but it's a starting point."

We walked inside and down a familiar corridor lined with ancient stuffed fish and mounted deer heads. The brass plates beneath the trophies were tarnished and the names unreadable. Most of those names would be engraved now on the local tombstones, I thought.

An old man in dungarees was washing the floor of the west meeting room, the old cigar-burned tables and captain's chairs pushed to one end. The restaurant that once was the pride of Linton had been sectioned off into office space. Three sections were empty. The other two held a construction company and a real estate outfit.

Voices came from the far end, competing with a televised soap opera and we walked down to the pair of half-opened paneled doors and pushed through.

This room hadn't changed. The great fifty-foot bar still stretched its length to the sliding serving windows in the wall, the gilt-framed mirror behind it reflected the hundreds of antique sporting weapons mounted on wooden pegs and the same six grinning bear heads taken by the long-dead Hiram Tod. When I was a kid the moths had eaten away most of the fur, now the toothy grimaces seemed to be coming out of mummified skulls, strangely livened by bright glassy eyes that lay loosely in dried sockets.

The pair of seedy customers drinking from schooners of beer had their feet propped on a gleaming brass rail while they argued about baseball. The skinny old bartender in the too-big shirt ignored them, polishing already shiny glasses to crystallike brilliance.

When we propped ourselves on the stools and called for a beer the two at the end stopped talking long enough to look us over, then went back to their argument. The bartender set down our glasses, rang up the money and pushed my change toward me. I looked at him carefully, studying his face, remembering the towering man with the huge gut that could bounce off full half kegs of suds onto the cellar chute, and the deep voice that used to make us hustle for the quarters we earned when we cleaned up the picnic tables.

I said, "Tod?"

The old man turned, his eyes focusing on mine. He nodded.

"You been on a diet?"

He grunted and a grin showed his false choppers. "I been on a cancer, son. Only that was a long time ago and hardly nobody remembers me fat. Who may you be?"

I stuck out my hand and waited until he took it. "Cameron Barrin was my grandfather."

He pulled his hand away sharply. "You ain't . . ."

Before he could finish I shook my head. "I'm the bastard one, Tod. Dogeron Kelly. Used to run errands for you when I sneaked out of the castle up there."

His grin got big suddenly and he grabbed my hand again. "Damn, boy! Sure I remember you. Hell, I remember you and that Polack kid fighting to see who got the swamping job at the hunkie picnic. I put up five bucks for the winner."

"That Polack kid sure could hit," I said.

"Yeah, but you won." He laughed again and pulled another beer for himself. "You know, I bet another five on the Polack."

"Tough."

"My own fault. I shoulda remembered you was your father's kid."

The beer stopped halfway to my mouth. "You knew him?"

"Sure, and your mother too. But that was before all the

trouble. What a wild-assed Irisher he was. He used to meet your ma right here in this place. Oh, nobody ever knew about it or anything. She used to sing when old Barney played the piano." He stopped for a minute, cocking his head at me. "I ain't talking outa turn or anything, am I? Sometimes an old guy like me . . ."

"No sweat, Tod. It was just something I didn't know but was glad to hear. I'm glad my mother had class enough to cut away from that bunch when she could."

"Dead, both of them, aren't they?"

"Uh-huh."

"Too bad. It ain't like before at all. What're you doing back here?"

"Looking the old place over."

"Not much to see anymore. Except for her." He nodded at Sharon, smiling. "This is your daughter?"

Sharon choked on her beer and grabbed for a paper napkin to wipe her chin. When she dried off she faked a sigh of exasperation and said, "Good grief!"

"We're not even married," I told him.

"Made another boo-boo, I guess," Tod said.

"Nope, you just proved a point, Tod. I'd just better pick on somebody my own age."

"Don't do it on my account," Sharon told me quickly. "I'm starting to enjoy all this after putting up with my New York image."

"Good thing she isn't my daughter," I said.

"It would be a very incestuous relationship if I were."

"I didn't mean that." I gave her a poke with my elbow and Tod let out a chuckle.

"Me," he told us, "I couldn't take the excitement you kids look for. I'm glad even the old pilot light's gone out. Now a woman is only something that goes to the ladies' room instead of the men's room." He finished his beer, filled all three and set them down again. This time he didn't take my money. "You still didn't say what you're doing back. It ain't really to just look around, is it?"

"In a way. I'm looking for information."

Tod folded his arms on the bar and nodded. "I see. Well, it ain't like it was, this being a place where you could learn anything, but I hear a few things now and then."

"About Barrin Industries?"

"Shot to hell, is what. Maybe half working what used to work there. They ever get busy, they're going to have to import a labor force. No more young people around here if they can help it."

"How about McMillan?"

129

"Shoot, man. He's the one that hired 'em all away for his factory in Aberdeen and the electronic plant outside Madrid. He even bought up a lot of property they owned so they could relocate."

"Adjoining lots, probably, and all on the right of way to the water."

"Correct. But who cared?"

"McMillan," I said. "He knew what he was doing.'

Tod shrugged again and spread his hands. "They was all glad to get out. They're probably still glad. This town hasn't improved none."

"Ever hear anything about my cousins?"

"Dennison and Al? Them two patsies? All they do is toss parties out at the country club. Society crap, y'know? I got a niece that waits on tables out there and she tells me everything that goes on."

"Wild?"

"Them old maids? All hankie waving and backbiting. Half the guys go only because their wives make 'em. They wind up talking golf at the bar and getting blasted. Sure not like the old days here."

"You mean Al and Dennie are boozers?"

"Nah. They're as bad as the old maids. With all them relatives watching an' the way their sisters hang on 'em, all they do is talk. Oh, they'd like to cut loose. That Dennie pinched my niece's ass once . . . sorry, ma'am . . . and Al, he took a short cut back to town with some lady entertainer they had out there and got stuck in a ditch by the river. Bennie Sachs was on night patrol and hauled them out. Old Al had some scratches on his cheek, but he said he got them from the bushes. The dame, she wasn't talking and never said nothin' anyway, so we made a few jokes about it, then it all died down." Tod let out a rumbling chuckle again and stroked his chin thoughtfully. "I still think he made a pass at her. It would take a blindman not to see that ditch in a full moon."

"Lousy technique," I said.

"You have a better one?" Sharon asked me.

"Later you'll find out."

"Ah, you kids," Tod muttered.

I finished the beer and pushed off the stool. "Where does that niece of yours live?"

"Over on Highland. White house at the top of the hill." He gave me a shrewd look. "You figuring to hang something on those cousins of yours?"

"I sure would like to have something to prod them with."

130

"Anything doing, Louise'll tell you. And good luck. I don't like them snotnoses. Just tell Louise I sent you."

"Thanks, I'll do that."

"You coming back?"

I nodded and pushed a pair of singles across the bar. "Hell, Tod, I'm already here."

Sharon was beginning to enjoy the game. Linton had been her backyard too and she knew her way around the streets and rear alleys better than I did, pointing out familiar landmarks, making me pause to look at her old school and stopping in a few stores to say hello to old friends. Of the dozen or so people I spoke to, she knew several of them, but all we managed to get was a blank as far as the Barrin family was concerned. The aristocracy was safely barricaded behind their fortifications on the estate with their private lives well hidden.

After supper she agreed to tackle Tod's niece, dropped me off at the local precinct station and drove off. I watched the taillights disappear around the corner, then went up the steps into the building.

A cop going off duty directed me to an office on the right and I walked to the door, rapped twice and walked in. The burly-shouldered guy at the filing cabinet with his back to me said, "Be with you in a minute," then flipped through a few folders, found the one he wanted and slammed the door in. When he turned around he was about to ask me to sit down, did a slow double take that wiped the forced smile off his face and just stood there, looking at me belligerently. "You, huh?"

"It was when I came in."

"Don't get smart, buddy." His elbow hitched the gun in the belt holster up in an involuntary gesture, remembering me from the beach.

I said, "Then let's start from the beginning."

Bennie Sachs wasn't quite used to being pushed. He had been a small-town cop too long, used to doing the pushing, and when it went the other way he knew he had to be up against some kind of power package. I took a seat without being asked and waited until he had settled himself behind his desk.

Finally he settled back, his face a mash of complacency. "Let's hear it, mister."

"Kelly," I said. "Dogeron Kelly, cousin to Al and Dennison Barrin. Cameron Barrin was my grandfather."

When I mentioned Al and Dennie I saw the cold look

131

come into his eyes, but that was all that showed. "Good for you," he told me.

"I don't dig my cousins anymore than you do, Mr. Sachs."

He watched me for a moment, then a twist nudged the corner of his mouth and I knew the ice was broken. "What can I do for you?"

"Drag something out of your daily reports. It goes back aways."

"Like to Alfred and that lady singer at the country club?"

"You nailed it," I laughed.

"Not much to it. They were sitting down there in the car when I drove up. I threw a towrope around his axle and hauled them out. I followed them back into town in case they had busted something."

"Al had scratches on his face, I understand."

"From the bushes he said, three nice long even ones, spaced about as far apart as a woman's fingers and nail deep. And there wasn't even a shrub near that ditch."

"How'd they do it?"

"Mr. Barrin *said* he lost control when he went onto the shoulder."

"But what do you say?"

"I can guess."

"So guess."

"He tried a little grab-ass and the dame clouted him one. Those tire tracks S'ed all over the road before he went straight into the ditch."

"Were they arguing?"

"Nope. All nice and neat. Real pals when I drove up. The dame wasn't even mussed. It coulda happened like he said, especially if he'd been drinking, but I didn't smell any booze on 'im and besides, I'd sooner think I had a dirty mind."

"That's all there was to it?"

"Got a case of booze the next day from an anonymous donor. Good Scotch. Seems like the Barrin butler bought it."

"Thought you weren't supposed to take bribes?" I said through a laugh.

"Hell, I told you it was from an anonymous source. By the time I inquired, the booze was all gone. Couldn't be sure anyway. Peggy over at the liquor store only hinted at it."

"So Cousin Al is clean as a whistle."

"No complaints lodged," Bennie Sachs said. "But I bet

132

he sure wanted a piece of that. Pretty nice-looking dame. Only trouble was, she had two broken fingernails."

"Observant, aren't you?"

The big cop shrugged casually. "Cops are supposed to be."

"How about Cross McMillan?"

"Heavy taxpayer. Minds his own business."

"Not the other day he didn't," I reminded him.

Sach's thoughts drifted back to the scene in front of the gates at Mondo Beach. He picked up a cigar, bit the end off and spat the piece out. "Mr. McMillan was planning on buying that place. He had money down on it already."

"His deal went sour. That place has been bought up."

Without looking at me, he held a match to his cigar and nodded. "That's what I heard. He ain't very happy about it. He had big plans for that place."

"Tough."

"Not on McMillan. What he wants, he gets."

"I've heard that before too. The only thing he can't get is his own wife."

Sachs shook the match out and flipped it in a corner. "I wouldn't make noises like that if I was you. He's pretty touchy on that subject. When he outsmarted Cubby Tillson on that land deal old Cubby mouthed off about the same thing and Cross knocked the shit outa him . . . and Cubby's a pretty big apple. Fleet title-holder in the Navy back in forty-five." He pulled on the cigar and blew a smelly blue cloud of smoke my way. "Who got the beach property now?"

"Somebody in the family, I hear."

"You hear pretty quick. The deed ain't even been filed yet. Cross McMillan's going to be pretty interested in seeing whose name is on that paper."

"Public information, Mr. Sachs. Just the property is private." I got up and put on my hat. "Thanks for the talk."

"Anytime," he said. He let me get as far as the door before he said, "By the way, Mr. Kelly, you got a permit for that gun you're wearing?"

"You're pretty good at guessing," I said.

His eyes gave me a smile and he stuck the cigar back in his mouth.

Sharon was waiting for me in the car outside the door and moved over to let me under the wheel. I said, "How'd you make out?"

"Zilch. They're as pure as a virginal bride, but if you could make a case out of subtle leers and vile thoughts, you'd be in. Louise even called a couple of her gossipy

133

friends, but the general consensus of opinion is that neither of them ever strayed from the bed of bachelorhood."

I said something nasty under my breath and pulled away from the curb. My mind kept going back to the gleeful look I saw on Alfred's face just before he smashed me off my bicycle with his new roadster, and the shrill cursing of Dennie as he tried to piss through a gonorrhea-infected dong. Mice don't generally sprout batwings and fly away to goodie land.

"There was one other thing Louise remembered," Sharon added. "Right after your grandfather died there was an explosion and a fire in the laboratory building of the factory. One of the older engineers who was alone in the place at the time was hit in the head and knocked out. The investigation later reported that it was an accident since some experimental work was under way, but the engineer kept claiming he was hit before the explosion. He kept claiming it was a bungled robbery attempt and that he had seen Alfred Barrin's car pull up just prior to the blast."

"Robbery?"

Sharon made a vague motion with her hands. "Apparently nothing was stolen. Alfred said he was at home with his brother and the engineer never quite recovered from his injury. He retired right after that."

"She mention the guy's name."

"In fact, she did. Stanley Cramer. He used to hang out at her Uncle Tod's place. Nice old man and he's still alive. Lives out in the Maple Hill section right near where our old house was."

"Curious," I said.

"Why?"

"Because any research the Barrin plant was working on then involved aluminum extrusion processes. The lab was just a highly refined mental shop."

"Well, that's what she said."

"Let's check on it."

The library was open, nearly empty, and the little old lady who ran it very obliging. Her cross-indexes were neat rows of cards in spiderwebby handwriting and after a thirty-second perusal she selected one, consulted it, then brought out an old library copy of the *Linton Herald*.

Page one held the item, a three-column piece with a photo of the destroyed laboratory. The essence of the story was much the same as Sharon had given me, but with the further explanation that the suspected cause was the collapse of the bins holding the acid containers onto the chemical storage area below. From the photo, it seemed as though the explosion had released its force against the inside wall and the damage was more superficial than anything else. There was no mention at all about my cousin.

When we were back in the car I asked Sharon where Louise got the bit about Al. "Oh, she just heard her uncle and aunt talking about it, that's all. Anything a Barrin does in this town is big news."

"Think you could find Cramer's place?"

"I guess so. Not many people live out there anyway."

It wasn't hard to do. Stanley Cramer was listed in the phone book and a light was on in the front room of the small cottage when we got there. Through the window, I saw him get up from in front of the television set when I rang the bell, a wizened old man with bowed legs and a shuffling walk. He had a full head of white hair and an old-fashioned handlebar moustache like the Polish papas wore when I was a kid.

The porch light flickered on and the door opened. Watery blue eyes blinked up at us and he said, "Well, well. Don't usually get company out here. You people lost?"

"Nope. You Stanley Cramer?"

"All day long."

"Then we came to see you."

"Now, isn't that nice." He smiled toothlessly under the flowing whiskers and swung the door wide. "You come right on in."

His place was a man's house, tidy and orderly. A collection of odd lever and gear miniature contraptions decorated the mantel over the fireplace and several framed photographs were propped on the small tables. One of them was a picture of him and my grandfather in front of the original Barrin building and must have been sixty years old.

He poured wine from a cut-glass decanter and offered it before he finally sat down opposite us and said, "It's so nice to see somebody I even forgot the introductions. Who may you be?" He squinted at us closely. "Don't know either one of you, do I?"

"You knew my grandfather," I told him. "Cameron Barrin. I'm Dogeron Kelly, the family secret."

Laughter flashed across his eyes and he shook a finger at me. "Ah, yes, I remember you, all right. Big stink about it when you came along. Old Cam was fit to be tied."

"This is Sharon Cass. She used to live here. In fact, her father worked at Barrin."

Cramer reached for a pair of glasses beside his chair and hooked them over his ears, then leaned forward to look at her. "You Larry Cass's daughter?" Before she could answer

135

he nodded vigorously. "Yes, ma'am, you sure are. Damned if you're not your mother all over again. Same mouth, same eyes. You even got your hair like she had it. Lovely woman, your mother."

"Thank you."

"Sure is nice of you, coming all the way out here to see an old fossil like me." He smiled again, sipped his wine and looked at me. "Kind of think there's more on your mind though."

"I thought you could help me."

"Nothing much I'm very good at anymore, son."

"Just a case of remembering."

"Oh, I can do that. About all I can do."

"Remember the explosion in the Barrin lab?"

The moustache twisted down when his smile faded. "Before and after, but not the explosion." He took his glasses off and scratched his head. "But I guess explosions are the things you're not supposed to remember."

"Once you told somebody that it wasn't the blast that got you."

He held out the decanter, refilled our glasses and poured another one for himself. "Did I?"

"Good wine," I said.

The watery quality had left his eyes and he watched me sharply. "You know, son, you got something of old Cam in you. He was a spooky character too. Sometimes he reminded me of a snake, other times he was all cat, smart and deadly as they come. The others, there's no part of Cam in them at all."

"I'm the only direct relative he had." Then I added, "Or rather, indirect. Nobody rang bells when I was born."

"Guess not," Cramer chuckled. "Cam, he didn't like to be bucked."

"About the explosion."

"See? Just like Cam. Wouldn't leave a thing alone." He tasted his wine again, rolling it around his tongue. "The explosion," he mused finally. "Must have been a little after midnight. I was working on a heat problem we had with an aluminum alloy. I thought I heard a noise and went to turn around. That's when I got cracked on the head. Next thing I know I was in the hospital."

"You're lucky you didn't get killed."

"Beats me how I dragged myself out of there. They found me near the front door later, but I sure don't remember getting there."

"You said you saw Al's car around earlier."

"Well now, it could have been or it couldn't have been.

136

About ten minutes earlier I went down to the supply room to pick up some solder. I thought I heard a car pull up and when I looked out there was a two-tone sedan something like Al had. He'd come down once in a while to go over the books and I didn't think anything about it. Hell, it was his place, wasn't it?"

"In a sense."

"So I got my solder and went back to work."

"That's all?"

Cramer just nodded, but his fingers pulled at his moustache thoughtfully.

"What could have blown up?"

"I was waiting for that," he said. "Nothing, I'd say, but I'm not a chemical engineer. Maybe those acids could have caused it."

"Somebody theorized about an attempted robbery."

"That's right. The explosion was against the wall where the safe was."

"Anything worth stealing?"

He gave me another one of those vague shrugs. "Depends on how badly you need four hundred dollars in petty cash and a lot of old papers. Used to be that old safe was never even locked. For a while we used it for storage. The only reason it was there was because the lab was part of the original office before Cam built the new wing. Any cash or other valuables were in the vault over there."

"And Cousin Al was in the clear again."

"I take it you don't like that boy."

"He's a meathead."

"You can say that again," Cramer agreed. "Yeah, he was clear. He was with Dennison all night. Anyway, I shouldn't've shot my mouth off. That car could have belonged to anyone. It wasn't like his big Caddie or that little foreign job he generally drove. Couple of guys at the plant even had one like it."

"But you still think it was his," I stated.

"Son, when an old man gets an idea stuck in his head it's pretty hard to dislodge, even if it's wrong. Age is funny that way."

"Sure."

"Incidentally, mind telling me why you're so interested in ancient history?"

"Curiosity," I said.

"It killed the cat."

"If you were right, it could kill Alfred boy too."

"And you'd like that?"

"Why not? He tried to kill me once."

Sharon put her glass down and looked over at me. "You must be aging too. You won't let ideas get away either."

Stanley Cramer let out a big smile and scratched his head again. "If I were you, I'd get ideas about the pretty little lady here and let the past stay buried."

"You may be right," I told him. "Let's go, pretty little lady."

It was old and musty, animals from the field had left their litter around and nested in the stuffing from some of the chairs. Moonlight through the cracked windows ran down the silky strands of cobwebs, giving the place a fuzzy appearance.

She had asked to see it again, and this time she wanted to go in. A pair of old hurricane lamps she dug out of a cabinet were the only light, the glow soft and feeble, but enough to reflect the wetness under her eyes as she touched pieces of tattered furniture.

Her old house was too far away from town to have been vandalized by kids or used by tramps, too remote and weed hidden to be a sex pad for lovers. Twice a bat flapped past and little scratching noises came from the woodwork.

"We always had mice," she said. "I wouldn't let Dad trap them. He didn't know it, but I used to leave scraps of food on the floor in the kitchen so they could eat."

I let her talk, listening to her ramble on about days in pigtails and pinafores or her father pulling her along on a sled. Finally she stopped at the foot of the stairs, hesitated a moment, then started up. There were three rooms at the top. The door to the smallest one was open and a foot-treadle sewing machine and a spindleback chair were waiting for another seamstress.

Sharon opened the middle door, the lamp outstretched in her hand. "My father and mother's room," she said. I edged up close to her and looked inside. Wind and rain from a broken pane had discolored the mattress and blown the covers across the room. The veneer tops of both dressers had warped off, the mirrors discolored, barely reflecting our images.

She closed the door gently and went to the last one on the end. It didn't open at first, then I twisted the knob, put my shoulder against the edge of it and leaned inward. It creaked open, then stuck halfway and we had to slip in one at a time.

The window was intact, and with the door wedged so tightly shut little dirt had had a chance to collect. A quilted spread still covered the bed, a few empty makeup jars and

138

a stack of movie magazines were on one end of the bureau, a rocker leaned quietly in a corner next to an old rolltop desk and a pair of shoes were on the closet floor under a few items of outgrown clothing. She had pasted up all her hero pictures, snipped from papers and books, interspersing them with school photos and pennants stenciled with the trademarks of various vacation spots.

"And you lived here," I stated.

Sharon walked over and put the lamp down on the dresser. "My own little sanctuary. I loved this room."

"You never really closed down the house, did you?"

"I couldn't. I just took what I needed and walked away. I never thought I'd come back here. Too many memories, Dog. I started out fresh."

"You don't wipe out memories, kid."

That oddball look came back in her face and disappeared almost as fast. "Yes, I know." She was looking at me in the dresser mirror, then her eyes went to one side and she picked a small photo out of the frame, smiled at it and dropped it in her pocket.

"Dog . . ." Her fingers were doing things with the buttons of her jacket, popping them open one by one. "Can we stay here tonight? Together?"

"You're mixing me up in your daydreams, kid."

"I had a lot of them in that very bed."

"Will you quit knocking me in the head? One night on the beach I could take. It was fun and it was funny. Another time and it won't be like that at all. You're no little girl anymore, doll. When you take off those clothes you're all lovely soft flesh and woman curves. I don't buy the frustration bit at all. It gets hard on the dingus. We used to call it lover's nuts."

She had the jacket off and threw it on the rocking chair. She started on the buttons of the blouse when I put my lamp down and grabbed her before she could get them open. Sharon smiled and shook her head. "The last time I wanted you and you wouldn't take me. Now I *want* you *not* to take me."

"You don't make sense," I damn near shouted.

"Please, Dog? Just this once? It won't happen again."

"Look, fantasies are fine, but . . ."

"Sometimes you live with fantasies a long time. Please, Dog?" She pushed me away with small, gentle hands and walked back to the dresser. I watched her undress slowly, feeling my insides go tumbling all over again. She was more beautiful than ever in that pale yellow light, but a different kind, a beautiful, a young, unself-conscious kind of beautiful. When she was all naked she tossed the single cover back and writhed down under it.

I looked at her, wondering what the hell I was letting myself in for, then I undressed too, but not with the same unself-consciousness. I did it fast, blew out the lamps and got in beside her.

"Just hold me," she said.

I wanted to say the same thing, but I didn't.

XII

The .45 was in my hand, the hammer cocked the second I touched the knob. Lee was a typical New Yorker who kept himself barricaded behind triple locks and now the door swung open easily. I had gone too far to pull back so I smashed on it, hit the floor rolling and ended up in a corner ready to spit lead at anybody who came at me.

I waited, changed positions fast and waited again. Nothing moved. Motes of dust danced in the late-morning sunlight streaming in the windows and from the street below the traffic noises were a dull hum. When another thirty seconds had passed I stood up and angled toward the door of my bedroom. It was empty, untouched and just as quiet.

On the other side of the living room Lee's door was closed, a half-dozen letters and the day's paper strewn on the floor. I reached it quickly, kicked it open and waited to see what would happen. Nothing did.

But this time I heard a noise, an almost inaudible murmur with odd bubbly overtones. The blinds were still down and I picked my way across the unmade-up bedroom to Lee's bathroom, the strange sounds getting faintly louder, seeming to rise, fall, then break with a weird hysteria.

Then I knew what the sounds really were, shoved the gun back and went through the door so hard I snapped the tongue out of the lock. Lee was stretched out in the tub, hands and feet lashed together behind his back, his mouth taped with wide surgical adhesive. The heavy metal desk chair had been tossed on top of him to keep him at the bottom and the tap turned on a slow trickle to make dying a long-drawn-out torturous affair. Muscles in his neck were taut cords as he stretched to keep his face above the surface, his eyes bulging wide with terror.

I turned the tap, flipped the chair away and dragged him out of the tub. When I cut through the tape that bound him the sudden release of his twisted body brought vomit spewing out of his nose and I ripped the gag off his mouth with one pull before he could choke to death. He looked up at me, groaned once and went into a dead faint.

Aside from a small discoloration on his temple there weren't any marks on him at all. I got Lee in bed, cleaned up and sat there mopping him with a cold wet towel until his eyes fluttered open. I said, "Take it easy, don't push it. We'll talk later."

His head made a small motion in acknowledgment.

"You hurt at all?"

One hand made a negative sign.

"Okay, then stay there."

I wet the towel again, laid it across his forehead and went out and locked the front door. I kept saying *damn* to myself for being idiot enough to think this wouldn't happen. I'd left everybody exposed I had touched because I didn't figure they'd be dumb enough to want to set the whole dirty machine in operation again and I was as wrong as hell. There wasn't any sense trying to follow up the attempted hit. The tub had been almost filled, which meant the water trap had been set long enough ago to give anybody a good chance to clear out. It had been a simple operation. They caught Lee coming up with the mail, held a gun on him, followed him in and sapped him.

I picked up the letters from the floor, then looked at the dateline on the newspaper. It was yesterday's. That meant they nailed him last night coming in from work. They had waited right through the night hoping to get me and when I didn't show, decided to leave a present for me.

When it hit me I let out another curse, ran into the bathroom, threw the drain on, flushed the tape down the toilet bowl and set the chair back in front of the desk where it belonged. As I ran past Lee I saw his eyes go wide again and said, "Get dressed and get ready to put on an act."

I barely had time to get my coat off, the gun stashed away and a call in to Leyland Hunter when the raps came on the door. I told his secretary to hang on, walked over and threw the lock open. The same two cops stood there, the one called Tobano and his partner, two guns pointed at my middle from either side of the opening.

"Don't just stand there," I said. "Come on in. I'm on the phone."

I started to walk back inside but Tobano stopped me.
"Hold it, buddy."

Everything was done with standard classical police procedure, even to the partner checking on the phone call. He told Hunter's secretary I'd call back and hung up. Before they had a chance to look through the rooms Lee came out in the bottom half of his pajamas and stood there scratching, a perfect picture of a guy dragged out of a sound sleep. He even managed a yawn. "What the hell's happening, Dog?"

"Beats me." I looked at the two cops. "Mind telling me what this is all about?"

"Mind if we check around first?"

"Go ahead."

"Make my bed up while you're at it," Lee told them.

Tobano stayed with us while his partner went through the place. He came out of my room shaking his head. "Clean." Their guns disappeared under their coats.

"Now?" I asked.

The big cop nodded. "We had a report there was a dead body up here."

Lee faked a grin. "My cleaning lady did that to me once when she found me passed out on the floor."

"This wasn't a lady," the cop told him.

"Anonymous?"

"Aren't they all?" he said to me. "That your room over there?"

"Uh-huh."

"It's made up."

"I'm neat."

"Here all night?"

"This an arrest?"

"Nope."

"Then let's skip the questions. You didn't even advise me of my rights."

"I said it wasn't an arrest. And we don't like games, either. If you know any practical joker who'd try this crap, you'd better tell them to knock it off."

"Don't worry."

The big cop gave me a disarming smile. "I'm not. I'm just wondering if this *was* a practical joke."

"Why?"

"Because we're not used to seeing the same two people so often. Seem a little odd to you?"

"Now that you mention it."

"Any explanation?"

I shrugged, picked up a butt and lit it. "I told a few

143

people about that last episode. Maybe one of them felt like having some fun."

"It's going to cost them if they keep it up."

Tobano didn't see the look on my face as I walked past to hold the door open for them. "You bet your ass it is," I said.

Lee couldn't hold his act any longer. It dropped as they went out and he sagged to the couch with a stifled groan and lay there shielding his eyes from the sunlight. His hands were shaking and a tic was playing around the corner of his mouth.

I went out to the kitchen, brewed up a pot of coffee and brought him a cup. "Drink it, you'll feel better."

He pushed himself to a sitting position and took the cup in his trembling fingers and sipped at it until it was gone. I took the cup away and lit him a cigarette. "Feel like talking?"

His eyes rolled toward mine in a face pasty white. "Dog . . . what the hell are you into?"

"Sorry, kid."

"They . . . tried to knock me off."

"I know."

"But I didn't even . . ."

"Just describe them."

His tongue tried to wet his parched lips and he nodded, his hand rubbing the bruise on the side of his head. "There were two of them. About your size. Those guns made them a lot bigger. Damn it, Dog . . ."

"Come on, Lee."

"Sure, come on. You know what it's like to think you're going to drown in a couple of minutes? You . . ."

"I have a good idea."

Lee squinted and propped his head in his hands. "They were in their forties, one wore a black suit, the other a sport coat and slacks. White shirts . . . patterned dark ties."

"Any definite characteristics?"

After a moment's thought Lee said, "Nothing . . . special, unless you want to call them kind of hard looking." He looked up at me then, his eyes still scared. "Dog, look, those guys weren't kidding around! They sat here all night without saying a damn thing, then all of a sudden one got up and coldcocked me. The next thing I knew I was tied up in the tub and they were turning the water on."

"They must have said something."

"Yeah, in the beginning. They wanted you. I didn't know where the hell you were. You didn't tell me you were going to stay out all night."

"How about their speech? What did they sound like?"

"You mean .. like a dialect?

"That's right."

Lee gave it a thought for a moment, frowning. "They spoke . . . well, pretty damn good. Like too good, maybe."

"What do you mean?"

"Sort of . . . like they studied the language. The one . . . he seemed to think first, then speak. The other had a funny inflection like . . . you remember that RAF pilot they called Big Benny?"

"Yeah."

"Like him, that kind."

"Benny was from Brussels," I said. "He went to England straight from college four years before the war started."

"Well, he didn't say much except to ask about you and he sounded like Big Benny when he did."

"Did they say what they wanted me for?"

"No, but one was going to search the place until the other one told him you wouldn't be that stupid. They were going to wait until you got here, make you talk and then kill you. They had a briefcase with them that had all kinds of stuff in it. Tools, bottles of stuff . . . scared the shit out of me. I guess they knew I wasn't lying or they would have tried something on me."

"They knew, all right. I just wonder why they didn't wait for me."

"One of them kept looking at his watch the last two hours. He was getting pretty fidgety."

"They could have figured I smelled the trap and would come back with reinforcements."

"But why those cops?"

"Another way to nail me down, except their timing was bad. They kept a watch on the door until I did show, then called the cops thinking I'd be grabbed in an apartment with a dead man . . . or trying to move a body."

"Trying to . . . geez, Dog . . ."

"Forget it. Nothing happened. I'm going to clear out of here and . . ."

"The hell you are," he interrupted. "I saw those guys and I can identify them. You're not letting me be a straggler on this raid. Man, I'm chicken. I don't go for this routine at all."

"Okay, okay, you may be right."

I got up and got another cigarette. When I turned around he was staring at me like I was a stranger "You know who they were, don't you?"

"No."

"Then you know why they were here."

"I got an idea."

"But you can't tell me."

"No," I said.

"You're wild," Lee told me, then he grinned. "I guess you know I really did shit my pants."

"I found that out the hard way."

"You ever do that?"

"Twice," I told him.

"Dog . . ."

"Yeah?"

"They were wearing brown shoes."

I snuffed the butt out and waited.

"In New York you don't wear brown shoes with a black suit or dark slacks. Like it's one of the gauche things out-of-towners do."

"Or foreigners?"

"Uh-huh. All the time."

"What else?"

"Everything they had on was brand-new. I saw the folds in their shirts from the packages."

"You notice the guns?"

"How could I miss them. One was a big bore, maybe a .38. Either a Colt or an S. and W. The other one was a .22 on a heavy frame."

"Nickel-plated?" I asked him quietly.

"Yeah. How'd you know?"

Below the penthouse level of the fabulous Chateau 300, New York City lay sprawled out like a gigantic Christmas tree, the lower branches sweeping into Queens, Brooklyn and the Bronx, then stairstepped up to the giant towers of Manhattan.

Cable Howard Productions had taken over the entire restaurant to celebrate its merger with Walt Gentry, announcing the forthcoming filming of *Fruits of Labor,* a current best seller of nineteenth-century sex. Lee had whipped up a guest list that included everybody who was anybody at all; football greats, movie stars, Wall Street financiers and a scattering of war heroes in uniform of all the services.

The press was all over the place, popping flashbulbs, rolling TV cameras and taking notes, living up to their reputations at the punch bowl and the three huge bars. A pair of name orchestras spelled each other at playing soft dance music for a change, with a concert pianist fresh in from an appearance at Carnegie Hall filling in the blanks between sets.

Walt Gentry presided over it all in his usual manner, pleasant and smiling, taking a few notes himself to break the monotony of his bachelorhood in the future. Sharon was at S. C. Cable's side prompting him with names and making the introductions. She had wanted to skip the whole affair, but her boss insisted he needed her and she was back in the big run again.

She saw me watching her and waved just as a glass tinkled next to mine. A voice said, "Enjoying yourself, Mr. Kelly?"

I threw a quick look at Dick Lagen and shrugged. "Not especially."

"Must be a bit dull after those lavish European affairs you're used to."

"Where'd you hear that?"

He swirled the ice in his glass, then polished half the drink off. "Several sources. You keep excellent company. Walking among the rich must be rather pleasant."

"I wouldn't know."

"Really? Doesn't being the guest of one of the richest men in Europe impress you? I understand Roland Holland owns nine separate major industries outright and heads one of the world's largest conglomerates."

"Rollie and I were in the same outfit during the war, Dick. Every once in a while I pick up on my old buddies. Lee Shay was there too."

"Your wartime buddy wasn't wealthy before the war, however."

"Nobody was, remember? Rollie was one of those types with a mind. A financial whiz kid. He parlayed a small bundle into a fat fortune and it couldn't have happened to a nicer guy. Plenty of others have done the same thing."

"Quite so, but they weren't friends of yours."

"That remark had a curve on it," I said.

"Your friends all seem to be very interesting people. Your seeming lack of friends is just as interesting. I still don't get very far researching your past . . . except for your immediate family."

"Read the society pages, Dick, you'll find out about them there."

Lagen let a waiter take his glass and picked another drink off the tray. "I found some interesting tidbits in the gossip columns . . . and a few police reports."

Now I knew where the needle was going in and beat him to the punch. "You mean about Veda and Pam? Those twists always were trouble. Veda's been in more night courts than a Times Square hooker. Pam's just as bad, but

147

if you want icing for the cake, try Lucella. She and that Fred Simon character cut a real wide path before they divorced. How the hell they could figure me for a black sheep is more than I can understand."

"The rest of the family seems to live with it."

"Bullshit. Those old biddies ignore it or are too old to remember. Besides, when you're top chicken in the pecking order in that social circle, nobody feels like promoting gossip and getting kicked off their rung."

"You ought to talk to Mona Merriman. That kind of talk would fill her columns for weeks."

"It's old hat, Dick. She'll get enough garbage for a month right at this bash."

Lagen let a smile play across his face and looked over to where the center of activity was. "She may get more. There's an old friend of yours here."

I followed the direction of his eyes but couldn't place anybody. "Who?"

"A Mr. Cross McMillan and his wife, Sheila."

"You really do a research job, friend."

"I've only just started, Mr. Kelly."

Walt Gentry was a large stockholder and a director of Wells River Plastic Corporation. Cross McMillan was the majority stockholder and chairman of the board. That afternoon there had been a meeting to consider a merger and, since Cross was staying in New York, Walt had invited his business associate to his party.

Until I joined the group he had been enjoying himself, then all those nasty memories of the past, the rock in the head, the standoff at the beach and the loss of all that waterfront he had wanted so badly etched a mask of concealed anger into his face. Walt's attempted introduction drew a curt "We've met," and upon seeing Sharon he threw a look at Walt as if he were being double-crossed. Walt got no part of the play at all and called him away to meet somebody else, leaving me standing there alone until a tall brunette with a figure and features so sensuous as almost not to be real sidled up and said, "My husband doesn't like you, Mr. Kelly."

I looked at her, puzzled. The sheer silk of her gown clung to the curves of her body, the open front of it the absolute minimum in modesty. At the point of cleavage of her magnificent breasts a huge pear-shaped diamond pendant dangled on a platinum chain throwing highlights of color into my eyes.

148

"No, we haven't met," she laughed. She held out her hand, cradling a drink in the other. "I'm Sheila McMillan . . . Cross's wife."

I took her hand and held it a moment. The grip was warm and firm, a little stronger than most women's. "Dogeron Kelly. I'm sorry."

"Don't be. Mona told me who you were, then I remembered Cross speaking about you."

"We're not exactly buddies."

Sheila laughed again and held the glass to her mouth. Even the way she tasted her drink was a pure sex act and I began to wonder about all those things I had heard about her. "You're the one who gave Cross that scar on his head, weren't you? You know, he's never forgiven you for that."

"Kid stuff," I said. "That was a long time ago. Besides, he never could stand our family. But at least we have something in common. I can't either."

"Yes, I know. Rumors circulate freely around Linton. I understand your coming home was quite a shock to them."

"More or less."

She looked past me toward her husband. He was shaking hands with a pair of uptown bank presidents and didn't see us. "Sometimes I wish Cross would get out of all this," she mused. "We have everything we need but he keeps wanting more. Money hasn't even got a useful purpose anymore. It's just something you need to play the game of business."

"High finance built this country," I reminded her.

"But it ruins people." She turned to me suddenly and smiled again. "Tell me, Mr. Kelly . . ."

"Call me Dog."

"All right . . . Dog" Sheila made a mock face at the name. "What do you do? Are you going with Barrin Industries?"

"Right now I'm doing nothing but relaxing. I don't think I could relax with Barrin."

"What a lovely evasion of my question."

"A month or two and I'll have it all figured out."

She patted my arm gently. "Best of luck to you then. I'm glad you aren't like the rest of the Barrins. I don't suppose I had better invite you to tea when you're in Linton, should I?"

My grin turned into a short laugh and I shook my head. "No, you'd better not. I wouldn't want Cross to blow a fuse."

I said "so long" to her, watched while she joined two other women and walked over to the door. The heavy-shouldered big guy by the entrance looked up when I approached and came from behind the table. "Everybody checks out, Mr. Kelly. No gatecrashers."

"How about downstairs?"

"A dozen or so autograph hounds, maybe. Joe's keeping his eye on them."

"You check the orchestras?"

"Sure. Two fill-ins for a couple who couldn't make it. They have ID's and union cards. Every one of those press guys here I know personally. The crews with those TV units are all vouched for. Waiters are all staff personnel."

"Okay, thanks," I said. Fifty bucks could buy me a lot of extra security.

Most of the evening I had been dodging Mona Merriman, but she caught up to me on the way to the bar and I had to escort her over for a refill. She stuck the ball-point pen in a clip on her pad and dropped everything in her purse with a sigh and snapped her fingers for a drink. "Someday," she told me, "I'm going to get an item that's true, not distorted or contrived and I think I'll fall over."

"You give the public what it wants to read." I raised my glass. "Cheers."

"Cheers yourself." She polished her drink off without a pause and told the bartender to fill it up again. She waved her glass at the chattering mob and clucked with disgust. "Look at them. Dig all the phony tits and store-bought hairdos. Everybody out making points."

"What for?"

My question caught her off base. "You kidding, my big friend?"

"Nope."

"Hell, there isn't a kid out there who isn't angling for a part in that new picture. Tonight everybody even remotely connected with Cable-Howard will be well bedded down and in hock for a line or at the very least a two-shot in a crowd scene. You watch the guys. They're pulling the same trick too. Two days after a working script is done, pirated copies will be peddled around town so that all the hams will be able to give a good first reading."

"Crazy," I said.

"Nice for all the studs, though. Watch the operators go to town. They'll move in on all the choice ass and cut them out before the idiot dames can find out that they're only flunkeys on the lot." She made a motion with her hand at an overly made-up middle-aged woman smiling up at a pair of good-looking young junior executive types. One of them seemed familiar. "It's not all the dames, either. That's

150

Sylvia Potter. Her husband's an assistant director for S. C. Cable. Right now she's picking herself out a playmate for this week who'll let her take out all her fetishes on his ripe young body because he thinks she might get him an in with her old man."

"Will she?"

"A lucky few will make it. Just a bit part that won't hurt anything. And Bibby Potter will go along or she'll blow the whistle on him and his philandering and wind up with half his estate." She took another drink of her highball. "It's a nutty business."

"The picture worth all that?"

"Oh, it'll be a winner. It can't miss. They'll drop five million in the production and bring back ten times that. You read the book?"

"Haven't had time. Is it good?"

"Big sex novel," Mona said. "Living and loving in an old-fashioned nineteenth-century manufacturing town. Pantalettes and petticoats lying all over the place, men struggling out of their waistcoats. You know, zippers were a great invention. Today a couple strips naked in ten seconds."·

I let her see my expression of disbelief.

"All right, wise guy, except me. At my age I have to have my undergarments engineered for me and they take time to dismantle."

"I bet it's worth it."

"Give it a try and see."·

"Careful, I might."

"Baloney, you belong out there with the studs. You see those kids eyeing you when they found out you knew Walt? If I were in your shoes I'd be getting all I could."

"Let's say I'm particular."

"Sure you are. Like with . . . Sheila McMillan?"

"You got a dirty mind, kid. I just met the lady."

"Then let me clue you . . . she's a teaser. That's what drives her husband nuts. Frigid as a penguin's balls and as beautiful as they come. You'd never know it to look at her, would you? All that meat just going to waste."

"Where did you hear that?"

"A bit here, a bit there. Cross let it slip to a business acquaintance who's a friend of mine during some bourbon blues. Most of it's servants' gossip, though."

"You believe all you hear?"

"Very little of it," she said, "but in this case it's true. Why do you think he's such a tiger when it comes to finance? He takes out all his frustrations raping the business world. He'd give his left nut just to get a hunk of his own wife and it's never going to happen."

"Then why did he marry her?"

Mona put her empty glass down on the bar and looked at me like I was a kid. "Because he's crazy mad in love with her, that's why. My guess is that she loves him too, but when it comes to sex, it's forget-it-time."

I finally found Cross McMillan and his wife across the room. They were standing there talking to a few others and Sheila was smiling at him, her eyes adoring, one hand on his arm. I suddenly felt sorry for the poor bald bastard and wished I hadn't planted that scar on his pate where everybody could see it. He would have been better off if I had castrated him.

Mona said, "What are you thinking of? You have a funny look on your face."

"Nothing printable, doll."

Her finger tapped the back of my hand. "I *do* have something I *can* print," she said mischievously.

"Oh?"

"About a possible romance between a Barrin scion and a certain secretary for a picture firm."

"Sharon?"

Mona's raised eyebrows gave me a positive nod.

"Kid, I'm damn near old enough to be her father."

"A perfect Hollywood twosome," she smiled. "How would you like to be a son to me?"

"You know what they'd call me then?"

"Sure. A son of a bitch. Very appropriate. You watch out for all those little hot-pants chippies out there, you hear?" Mona said and left.

My watch said ten forty-five. The call should have come in by now. I waved Lee out of the group he was with and made sure he had reservations at his club. He and another member were going to drive Sharon home, be certain she was locked in until I called her, then go directly to the Ryder A.C. where no one except members were admitted. I went out into the lobby, picked up a copy of *Fruits of Labor* and headed for the elevator.

XIII

My contact at Weller-Fabray answered my coded inquiry in French with the statement that they were closed until morning, which meant I was to call back on the hot line that had a scrambler attachment. I redialed and asked, "Your lines bugged?"

"They could be. We had Treasury Department agents in here this morning. Apparently the Sûreté in Marseilles are monitoring overseas calls. Jason placed two to us from the Pavilion of Crosses restaurant just before one of the couriers from Istanbul was shot to death. He had twenty kilos of heroine in a suitcase prepared for shipment to the United States."

"Who hit him?"

"Nobody knows. They seem to think it was an attempted hijacking. The murderer escaped completely."

"Damn," I said. "Who got the stuff?"

The voice on the other end chuckled. "That is the joke. Nobody. The courier had anticipated a possible double cross and had substituted packages. The genuine stuff is still hidden somewhere. Had all gone well he would have accepted the money and told the transfer agent later where to recover the proper goods. Unfortunately, he didn't anticipate being killed."

"Any leads at all?"

"So far, none. The courier was a professional. Now the big hunt is on. It will be . . . how do you say? . . . finders keepers"

"Who's working our end?"

"The Irishman O'Keefe and Pierre Dumont."

"Hell, O'Keefe has a record in Berlin and . . ."

"A simple assault charge. It's not very likely he'll be

153

recognized. Besides," . . . he chuckled again . . . "you should be the one to worry."

"Now what's up?" I asked him.

"The affair had your stamp on it. Your MO, so to speak. It is being rumored that the courier didn't know a switch had been made and it was a first-class hijacking with the killing only a red herring thrown in to confuse everybody."

"Nice."

"Certain parties are very angry. Le Fleur himself has directed a bonus for either the recovery or your demise."

Le Fleur, the flower. A gentle name for a human fungus. Someplace the bastard sat in royal opulence and pushed the buttons that could trigger the kill of anyone from a dope-head to a diplomat. Narcotics built his empire and the ones he couldn't squeeze out he eliminated or organized. The only ones he couldn't control were nibbling holes in his elaborate structure and if it happened often and success-fully enough the whole damn thing would fall apart.

I said, "This may bring him out into the open."

"No, I'm afraid not, although there are many who would like to know his true identity. Once that happened any one of the others in a fairly strong position would take steps to have him removed. These are the days of science and equip-ment. An aerial bombing raid on a stronghold is not an improbability and financially simple to arrange."

"But complicated," I told him.

"Quite. Therefore it is simpler to pick the fly out of the ointment, which, in this case, they think is you. One mem-ber of the syndicate has been selected to act as your exe-cutioner, especially in view of the fact that his natural animosity and suspicion has led him into instigating a kid-nap order on you . . . followed by your death, of course."

"The Turk?"

"Exactly. They already know what has happened to his two men. Either they succeed in the near future or The Turk becomes the object of Le Fleur's attentions. This he certainly doesn't desire."

"Hell, he's working at it. They tried again and I was lucky. They missed me. My friend wasn't so lucky and they damn near killed him."

"You shouldn't expose your friends to yourself, Dog."

"The Turk should know better."

"Perhaps he didn't take your retirement seriously."

"But he's going to. Who's come in the last few days?"

For a second he didn't speak and I could hear his fingers tapping against the phone. "Nobody we know of through routine channels, but that means very little. I understand they landed a shipment through Mexico and into Nevada a day ago. Someone could have come in with that. And the Coast Guard missed a night interception of a fast cruiser that was heading toward Miami, so who can be sure?"

"Okay, then we'll take it from there. I want two foreign types about my size with no outstanding characteristics. They speak English with an accent, possibly Belgian. Their clothes are all new and expensive, but they're wearing brown shoes with dark outfits, so that might give you a lead. Check into foreign-language movie houses, hotels catering to people from that area, restaurants . . . you know the scoop."

"I understand."

"Somebody's laid the groundwork for them here, so they have a contact. I doubt if they've had time to establish any kind of reliable identification, so that might help. They'll be operating on a cash basis in a credit card economy."

I could hear his pen scratching as he wrote it all down. "Another thing . . . one had a .38, the other guy packed a .22 on a nickel-plated heavy frame."

The writing stopped a moment. Then he said, "Arnold Bell."

"A Belgian national."

"Dog, you know what kind of a man this is, don't you?"

"I've heard the stories."

"No one's better. He works in close because he likes to do it that way. He has been the hit man on eleven important people. His only failure was an attempted assassination of General De Gaulle. He was almost caught then. Almost. So far he has been apprehended for nothing. Dog . . . they must want you very badly."

"Why would he use a backup man?"

"Most likely because he is unfamiliar with the country. Like you say . . . the brown shoes?"

"Looks like they both need a refresher course," I said.

"When will you be calling in?" he asked me.

"Tomorrow."

"That isn't much time."

"Do what you can," I said. "Incidentally, how did you explain the scrambler phone to the T-men?"

I could almost see him shrug. "A business necessity. The competition would most like to have the identity and whereabouts of our very select clientele."

Leyland Hunter's friends in the right places had made it easy for me. Both Bridey-the-Greek and Markham were released from the hospital at their own request and against

155

the advice of the doctors. The only thing they forgot was that cops can be curious creatures of habit even in matters that don't necessarily concern them. One detective had left word to be notified if there was any unorthodox departure. The clerk at the desk, who had a brother on the force, complied.

The cop's name was Sergeant Tobano.

He didn't get in from a special assignment until a quarter past two, booked the two punks he had with him, then turned around when the uniformed desk man pointed to me at the bench in the back of the room. He was tired, unshaven, his clothes rumpled and he looked annoyed at the world.

His eyes had that universal flat look and he shoved his hands in his pockets. "I was wondering when I'd see you again."

"Why?"

"One of those feelings."

"Let's go talk," I said.

"There's an office back here."

I followed him through the gate and into a wood-paneled room that smelled of a century ago, waited until he had closed the door, then sat in the chair on the other side of the cluttered table facing him. "Let's hear it," he said.

I reached for a pencil, wrote a number down on a piece of scrap paper and pushed it over to him. "Make a call first."

"What?" The word had a sharp, nasty tone to it.

"Just call. It's a local number."

Tobano didn't do anything at first. He sat there watching me with those dark hawk eyes, imprinting me in his mind. Finally he reached for the phone. "If you're another joker, your tail is in a sling." He dialed the number, and when it answered his eyes went from the paper in front of him to me, narrowing slightly. He identified himself, then started to say he was interrogating a person named Dogeron Kelly. He didn't get much further. He nodded absently twice, said okay and hung up. Then he called another number, ran a check on the first one and cradled the receiver. "You got some pretty important friends, Kelly."

"It helps."

"Right now I'll let it go. Just keep in mind that I don't give a shit who anybody is when they get out of line or interfere with my business. All you have coming is ten minutes' worth of talking."

"You kept a surveillance on those two guys who got clobbered in the garage toilet."

156

"A normal precaution."

"They ducked out."

"And you want to know where." He made it a flat statement.

"Right."

"Why?"

"I could go to the trouble of running them down myself if you want."

He ran it through his mind, knew it could be done and nodded. "The Greek's in a rooming house on the West Side." He scratched an address on the same paper I had given him and shoved it back. "Markham checked into the Ormin Hotel. They left at different times and each one took two different cabs getting to his pad. It didn't work."

"They weren't charged with anything, were they?"

"You don't book a guy for getting beaten up. They even paid the hospital bill."

I pushed the chair back and stood up. "If you managed to snag prints from those two while they were unconscious, tell the boys in Washington to process them through some of the European departments."

"I'll do that."

"You still covering that pair?"

"The message went to the right ears."

"Don't bet on it."

Tobano's face was thoughtful. "Why did they skip out of the hospital?"

"Maybe they were afraid of me," I said.

Fifty years ago one of the steamship tycoons had willed his midtown East Side mansion to a young legal fraternity. What had at one time been a handy dormitory for impoverished legal beagles now was one of New York's most exclusive private clubs occupied only by the mighty of the profession who constructed or destroyed empires.

I sat across a black walnut table from Leyland Hunter nursing my drink, picking out the faces I knew, aware of the acoustical quality of the room that totally muffled all but the loudest voices into a soft hum. "You live well," I said.

Hunter gave me a little smile and shrugged. "Protective coloration. Besides, it intimidates the more reluctant clients. Care to order?"

I nodded and he touched the button that brought the waiter, ordered for both of us and picked up his drink. I said, "I hope the cops didn't ruffle you any, Counselor."

"They didn't. Although I must say it's been some time since I've had communication with them."

"Want to know what happened?"

"Not particularly. You haven't asked for advice yet. Do you intend to?"

"Nope."

"Very well then. What else is on your n.ind?"

"The Mondo Beach property set?"

He sipped his drink gently, savoring the taste. "Completely. I expedited the deal and as you supposed, your cousins assumed the money came from the long lost relative. I suspect they intend renewing the friendship before long."

I grinned at him and flipped a cigarette out of my pack. "They're really hurting for cash then. I figured they would." I lit the butt and blew the match out. "I don't think that old boy would buy in anyway."

His nod was a solemn one. "I rather doubt it. He died ten years ago. Out of curiosity I made some inquiries and only by sheer luck managed to find out about it. He was gold rich, all right, but blew it all on uranium exploration during the boom and went totally broke. He died in a mine cave-in trying for another lucky strike."

"I guess he had his fun."

"Probably, but what joyful pleasures are you contemplating?"

I took the check out of my pocket with the note of details stapled to the corner and handed it to him. "Buy me a house, Counselor. Then get a crew in to repair everything as it was in its original condition."

He studied the note and the check, then looked over the rim of his glasses at me. "This isn't to be in your name?"

"You see what I want."

"Aren't you a little too old to be playing games like this?"

"It isn't a game, friend."

"Can I ask why?"

"Sure. I never had a house. I like somebody else to enjoy the pleasure. Any complications?"

"No. I suppose I am to expedite this too?"

"From the size of that check," I told him, "it's pretty obvious."

"Dogeron Kelly," he laughed, "you are a pisser."

"Terrible language from one of your stature."

"Balls," he said. "Now, is that all?"

"No."

"I was afraid of that."

"Just a question now. Why haven't Dennie and Al married?"

Hunter looked at me several seconds then finished his drink. "I was wondering when you were going to ask that." The waiter came, put down our plates, and when he had left Hunter tasted his food, approved and wiped his mouth with his napkin. "Several matches were arranged for both of them shortly after the war. I assume you remember how the family handled such things."

"How could I forget?"

"Unfortunately, your female cousins made a botch of things with their errant behavior. Although the Barrins are mere upstarts, those doing the arranging were quite chagrined about the whole episode and let the matter drop right there."

"That all?"

"Not quite. I have to go on hearsay now, but both Dennison and Alfred never seemed to pursue marriage as a career. Both preferred their position of heading the Barrin estate. At one time Dennie showed an interest in the Havelock widow, but she married into an old chain-store family with all her wealth. Cousin Alfred squired several unattached, and, I might add, unlovely daughters of riches here and there, but nothing seemed to take. Those people with all their war profits didn't buy Alfred's type at all. I think they knew what he was after."

"But nothing now?"

"Neither is of choice marriageable age at the moment, Dog. Financially, they aren't the best risks, either." His eyes had a strange glint to them. "I went over the books last week when we were in Linton. Your cousins have accepted several large and important contracts. On paper, everything looks quite sound, but the reports from the plant managers are pretty disturbing." He paused a second and let it sink in. "Barrin isn't going to be able to handle them unless they retool and they haven't got the money for that."

"Come on, Counselor, they can't be that stupid."

"Then the answer is obvious, isn't it?"

I nodded. "They're figuring on some sort of financing. But how?"

"That, my friend, is up their sleeve."

"Any estimates on the retooling job?"

"Roughly several million."

"How rough?"

"About fifteen million."

"That's pretty damn rough," I said. "They're not looking to start the job and then plead for an extension, are they?"

"Not with these contracts. No, they're hoping for something."

"Grand Sita up for sale?"

"Oh, they'd sell, but there are no buyers. Maybe in two years the picture will change, but they couldn't wait that long. Those contracts will go into effect next month. They've already invested the Mondo Beach money in factory renovations, so they are definitely going ahead."

"This ought to be good," I told him.

"It's going to be better. I've heard a rumor."

"Oh?"

"Cross McMillan is ready to move in at the next board meeting. It's scheduled a week before the contracts are formerly activated. Barrin Industries will come crashing down."

The thought pulled my mouth apart and I said, "How about that?"

But Hunter didn't grin back. He just sat there looking at me, then finally said, "That bastard streak in you sure shows. Eat your lunch."

I had the cabbie drop Hunter off at his office, then head back down to the Flatiron Building. Al DeVecchio was still eating salami and slopping coffee from an oversize mug with one ear glued to a telephone. When he hung up he invited me to a snack, but I refused and sat in the empty rocker.

"You made the papers, kid," he told me. "Both Madcap Merriman and Lagen have squibs about you. See it?"

"Nope."

"Merriman's description makes you out better than a movie star. A real sex symbol."

"Good for her."

"That Lagen's a corker. He's posing hypothetical questions . . . have you come back to take over the ailing Barrin Industries and all that."

"Should be good for a rise in the stock price."

"Not in today's market." He put his cup down and leaned back in his rocker. "What's bugging you, Dog?"

I stared out the window toward uptown Manhattan. The haze was thick and the outline of the Empire State Building was barely discernible. "You have any mob contacts, Al?"

He stopped rocking, his eyes squinting at me. "What?"

"Rackets. Mob. Organized crime."

"Look, because I'm Italian . . ."

"Don't give me any ethnic crap, Al. You handled the bookkeeping on the Cudder Hotel chain. You set up Davewell Products and engineered all the business details for the Warton merger."

He came halfway out of his chair. "How the hell did you know about that?"

"I do some homework too."

He sat down slowly, the amazement on his face. "Some damn homework. Those were all clean deals or I never would have touched them."

"How did you feel when you found out who was behind them?"

Al took another sip of his coffee and put it down with a grimace. "Shitty," he said. "Old buddy, I'm giving you grudging respect, which is something coming from me. As for your first question, my mob contacts are nil and they stay nil. They offered me two more fat deals I told them to shove all the way and that ends it there."

"Why did you get involved in the first place?"

"Easy, friend, real easy. They maneuvered through topnotch people I thought were clean and it wasn't until a long time afterward that I found out I was putting dirty money into legitimate businesses. I even turned the information over to the feds, and right there it stopped. Graft can go into some pretty high places. Some of our elected or appointed officials have hot, sweaty palms." He gave me another stare and shook his head. "Man . . ."

"How about the contacts?" I repeated.

"Forget it." I waited for a good minute, then: "Why?"

"A consignment of heroin for delivery here was sidetracked in Marseilles. I want to know who the receiver was."

"Dog, you are out of your fucking mind!"

"I'm not in the business if that's what's bothering you."

Al got up, paced the room once, then stood there glaring down on me. "What the hell business are you in?"

"Trying to stay alive, for one."

"Man, you're nuts. You think I'm going to ask anybody questions like that? You think I'm going to stick my neck out that far? You think I'm going to get involved with narcotics?"

"Sure I do, Al. Why fight it?"

"Go frig yourself."

161

I grinned at him, a big fat grin. "You can't help yourself anymore. Now you *got* to know what it's all about."

He let his hands drop helplessly by his sides, then turned them palms up in despair. "Where the hell did I go wrong? I put money in the poorbox, I support my family, I belong to the right clubs . . ."

"Quit clowning," I said. "Wait until you hear the facts."

"Sure."

"You'd better sit down."

I didn't tell him too much. There are times when it's better to let them figure things out for themselves. Conscience and guilt complexes are factors that can throw a monkey wrench into anything and Al DeVeccho had more than enough of both. All I wanted from him was a probable lead on who was handling the big buys of heroin. There were other ways of finding out, but Al had an in and if he listened right even a hint could point in the right direction.

It took a while, but eventually he decided to go along because my ass was in a sling and for no other reason. I said, "How long do you think it will take?"

Al shrugged his shoulders. "The Davewell bunch wants me to do another audit. I was going to turn it down. Maybe I'll start there."

"When?"

"Tuesday. You care if I get somebody else in on this?"

"Use your own discretion."

"If I did, I'd tell you to go piss up a stick. I never had any urge to go back into the gun business."

"Just watch your step and you won't."

"I don't want any bathtub treatments, either."

My knuckles whitened when I squeezed my hands together, remembering what almost had happened. "That was before I smelled what was going on. Now I have Lee's place locked off, a private security guard is on the floor and Lee knows enough to stay on his toes."

"What about your other friends?"

"I'm the target. They know damn well I've never been connected with anyone on this side of the Atlantic. I'll either be walking alone or ready to cover anything that happens."

"You'd better have eyes in the back of your head then."

"Don't sweat it," I said. "They may even get the picture that I'm out of the action all the way."

"You know better than that."

"It's still a possibility."

"Okay, have it your way. I still think I'm a nut for getting talked into this. At least you can keep the hell away

162

from me for a while. If I learn anything, I'll call that number or get you at the apartment."

"Fine."

"What are you planning on doing now?"

I smirked at him and got out of the rocker. "I got a date with a teenybopper named Sharon Cass who's taking me to supper with Walt Gentry and her boss. Nothing like living big, old buddy."

Al let out a few choice barracks words under his breath and didn't even bother to say so long when I left.

Ordinarily, S. C. Cable could field any question with the nimble dexterity of the professional con man, but when Sharon threw the curve at him he was stopped cold and looked across the table at Walt Gentry in absolute amazement, groping for an answer. Walt just smiled his silly little smile that showed which side he was on and left the big tiger of Hollywood dangling.

Sharon wasn't about to let it alone. "Well, why not?" she insisted. "It saves months of exploring for a practical location site, there's power facilities, plenty of room, authentic period buildings and a cooperative management." She probably had her fingers crossed under the table when she made the last statement, but I wasn't worried a bit about it.

S.C. finally found his voice someplace under his mottled chin. "Are you mad, Sharon? We haven't even got a working script yet. The budget isn't . . ."

Sharon's smile had a dagger in it. "You haven't signed the contract with Walt yet, either. And since you expect me to put my virtue on the mattress for your gigantic production, the least you could do is humor me."

"Humor you!"

"Exactly, or Walt cancels the deal. It's as simple as that."

Cable suppressed a choking cough and looked at Walt again. When he saw the affirmative nod he turned to me. "Are you the instigator of this . . . this . . ."

"Don't look at me," I told him. "I'm only going along with the idea. Frankly, it sounds pretty realistic . . . if you like realism . . . and I'm in a position to push for that management cooperation Sharon mentioned. I read the book and as far as the Barrin factory in Linton is concerned, that place has everything you need including the historical details. In fact, some of the truths about that place would goose your story up a little."

"This is blackmail," Cable said. "It's illegal."

"So is assigning women to perform an immoral act for profitable purposes," Sharon purred.

"You're fired," S. C. Cable said.

"You're hired," Walt Gentry told her. "The project is now in your hands."

Cable looked at me helplessly. "See how they trap you? Business ethics mean nothing. A deal is only words. You try . . ."

"Nobody called the deal off yet," I reminded him. "Looks like your move now."

"Shit," Cable said, "so we'll look over the factory. So if it's okay, why not? Any more problems?" He looked around and nobody said anything at all. "Can I hire this broad back? I can't afford to let her go working for anybody else."

"We'll talk about my raise later," Sharon said.

"Oh, boy. I'm broke before I start," Cable moaned. "Now let's eat while I still got an appetite."

Under the table I gave Sharon's hand a squeeze. My finger felt the funny little ring on hers. When she realized I was touching it she looked at me with a quiet smile and eased her hand away.

She had left the sleek business facade back at the restaurant. The hard maturity, the total awareness the city seems to nurture to a peak was gone now. The velvet claws that could bend the business giants with a single soft silken scratch were sheathed. She had unfastened a golden pin so that her hair could swirl around her face and had changed from the black chiffon into tight little short shorts and an even tighter halter that form-fitted into every crevice and curve of her body. The little girl was back, but the woman was still there and it made me uncomfortable to look at her.

There was that strange something about her. Purpose. Call it purpose. Then again, all females were dedicated to something or other. Sharon saw the way I was looking at her and smiled, a cute little feline smile that made me want to lay my hands on her and squeeze a little bit. But even little felines could bite back and I had just seen her nip two of them.

"What made you pull that off, kitten?"

She crossed the room and turned down the volume on the record player, then brought me my coffee. "I don't know. Maybe I was just thinking . . . well, Linton was my home too. It might be nice to see something good happen there again."

"What do you figure the rental for the site will be?"

Her shrug was a little wistful. "Not all that much, really. What I had in mind was some of the other locations. There

164

are people who can use the money a lot more than the Barrin clan."

"You're a sentimental do-gooder," I told her. "I thought you hated that place?"

"I guess I did. Seeing the beach and my old house . . . well, a little nostalgia set in. Did I do wrong?"

"How much do you figure the company will drop in the town?"

"They won't budget less than five million. At least two will go directly into the economy of Linton for housing, subsistence, rentals and all the other details."

I let out a little laugh. "Those cousins of mine are going to be obligated to take the deal if they want to retain their public-spirited image."

"You think there'll be any trouble?" she asked me.

"Trouble, but no difficulty. Not from them, kitten. If there's any roadblocks they'll come from another angle."

"Cross McMillan?"

"That slob won't cooperate with the Barrins to wipe his own tail," I said.

Sharon refilled her coffee cup and smiled. "But he'll cooperate with Walt."

"What makes you think so?"

"Because the handsome young bachelor prince owns a big chunk of McMillan holdings and that cute little-boy smile of his holds a mouthful of tiger teeth. No, Cross won't buck Walt, and Walt won't buck me."

"Nice," I said.

"Or you, Dog. Walt thinks you're a real cobra."

"Oh?"

"I think you are too." She put her coffee down and came over and sat beside me. "You're a snake, my friend. You don't hiss and you don't rattle. I haven't decided if you're a constrictor or venomous. I'm wondering what it would cost me to find out."

"Some one of these days you're going to lay your virginity on the line and I'm going to pop it, kid." I looked at her and let her see a face full of teeth. Getting played with by a slippery, beautiful blonde wasn't my idea of fun when there wasn't sand around to make up some friction.

"Keep talking, Dog."

I handed her my cup and stood up. "Screw you, little girl, I'm not all that moral. I wish I knew your fiancé. I'd slam him on his ass and make him marry you just to take a walking land mine out of circulation. I heard you put down that lover boy . . . what's his name?"

"Raul?"

165

"Yeah. Just don't give *me* that garbage. Not again. You got a hot wet body, sugar. I like it. I shouldn't but I do. No more skinny-dipping like Hunter and old Dubro and no more sacking it in cobwebby houses. I couldn't take it."

"Dog," she said softly.

"What?"

"You love me?"

"Hell no."

"You bastard."

"Yeah, I know."

"I didn't mean it that way."

I grinned at her and slipped into my coat. "You love me, kid?"

"Certainly," she said matter-of-factly.

"A terrible affliction I infect all the women with," I said.

"You really are a bastard, Dog." She smiled back at me, her teeth white and shiny.

"A cobra, remember?"

XIV

Next to the Ormin Hotel, the shattered remains of a row of tenements gaped out at the street, windows smashed, the frames smoke blackened and whole areas of brickwork crumpled in a miniature landslide to the sidewalk. Somehow one building still stood between the ruins and the hotel and a lone figure curled in the shadow of the stoop.

There was no Markham registered, but the clerk remembered the guy with the torn-up face and gave me the room number for a five-dollar bill, then went back to his scratch sheet on a stool behind the counter. The only thing that surprised him was the five. It was four more than he'd usually get for the same information.

His room was on the west side of the third floor at the far end of a corridor lit by two hanging bulbs. I stayed close to the wall trying to be as quiet as possible, reached the door and stood there listening for any sounds inside. All I heard was the rats scratching inside the wall. I waited another minute and tried the knob, letting it twist slowly and gently under my fingers. When the latch was all the way free I pushed the door in gently, waiting to feel the bite of a chain, but it went past the distance a chain would have held it and I didn't bother waiting anymore. I shoved it open all the way and it clattered back against some barrier and stayed there.

The hammer going back on the .45 was enough for anybody to hear. I said, "Markham," and waited. I could see almost one-half the room in the dull light from the corridor, the dresser and chair with the pants thrown over the back, even one corner of the bed that nestled out of my line of sight. I said, "Markham," again, then rolled inside

167

in a tight ball, spun on my stomach with the gun ready to cut loose and nothing happened at all.

But I could see Markham. He was on the bed with one arm dangling over the side and there was just enough light to see that his eyes were open. I found the switch on the lamp beside the bed and flipped it on.

My strong-arm friend was out to lunch. Somebody had retired him from the land of the living with a single tiny puncture square in the middle of his forehead halfway between his hairline and the bridge of his nose. There had been no fuss and no mess. There was a half-empty bottle of codeine tablets on the night table and Markham had bought his ticket in the middle of a deep sleep he needed to deaden the pain from his smashed face.

I went over and took a look at the door. The lock was old-fashioned and simple, easy to open with a skeleton key or a pick. There was a chain lock too, but it dangled free because whoever installed it put the catch too close to the edge of the door and there was enough play for it to be opened by reaching in from the outside and flipping it back.

Markham had made too many other people hurt without knowing the bite of pain himself. He forgot that it could make you careless about the things that could get you dead fast.

I went back to the body, felt the clammy skin and lifted the arm that dangled so stiffly, then went out, closed the door and went back downstairs. The clerk looked at me over his scratch sheet and said, "Find him?"

I nodded. "He get any other visitors?"

"Nope."

"Anybody check in the last twelve hours?"

"We don't get much trade, feller. Like I'm only here to see nobody tears the place up. In this neighborhood . . ."

"I didn't ask you that," I said.

He faked a smile, waiting to see another bill in my fingers, but he saw what was in my face and the smile turned sour. "One guy comes in. So I give him a room."

"He there now?"

"Nah. I figured he needed it for a broad. He went out maybe a half hour later to get one. He ain't shown yet."

"Luggage?"

"When they pay in advance, they don't need it. Besides, you think we got fancy trade yet? Here they come in with paper bags. This guy was looking for a quick shack, that's all. The way he was dressed he could do better uptown."

"Describe him."

"Mister, I don't look at my customers. You I'll remember from talking. You want that?"

"I don't give a shit, buddy. Where's your register?"

"Hell, I'll tell you his name. Peterson, that's what. Newark, New Jersey. Look, what's . . ."

"Give me your phone."

"Pay phone's on the wall."

I looked at him for about three seconds and he handed me the phone. I had to go through the police emergency number, but I finally raised Tobano and said, "I found Markham, Sergeant. He's nice and dead."

For a minute I listened, then said into the mouthpiece, "Ease off. He's cold and rigor's set in. I'm covered for every minute of the day. If I were you I'd get to the Greek He might have been a little luckier."

Tobano finally calmed down, but the annoyance was still there. "You stay put until we get there, understand?"

"Unh-uh, pal. Consider this call from an anonymous source. I'll check in with you later. By the way, did you get a report on those prints?"

His voice was quiet and hard. "I did," he said, and hung up.

The night clerk had put down his paper and was trying to light a cigarette. I handed his phone back and held a match under the butt in his lips. "Don't bother going upstairs, mister. Just stay here until a squad car shows. After that tell them anything you know."

He sucked in a lungful of smoke, coughed and nodded. "If that guy comes back . . ."

"He won't," I told him.

The pancakes and sausages weren't sitting very well with Lee at all. He couldn't keep his eyes from drifting to the front page of the *News* where the body shots of Markham and Bridey-the-Greek were laid out side by side with the "Mystery Murders" caption hinting at some dark intrigue. The same .22 caliber gun had killed both of them, but Bridey had tried to scramble out and it took four shots to pull him down. The last was through the back of the head and he lay face down halfway out the open window leading onto a fire escape.

Lee finally pushed his plate away and tried to swallow some coffee. It was a bad try. His hand was shaking and coffee spilled down on his shirt. I said, "Relax, buddy."

"Sure, relax. Easy to say, isn't it?"

"No trouble at all."

He stopped dabbing at his clothes and looked up at me

"If I were you I'd be scared shitless. How the hell can you sit there like that?"

"Look at the bright side. Two of those punks are ooled. The odds are going down."

"Why, Dog? Hell, if they were after you ."

"Object lessons. You screw up an assignment and you're in line for a tapout yourself. The lesson goes a little higher than to the hit men themselves."

"Dog . . ."

I knew what he wanted and shook my head. "Don't ask me, kid. From now on I'm not going to be close to anybody so there's not much chance of anybody trying the bathtub routine again. That little bit didn't work either, so the next time out it will be the direct approach. There's a cover on you and Sharon just to make sure, but my bet is they'll go straight after me."

His clenched knuckles rapped against the edge of the table with impatience. "Damn it, Dog . . . why?"

"Because sombody thinks I had something to do with a situation I wasn't involved in at all."

Lee pursued his mouth, then nodded with his eyes tight. "Okay. Just one other thing. Did you ever have anything to do with something *like* it?"

I picked up my coffee cup and watched him because he was looking to see if my hand was shaking too. It wasn't. "All the time," I told him.

"You know, Dog. I knew it when I opened that damn suitcase. I could almost taste it. And I wasn't the only one. Everybody else could feel it too, except they didn't know it for what it was. Remember how we always seemed to know when there were krauts hanging around in the sun overhead or on the other side of a cloudbank? That's the way it is with you now. You're *there* and you're trouble. It was better with the krauts when you had some sky to maneuver in, but with you it's like being on a strafing mission when you lose one of those beautiful dimensions to run in and the krauts could pick you off like flies because they had the altitude and the speed and you were all wrapped up in trying to keep your K-14 sights on a fat-bellied locomotive.

"It was all so nice and easy when you weren't here. Life was one big ball with a lot of laughs and just the normal tangles that make it interesting. Everybody was getting laid and nobody was getting killed, then you decide to pick up a lousy ten-grand bonus to add to that suitcase and it was like *Titanic* time. The fucking ship is sinking only nobody knows it. They keep eating and singing and when it comes

170

time for the big bailout there aren't enough lifeboats and the only ones having a ball are the sharks."

"You think too much," I said.

"What happens to your little doll, buddy? Suddenly you got her all turned upside down too." I went to talk but he stopped me short. "Shit, man, don't put me on. Everybody knows *everything* in this town. That kid's turned colors like a chameleon since you gave her that tingly look of yours. You melted the ice, now you're going to let her drip all over the place. What happens if they try giving her the bath too?"

"She's got a cover on her."

"Great. Fine. Beautiful games you play, kiddo. For what? Just what the hell are you *after*, Dog?"

I snubbed out my cigarette in the coffee cup and looked at the wet filter floating in the dregs. "I keep saying it, but nobody wants to believe me. I don't want anything. Just my ten grand."

"Suppose they keep on not believing you?"

"Then they're going to have to find it out the hard way."

The late editions of the papers carried a bigger story on Markham and Bridey-the-Greek. A reporter with an inside track to classified information blew the whistle on their being contract men and the six o'clock TV news report confirmed it with an overseas source tying them in with The Turk's operation in Europe. One of the wire services had managed to contact The Turk, but he claimed he was a legitimate businessman and denied the connection. The analysis mentioned the suspected killing of a narcotics courier in Marseilles and the furor in certain circles because a multimillion-dollar shipment of heroin was supposedly sidetracked and hinted at a connection between all the events.

Al DeVecchio gave the new color TV a disgusted slam with the flat of his hand and switched the set off. "Now we know," he said.

"Now you know nothing."

"I made some calls today," Al told me. He eased out of the sofa and poured himself another beer, watching me in the mirror in the back of his bar. "I finally got to a police chief in the south of Spain who was willing to talk upon recommendation of a certain friend."

"So?"

"There was a shadowy figure they referred to as *El Lobo* who raised all kinds of hell over there. Nobody ever identified him and very few knew him. One that did claimed he

171

died in the hills just outside that city in the south of Spain."

"So?" I sipped my beer and waited.

"*El Lobo* seemed to take particular pleasure in muscling in on the activities of another shadow figure they call Le Fleur. In fact, he was so damn good at it that he was inching his way up to being top man in the narcotics racket."

"If he's dead, why worry about it?"

"Because nobody has ever seen the body and his handiwork is still being felt."

"That's a police problem," I said.

Al turned around, walked over and stood in front of me and dug his eyes into mine. "It goes a little bit further. The police are on one side and those pretty deadly organizations are on the other. The cops are restricted. The others aren't. They got the money, the men and the expertise to enforce their own rules and they couldn't care less who gets in the way. They don't think *El Lobo* is dead at all."

"Get to the point, Al."

"It's not the first time I've picked up the similarity between *El Lobo . . . the wolf . . .* and your name. Tell me, pal, did anybody ever refer to you as *The* Dog?"

"I've been called worse."

He shook his head and waited. I nodded. "Come on," I said, "it's a natural for anybody with my name."

"All right, Dog . . . just don't lie to me this time. It's something I can do very few other people can do. I can tell when you're lying without any doubt at all. Are you . . . were you *El Lobo?*"

This time I let my own eyes do the digging. "Nope. Sorry to disappoint you."

Across the room the clock ticked on the wall. It was a long time before Al gave me a tight little smile and took another pull of his beer. "Okay, Dog, I believe."

"I'm glad somebody does."

He eased back down on the sofa again and crossed his legs. "I cross-checked on Roland Holland today too. Our old buddy is sitting pretty."

"Smart boy, that one."

"You guys were pretty close at one time.'

"Hell, we flew together," I said. "You knew him as well as I did.'

Al nodded, finished his beer and got up for another one. "Funny, him taking his discharge overseas the way you did."

"He didn't have anything to come home to either."

The beer can popped open in Al's hand and he sipped the foam off before it could spill. When he wiped his mouth he said, "Rollie was a Phi Beta Kappa man. Masters degree and all that stuff. Pretty brilliant guy with a hell of a lot of potential."

I knew what he was getting at. "That's why he stayed in Europe. That's where all the big opportunities were. If you checked on him you damn well know he didn't make any mistakes. Right now he heads up some mighty big industries. Hell, even government leaders consult him before they make any moves."

"Does he ever consult you, Dog?"

I let out a laugh. "Sure. Who do you think is the brains behind all that Phi Beta Kappa business?"

Al grunted and tried his drink again. "Not you," he said. "You never could even count."

"Then why the interest in Holland?"

"Because, Doggie boy, friend Roland Holland comes across as thinking you're the greatest and praise from somebody in that quarter is praise indeed, especially when you balance it against the fact that you have an unexplained source of wealth, your name seems to draw a clamlike silence in certain quarters, you're a target of attack by a couple of killer and you're damn inquisitive about the machinery of narcotics traffic."

"I'm an enigma," I said.

"You're a pain in the ass and you scare me."

"Did you get what I asked for?"

He put the beer down on the table beside him and made circles on the polished mahogany with the wet bottom of the can. "I got some information by not asking anything. Two important parties were conspicuously absent from our meeting and from what I overheard during a phone conversation, and extrapolated from the tone of voice, those two parties are not in good standing with key figures because of a bungled operation, and unless they come up with the answer . . . and a missing product, the situation is likely to turn into one of those concrete overcoat affairs."

"You extrapolate pretty well."

"That's my business."

"Who's holding the dirty end of the stick?"

"Familiar with the Guido brothers?"

"Didn't they work the waterfront and the airport rackets?"

"They moved up," Al said. Then he paused and gave me another hard look again.

"For a guy who's been away, you're pretty knowledgeable."

173

"We have newspapers in Europe. They go in heavy for sensational crime in America."

"The Guido brothers handle narcotics. The state and the U.S. Senate ran two investigations on them and couldn't get past their cover. Neither one ever took a fall. They lie behind a legitimate front and play it from there."

"If they're that good, then why the sudden heat from their friends?"

"Good question," Al told me. "I'd say their track record. It was rumored that they used to hold out on the organization. They weren't as big then and it wasn't all that uncommon a deal at certain levels and for the sake of keeping peace in the outlying areas the organization let it pass. Now it doesn't smell so good. The in boys think the whole thing could be a fast play to gain leverage or to buck the syndicate. It's been done before in the days of the beer barons. They don't want it to happen again. Narcotics comes in a small package with millions in profits, easy to ship, easy to dispose of, and with enough laid by, a smart operator could buy his own organization."

"Brothers Guido couldn't be that stupid," I said.

"Maybe not. Right now they're trying to prove it. I wouldn't want to get caught in the crossfire."

"Not you, Al."

He grinned at me and stopped swabbing the tabletop with his beer can. "Dog . . . I don't give a damn, but my curiosity is killing me."

"What?"

"Guys can get themselves in trouble all kinds of ways. Sometimes it's not just the direct action . . . it's more like the links that tie one thing to another."

"You're not making sense, kid."

"Somebody's tagging you on this narcotics deal."

I shrugged, not answering him.

"All my phone calls got me some other information too."

I waited.

"You got wrapped up in black marketeering right after the war, didn't you?"

"Asking or extrapolating again?"

"That was something you could handle. You still had all that war craziness inside you. You liked the action as long as it spiced up the day and Europe was just the place to find it. You were big and tough and could handle trouble with even bigger trouble and enjoy every minute of it. Killing was nothing new to you and by that time it was simply a natural function of things."

"That's what you think?" I asked him.

174

"That's what I'm going to find out in a minute," Al told me.

"I hope you enjoy the answers."

His eyes had that quizzical expression in them again, deep and heavy, partially closed. "Were you in the black market?"

"Yes."

"That whole operation was tied in with narcotic traffic, wasn't it?"

I nodded.

"You ever kill anybody since the war?

"Quite a few," I said.

When he finished studying my face he said, "I'm sorry I asked."

I got up and put on my coat and hat, picked the last butt out of the pack and lit it.

"What are you planning to do, Dog?"

"Take a little trip to my old hometown. Just simple business like the way I hoped everything would be."

"Watch it. You're leaving pretty deep tracks."

I walked to the door and opened it. Al was sitting there watching me and tossed me a sad salute. I said, "There's a question you didn't ask, buddy. You would have liked that answer."

XV

I changed rental cars twice before I reached Linton, threading my way over a prearranged route I had picked out on the map, driving at night so it would be easier to spot a tail and easier to lose if I had one. Before the first switch I thought somebody had picked me up, but I got off the main road and the other car went by, its headlights out of focus and didn't show again.

Now the early glow of dawn was winking off the buildings up ahead and I pulled into a diner just outside of town, found a booth in the back and ordered breakfast. Traffic hadn't gotten started yet and outside of a lone trucker at the counter I had the place to myself.

Back in the city, Hobis and The Chopper were staked out where I wanted them, two others ready to stay in close on Lee and Sharon, all the little wheels were put in motion and I was wound up so tight I could hardly eat.

I was back in the game again. Hell, I didn't want it that way. They could have laid off me and the whole stinking mess would have stayed in the usual state of ferment. Now it was getting ready to explode. And that was the trouble with an explosion . . . it took everything with it, the good, the bad and the neutral. All that was left was ruins until somebody else built on the rubble and let that ferment into an explosion too. For twenty years the crashing thunder of the blast had been all around me and I was tired of it, the kind of tired that makes your bones ache and your mind want to get off into a lonely space and just sit and sit and sit forever.

Home. There never was any such place. It was just something you thought you had and something you thought you wanted, but when you went to find it, it wasn't there at all.

I was playing kid games with myself, using a penny ante inheritance for a ticket to find home again.

My ticket had been punched a long time ago.

Home wasn't any place on the line.

I reached for a cigarette and pulled Lee's note out with the pack. He had left it on my dresser and I had stuck it in my pocket without reading it. I unfolded it and laid it on the table.

Across the top Lee's scrawl read, "Doorman gave me this." The rest of the note was only two words and a number printed carefully in pencil with an odd flourish to the letters. *"Dog. Ferris. 655."* It didn't make sense at all. I turned it over, but the other side was blank and I looked at the message again. The paper was cheap, but watermarked and seemed to be the bottom half of the small stationery sheets you find in hotels. There was some odd familiarity about the whole thing, but nothing that wanted to come out of my memory.

Yet somebody knew where I was. Somebody delivered it and somebody expected me to understand the cryptic message. Had it been from any of the old bunch it would have been coded so that I could decipher it. Of all the shiny new faces I had met since I got off the plane, I couldn't pick one who'd bother corresponding this way. And it wouldn't be the hunters. They didn't write notes. They just tracked you down and killed, picking their own time and place.

When the details of each letter and numeral were clear in my mind I touched a match to the note and let it burn in the ashtray on the table. The counterman looked over at me curiously, then shrugged and turned away. The trucker finished his coffee, paid his bill and left. Outside, the sun had pushed up over the horizon and Linton had started to come alive. I picked up my check, handed the guy at the register a five, took my change and left.

At the corner of Bergan and High, cars flanked both sides of the street outside Tod's and men in working clothes were drifting inside in groups of twos and threes. I parked at the end of the line, cut across the street and went in with a couple of men in their fifties who looked at me curiously.

One said, "You with the union?"

"Nope. Just a visitor. Used to live here."

"Come back for a job?"

I grinned at him and shook my head. "I'm in a different business. I know Tod, that's all. What's going on?"

"Barrin's taking on more men," the one guy told me. He

177

gave me a wink over his glasses. "They won't have much to work with. They could use some young blood like you."

"You flatter me, friend, I'm one of the oldies too."

"Not like us, son, not like us."

Tod had given up in exasperation and put three girls behind the bar. A couple more were hustling coffee in the next room where all the noise was coming from and Tod was sitting it out at a back table with a schooner of beer in front of him and his ear glued to a portable radio. When he saw me his eyebrows went up and he pointed to the chair beside him.

"Hi, kid. I shoulda known something would happen. You're like your old man, always action when he was around. A good fight, maybe, plenty of singing, lots of action."

I took the beer the girl brought me and let it sit there. The suds wouldn't go right on top of breakfast. "Don't look at me, Tod. Whatever's going on isn't my bit."

"Pig's ass. Maybe you just stirred the soup."

"What's happening?"

Under the sweater the bony shoulders that used to be weighed with solid muscle gave a small shrug. "Barrin's got new contracts, that's what. They're hiring again."

"The labor pool looks a little sad," I said.

"Good guys, but old-timers. Half of 'em have been on welfare for years. The fuckin' union's flipping. They can't get anybody down here since McMillan's paying higher than union wages and these old coots'll do anything to get back on the job again. You know what this meeting is all about?"

"I just got here."

"Barrin wants to go under union minimums and the labor leaders are screaming. This bunch is about to tell the unions to go frig themselves and cut out. All they want is work and they're not going to let them city boys tell them they can't."

"What's going to happen, Tod?"

"You ought to know, kid. They'll picket, run goons up here and try to stop the contracts. Those city boys know all the cute tricks. Right now they're meeting with some of the Washington boys and putting on the big squeeze."

I wiped the sweat off the cold beer with my fingers and let out a laugh. "You got it wrong, Tod."

"Come on, bucko."

"Labor's running scared on this one if you're telling it right."

"Oh hell!"

178

"Take a good look," I said, "a dying town, impoverished workers who want off public welfare and an opportunity to get back on their feet, blocked by fat, rich, politically oriented organizations howling for dues money."

"So what?"

"A newspaper's dream story and a labor lobby nightmare."

Tod watched me for a moment, then shut the radio off impatiently. He took a long pull of his beer and put the stein back down. "I'll be a son of a bitch," he said. "You know, you may be right."

"They won't picket and they won't run in any goons," I said. "They're a little too smart. They'll let it go ahead. If it falls, then it falls. If it works, then they'll wait until they have the power back again, then move in for a reorganization. By then all those old boys who are voting now will be smothered by the newer ones. The game never changes, Tod."

"You said . . . 'if it falls.'"

"Something looks pretty damn spooky to me."

"Maybe you ought to know, kid." His tone didn't sound friendly anymore.

"I'm sure going to find out, Tod. There's always a winner in every game."

"Who wins in this one?"

"Right now there's a couple leading the field."

"Old Alfred and Dennison Barrin?"

"How can they lose?"

"That's what I figured. The rich get richer."

"Not in this case," I said. "I think they're trying to hold on to what they'd like to have."

Tod finished his beer, got a refill and looked at me with a direct, earnest glance. "Tell me somethin', kid. Are any of those old guys gonna get busted?"

Something funny crawled up my back and I had to take the top off my drink so he didn't see what I was thinking. I put the glass down and looked back up at him. "Not if I can help it."

"Will they get hurt?"

Now I could see him back the way he was behind the bar in the old days, ready to pick somebody up by his neck with one big, beefy hand and toss him into the wall. He was watching my face and whatever he saw put the assurance back into his expression, and when I said, "No," Tod nodded slowly.

"Just like your old man," he said.

"Thanks."

"Too bad you never met him."

"I can look in the mirror, Tod."

"Ah, that you can, that you can. You might even see your grandfather, the old bastard."

"That's *my* title, Tod."

"It means something different the way I'm saying it. You know, he woulda liked it right now."

"Hell, that's the way he started."

He put down the rest of his beer in a single big gulp. "And you're going to finish it."

I grinned at him.

"You haven't changed either," he said.

"Don't fool yourself."

"The only thing's missing's the pretty lady."

"She's working," I told him. "Too much of me is no good."

"Sheee-it." One corner of his mouth turned up in a smile. "The little lady is all yours, Kelly." He ran the back of his arm across his mouth and let his eyes dance across the table. "I got to asking questions after you left."

"So what's new?"

"Fuck you, Kelly. Find out for yourself."

"You're a big help."

"Sure I am."

"Where's your pay phone?"

"Outside in the hall." He sat back and folded his hands across his stomach. "You gonna raise some more hell?"

"Just a little," I said.

"Damn," he told me, "you kids have all the fun."

Nothing could perturb the butler. He was too coldly professional, too remote. In his own way he was a contract man too, ready to protect his own as long as the pay was right, but not quite ready to go beyond the bounds of his limitations when it came to Big Casino time. I said, "Hello, Harvey," and Big Casino time was there and Harvey smiled with a facial expression that didn't mean anything at all except to me and opened the door.

"Miss Pam and Miss Veda are inside, sir."

"Where's Lucella?"

"Drunk, sir. May I be so bold?"

"You may be so bold, Harvey. And my male cousins?"

"At a meeting, sir."

"Great. I have arrived at the opportune time."

"I would say so, sir."

"And why would you say so, Harvey?"

There was no smile, no raising of the eyebrows, just the

simple, unspoken acknowledgment of small dog to top dog, and he said, "Because you have been the subject of countless discussions since your last visit, sir."

"I hope they didn't say anything good about me."

"You can be sure of that, sir."

"They're afraid the plans of mice and men may get screwed up, I guess."

Harvey almost smiled, but didn't quite make it. "A rather awkward misquote, sir, but the inference is correct."

I gave him my coat and hat. "You know, Harvey, I'm beginning to like you."

"Thank you, sir. This way, please. Shall I announce you?"

"Don't bother."

I could hear the two of them before I ever got near the library. Age had touched everything except their voices and to me they were still pigtailed brats laughing at me behind the curtains when I was catching hell, and sniveling slobs when they got caught with their hands in the sugar bowl.

Right now they were hissing at each other like snakes and never heard me come into the room until I said, "Why don't you flush all that shit, ladies?"

Veda spun around with all that acquired arrogance ready to lash out at me with that venomous tongue of hers, then stopped in midsentence with a startled expression that was almost matched by Pam's.

I said, "Sit down and shut up," then walked over to the desk and picked a cigarette out of the cut-glass container. I lit it, gave the butt a disgusted look, then dropped it on the rug and squashed it out with my heel. My own brand tasted better and when it was fired up I turned back to my two cousins and smiled just enough so that they sat down fast without ever taking their eyes off me, their hatred filling the room like smoke.

It was a good scene. Hell, it was a beautiful scene. I leaned back against the desk and soaked it all in, letting them take their time to see what I was really like and when the tight lines in their faces started to droop into age wrinkles around their chins and the flab let loose under their arms I took another long drag of the butt then moved around the desk and sat in my grandfather's old chair and leaned back nice and comfortable like he used to do and they were seeing him as well as me with scared little eyes and micey moving hands.

I said, "The last time was only for fun, girls."

Veda tried the bluff. For a lifetime she had been pulling it and for a while it had worked, until she hit the tables at

Vegas and Monte Carlo where the experts were better at the game. She started to say, "Dogeron, I will not have this . . ."

But I was holding the cards and stopped her. "Cut the crap, Veda, we're not kids anymore, but I took enough cuts across my ass for you to keep those days in mind. You try playing cute and I'm going to hoist your white tail over the edge of that chair and whip the skin off it with my belt. You looked up my bleeding asshole for the last time and now it's my turn."

"Well!"

"The sight of it might make me sick, Veda, but I'm willing to try. Just open your big mouth."

She seemed to push back into the chair, her hands tight on the arms. I looked at Pam.

"The same goes for you, only your ass gets kicked, not whipped."

If Pam had had a gun she would have killed me. For some reason she couldn't seem to get her mouth shut and I could see her mind working for something to say. When she finally found it she couldn't get it out and I grinned at her.

"Where's old Marvin?" I asked her. "Your husband," I reminded her.

Every word was stiff and forced. "Out. He's . . . downtown."

"I can't blame him. If he's lucky he's screwing some bag in the back seat of the car. He sure never gets any from you."

Pam arched with indignation and almost spoke again, but I added, "Cut it, baby, I remember you getting your first taste of love when you were fourteen and thought nobody was watching. And I mean taste. That delivery boy was a big stud, wasn't he?"

My cousin damn near fainted. Her face got red to the roots of her dye job and she gave Veda a helpless glance that was returned with equal amazement, then she almost raised one hand for me to stop.

I wasn't about to. "Don't sweat, Pam. You liked it. You tried every guy who used the delivery entrance until one wanted it straight and stuck it in you. Lest you forget, gal, all that screaming you did you blamed on me for knocking you down the back porch and I got jumped for that one. Hell, all I did was walk into the laundry room to get a shirt at the wrong time. Incidentally, what ever happened to your bloody panties?"

I took another drag on the cigarette and watched Veda

182

staring at her sister as though she were something from outer space. Then I had to tell her. You don't miss opportunities like that. I said, "Veda baby, don't get rough on her. There was you and the governess from the Forbes estate, you and the cute black-haired girl from school you brought home one holiday, you and that interior decorator the old man hired to do over the Mondo Beach place . . . so don't look at Pam. Hell, you only liked broads until you were seventeen. How you doing now?"

Both of them sat there like lumps, hands fidgeting nervously in their laps, trying to play the elegant matrons listening to some horrible diatribe, but each of them knowing it was true.

"In case you're worried, Lucella isn't any better. She's just more honest. She was a straight-out fucker who always got caught and wound up marrying a nithead she had the good sense to divorce. Too bad. She's still young enough to enjoy a good piece now and then. At least she can booze it up enough to lose all those sexual urges in a good sleep."

My cigarette had burned down to the filter tip and I scraped it out on the jade ashtray. The old man used to do the same with his cigars. The ashtray was worth a cool ten grand, but the old man liked to live big. I looked at his picture over on the wall, the one with the scowl and the two pheasants in his hand, the unloaded and open shotgun crooked over his other arm. The pheasants looked stiff like they had been stuffed. They must have been, otherwise they would have stunk before the portrait was finished.

Old Cameron Barrin's frown wasn't as fierce as I had thought it was. As a matter of fact, now that I looked at it closely, it was a worried expression. I winked at the picture and mentally told him not to worry, the seed was still there and even if it was a bastard seed it still had some Cameron genes in it straight from the source of his own balls and not his stupid brother's.

"Little old ladies," I said, "you are impoverished."

Pam reacted first, coming out of her chair in a defensive gesture that almost looked real. Her voice was deliberately controlled as though she was taking care of an obstreperous bridge club member. "You are not about to come in here and . . ."

"I *am* in here and like I said, stop the shit, both of you." I dropped my feet off the desktop and pulled my chair up to the edge so I could prop my arms on it. I didn't realize it until I saw their faces change, but that was exactly what the old man used to do when he was about to pull the cork.

"Your stock is gone," I told them. "Now look at me."

Their attention was undivided. I didn't have to tell them because they felt it coming, but I wanted to make it all very sure in their minds so once and for all it would end. They didn't even suspect what the tag scene was going to be.

"I have it all. That and more. I'm about to control the Barrin Industries."

Veda's lips were white. Pam kept pulling at her sleeve.

"Alfie boy and Dennie don't know about it yet, do they?"

Veda's mouth was a thin, colorless line. Pam just sat there.

"You've been playing the game on empty pocketbooks, ladies. It's a good thing the old man left everything free and clear. Barrin stock is down in the peanut class and the boys are still trying to ride a stallion. All you have is some property, antiquated factories and contracts that can be yanked and you're all sitting on a lousy watersoaked log floating downstream with the vultures circling overhead."

"Dogeron . . ." Pam said.

I ignored her. "And do you know who the vultures are? You got me and McMillan and the Securities Exchange Commission who are going to move in pretty damn soon and if I don't get it, or McMillan doesn't get it, the SEC will chew you to pieces."

"Dogeron . . ."

"What?"

"How . . . can you do this?"

"No trouble at all, Pam. Like I said, you looked at my bleeding asshole once too often. I'd like my turn at bat."

"The family name . . ."

"My name's Kelly, or did you forget?"

"That was so long ago."

"Look at the calendar and look at the clock. The time is now, kid. The game is over. You all lost it in the locker room."

"Dog." Veda was sitting back, studying me with callous eyes. "You didn't have to come here to insult us." I grinned again, and she knew what I was grinning at and waiting for, so nodded and added, "Or remind us of the truth."

"That's right."

"Why are you here?"

"I was wondering when you'd ask."

Both of them wanted to look at each other, hang on to lines of communication and get mutual support like they used to, but neither of them dared to.

I said, "Unless all of want to find what it's like to be out on the street, you'll do exactly what I want you to do."

"What . . . will that be?" Pam managed to say.

"As far as Alfred and Dennie are concerned, you still have your stock. Condition *one* is, you'll vote it the way I tell you to no matter what they say. You don't have any choice, so it's an easy condition. Be nice and I may drop some of those Barrin paper goodies back in your hands. Try any tricks and the shit hits the fan. I haven't got a damn thing to lose, but your feminine dainties can get put up for auction. Clear?"

Neither of them was stupid. They didn't have to look at each other for the answer. They knew I had it all in my hands and weren't eager for any further clarification. The hard work of generations had slipped through the greasy fingers of avarice and they were beginning to find out that you don't crap in a rose garden because human feces aren't as adaptable to soil culture as animal dung and the stink is pretty damn distinctive. And even worse when you kicked the topsoil off and let them show.

Ladies. They sat there as if I were the liar, trying to compose themselves with all the Victorian demeanor of royalty looking down their noses at the hun upstart and I knew Veda would be the one to have to shed her wig.

She fell right into the trap. "And condition two?" she asked with that same ridiculous haughtiness.

The crunch. The tag line. She never should have asked it and suddenly she knew it. I lit another cigarette and put my feet back on the desk.

"Stand up," I said. "Both of you."

This time they got in that mutual glance, but they both stood up.

"Take off your clothes," I told them.

Horror has to be seen to be enjoyed and I enjoyed it. Only seconds ticked by, but their faces went from indignation to anger, then a plea for pity, finally disintegrating into abject subservience when I gave them a narrow-eyed look to remind them of the delivery boys and the governess and the other things they didn't realize I knew and they took off their clothes.

Everything they had was piled in a heap on the floor like I told them to do, then I made them turn around, then face me again. I dropped the stub of my cigarette in the old-fashioned inkwell and pushed the chair back.

I called out, "Harvey, bring my stuff in here."

When the butler came in with my coat and hat he barely paused at the threshold, his eyes taking in the entire scene. I put my coat over my arm, put on my hat and looked at the two women. "Sloppy," I said. "Pam, you ought to shave. You're the hairiest broad I ever saw in my life."

Harvey opened the door for me and this time he couldn't quite hide his smile. "Will there be anything else, sir?"

I gave his shoulder a squeeze. "I don't think so."

"Very good, sir."

Two steps down I heard his chuckle. Softly he said, *"Very* good, sir."

The pale-blue pickup was behind me for the fourth time. I stopped at the post office and bought a folder of airmail stamps and looked at the driver of the truck who was mailing a package at the parcel post window. He was about sixty, dressed in faded blue denim pants and a torn sweater. The clerk was giving his receipt when I went back outside. I waited in my car until he came down the steps, drove off and turned right at the first intersection. He turned left and in the rearview mirror I saw him pull into a parking slot outside a small appliance store.

I was getting edgy again and even the thought of my naked cousins couldn't take the bite out of things. I kept thinking, DOG. FERRIS. 655, wondering what the hell it meant.

He was young and had blond hair and didn't have time to grab his helmet. He was a young, grinning kraut and he damn near took me out after he shot down Bertram and all I had was that one look at him and the name Helgurt under his canopy and the five insignias, three American and two British under that just back of the yellow spinner on his ME 109. He lifted his wing the same time I did and we slid together like lovers waiting to kiss in a monumental close-up of flame, but air pressures and engineering combined to keep those lips apart and we hauled back on the controls into tight, stall-vibrating turns that dragged the blood from our eyeballs and there he was coming into my reticule before I came into his and my fingers squeezed the trigger on the stick and six fifties went off converging into a cone of fire at four hundred feet that took his yellow spinner off with the prop and chewed a beautiful flying machine into a pile of junk within three seconds leaving the young, grinning blond-headed kraut without any helmet and without any head or body parts anybody could remember. He had five kills and I had a hell of a lot more, but I remembered them and his name, Helgurt, and his yellow spinner, so why couldn't I remember DOG. FERRIS. 655?

Somebody had left the brochure on the desk, a four colored come-on with block-lettered Farnsworth Aviation, Inc.

186

headlining the aerial photo of the sky over the mountains with the latest Farnsworth executive jet streaking by under a high band of striped cirrus clouds.

"Nice plane," I said.

"Who may I say called, sir?" the receptionist asked me.

"Just a friend of the family," I told her. "I'll come back."

She poised her pen over the lined pad and gave me an annoyed grimace. "Ill be very glad to . . ."

"I know you will, kitten, but I won't," I said. "Don't worry. I'll see you again."

Behind me, the stout man in the pin-striped suit coughed behind his hand and I moved out of the way. He said his name was Meehan and he was expected at the conference. The receptionist pushed a button on her intercom, made the inquiry, then admitted him through the gate with a practiced smile. I went back to my car and drove away from the parking lot. On the other side of the building a double line of men were strung out for a good hundred yards. Two other men were taking down their information on clipboards, then admitting them into the main building.

The time was sixteen minutes after two in the afternoon and Barrin Industries looked for all the world like a thriving enterprise. I drove around the factory complex, took a side road through the old section up to a saloon, went in and had a beer and, halfway through, picked up my change and made a phone call from the booth at the back of the bar.

Sheila McMillan laughed when I told her who I was and dared me to come out for lunch. I told her to climb a tree and to meet me at Tod's if she wanted to really know how her husband got that scar on his skull and when she said she would I hung up, finished my beer and drove down to Bergan and High, parked and went in where the moths were still gnawing at the stuffed dead heads of all those beautiful animals.

All the old men were gone now. The sun was on the other side of the room throwing a rosy glow through the dirt-streaked windows and the heavy tones of the Dante Symphony from Tod's radio had quieted the three at the bar. I wouldn't let Tod change stations and the mood had diminished the baseball talk, turning it into nostalgia and latrinograms of what might happen to the big smog mill on the riverbank and Tod didn't know whether to shit or go blind.

Hell, he knew Sheila even if nobody else did. He had

187

known Cameron Barrin and he had known my old man. He remembered my mother and he knew Cross. Now he was knowing me and trying to put all the pieecs together and all he could do was look at the two of us back in the corner sitting together and all he could imagine was the wires touching and the bomb going off with him in the middle and everybody else fat and happy minding their own business.

She didn't have to turn up in those crazy hot pants under the leather skirt. She could have worn stockings instead of letting all the skin show. The fringed buckskin jacket didn't have to be tied with a rawhide thong that let her breasts peek out almost to the nipples showing all that tanned flesh from the top of her navel to the jutting rise of her bosom. But it was.

"Why is Tod looking at me like that?" she asked me.

"You're a walking orgasm, doll," I said.

"To him or you?"

"Skin isn't new to me, sugar." I told Tod and he looked back at his customers. "You're sure kicking him around."

"Legs or tits?"

"All one big package, and he can only take a little bit at a time."

"Which one first?"

"You mess with Tod and you'll get your face splashed up."

"So I'll mess with you."

"I can do worse."

"Talk."

"Look at me," I said.

"I am."

"Don't you know yet?"

"You must be kidding."

"Sorry, baby. It's real. Watch it."

Her smile came on so slowly it was like the sun rising. I watched her lift her drink and sip at it deliberately, with eyes so deeply blue it was incredible washing over me like a gentle, laughing waterfall.

"Tiger?"

"Of a sort. Just be careful. Even tigers can purr."

"You're a mean one."

"Don't go to too much trouble finding out," I said.

"Somebody's been telling you lies, Dog."

"Don't you think they'd waste their time trying that?"

"Would they?"

I nodded.

"How did Cross really get that crease on his head?"

188

"He probably told you the truth. I hit him with a rock. I was too young to do anything else. My baser instincts took over at the moment."

"Oh, how he hates you."

"Nuts. He hates the Barrins."

"Only you're not a Barrin."

"But I'm the one with the rock, remember?"

Sheila held her glass up and looked at the sunlight coming through the ice and the liquid. A spectrum of color danced across her face for a moment, then she put the glass down. "You know what he's going to do to you?"

"He's going to try," I said.

"All the way."

"That won't be enough," I told her. I finished my drink and waved for Tod to bring me another. "Are you as pretty all the way naked as you are now?"

I watched her eyes change shape, then go back to their original oblongs and heard her laugh. "Prettier."

"Hair color the same?"

"Identical."

"Leggy?"

"All beautiful thighs right up to my whoosis, then down again."

"Nipples sensitive?"

"See them pointing at you?" she smiled.

"Come fast?"

"Oh, yes."

"Often?"

"Certainly."

"Only when you're doing it to yourself?"

She twisted the glass in her hand and held it up again. The sun had gone down and there weren't any multicolored spectrums showing on her face now. "You really *are* a tiger, aren't you?"

"Want to find out?"

"No."

"Better to just talk about it?"

"By far," she said.

"We have a lot of talking to do, haven't we?"

Sheila finished her drink and set the glass down gently. Her eyes came up and smiled at me. "I think so," she said. "You know women pretty well, don't you?"

"I think so," I said.

"Can we go someplace and talk?"

I put a bill on the bar and helped her into her jacket. Tod was looking at me as if I were in a cage and shook his head, then threw a wave as if he were giving up all hope

189

and took the curse off with the kind of grin only one man can give to another. I grinned back and Sheila walked out ahead of me. When we reached the car she got in, sat there looking straight ahead a second, then said, "Somebody's got to lose."

"Always," I told her.

XVI

She opened the buttons on my shirt down to my belt buckle and let the edges of her nails trace little lines of fire down my chest. "Like?" she asked me.

"Nice," I said. Overhead, the moon was a thin crescent in the black of night, fuzzing out occasionally behind the cloud barrier. The dim glow of Linton outlined the turrets and the Moorish-looking left wing of the old beach house and when I looked back over my head I could see the corner of the widow's walk I had fallen from when I was six years old.

"You're not paying attention," Sheila told me.

"I'm enjoying myself," I said.

"Men are supposed to be aggressive."

"When the need arises."

"I felt you. You have arisen."

"Sheila, I think you have penis envy."

"Weren't we going to talk?"

I reached over and ran my hand down her leg. I could feel the muscles tighten under my fingers, then relax as if somebody had pulled down the handle on a rheostat. Her fingers on my chest stopped a minute, then started the tracing action again and ran under my belt, but it was still mechanical and forced, an actress on stage doing her part the way the script called for.

"What's Cross doing?" I asked.

The tips of her nails dug in just a little bit before they softened. She didn't even know what had happened. "Working. He's a very dedicated person when it comes to business."

I took my hand away and put it back under my head. Her fingers started teasing again and she rolled onto her stomach to look down at my face. "He should be home dedicating himself to you," I said.

"We've been married quite a long time." Her fingers tugged at my belt buckle and opened it. "I was seventeen on my wedding day."

"What difference does that make? You should improve with age."

"Perhaps if there were a difference, I could explain it. Indifference is the trouble. I told you he was a dedicated man."

"You love him?"

"By all means."

"And he loves you?"

"Yes. Certainly. But there are things other than love, aren't there?"

She was propped on one elbow, her chin in her hand. I eased my arm down and ran my fingers in the naked valley between her breasts. I felt the muscular tic run across her shoulders and the fingers at my belt twitched slightly and become motionless. I patted her cheek gently and put my hand back under my head. The fingers started in again. This time the snap popped loose and she pulled the zipper down halfway, then started rubbing soft circles into my belly.

"What things?" I asked her.

Now the soft circles widened and deepened and the fingertips were delicate feathers searching, finding and barely touching. "Understanding, for one thing." She squeezed gently and her breath caught in her throat. "You understand," she stated.

"Sometimes you have to tell them, Sheila."

Her hand paused and her eyes lifted to stare into the darkness. "I . . . can't."

"Why not?"

"Because there's nothing to say." She looked back at me again and I knew she was smiling. "I'd like to hit you with a big stick," she said. "You know too damn much." Her fingers squeezed again, deliberately hard and my breath hissed in between my teeth. "You're awfully ready, aren't you?"

"Obvious, isn't it?"

"Really ready?"

"Really," I told her.

"Let's find out," she said, and I lost her in the darkness,

only the outline of her hair moving with the fluid motion of the waves that were breaking in the background, each roller seeming to come in with greater force until the tidal inundation swept up and over me in a thunderous crescendo and then the crescent moon fell back into place among the clouds and she was smiling down at me again.

"Nice?"

"Beautiful," I said. "Nice?"

"Lovely," she told me. She did all the little things and finished with the buttons on my shirt, then stood up, reached out her hand and pulled me to my feet. "Can I ask you something now?"

"Go ahead."

"Why did you want to see me?"

"You invited me to, remember?"

"Don't hedge."

I dug cigarettes out, gave her one and lit them. "I was going to see if I could get anything out of you about your husband's plot to grab Barrin."

"Change your mind?"

"Nope. Just my approach. I should have simply asked, right?"

"The answer would be the same," she said. "He wants Barrin. It's not just a toy like the other organizations he controls, it's a project." She took my hand and we started down toward the water to skirt the edge back to the path. "It's a hangover from when your grandfather was alive. Cross was determined to be the biggest and Cameron Barrin was the only obstacle he had to hurdle. Poor Cross, he never could make it. That old man tripped him up every time he tried to move."

"Now he thinks he has it made?"

"Well, he's gloating. I've seen him do it before and when he gloats it means he's won."

For a minute we just walked, kicking at the sand. We reached the path and turned up toward the dunes. I said, "What's he going to do with it if he gets it?"

"Have you ever seen a company raided, Dog?"

I nodded and helped her over a grassy mound of sand.

"He says it won't matter because there's nothing left to salvage anyway. He's looking to the future when everything here can be his to do with as he likes."

"Then he can't be very happy," I said.

She stopped and looked up at me. "You know about the beach being sold?"

"Somebody in the family bought it, I understand."

193

"That somebody could be in trouble if there's any way at all to do it. He'll spend everything he has to get his hands on the Barrin property."

"Hasn't he got enough now?"

"Until he has it all, he'll never have enough. I told you, Cross is dedicated."

"Too bad."

"Why?"

"Guys like that ache pretty bad when they can't get the things they want."

She caught the inflection in my voice and I felt that shudder run up her arm again. "Some things are just impossible," she said.

"Not if you think about it. Now suppose I ask you something."

"I'm all ears."

"Why did you bother seeing me?"

"There was something I wanted to find out about you."

"Did you?"

"Yes."

"Sorry?"

"No guilt complex, Mr. Kelly. My curiosity has always led me into odd situations."

"It can get you into trouble."

"That I found out a long time ago."

I was going to say something, decided not to and steered her toward the end of the path. When we reached the car I held the door open and she got in. She had a pixie tilt to her eyes and she was smiling again. I got behind the wheel and turned the key.

"Are you taking me back to my car?"

"You've had your curiosity satisfied for one night, doll. Besides, I have a conference to attend." I looked at my watch and it was a little after nine. "My cousins are finishing their meeting in thirty minutes. Then it's my turn."

"Dog . . ."

"Uh-huh?"

"We had a very interesting evening. Will you ever see me again?"

"Indubitably, kitten."

"Even if Cross wants to kill you?"

"He'll have to stand in line," I said.

Hobis and The Chopper hadn't had any trouble since they took up the stakeout. Three hours ago Hobis had reported that he thought there was a surveillance on Lee's apartment but didn't want to expose the setup by checking it out. I passed the word for him to get in somebody else if he wanted to assign a tail to be sure of it, but for him to hold his position.

My man at the other end said it would be done, coughed and lapsed back into French again. "I've had a call from the Continent."

"So?"

"Pierre Dumont was shot just outside Marseilles."

"Bad?"

"Superficial wound in the leg, but O'Keefe is sending him back. That shipment apparently was bigger than anyone realized. Every possibility is being covered and the city is a focal point for every assassin that can be bought."

"Don't write me a story. Just tell me what the scoop is."

"Pardon?"

"Just tell it."

"I see. Yes. Le Fleur has posted a . . . a . . . how do you say it?"

"Reward?"

"Exactly. The shipment is worth approximately seventy million in street money. The loss cannot be tolerated. The government has confiscated the last two and this one was to make up the deficit. There are some stories circulating that it has already gone out."

"To whom?" I asked him.

He coughed again and was hesitant with his answer. "To you," was all he said.

"Somebody's got their wires crossed."

"I have been advised that we should sever all connections."

"You've been advised wrong, my friend. Just don't cross any of *my* wires."

"It isn't like . . . before, Mr. Kelly."

"Nothing has changed at all, old buddy. You're getting your fat deposits in the bank and let it stand just like that. I don't like this shit any more than you do, but when the heat's on, don't try ducking out or you're the one who's liable to be caught in the middle."

"Mr. Kelly . . . it isn't just me."

"Take your pick then . . . which one are you afraid of the most?"

"Sir?"

"You got the picture," I said. "Now I'm going to add to it. You know the Guido brothers?"

"Mr. Kelly . . ."

"They were the consignees. They're looking hard too. There's no way that stuff can get to me, but all that flap

195

is making me one special kind of a target I don't like, and this thing gets ripped apart in a hurry or this here dog is going to lay somebody out, you understand?"

"I understand."

"Okay, then pass the word. I'm out. The thing is sour. I'm getting bugged and when I get bugged somebody gets hurt and that somebody is plural. Does this message get through or not?"

"Yes . . . I believe I understand."

I hung up the phone and walked back to the bar where Tod was polishing the mahogany top to a glossy finish, a stalling operation that gave him an excuse for not having to talk. He barely gave me a glance, but I picked up my glass and moved down to where he was so busy rubbing and pulled a stool up with my foot.

"What's the beef, Tod?"

"No beef," he muttered.

"Think I'm upsetting the applecart?"

He shrugged and spilled some more oily liquid on the aged wood, rubbing it in with the rag. He finally stopped, cranking his face up to mine with worried lines creasing his forehead. "Cross is going to find out, kid."

"Who'll tell him?"

"Things don't get hidden so easily around here."

"Linton's been a burial ground of big secrets for a long time, Tod."

"Not anymore."

"I told you," I said, "it was just a friendly visit."

Tod scowled, trying hard to believe me. "So why bother?"

"You got to keep looking for the leverage, Tod."

He nodded as if he understood, then capped the can of polish and put it under the bar. I finished my beer while he washed his hands and when he walked back again he held a folded sheet of notepaper and handed it to me. "Stanley Cramer said to give this to you."

The note was brief, a simple *"Stop by and see me,"* signed with his initials.

"He say what this was about?" I asked him.

"Nope. Said to bring the little lady too."

I rolled the note up and dropped it in the ashtray. "She's in the city."

" 'S okay. Stan's outa town too. Said he'll be back in a few days. Looking up a couple of his old buddies, I think. The kid's father used to work with him." He looked up for confirmation.

"A long time ago."

196

"Funny bunch, those old-timers. Good company men. Be nice if things work out around here."

"They will, Tod." I said. I picked up my hat and dropped my change in my pocket. "Incidentally, did Sharon Cass ever go with anybody from around here?"

Once again I got that quizzical look and his mouth thinned out. "Don't all girls?"

"She's been in New York quite awhile."

"First she lived here."

"The other day you said you heard something."

His mouth tightened again. "She's engaged."

"So she told me."

"You figuring to break up the engagement?"

"Maybe I don't want that to happen."

Tod stood there leaning on the bar. After a moment he nodded sagely. "You're a big boy now, kiddo. You look like you've been takin' care of a lot of problems and a lot of answers up till now, so you just keep right on doin' that and you can never blame anybody else for giving you bad advice."

My face cracked into a grin. "Okay, philosopher." I put on my hat.

"Just don't hurt her," he added.

"Hell, she's still a virgin."

"That's what I hear," he said. He wasn't grim anymore. He reminded me of a schoolteacher I once had.

Alfred and Dennison weren't good listeners. Their guts had been churning ever since I had arrived and now they sat tight-lipped with untasted drinks while I told them what they were going to do.

The funny part was that I didn't even have to lay it all on the line. Their three sisters had picked up the pace the minute I made the statement and were bubbling over with enthusiasm about having a motion picture made in Linton with the Barrin complex an integral part of the background. There was absolutely no doubt about which way they wanted things to go and from the indirect looks Al and Dennie were exchanging the message was loud and clear. Either they'd have to indulge their sisters' whims or find themselves possibly bucked in laying their hands on the Barrin stocks they thought the girls still owned. Somebody had clued Lucella in and she played the game with school-girl anticipation, except that with her the humor of the situation seemed more real. Ever since she had divorced Fred Simon she had been put down in the family and now

197

she was finally one up on them, not having been made to pull a nudie in her own front room.

But the only one really enjoying the situation was Pam's husband. Marvin Gates had to hide his laughter behind a constantly uptilted Martini glass and when it got too much for him he excused himself to get a cigar.

I wondered how he had found out.

My cousins had the escape hatch opened for them when I dropped in the bit about the public-spirit angle. There were others who would benefit with movie company paychecks and the publicity would smother any adverse criticism the unions might give the press.

But they couldn't give a quick affirmative. There had to be some show of strength and after a forty-minute private conference they came back to the library and agreed that as long as nothing interfered with factory operation they didn't see why it couldn't be done.

Very grandiosely Alfred managed to add, "It's nice to see you taking an interest, Dogeron."

"Think nothing of it," I said.

"Although it has little or nothing to do with our previous situation."

"None at all," I stated. I tasted my drink and put it down again. I never did like Martinis.

"You might be interested to know I have uncovered certain information about your past," he continued.

"Oh?"

"There was a woman of nobility in Europe . . ."

"There were two," I interrupted calmly, "although you'd hardly get them to admit to it."

"Certain evidence is in existence."

"I heard about those photos. I also heard that the guy who took them is dead. A hunting accident with the husband of the countess he tried to shake down. The husband insists the woman in the photo is not his wife."

Alfred's mouth had the upturned corners of a rattlesnake smile. "There are other things."

"Perseverance. That's what I like about you, Alfie boy." I picked the olive out of the Martini, ate it and got up. "You'll be hearing about the movie details in a day or so. Should be fun."

Nobody bothered to say good-bye when I left. Only Marvin Gates rose to walk me out. Somehow he still looked like one of those old-time directors, his eyes a little bleary now, his walk unsteady.

Harvey, the butler, met us in the foyer and held out my

coat and hat, then retreated to the pantry. Marvin gave me a friendly pat on the shoulder and let the big smile he had suppressed all evening come through. "Good show, old man. It's a great thing to see them on the run. The ladies have changed considerably since your last visit."

"Who put you wise, buddy?"

One eye crinkled in a wink. "We drinkers exchange confidences out of sheer boredom. Seems like Lucella awoke to hear voices and came downstairs to catch the play. Needless to say, she hurried back up again at the final curtain and seemed to find it all very amusing. As a matter of fact, I'm sorry I missed it. That night I was . . . ah, engaged myself. Nothing quite as exciting as your scene though."

"Now everybody's got a secret," I said.

"Indeed we have. A lovely one to be let out at the proper moment."

"When will that be?"

"After it has been savored to the last. Ah, yes. I have the distinct impression that everybody is sitting on a time bomb."

"Enjoy yourself," I told him.

"Totally," he said.

I heard the cough from the bushes just as I reached the car and spun, dropping to the ground on one knee with the .45 in my hand. The voice had a note of sudden fear when it said, "It's me, sir. Harvey."

"What a way to get yourself killed," I told him.

He came out of the shrubbery while I stuck the gun back, a little shaken by what he had seen. "I'm sorry sir. I didn't mean . . . but I thought you should know."

"What is it?"

"Have you anybody waiting for you, sir?"

"No. Why?"

"A car has circled the grounds several times. Right now it is parked about fifty yards south of the main gate drawn back into the trees. The occupant is across the road watching the house."

"How'd you spot him?"

"I didn't, sir. It was my nephew." He fidgeted a moment, then: "Well, his family is rather impoverished. Every week I manage to see that he gets a supply of groceries to take home."

"Toting privileges?"

"Something like that, sir, if you don't mind."

"No sweat."

"He saw the car and thinking it was the police, waited to see what was happening. The person never left so he came in the old way."

"Why bother telling me about it?"

I saw his eyes drop to where I had put the gun. "I'm rather glad I did now, sir."

"The old way out still big enough to get a car through?"

"Possibly. It is pretty well overgrown but the gardener takes the refuse out through there with the small tractor."

"Okay, Harvey. And thanks."

"Sir . . . will there be any trouble?"

"Not now," I said.

Sergeant Tobano had glowered through two cups of coffee, listening to me, saying nothing, but never taking his eyes from mine. Outside the all night restaurant the sun was filtering through the heavy air, pressuring the light onto the city. The couple with the jangling hangovers had left and two hippie types took their seats, but not before the counterman had scooped up the change they had left as a tip.

"We got a rumble on the Guido brothers," Tobano told me.

"You'll be getting more."

"What are you getting out of this?"

"Out is *what* I'm getting. Nobody seems to believe me."

"Can't blame 'em, with your history. The packages on you are pretty thick."

"People must like to speculate."

"Crap."

"Look, I'm giving you what information I have. What else do you want?"

Those searching eyes beaded up again. "I don't know. When I get an informer like you I want to check it out. All the way."

"Then you damn well better hurry."

"Kelly," he said deliberately, "time is funny. It has a way of taking care of things all by itself. Sometimes we can help it along and sometimes all we have to do is wait."

"Too much time gets people knocked off."

"Isn't it a little late to be worried about that?"

I dunked the end of my doughnut, washed it down with the rest of my coffee and lit up a cigarette. "I'm not worried about myself."

"Innocent bystanders?"

"A few."

"I don't like you, Kelly. I used to hate you guys, but

200

I'm too old to be bothered hating anymore. Now I just don't like. Catch?"

"Loud and clear, Sergeant."

"In or out, you're nothing but trouble. Any information you have is only more trouble. You got a little hold with the executive suite and the men don't want you tipped, but tipped you'll get yet. There's even a precedent for it . . . a guy they called Lucky."

"Luciano?"

"The same. Drags a stretch in the pen and because he has pull in the old country and makes it look like he helps out the country in the Italian campaign during the war, he gets paroled."

"He was deported."

"Sure, and right back into the narcotic traffic again from his old backyard."

"He died pretty late in life, Sergeant."

"It would have been better if he'd died at birth."

"There's always somebody else," I said.

"Exactly what I mean. There's always somebody else."

"Didn't mean to bug you, kid."

"You don't. It'll just be a pleasure to see you get your lumps."

"Thanks," I said.

"Don't mention it."

Lee and Rose were tired lumps under a tangled heap of bedclothes, both of them blubbering soft snores of applause. I went into the other room, packed my clothes in my old bag, showered and shaved, then made a sandwich. I was all set to leave when I turned around and saw Lee standing in the doorway with scratch marks all over his chest and wearing that same silly pair of shorts with the LOVE button pinned to them.

"Where the hell have you been?"

"Around. Go back to bed," I said.

"Sure. Just like that." He eyed my bags and frowned. "Where you going?"

"Clearing out, buddy."

"You wait until the shit hits the fan, then you blow. Nice."

"What're you talking about?"

"Read the papers."

I knotted my tie and pulled my jacket over the gun in my belt. "Let's hear it, Lee."

"I was with Dick Lagen last night."

"So?"

"Money and the power of the press can move mountains."

"Bulldozers are quicker."

"You're tagged, Dog. He came across something in Europe and now the walls are going to tumble down. He wouldn't say what it was and now he's just lying back waiting for something else to come in and the boom gets lowered."

"Buddy . . ." I looked at him with a wry expression. "You've been civilized too long."

"Cold, Dog. You're cold. I remember you when you were a nice guy."

"So do I."

"What happens with Sharon?"

"Nothing happens."

"That can be the worst part. She's all fired up over this movie shit. All she talks about is how Linton is going to start over. You're going to bust that girl wide open."

"She's a tough little cookie, Lee."

"Not that tough." He paused, leaning against the door frame. "The cops were back again."

"Yeah, I know."

"There was another one with the big guy this time. A federal agent. Treasury."

I didn't answer him.

"They didn't get anymore this time in case you're wondering."

"I'm not wondering."

"Dog . . . there's somebody tailing me."

"That's right."

"Your side?" He sounded surprised.

"An old friend."

He nodded, thought a second, his mouth twisted, gnawing on a idea. "Sharon too?"

"A precaution."

"I see. You get that note the guy left?"

"Yeah."

"He left another one. Same thing. *Ferris* and some numbers. It's on the table outside."

Back in my mind the seed started to germinate. It popped open with the heat of repetition, but it wasn't in fertile soil yet, trying to blossom in the crack of a concrete slab. I could see it and I could feel it, but I knew damn well I wasn't going to be able to identify it until the bloom showed on the stalk.

I picked up the bags and Lee stood aside to let me through the door. "Mind telling me where you're going?"

"Tonight I'm going to a hotel, get a damn good sleep, make a lot of phone calls, then pick up a car and go back to a crazy old building on the waterfront at Mondo Beach, do some thinking and begin to enjoy myself."

His face seemed to change and suddenly we weren't here any longer but looking across a few feet of high sky through the bubble canopies of P-51s, props synced and in tight formation, waiting to pounce the krauts moving in on the bombers below.

"You're looking for some running room," Lee said.

He didn't know how right he was.

XVII

Dick Lagen hadn't closed in yet, but his last paragraph hinted at a pending story that was going to be shattering in certain circles. Mona Merriman was doing the big thing in her gossip column, telling all about the workings of S.C. Cable and Walter Gentry in locating their new picture at an old picturesque factory site northeast of New York. Several prominent motion picture stars had already been suggested for leads in *Fruits of Labor* with the female slot being pretty well tied up by a current English beauty. My name was right up there with the rest of the Barrin clan as having been instrumental in bringing the picture to an eastern location rather than going onto California sets which were beginning to lose their appeal to total realism.

On the inside pages there was a one-column item about the two "mystery murders" as yet unsolved, but identification had been made and the usual solution was in the immediate future. I said, "Balls!" to myself and tossed the paper down just as the phone rang to tell me Al DeVecchio was on his way up.

Without his rocker, coffee and salami he was uncomfortable. He sat in a straight-back chair fiddling with the papers on his lap, shaking his head at the stupidity of it all and when he found what he was looking for, held it up as though he really needed it and said, "You won't make it, Dog."

"Why not?"

"McMillan figures to edge you out by at least five percentage points. That's enough for control."

"All proxies?"

"Who needs anything more? He's got Farnsworth Aviation interested and with those contracts he gets the stock-holders interested. There's no more nostalgia, buddy. Anybody holding Barrin stock wants dividends, not fond memories. Most of what's out has been inherited. It's in new hands that couldn't give a damn about anything except money."

"He's going to raid Barrin, Al."

"Sure, I know it. He can take the contracts to his own factories and do the job better, but he isn't holding that out in front of the people holding odd pieces of Barrin paper. He'll make a shambles out of Barrin and couldn't care less."

"How come Farnsworth is interested at all?"

"Barrin reputation for excellence. They still use some of the old extrusion processes and that's what Farnsworth wants. They don't know it, but McMillan will probably screw them too. Prices aren't about to go down no matter how you do it. He's sold them a bill of goods somehow. Now he's making it all look good to the little people."

"What do I need?"

"Nothing you can get. McMillan has his shares and the proxies. You can get a seat on the board but it'll be stacked against you. It's his ball game."

"How about the SEC?"

"Old Cross has got that licked too. He can always produce for a little while. Come on, Dog, you know what he's really after."

"I think I'm the only one who does," I said.

"What?"

"Nothing. Just mumbling."

"You wasted a lot of dough, pal."

"Not yet."

"Remember, I told you that you never even could count."

"I hire people who can count, Al."

He let the paper slide back into the pile and relaxed back into the chair, his face all funny. "What have you got going?"

"Just a lot of odd ideas. Barrin isn't all that much to fight over."

"So?"

"There's something else."

"Care to tell me?"

"I will when I can." I lit a cigarette and held one out to him. "What happened to the Guido brothers?"

He took the light I offered and blew a stream of smoke across the space between us. "You like to put a chill on the party, don't you?"

I waited.

"Everything's come to a screaming halt until the Guido boys come up with the goods. I'm not in anybody's confidence."

"Then extrapolate. You're pretty good at extrapolating."

"I extrapolate a hell of a lot of money wandering around someplace where nobody can find it. The button boys are back on the streets again and small talk has it that contracts are ready to be handed out. The older Guido laddie got his family into South America just in case, but the other one didn't think fast enough and his place in Jersey is staked out by a team over there. They're scared shitless is what I know and they have heavy dough out to dig up that missing shipment."

"Good for them."

Al folded the papers into their envelope and tossed them at me. "And now, my old buddy, I want out of your life. I'm paid to date and I don't want any more complications. You have all I'm about to give you and if you throw any of that old wartime camaraderie jazz at me I'll tell you where to put it."

"I'll call you."

"Anytime. For lunch, dinner, a squadron reunion, but stay out of my working life."

He started to the door, stopped and turned around. "It's been fun, Dog. Just enough to keep the old pecker up as the British used to say."

"You'll be missing the best part," I said.

"I hope so." He grinned at me and tossed his cigarette butt into an ashtray. "Incidentally, I had a long talk with Roland Holland."

"Oh?"

"Let's say I extrapolated again." He paused and let his grin get wider. "You're a sneaky slob," he said.

When he closed the door I looked at the doodles I had scribbled on the pad. Circles were drawn around the name *Ferris* and sixes and fives were intertwined around the edges of the paper. Straight lines from the name went out to each of the numerals and the seed grew a tiny stalk but still went unidentified. Out of habit I got up, flushed all the paper on the pad down the toilet, burned Al's sheets in the sink and went out to meet my contact.

His French faltered and burst into rapid Spanish punctuated with little taps of his forefinger on the tabletop. "No, I am sorry, Mr. Kelly, there is no more. Everything is completely out of hand now."

"Tell me what O'Keefe said."

Sweat dotted his forehead and ran in a rivulet down his temple. "Please."

I could see my face in the mirror behind him and it wasn't something I could enjoy either. He had been too long in the easy end of the trade and now he was knowing what it was like on the other hand. He swallowed hard, trying to cover his shakiness by sipping his drink, but it didn't work and I waited him out.

"For you," he said, "it will be as a favor."

"As a favor," I repeated.

"It has left the country. The courier who was killed . . . he entrusted it to somebody. The one called LeFleur . . . he suspected it went to that bookstore in Soho . . ."

"Simon Corner?"

"That is the one. Simon Corner is now dead. He did not have it either. However, it has given the English police a chance to locate the mysterious Le Fleur. As the Americans put it, all hell is breaking loose over there. They may now have the opportunity to break the entire structure of the apparatus. The monetary loss of the shipment was too much for any organization to stand. They cannot recoup unless it is found."

"What did O'Keefe say?"

He took another taste of his drink and nodded slowly. When he put the glass down he patted his mouth, then licked his lips nervously. "For some reason they have decided to concentrate totally on you. People are . . . being alerted. O'Keefe says . . . for you to . . . take off."

"It's screaming halt time, isn't it?"

"Pardon?"

"I'm like *persona non grata* now."

"Precisely, Mr. Kelly. All indications point to you as not being able to live more than a few days unless . . ."

"Unless?"

"Yes. Unless . . . you surrender the shipment."

"The real big guns are coming out now, aren't they?"

"I'm . . . afraid so."

"You were authorized to make this meet then?"

"Yes."

"Tell them to go fuck themselves," I said.

When you can't run and you can't hide, you do a little bit of both and bring them out into the open. In the weeds you make yourself a weed while they're rocks and in the rocks you're a rock while they're weeds. But you keep them

207

visible and not you, always keeping the back door open and a few birds around to caw and scream when the intruder shows up. You find your own backyard where you know all the crevices and trip wires and you're safe until they break the defenses and if you're lucky, by then you're in another backyard you know equally as well and start all over again. But you had to remember, it wasn't the hound tracking you who had the worst bite. It was the strange dog in the other yard who got you from behind.

I turned the television on, caught fifteen minutes of worthless news and switched it off again.

Sharon Cass was out to lunch and couldn't be reached. I left a message that I'd see her at her apartment that night and stretched out on the couch. The seed in the back of my mind grew another inch, but it was just a tiny thing and I said the hell with it and went to sleep.

It was a nice party. Only a small ten-piece orchestra and a few hundred important people in a tidy twenty-room penthouse belonging to S. C. Cable.

The noise of the crowd rose above the soft music, drowning it out completely, bass laughter and the tinkle of glasses making it seem as if it weren't there at all. Flesh was rampant in see-through blouses and plunging necklines or backs designed for a maximum of exposure. Skin-for-sale time. Feel for texture, pluck for resiliency, poke for resistance. Body fragrances were mixed into a cesspool of heady smells that had no individual identity. Uniform of the day, nearly exposed, jutting tits. No underwear. Crotches thrust forward, eyes seductively lowered. Lips wet. Face the tuxedos and black business suits, for here is the enemy who might drop a piece of priceless information for a closer look at those bulging orbs, or, for the comforting rub of protruding genitals against a girdled thigh, the little fat lady with the diamond rings might just hint what agency contact to see about a part.

Sharon said, "I knew you'd hate it, Dog."

"It's not all that bad."

"Not if you like the sex routines."

"Right now that's all you can smell."

"That's movie business."

"Any business, kitten. How long do we have to stay?"

Her laugh was gentle and low. "I thought anyone who spent time in Europe would be used to the sophistication."

"They're a little more subtle about it over there," I told her.

208

She handed me a glass from the tray that was offered her by a pert little waitress. "What's wrong, Dog?"

"Nothing."

"Those girls are giving you that look again."

"Screw them."

"You aren't very sociable tonight." She touched my arm and smiled at me. "I'm sorry. I shouldn't have made you come along."

"Nobody makes me do anything." I laughed and gave her hair a little tug. "I'll ease off. Too many things have been happening."

Sharon nodded toward the door. "There's Lee. He's the one who talked the English actress into signing with S.C."

"Cable have him on the payroll too?"

"For the duration of the picture. Good choice. I wonder why he doesn't seem all that happy about it."

"Broads on his mind maybe. He's a horny character. Right now he could have a feast."

"Couldn't everybody?"

"I don't enjoy eating at the trough, honey," I said. "It's better at your own dinner table."

"Trying to tell me something?"

"Nope. You're a spoken-for woman." I dropped my empty glass on a passing tray and waved off a refill. "When do I get to meet your fiancé?"

Almost absently, she said, "He'll show up when he's ready."

"Independent slob."

"Yes," she told me. "Quite."

"Somebody ought to warn him."

"Why don't you?"

"Let the prick watch out for himself."

"There you go again with that dirty language."

When I looked at her there was a far-off smile on her face that reminded me of something else and the calendar started turning over backward, dropping the years away, one by one. The seed was growing now and a leaf was sprouting from the stalk. It had a vague number on it but too distant to read.

Somebody came and took Sharon to the other side of the room while I was thinking about it and a pair of blondes filled her place with small talk I answered abstractedly until Mona Merriman came up with her usual brassy style and told them to bug off because I was all hers, and with imperial pomp introduced me to a few friends before getting me off alone.

I said, "What?"

"You weren't listening at all."

"Sorry, doll."

"I said, what has Lagen got on you?"

"Beats me."

She turned me around so nobody could see her face and looked at me seriously. "They take me for a gossipy old woman, Dog, but I was a damn good reporter long before I hit the money line. He's got something and he wants you crawling."

"Forget it, Mona."

"Son . . . I said I was a reporter. My staff passes me interesting tidbits of information."

She was a strange broad. Suddenly there was no flabbiness in her face at all. It was all hard, questioning planes with a fire dancing out of her eyes.

"He thinks I was a big hood in Europe," I said.

"Were you?"

"The biggest, kid."

"And now?"

"Out."

"Damn. For real?"

I nodded slowly.

"He can prove it?"

"No chance."

"Baby, I could make music with you. Real typewriter music."

"Don't. There's other music that's louder."

"And much more staccato, I suppose?"

"If you want to put it that way."

"The crashing of cymbals?"

"The big brass drum, Mona."

"Who's the drummer?"

"Sometimes a guy can be lucky all the time," I said. "Let's go join the party."

"You won't want to."

"Why not?"

"Cross and Sheila McMillan are here. He seems quite perturbed about the entire arrangement."

"Only he can't do anything about it, can he?"

"Not since your cousins okayed the deal." Mona's fingers squeezed my arm. "You really put the heat on, didn't you?"

"A public service."

"From what I hear, it was plain heat."

"They needed it."

"Doggie, I'd like to take you to bed with me."

"I'm not exactly a Teddy bear, Mona."

"You're better than a two-battery vibrator."

"You're wild, baby. What do you do for fun?" I let out a laugh and put my arm around her shoulder.

"Mainly play with the children who would give their dingdong for a chance like you have, knowing how I'd give them paragraphs for their scrapbooks."

"Write me out then."

"You never even were penciled in, Doggie. Your type is alive in the wrong era."

"Perceptive cunt, aren't you?"

"That's the nicest thing anybody's said all week. And true. Very true. Maybe that's why I like you. Now be a smart boy and get you and your little blonde out of here. The glacier has been looking this way and I can read all the signs."

"Who?"

"Sheila McMillan. I'm an older pussy than you are a dog and I can read all the signs too."

The years were catching up. I was tired and annoyed and it wasn't fun anymore. I thought I was out of it, but nothing would let go. Somehow it was like waking up and thinking the dream you just had was real, then you saw a different room in the cold light of a bright sun and knew the dream was fake and what the judge said was the true thing and if you waited a little while longer you'd hear the feet coming down the corridor, feel the scissors against your leg slicing the trousers and sense the razor shaving that small bald spot on your skull. You could wait a little more after that and they'd put the hood over your face with the metallic plate under it, then somebody would hit the switch to let the voltage sweep through all the tissue in one monstrous sheet of pain and you could call it quits for good.

Or was life and memory so accelerated at that last moment you lasted for another lifetime of absolute agony smelling the searing flesh and knowing the excruciating pain of muscles knotted in horrible spasms? Was it really like that?

Maybe I had seen them die too often. Maybe I had been on the line one too many times. You shouldn't think about things like that. Or was the thought for somebody else? I used to believe they went quietly, realizing that it was their time, and almost glad to go to be away from all the things that led up to that last second. Two of them had even smiled at me because eventually the wheel would turn and I'd be the one dropping off. I had lasted longer than

211

*most of the others, but now it was the ninth inning, the
score was tied, two out, nobody on base and I was up to
bat with a hostile grandstand behind me.*

Kelly at the bat. Forget Casey. Now it was Kelly.

"What are you thinking about?" Sharon asked me.

"I'm thinking why the hell you don't put some clothes
on."

"After all those naked females tonight I'm positively
decent," she said.

"Not in a chiffon nightgown with nothing on underneath."

"You haven't felt me yet. How do you know?"

"I can see your snatch, kid."

"Like it?" She grinned at me deliberately.

"Love it, so scram, virgin."

She handed me the coffee cup, spooned in the sugar and
added the milk. "You resent my maidenhood?"

"Horseshit, lady. After a while it'll get tough rubbery."

"Not according to medical statistics."

"So it'll atrophy from disuse," I said.

I got another of those funny smiles and she turned and
sat down opposite me, making a project of crossing her
legs. The nightgown split open, exposing those lovely legs
and her eyes laughed too. "How many women have you
had, Dog?"

"Plenty." I took a pull on the coffee and burned my
mouth.

"Virgins?"

"Numerous."

"About how many?"

"What kind of question is that? Come on . . ."

"Make a guess."

"A dozen. I never made it a practice of fooling around
with virgins. They were all accidents of nature."

"Does it hurt?"

"How the hell would I know!"

"Well, did they scream?"

I burned my mouth again and put the coffee down for
a cigarette. "They all scream when I'm laying them." I
thought that would shut her up but it didn't.

"I mean the first time."

Even the cigarette burned. I took another drag and
stamped it out. "No," I said. "When I found out they
hadn't been hit I went classical. They loved every damn
second of it and screamed for more. I know all the tricks,
all the techniques, all the little nuances from foreplay to

212

afterlove and I'll be damned if I'm going to set you up for somebody else."

"I know some tricks too."

"Yeah," I said. "I heard you telling Raul about them when I first saw you."

"Jealous?"

"Nope. I even appreciate your attitude. Like total understanding. Why don't you let your boy bust it for you and be done with it?"

"Because he may be dead." The way she said it was so simple I should have known.

"Serviceman?"

"Yes."

"Overseas?"

Sharon nodded and sipped at her coffee.

"When did you see him last?"

"The day he left. It was the day we became engaged. There wasn't time to do anything else so he gave me this." She held up her hand with the cheap little ring on it.

I said, "I'm sorry, kid."

"That's all right."

"Love him?"

"I've always loved him."

"Get letters?"

"No."

"How long do you expect to wait?"

"Until I'm sure he's dead."

"Meanwhile?"

"I play my own tricks. And techniques. And nuances."

I pushed out of my chair. "He doesn't have much more time," I told her.

"Yes, I know."

Thunder rumbled outside the window and I walked to the French doors and looked down at the big-bellied city that squatted underneath me. Headlights of the cars probed through the darkness, their horns demanding pathways and tiny dark things scuttled across between traffic lights whose WALK and DON'T WALK became another commandment to the mice caught in the concrete maze of the city.

"When does the picture move out to Linton?" I asked her.

"The crew will be looking for location sites the end of the week."

"You coming out?"

"I have to go."

"The old house on Mondo Beach . . ."

213

"Yes?"

"I'll be there."

"Dog . . ."

I turned around and she was standing there in front of the chair with the nightgown in a puddle around her feet. She was a naked picture of beauty that made everything inside me tingle for a short second before it went sour. In the dim light she looked slippery and wet again, all gorgeous thighs and bushy-haired belly surmounted by high-aiming breasts, but I could see her teeth and I couldn't tell if it was a smile or a laugh and I thought it was a laugh. I grabbed my coat and hat, grinned back a little bit and headed for the door.

It was raining out again. The night blanket of dark and haze cut all the buildings off like a soft, cheesy knife, muting the roar of the city lion to an angry growl punctuated by the irritated snarls of taxi horns at intersections where the red hadn't quite changed to green. On the avenues, cars drifted by nearly empty buses, reluctant to get to their destinations, and what few people walked the streets huddled under the canopies of umbrellas or just walked, heads lowered, not caring where they went.

It's a funny city, I thought. It only went in two directions, up and down and across. Somebody had laid it out like a grid on a tactical map and there it was. It didn't go in circles like London; it didn't ramble and squeeze and evacuate its bowels like Rome and Paris and Madrid . . . it was just there going north, south, east and west unless you got to where they forgot directions and called it the Village, or Brooklyn, then it was something else. But when you said the City, it meant Manhattan, the head of the world octopus that was all computers and vaults and money and the big rich and the little poor and the idiots trying to make the poor rich and the rich poor to pocket the votes and not once did they know that you can't do either one. You were either rich or poor, so enjoy it, citizens, and squawk your fucking heads off if you feel like it, only remember, it won't do you any good at all. The poor try to take, the rich intend to keep and anybody who gets rich is going to damn well keep it because only idiots stay poor anyway. Like the alive stay alive and the dead stay dead.

And it's funny to be dead. Civilization was nourished on the dead. Cultures and religions and even governments flourished on the dead. But all the dead do is smell. It's

214

the alive who can hurt you. But sometimes the dead smell in advance.

And that was a smell familiar to me. It was behind about a hundred yards and holding. In another few blocks it would come closer.

I had spotted him when I left Sharon's and wondered what had happened to all that jungle knowledge I had supposed them to have. Hell, it was a setup, a plain simple setup all the way. I had laid on three alternates if they had spotted the first one and they had gone for the initial track. All my fancy prearranged signals on the alternates reported all clear so I didn't have to sweat out being flanked.

There was only one guy back there.

In a way, he was like me, but not quite. *He* didn't know the city. To him they were all the same. Not to me, though. The bricks and concrete were another world and I led him through the maze to the hole in the wall and when he reached it I was waiting for him.

He was almost as fast and almost as wary, but that little edge is what makes the difference between living and dying. The gun was in his fist, but I had the .45 in my hand and it makes one hell of a hole when the lead goes through flesh and intestines and tears the backbone right out of a man. It blows you back six feet, all doubled up, living long enough to wish you were dead, and when I picked the .38 out of his fingers I looked at his face and said nice and quiet, "You only got ten minutes to go, buddy, but it can be the worst ten minutes of your life. You want me to shorten them or make you really hurt?"

Somehow he managed a crooked smile, all greasy with blood and spit. He lay there, letting the initial shock wear off, knowing what would happen when all those nerve endings registered incredible pain in another ten seconds. *"El Lobo,"* he said.

"I killed *El Lobo* ten years ago," I told him.

"The Dog?"

I nodded.

He pulled the trigger on a gun that wasn't in his hand anymore.

"One more time," I said.

He shook his head.

"Who?"

The guy smiled and gave me that same negative sign so I let him look down that big black hole of the .45 and for one second he wanted to tell me but that one second was too late. The blast of the shot was muffled in the small

215

roll of fat around his belt and I remembered the others, with Lee last in the bathtub, and while he was dying I said, "Good luck, sucker," and got out of there while the woman was still screaming in the window and the sirens were whining their way up the avenue.

Before I cut out I took a look at his shoes to make sure. They were brown.

XVIII

It was just an old dirty beat-up pile of junk, but it smelled nice and it looked nice and after I clawed my way through the spider webs and the warped boards I found the old room where my father screwed my mother and got me out of the bargain and it still smelled of their compact, that wild love that put them both in the tall deep where the sod falls in on top of you.

She had told me of that room and until now nobody had ever let me look inside, but now it was mine and there was no old man, no costumed guards at the gates, just mine where my father fucked my mother when nobody was watching in that little lonely cot in the topmost room with the moon coming through astride the salt air with the continuous, monotonous roll of the breakers.

I said, "Hi Ma."

Something said hello back.

I said, "Hello, Dad."

The wind sounded a laugh.

"I'm home now," I said.

Nothing.

"I love you. Tough, and it's all over, but I love you."

Nothing. Hell, I didn't expect anything anyway.

"Ma?"

Nothing.

"Dad . . .?"

Nothing. It was all shit and why bother? Okay, fuck the shit.

Such a tiny room. Here was where I was conceived, the act of love in the midst of nothing, a single, one-screw generation ago. And now I sit on top of the throne, the issue, the residue, the bastard. The damn lousy killer and all I want to say is *Ma . . . Dad . . . what the fuck can I do?*

Think, son. They took it all away from us a long time ago. Now it's your turn. There aren't many big ones left anymore.

I lay on the bed where my dad screwed my mother when nobody was watching and I felt very comfortable. For the first time I realized what she was like.

Outside somebody was going to kill me.

Like maybe.

I took my pants off and made myself come.

The rain was a dismal thing, one of those downpourings that squash the little people inside, cringing around a sink or using the weather for an excuse to vacuum. . . .

I said, "Lovely," and walked out into it, breathing the soft, salt spray with that luscious sexy tang and wondered where Arnold Bell was with his muffled .22-caliber job and what he was thinking ever since his partner had been carried away in a rubber body bag into the New York City morgue. Damn. They won't move in so fast now, will they, Dog?

Oh? Wait until Tobano checks it out . . . and he will, you know. Just wait. Crazy cops, I thought. Dedicated, honest, determined. What the hell did they ever know about people like me?

Maybe too much.

I have lived too long.

No ballistics man has a copy of my gun barrel. The dead guy back there in the city is only a corpse and when they process his prints the feds will close the book on an overseas brownshoes, a high priority shooter who didn't quite make the grade.

But there was another one still left.

The really big one.

Arnold Bell.

He was the hit man and I was his hit.

Shit.

Then suddenly the sun was up and shining with the rain only a faint misty gray away far to the north and a fat, sooty-looking sea gull was squatting on the porch roof outside my window and I damned near said hello to him. A few miles in the background a triple tendril of smoke began to vomit from the chimneys of the Barrin plant and I had that foolish feeling that all was well with the world.

218

And I had the chance to be Robinson Crusoe again for three whole days like I had always wanted and it felt good until it got dark at the end of the last day and I was looking up at the stars and they formed numbers so that the stalk sprouting out of the seed had another branch and the blossom was ready to unfold.

The .45 was back on the bed, snug in its holster, a dirty, biting serpent but no good at all unless somebody was there to pinch its tail. I heard the rustle of the sand weeds and felt the slip of the sand and when I had my hands on his neck he was five seconds away from dying and all Marvin Gates was aggravated about was that I had made him spill his drink.

"You and Harvey," I said.

"There's no reason for knocking me down like that."

"Don't ever sneak up on me."

"I thought I was whistling."

"You were drinking."

"Sorry, old man."

"Speak," I said.

"Can't we go refill my glass?"

"All I got is beer in the house."

"Plebeian, but it might do. I haven't slummed for a long time."

I had to grin at the idiot. He had missed his big pitch but was still swinging. "So slum," I informed him.

The driftwood sputtered and burned with a dull glow and pop onto the bare floor, sipping a cold Blue Ribbon beer without bothering to talk. An hour squeezed by and the fire died to a ruby glow of ashes along the logs and I said, "How'd you find me, kiddo?"

He tore the top off a beer without looking at me and answered, "You had no place else to go."

"I own the joint."

"That's what I figured."

"Why?"

"Why?"

"Somebody bought it," he told me. "I didn't buy the Canadian story after I saw you, so all I did was put the pieces together."

"Maybe I'll rap you right in the mouth."

"What for? Who wants a born loser anyway?"

"Pam seems to have held onto you."

"She's a slob." He took a real long pull of the Pabst, put the can down and flashed a smile at me. "I wish I could win," he said. "It's hell living in the garbage can."

"What do you want, Marv?"

"Is it all that obvious?"

"Kill the shit, kid. What do you want?"

Something happened to his face. The mouth was tight and his eyes had a funny color to them. "Maybe I want my balls back."

"You're a fucking swindler, Marv," I said.

"Not really." He got up, walked to the ice chest and pulled out another can of beer. This time he popped the top and didn't bother pouring it into a glass. "I'm a stupid, Mr. Kelly. Is that bad English?"

"Pretty bad."

"I have the unfortunate attribute of loving my wife even after I was trapped in a terrible affair that totally deballed me."

"You deballed yourself, buddy," I told him.

"The story is rather old now, isn't it?"

"Sure, for deballing." I topped off my beer and got me another one. "Let's speak, Marv."

"What makes you think . . ."

"Cut the shit and speak, Marv. You didn't come here to slop up my brew."

"Alfred and Dennison are both homosexual."

"So what else is new," I said.

"You know?"

I gave a little shrug.

"But how do *you* know about it?"

"I have, er . . . some oddball associates who are rather astute at recognizing their own kind. They pointed the finger at both of them. Oh, nothing definite, nothing provable, but I respect their judgment. Since your first night here I have made a few inquiries, but if those two *have* been indulging, they've been quite shrewd about it. The ones they call friends are all very proper and very straight, but there have been many times when they've been gone a day here, a few days there, on somewhat mysterious so-called business trips that required rather tedious explanations in detail when they returned home. At least on Dennison's part. Alfred isn't given to loose talk unless he's pressed for it."

"Not many people would pick Alfie for a queer," I said.

"He has the sadistic streak for it. He'd be one of the mean ones."

"At least Dennie has an excuse."

Marvin looked at me questioningly. "He picked up a dose of clap from a whore when he was a kid and it probably scared him away from all women after that," I said.

"Understandable." He had another swallow of his beer

220

and nodded. "That could explain a lot of things. I'm surprised that you knew."

"I didn't. It's just something that's been on my mind like a dirty joke you can't quite remember."

"Well, this isn't exactly a confirmation, simply an educated guess. I got to mulling it around in my mind and thought it might be an interesting point to pursue in your, er, morals clause combat."

"You sure have a bad taste for those guys, Gates."

He turned the can around in his fingers, studying the label. "The venture into the field of swindling wasn't all my own idea. It's taken a long time to resurrect the details, but they set me up for it."

"You didn't have to take the bait."

"Ah, but I did. It isn't very pleasant to live off the bounty of a demanding woman. One sometimes stretches too far for independence. I was outclassed, outmaneuvered and out on my ear before I realized what happened. Life has been pretty miserable ever since. I presume you know all the details?"

I nodded.

Gates put the can down and got up. "Well, good hunting. Didn't mean to waste your time. Thanks for the drinks."

"Any time," I told him.

When he had gone I finished the last of the groceries I had in the house, cleaned up and dressed, then drove back toward Linton and took the road that led out to Stanley Cramer's house.

All the lights were on downstairs and through the open curtained windows I could see three old men grouped around a table playing cards, each wearing a plastic eyeshade like an old-time faro dealer, hands held close to their vests.

From out of the night a little dog came up and yapped happily at me and before I reached the porch Cramer had the door open and was waiting for me. "Come on in, son. We'll finish the hand, then we can talk."

The bald-headed guy was Juke, the other one was Stoney and they had all worked together for my grandfather back in the old days until age had put them on the shelf. Their weekly card game was a ritual they never interrupted, but I was an oddity and part of the past they kept so close to them and an hour went by in small talk about Barrin Industries before Stanley Cramer finally got to the point.

"You know," he told me, " I got to thinking after you left. About that explosion and all."

I lit a cigarette, sat back and waited.

"Went over to see one of the old chemical engineers who was there at the time and he said for the life of him, he couldn't figure what made the place blow like that. When they were investigating he never spoke up because he kind of figured somebody might of messed around with those acids, left something open and it spilled . . . and since nobody was bad hurt and the damage was minor, he just passed it off. But it just beats all how that safe got blown outa the wall the way it did."

"You said there was nothing in it."

"Only petty cash and old papers and plenty of the cash was still laying around, so it couldn't have been robbery."

"Remember any of the papers stored there?"

Cramer looked at the bold guy and nodded. "Tell him, Juke."

"Old company formulas for metal alloys. Secret stuff at one time. By the time of the blast it was out of date, so nobody could have wanted them. They was scattered around too. I had a pound can of good tobacco in there too. The other stuff was all put in the new vault."

I tried to pick the meat out of what he had said but couldn't, so I waited some more. These old guys had their own way of doing things.

"Anyhow," he went on, "I never gave this next thing a thought until Stan brought it up the other day, but about a week later they needed something out of the new vault and when they went to get it open the dial was jammed and they had to call in a guy from the safe company. He said somebody had tried to pry it off or something. I forget. Now, that there Alfred, he said the forklift they had in there the day before when they was moving in some office machines probably banged the safe and damaged it."

"Possible?" I asked.

"The kid who ran the forklift was too damn careful for that. He sure would have reported it right away if he did. He said it never happened, but that Alfred gave him a chewing out anyway and the kid quit. Well, when they got the safe opened, the two of them, Al and Dennie, they spent half the day in the vault going through the stuff and when they came out they looked meaner'n snakes trying to swaller an iron egg."

"Tell me something, didn't they have the combination to that vault?"

"Nope. Not until the old man's will was all probated and they took over. Until then only your grandfather and

Jimmie Moore had the numbers. Now they're both long dead."

"What about the combination to the old safe?"

"Hell, no trouble to that. Stoney here reset the combination to ten-twenty-thirty so we could all remember it. Maybe a dozen of us knew it, but like I said, wasn't anything in there worth stealing and if it was one of us it woulda been easier to turn the knob."

"Makes you think, doesn't it?" Cramer suggested.

"They hold an inventory the second time?"

"Damn right. The payroll was in there, in cash. Nothing missing though. Everything checked out against the books. Old lady Thorpe, the comptroller, she's dead now too, she checked out all the files against her own memos so nothing happened. In fact, Jimmie Moore was in the vault with your cousins and watched while they counted up the cash. Alfred, he was more interested in the papers, but what the hell, it was all going to fall into their hands in a little while so he didn't ask any questions."

"Odd," I said. I took another drag on the butt. "Looks like somebody wanted something."

Cramer nodded slowly. "But didn't get anything."

"What could they be after?" I asked him.

He gave me a funny little grin. "That's what we're wondering. Now, old farts like us got holes in our memories, but if we keep thinking long enough, we might find out what it was all about. We still got a few friends around who remember a little better and we'll ask around. You going to be in Linton long?"

"Know the old house at Mondo Beach?"

They bobbed their heads in unison.

"My hidey-hole, and keep it under your hats." Then I told them what was going to be happening around the plant when the movie company moved in. Their seamed faces broke out into broad smiles.

Stoney said, "Damme, all them girls around. Think we'll get to see any of them flesh scenes they make nowadays?"

His baldie friend looked at him and grunted. "Hell, why bother? You can't get it up anymore anyway."

"Like hell I can't! Why just last month . . ."

He was still telling the story when I left.

Bennie Sachs wasn't comfortable talking business at his home. He was still in his uniform with his gun belt hanging on the back of his chair and he looked tired. In the kitchen his wife made rattling noises at the sink and the two kids were asleep. Now he ran his fingers through his

hair and watched me through those smoky eyes of his.
"You're really going all out, aren't you?"

"Not yet," I said.

"Look, you don't go dropping fag charges on anybody
to start with these days. You never can tell whose toes
you'll step on."

"All I want to know," I said, "is have you ever heard
any noises in that direction?"

"I hear all kinds of noises, Kelly. I don't sit in judgment
on moral issues, I simply enforce the laws."

"Tangling with the Barrins got you shook?"

"Not one flipping bit, my friend. If they got out of line,
they'd go the same route as anybody else. And let me add
something before you try it. Yes, there are certain prefer-
ential treatments you give local citizens of justifiable character, otherwise, you'd be batting your head against the
wall. There's no harm in going out of your way a little bit
to do favors either, just as long as you spread the joy in
other directions too. This isn't all that big a place where a
cop can be totally impersonal and all the way out of it. I
live here too. I know people. They know me. If there are
strangers around here, you're one of them."

"Let's get back to the first question with something
added."

"Look . . ."

"You know about the picture that's going to be made
here, don't you?"

He stopped swinging in his chair and watched me.
"Yeah, they've already applied for permits."

"Not because my cousins like the idea, buddy. I'm
squeezing them. There'll be money in this town if the deal
goes through, but that's not the end of it. I have to keep
squeezing if I want Linton to stay alive."

"Come off it, Kelly, the factory is going to . . ."

"That's a lot of bullshit. There's a back alley fight going
on that will probably make a junk pile out of the whole
shebang if it works out wrong. Now look, I'm not asking
for information. I'm looking for an opinion. I can go
around you easy enough, but I haven't got the time and
you're the most direct route."

Something seemed funny to him and he let me see a
begrudged smile. "People are known by the company they
keep," he said.

"What?"

"An old adage, Kelly. Like princes shouldn't consort
with clowns. The stage makeup might rub off on the wrong
sleeve."

"Skip the philosophy."

He stared at his hands and rubbed them together. "One of our proper but sissy citizens was up on a morals charge. He was bailed out, defended and released all through the efforts of an anonymous benefactor. It happened to another a year later and we put the hints together, but that ended it."

"No name?"

"Draw your own conclusions," he said. For a few seconds he sat there in thought, then turned around in my direction again. "In five years we had four cases of extreme brutality reported. The pattern was always the same . . . a young whore all beat to hell but not willing to make any charges. Always a screwy story of falling out of a window or something. Invariably, big medical bills would be paid in full, in cash, and the twist would leave town for greener pastures well bankrolled. The last one was two years ago."

"Just four?"

"Only that many were reported. Finding a beat-up whore isn't all that unusual. Finding four in the same age group is." He was studying my face, then said, "What's wrong?"

"It's backward, that's what."

"What's backward?"

"Nothing you'd be interested in, Mr. Sachs. I just think you blew a cute notion of mine to bits."

"Maybe it's a good thing."

Leyland Hunter sounded tired and told me that an old man needed sleep a lot more than the young studs, but he came out of his grouch when I asked him if there had been any news on a street kill a few days ago.

"That's been in all the papers, Dog . . ."

"I haven't seen the papers."

"May I ask why . . ."

"Did they get an identification?" I insisted.

"Yes. It seems the deceased was connected with the European underground. Incidentally, he apparently was in this country illegally. He was a French citizen with quite a lengthy criminal record."

"Nothing more?"

"His . . . killer hasn't been identified," he told me. "Dog, look, if you're in some sort of trouble . . ."

"I'm not."

Hunter didn't sound a bit reassured. "I hope not."

"Look," I said, "how about standing in for me when that stockholder's meeting comes off."

"I expected to, not that it will do much good. Nothing

has changed except the fact that McMillan has picked up a little more support. They can still outvote you. Oh, you'll have a seat on the board if you want, but he'll hold the reins. The first thing that happens is that your cousins will be ousted and you'll be left like the rest, holding a lot of worthless paper."

"Suppose I could force his hand."

"Dog. Nobody forces Cross McMillan's hand. He's a friend to no one and an enemy to most. You're in a losing game."

"You know what's happening at the plant?"

"All eyewash, Dog. The picture being made there will be of temporary human interest, coupled with the fact that Barrin has a minor resurgence of activity, but after that it will be all over. Sometimes I'm sorry you even bothered to come home."

"I'm not all the way home yet, Counselor."

"What do you mean?"

"Let's say it's like I'm on third base."

He grunted and I could picture him shaking his head. "Then let's say it's like the bottom of the ninth, a weak hitter is up and there's already two strikes on him."

"That leaves only one answer then, friend."

"Oh?"

"Sure, I steal home with the winning run."

"Impossible."

"At least it's a chance," I said.

XIX

S. C. Cable moved his company into Linton with all the fanfare my buddy Lee Shay and a top publicity outfit could muster. The caravan was quartered at two motels with offices in the old hotel uptown and the production crews getting the sites ready for filming. Somehow there seemed to be an aura of prosperity hanging over the town and everyone moved a little quicker and a little happier.

McMillan was playing his cards right too, making the front pages of the local paper with photos of himself, Walt Gentry and S. C. Cable, the story recounting his association with Walt in other ventures, and to the casual reader the whole deal looked like his idea to start with. It was going to make a big impression on the stockholders when the meeting took place and if there were any swing votes left, they'd damn well go to his side. Old Cross was a real cutie, all right. Funny thing was, I was beginning to like him. Good enemies were hard to come by. When he wanted something he'd go all out to get it.

The sun was starting to set in the west and I climbed up to the widow's walk that jutted up from the roof, lay down on the weathered boards and scanned the beach area with my binoculars. A few birds were still charging at the surf, pecking furiously into the wet sand for late tidbits and the tall grass rippled under the pressure of the breeze. A quarter mile away a large stray dog sniffed among the dunes, but outside of that, the beach was empty. A pair of fishing boats cruised by, outriggers up, heading for home. The lone sportsman in the second one was stretched out on the deck enjoying the late sun. He's lucky, I thought. Not a damn thing to think about except who was going to clean his fish.

I put the glasses back in the case, went downstairs and got into my car. It was getting to be about that time.

The few that were left were older now, wearing their regal armor of corsets and tiaras with a posture two generations old, beat-up old biddies with their aging consorts and subservient relations in strict attendance somehow dominating the ballroom of the hotel.

Rose said, "They belong to you?"

I grinned at her and shook my head. "That's another end of the Barrin chain. The ones who made sound investments and held onto their dough."

"Society, huh?"

"High, kiddo. Real high."

"Your cousins are stupid. Look at them kissing hands."

"They'll kiss more than that to stay in good with the family. Those old dolls pull a lot of weight."

"Which one am I supposed to go after?"

"Alfie. The one with the snake face."

"If what you think is true . . ."

"It won't go that far. I'm just hoping you're as good an actress as you say you are."

"When it comes to johns, I'm the best." She looked at me over her champagne glass, one eyebrow cocked. "And if I pull this off I get a part in the picture?"

"Uh-huh. Guaranteed."

"You sure Lee knows about this?"

"Up to a point. He's shaky enough without giving him all the details."

"Suppose I have to ball him?"

I laughed at her then. "You're profession sort of calls for that sort of thing, doesn't it?"

"So I want a bigger part."

"Okay, another page of script."

Her laugh tinkled out and she dipped her tongue in the champagne. "Only kidding, Dog. I'll take care of my end." She glanced over to where Alfred was hanging over the oldest aunt in the family, studying him carefully. "You know, *if* you're right, he won't be capable of balling anyway. I've seen those types before. They take out their inabilities in other ways. I still have a few scars to show for it."

"Then you'll know when to cut out."

"You have the room all set?"

I handed her the key and she dropped it into the tiny

228

purse she carried. "Exactly as I diagrammed it. Everything is preset, available light is all you need, the activators are in four selected positions and if things get touchy, you bust out through the closet in the bathroom to the next suite. Extra clothes are there if you have to run bare-assed."

"Money sure can buy everything, can't it?"

"Not everything," I said.

"How do I look?"

"Like you took off ten years someplace. How'd you do it?"

"Cosmetic science, a clear conscience and a happy mind."

"Kid, you can sure rationalize."

"A girl in my position has to. I don't want to be a whore all my life."

"Then marry Lee."

"I'm thinking about it. He's asked me twice in the last three days."

"Why didn't you take him up on it?"

"Because I'm not too sure he won't have regrets about my past. Most men want to start out with a fresh one."

"Not Lee, baby. He wants to ride a mount already broken to the saddle. He means what he says."

"You sure?"

"One hundred percent."

After a few moments she smiled and nodded, her lips pursed in thought. "Okay, I'm convinced."

"Then get to work."

"Roger, boss man."

Leyland Hunter waited until she left, then walked over to me. "You're taking a big chance."

"Not really," I said. "One of my guys will be standing by if things get rough." I stayed in the corner out of sight scanning the faces of the crowd. Another bunch had come in through the main entrance and were shaking hands all around. In the center of the group, Cross McMillan had Sharon on his arm and Walt Gentry escorted Sheila. S. C. Cable was a smiling producer with a bundle of white fox with hair to match holding his hand. His new leading lady was strictly from England via old-style Hollywood.

I said, "Take care of things, mighty Hunter."

"Yes, I suppose I had better pay my respects to the rest of the tribe. For old times' sake, of course."

"Naturally. Be sure to line up their proxies."

"I'm afraid there won't be that much among them to help. They'll commit to your cousins out of family loyalty, but their shares are nominal. Am I going to be able to reach you if necessary?"

"Let me call you, Counselor. I don't want you exposed to my presence any more than necessary."

He gave me one of his courtroom glares, nodded and walked off, picking his way through the chattering crowd of minor celebrities and local big wheels.

A lone waiter spotted me in the dim corner, cut around the piano and held out a full tray of bubbling champagne. "Drink, sir?"

"No thanks."

"Very good, sir." He started to swing around when the nameplate on his jacket hit me like a short hard jab.

I said softly, "Ferris."

He kept on walking.

"Ferris!"

"Sir?"

I tapped his plastic nameplate.

He glanced down, then smiled and shook his head. "Oh ... I'm sorry, sir. No, I'm not Ferris. I'm Daly, John Daly. Apparently the jackets they fitted us with got mixed up. You see, we were only hired for the night. Ferris must be here someplace wearing my name tag."

"Who did the hiring?"

"There was an ad in the paper two days ago. We simply answered it."

"All local help?"

"Well, I do know most everyone who applied. A few were strangers to me. If I see the one with my tag shall I send him over?"

"No, I'll find him. And thanks."

"Certainly, sir."

Contact made. But from which side? Ferris 655 had run me down and found a way to reach me. It had to be an alternate route because he couldn't have been sure I'd be here, but it was a cute arrangement and deliberate as hell. I knew there wouldn't be any Daly nameplate circulating and spotting the one with Ferris meant that I was either tagged or supposed to get thinking. But what would any other alternates be?

Ferris 655. The seed in my mind that had germinated into a stalk that bore leaves now began to sprout a blossom that would erupt into fruit. Ferris. Ferris. It was something from a long time ago. Something obscure, but supposed to be remembered.

I went out the side door of the ballroom, took the back corridor that led to the parking lot, let my eyes get adjusted to the darkness and picked my way between the cars to the street ramp. Traffic seemed normal enough and the few pedestrians on the sidewalk didn't pay any attention to me at all. I stayed in the shadows, found my car two blocks away, checked out the one parked in front of me, then got behind the wheel and sat there looking up at the stars. *Ferris,* I thought.

Hell, I had been concentrating too long on the name. I had damn near ignored the numbers, and now I had half of the cryptic message right in front of me.

Twenty-three years ago, 655 was a post office box number and a picture postcard to that address was an alert signal that a shipment of contraband was ready for a drop and I had to designate the time and place through old Mel Tarbok. But Mel had been dead for fifteen years now and that post office box had long been discarded.

Which left *Ferris* and I didn't have the slightest idea who or what *Ferris* was.

I turned the key and let the engine idle a minute, then pulled out into traffic behind a bakery truck. I turned left at the next intersection when I saw the car behind me finally flip on its lights and when it slowed for the next turn it was still behind me. When it turned I was already parked and waiting in a doorway with the .45 in my hand. The lights from the window threw a good, solid glow across the roadway and lit up the faces inside the sedan. A pair of teen-agers were laughing and one was taking a pull from a can of beer. They cruised right on past and farther down the street one leaned out the window to whistle at a lone girl walking by.

I put the gun away and got back in my car. I was getting spooked again and almost got annoyed at myself until I remembered that getting spooked easily had saved my neck more than once. This time I made sure nobody was behind me and I picked up the old Stillman road that headed out into the country hoping I could remember Tod's directions.

Curiosity had made me look over the old bawdy house that was falling apart, then led me into making an inquiry at a real estate place. The old man told me the place had never been put up for sale as far as he knew and Tod had confirmed it. Over the phone he had told me, "Hell, Dog, Lucy Longstreet never did go far. She and that colored maid moved out on a little farm where the old way station was when the buses first started coming through. Still there as far as I know. Saw them about a year ago, playing Scrabble on the porch. Doesn't want nothing to do with nobody, though."

And now she was still there playing Scrabble on the porch with Beth, the colored towel girl, both of them old and tired with screechy voices, armed with huge, dog-eared dictionaries. Years had taken the fat off Lucy, leaving the flesh dripping in folds from her arms and chin, but her hair was still the same off-color red that didn't belong there at all and the diamonds still glinted on her fingers, only this time the pudginess wasn't there to hold them on and the jewels hung on the underside of her hand.

It was Bath, aged but timeless, who recognized me and simply said, "My, oh my, look who's here, Miss Lucy."

Madam Longstreet had a mind that could dip back, bend and reform like a steel spring and after a five-second inspection she closed her dictionary and nodded. "Cameron's bastard grandson with the idiot name."

"You made me, Lucy," I said.

"Been reading about you too." She pointed to a chair. "Have a seat. Beth, go make us all a drink." I tossed my hat on the table and slid into an overstuffed wing-back. "Good to see you, kid," she told me.

"You haven't changed much."

"Who you kidding, sonny? Take a good look."

"I was talking about your attitude."

Beth came in with a bottle and three glasses on a polished silver tray. I remembered that being passed around her old parlor. Beth poured out the drinks over ice, added some ginger ale and went back to her dictionary. "Don't mind me," Lucy said, and spilled down her drink in one long pull. "Very seldom get a chance to have one anymore."

"Maybe you shouldn't have retired."

"Hell, the amateurs get all the action these days. Nobody can run a decent operation anymore." She pulled a long cigar out of her pocket, stuck it in her mouth and held a lighter to it.

"At least you could have bitten the end off of it," I said.

"I ain't no woman's lib type, sonny."

"You never were."

She sat back puffing on the stogie, her legs crossed, then let a smile flash at me. "Got the word you might look me up."

"Who's that smart?"

"Cop named Bennie Sachs. Aren't many people who know I'm alive, but he had some funny ideas about you and passed the word."

"About what?"

232

"Something about those cousins of yours."

I shrugged my shoulders and tasted my drink. It was a real powerhouse. "Why bother if you're out of circulation? This could be a visit for old times' sake."

"Pig poopie, sonny. I have a telephone, an ear for gossip and a few select old pals I enjoy talking to. Beth there, she goes to town right regular and picks up things from other quarters. Whether you know it or not, the old clearing house of information is still in operation. Now, what's on your mind?"

"An angle on Cousin Dennison."

"How about Alfred?"

"I got that one from Sachs."

"My money says it's true."

"A real bet?"

"Down the line," she told me. "One of the girls was the daughter of a kid who used to work for me. And that's as far as I go, sonny."

"Then give me Alfred."

She made three smoke rings, then blew them apart. "He plays, all right. Nice and quietly, but he plays. You know how many gays are running around you never know about?"

I nodded.

"You won't catch him at it," she said.

"I don't have to," I said. "All I have to do is *know*."

"Now you know."

"But I could push him into it. You'd be surprised at the people I know who would be glad to cooperate or else get twisted a little."

"I wouldn't be a bit surprised at all, sonny."

"Should I?"

"Why bother. You'd do better concentrating on the other one."

"How bad is he, Lucy?"

"Dangerous, sonny." She took another drag on the cigar and let the smoke curl out of her nose. "He'll kill the next one."

I felt my hands tighten up around the arms of the chair and swore silently. She must have seen what was in my face and the cigar came out of her mouth. "You got him set up already?"

"Yes."

"Be careful, sonny. Be damned careful."

"I try."

Lucy yelled for Beth to refill her glass and when she had

233

it poured she sat back contentedly and flicked the inch-long ash from her cigar onto the floor. "An old friend came to see me awhile back."

I looked at her, waiting.

"Stanley Cramer. Seems like you're digging around a lot of dried-up garbage heaps these days."

"Just picking up the pieces of the past."

'Asking a lot of oddball questions too."

"So?"

"Nobody else ever bothered," she said. "You got Stan all primed up and he wanted to know where you stand."

"Outside the back door is where," I told her. "They don't let the family bastards at the dining table."

"Quit feeling sorry for yourself."

"Come on, Lucy."

"No shit, sonny, don't let it reach you." She gave me a sudden smile and did the same thing with her drink as she did with the first one and put the glass down with a sigh. "Those old boys who used to be with old Cameron were a pretty terrific lot."

"They made the business," I said.

Something far away touched her eyes. "They could have made it even bigger."

"How?"

She threw her hands open with an impatient gesture. "Oh, hell, I guess I'm getting old myself."

"You'd never know it."

"Ho, I'm living on memories. I go back too damn far. I've listened to too many stories and held too many heads on my lap while I stroked their foreheads. Good fun, though, and I'm not complaining, but sometimes I wonder if the things they told me were real or just pipe dreams. The old days were better." She looked back at me again, her face serious. "Stan and the boys are your friends. Look out for them."

"Sure, Lucy."

"There are a lot of strange faces in town. Your name has been coming up here and there. The ones who ask about you speak with forked tongues, sonny. If I were you I wouldn't stay in any one place too long. Even here. I'll listen around and if I hear anything I'll pass it on. Don't worry, I know where to reach you."

I got up and grabbed my hat. "Good to see you again, Lucy."

"Anytime." She put her cigar down and pushed herself out of the chair to walk me to the door. "Incidentally, what's this stuff with you and the Cass kid?"

234

"Just friends. Where'd you pick that up?"

"I read the columns. Heard about you two being in Tod's together. Doesn't sound like friendship to me."

"You're a nosy old biddy."

"Always was."

"Had her down on the beach too, didn't you?"

"Bennie Sachs again?"

"Nobody takes a friend on the beach like you did unless you were pretty *good* friends."

"She's engaged, Lucy."

"Yeah, I know the guy."

I stopped in the doorway and turned around. "Who is he, Lucy?"

She looked at me, her eyes bland, then shook her head. "You wouldn't know him." She reached out and caught my wrist. "Go easy on the kid. She's okay. I knew her old man real well. Beth there midwifed her birthing."

"She won't get hurt."

"I don't know. You're just like your old man. And your grandfather. Sometimes they got a little out of line too."

I patted her shoulder. "Sure. Take care, Lucy."

"You don't see me with any brats around," she answered. "I always took care."

I was running out of choices. I couldn't stay in the corners anymore or let the shadows keep me covered. Ferris was going to have to make contact and I'd have to stay available, And if I was available for Ferris I was available for Arnold Bell.

Hell, I tried to stay out of it. I had left myself wide open so everybody would know I had cut out, but the game had its own rules and they didn't want you to cut out unless you did it on a slab in the morgue. Only then could they be sure. Time and distance didn't mean a damn thing. They were always those gnawing suspicions that you were just sitting by, waiting to pounce and start all over again.

Okay, I was back in the running again, all the way. It was hare and hound, but the rabbit had sneaked out in front and now the hounds were baying at its heels, but this rabbit was jungle bred and had fucking big teeth and fucking long claws with a tiger for its father and a lion on its mother's side and the end of the canyon was coming up where the rabbit had to turn and let loose with all the armament and screw the odds. You died once . . . that was it . . . time's up, Charlie, and hope you had a nice life. Up your ass, Mac, just make sure I'm dead, that's all.

The party had thinned out and separated into tight little groups making their own points with champagne perfection. A tired orchestra played to a half-dozen couples rubbing pelvises on the small floor. Walt Gentry was smiling at the blonde leading lady who had left her white fox somewhere and was holding him off in a dance designed to give him a full view of her chest that was barely encased in swath of see-through chiffon. His demeanor was one of total satisfaction, like the deal had been made hours ago.

Cousin Dennison was hovering over Leyland Hunter who was drawing up some kind of a document, with Cross McMillan gloating beside them, and S. C. Cable was busy talking to Sharon. She was taking notes, consulting the two elderly gentlemen alongside who were apparently quite happy with everything. One owned a whole tract of downtown property and the other was the mayor of Linton.

I didn't see Rose and I didn't see Alfred.

Nobody had seen a waiter with a Daly nameplate, either.

Over in the Corner Sheila McMillan was holding a glass of champagne in either hand and when she saw me standing by myself beside the piano she put the glasses down and walked around the edge of the crowd to my little nook and said, "Take me out of here, Dog."

One of the waiters brought her jacket and we walked back through the kitchen to the side entrance I had used before. She was weaving a little bit and her face had a peculiar set to it. "Why this way?" she asked me.

"People talk," I said.

"I don't care about people anymore."

At the door I flipped the overhead light out and she leaned against me for a moment breathing the cool air. "Want to walk?"

"Yes. I need it."

The parking area was half empty, but I never did like rows of quiet cars and took the path to the right that led behind a row of bushes and cut into the main entrance.

Under the light at the door Bennie Sachs was talking to another uniformed cop and I didn't like that either, so I led her across the grass and angled toward the corner of lawn to the street and stood in the darkness of the trees a minutes to look around.

"You're waiting for somebody," Sheila said.

"Not really."

"Somebody's out there."

"Everybody's out there, kitten."

I felt the shiver run through her and held her hand. "Get me away from everybody, Dog."

"Come on, I'll take you home."

"No, not home. I took a room at the hotel for the night.

Cross is going back to New York and I didn't want to stay in the big house alone. I'm tired of being alone."

"What's bugging you, kid?"

"Nothing. Please, just take me to the hotel."

So we walked to the car, listening to the night sounds, my ears trying to pick up anything that didn't belong to the night alone. I got her inside, went around the car and shoved the key in the lock. She shivered again and stared straight ahead. "Trouble?" I asked her.

"Why do people do things to people?"

"Beats me, sugar." Inadvertently, I put my hand on her thigh and although it was only a quick touch I felt her contract in a spasm of emotional anguish that only stopped when I had both hands on the wheel.

The inn was a two-storied affair with a semicircular drive that cut in front of the main entrance, with a cut-off drive for deliveries that circled the building. Just to be sure, I went around the back and stopped when the taxi drove up to the front to unload a foursome.

The taxi driver took his money and drove off and I shoved the car into gear and that was when they jumped me.

Their only trouble was that I had seen them coming and shot one right through the middle of his forehead and left him standing there with only a mangled mess from his eyes up until he hit the ground and ran over the other one with both wheels, then backed up over him with the same two wheels in a sound like running over a wooden bushel basket.

I was out and rolling when I spotted the third one coming in fast to see what the hell had happened and just as he saw the tangled heaps on the ground I broke his arm with one smashing chop and his neck with the next.

All three of them had guns with full loads, two .38s and a 9 mm. P-38, all with the hammers back and ready to go, but they hadn't been fast enough to use them. It only took a few seconds to go through their pockets. The one I had shot was unrecognizable and his name didn't mean anything at all. The other one's face was contorted in some exquisite agony, but I recognized him. Up close he didn't look like a teen-ager at all, but he was the side man in the car that had followed me earlier. The guy with the broken neck had a very familiar name. He was one of the Guido brothers' hit men, a backup on what was expected to be a sure kill.

When I looked up, Sheila's face was framed in the window of my car, one eye looking at me through the hole the .45 had punched in the glass. She was smiling distantly and

237

I could sense the waves of shock and terror that were sending signals through every nerve of her body. I got in the
car and this time when I put my hand on her there was no
response at all except a slight widening of her eyes that
didn't mean a thing.

They were all around me and there was no place to go
except a beat-up old clapboard house on the ocean.

There was an oddity to her state of shock, as if she had
been squeezed dry. She walked with a strange lightness,
her smile an enigmatic Mona Lisa twisting of the lips with
no desire to explain her attitude. She neither complained
nor resisted, simply going where I directed her, across the
sandy hillocks to the warped boardwalk and into the house,
where she stood quietly until I pulled the blinds and lit the
kerosene lamps.

"You all right?" I asked her.

She waited, turned her head slowly and one corner of
her smile twitched. Her eyes were much too bright. I took
her hand, led her to a chair and sat her down. "Wait here."

In the kitchen I turned on the gas stove, set the kettle
over the burner and while the water was getting hot, dis-
assembled the .45. I fitted in a new barrel, took the old one
and the ejected shell that had flipped onto the dashboard
and buried them under the sand. When I was finished the
water was boiling and I made us both a cup of coffee.

Sheila was still sitting where I had left her in exactly
the same position. I didn't like it a bit. For ten seconds I
held the coffee cup out to her before there was a semblance
of recognition, then she took it from my hand with a tiny
nod and lifted it to her lips.

There wasn't going to be any way of getting through to
her for a while so I just sat there toying with the coffee,
watching her face.

By now they should have found the bodies, I thought.
Or perhaps not, too. Maybe that service drive wouldn't see
any use until the deliveries started tomorrow. I had fired
the shot from inside a closed car on the dark side of the
building and even waited a reasonable length of time before
moving out. There had been no alarm, nobody around to
investigate, so in all probability the sound of the blast
hadn't been heard at all. There hadn't even been a yell from
any of the punks who were mashed to pieces back there.
Overconfidence had caught them asleep and all they knew
was that last second of horror.

Tomorrow I'd have the window glass replaced and the
tires changed on the rented car and I hoped it would give

me the time I needed. There was still the problem of a witness who sat across from me in a stupor. Maybe she would talk, maybe she wouldn't, but to let anybody see her as she was now was inviting immediate disaster. Right now Sheila McMillan's mind was one huge mass of turmoil trying to bury itself in some deep, dark place and anything could trigger it in the wrong direction.

She had finished the coffee and I took the empty cup from her hand. "Come on, Sheila," I said. My fingers went under her arm and she responded to the touch, rising slowly, clutching her pocketbook. I picked up a lamp and led her upstairs to the one bedroom I had fixed up. I put the lamp down and turned back the covers while she stood in the middle of the room staring at the wall. When I crossed her line of vision her eyes seemed to follow me vacantly and she was still smiling that faint smile.

She was easy to undress. I simply unzipped the back of her gown and let it fall to the floor. She didn't have anything else on except her shoes. I took them off when I lifted her feet from the tangle of fabric around her ankles, then put my arm around her and made her sit on the edge of the bed. I pushed her back gently, took her legs and stretched them out, then brushed her hair away from her face.

She was beautiful, all right, soft skin nicely tanned that was white across her breasts and thighs, a body lushly mature with hidden sensuality in the mounds of her pink-tipped bosom and the tawny triangle of hair where her tapered legs met.

For the first time her eyes moved and the smile relaxed from its fixed position, her face watching me almost absently. I took the tips of my fingers and drew them slowly down her body, over the rise of her breasts, across the flatness of her belly through the soft vee of hair and in a wavy line down her legs. I gave her toes a little squeeze, pulled the covers up under her chin and patted her cheek.

"Poor kid," I said softly.

The brightness in her eyes seemed to mist over, then the lids closed over them, her mouth softened and her chest rose in the regular rhythm of sleep.

XX

The local newspaper ran a special edition to contain the events of the previous night. The triple killings took precedence on the first page with four photos of the bodies where they lay and police mug shots of what they had looked like previously. Identification was immediate and positive. All three were members of the mob led by the Guido brothers but no motive for their deaths had been uncovered. At present it was suspected that, since the Guido crowd had been engaged in illegal strong-arm union tactics on the waterfront, they might have been in Linton to muscle in on union activities going on with the reactivation of the Barrin plant. Local police were working in conjunction with New York City departments and other state authorities and expected immediate results.

Balls.

Inside pages of the edition covered the activities of the S. C. Cable production crews setting up for the forthcoming *Fruits of Labor* picture, the society pages went all out on the party given for prominent local citizens and the picture company and the rest of the world news was sandwiched in the last section.

Even the New York papers were having a field day with the topic and even if *Fruits of Labor* hadn't been a great book to begin with, it sure was getting one hell of a push with all the notoriety going on around it. Mona Merriman ran a full-column plug with details obviously supplied by Lee and the publicity department, another Hollywood columnist gave it two paragraphs and Dick Lagen hinted at a more sinister possible aspect and stated flatly that this was only the beginning of the unrest that was bound to come.

If he did have anything substantial, either it wasn't provable or he wasn't ready to break it yet.

Chet Linden had listened while I told him what happened and told me to get lost.

I said, "Buddy, I'm getting highly pissed off and I don't want any crap from you at all. I told you what could happen and you wouldn't listen and if you feel like stranding me, old pal, I'll blow the whistle on the whole damn shebang and bring it down on everybody's head."

His voice was flat and cold. "We don't take that stuff, Dog."

But I could be just as cold and a lot more deadly I had four more kills in my pocket to prove it and he damn well kept count too. "You don't have any choice, Chet. Just do it."

I heard him suck in his breath with disgust. "Okay, where's the car?"

When I gave him the directions I said, "They have tire impressions from the area, so just switch shoes of the same type and the rental company will never notice it. Do the window, wash down the undersides, run it through the countryside a little bit to pick up traces of dirt other than that beside the hotel and leave it where you found it."

"You think their labs can't pick up something if they nail you?"

"They won't have time. I'm not on anybody's list yet."

"You're on ours now."

"Come get me then. And, Chet . . ."

"Yeah?"

"Don't try booby-trapping the car. I know all the gimmicks too . . . and you just might get some innocent slob killed."

He didn't answer me. He just hung up and I grinned because the choice was all mine. But from now on I had something else to look out for.

Rose was waiting for me at the back table of the Arcade Bar and Grill, a little place struggling for survival without seeming to care what happened. The couple who ran the place had aged along with the building and looked more like wooden fixtures than people. She had gotten there five minutes early and had ordered a hamburger, getting ready to bite into it when I arrived. I called for one myself and sat down opposite her.

She smiled a faint hello, but there was a cloud across her face that hadn't been there before. I said, "How'd you make out, kid?"

"You picked a live one."

241

"Any trouble?"

She shook her head. "He took me out for a snack and a drink, then dropped me off at the hotel."

"You didn't invite him up?"

"Let me play the johns my way. He wants to be the aggressor."

I took my hamburger when it came and doused it with ketchup. "I may be wrong."

"You aren't wrong. I know the signs. I told you, I had it happen to me before." She looked at me a few long seconds, the cloud still there veiling her feelings. "I thought I could handle this when I took you up on the deal. Now I'm not so sure."

"Why?"

"Dog . . . if this were just a badger game . . ."

"It isn't," I said.

"Your games are all for keeps," she told me softly. "Like last night."

"Last night?" I took a big bite out of the hamburger and watched her.

"Don't be so damn cool, Dog."

"See me in jail, Rose?"

"Maybe they haven't caught you yet."

"Let's wait until it happens."

I saw her eyes go past my head and she nodded. "Could be it's about to."

But I had seen Bennie Sachs in the mirror I was facing and was all ready for him when he walked up and gave a curt nod to both of us. I stood up, still chewing and offered to buy him coffee.

He said No, glanced at Rose, then back to me and said, "Can I see you alone, Mr. Kelly?"

I put the rest of the hamburger down, wiped my mouth and nodded. "Sure. Where?"

"They got a back room here."

"Let's go."

"You first. He pointed toward a door in the far corner. "Over there." He kept his hand close to the police special on his hip and followed me through the door into a storeroom, then into a smelly toilet reeking of filth and stagnating water on the floor.

"Now what?" I asked him.

"Let's see that rod of yours."

I handed him the .45. He smelled it, checked the action, snapped out the clip then slammed it back in again. "Stand against the wall," he said.

I shrugged and did what he told me. Bennie kept me in

242

sight while he took the lid off the tank of the bowl. The water was low so he held down the float until it was brimful, then raised my .45 over one corner at an angle and fired. The damn blast nearly wrecked our eardrums and the burst of spray drenched us both. He let down the cocked hammer with his thumb, pushed the flushing lever and when the tank had emptied, spilling its guts out all over the floor because the drain was clogged, reached down and picked up the spent slug from the bottom barely getting his fingers wet.

"Neat," I said.

"Consider yourself getting VIP status," he told me.

"If you'd have asked I would have given you the piece to check out without all the fuss."

"I like it better this way."

"Suit yourself."

"Mr. Kelly . . ."

"I know. Don't leave town. Incidentally, if you want my car . . ."

"We've already impounded it. I called a cab to take you home."

"Very efficient."

"You should know cops."

"That I do, my friend. Have my car delivered when you're done with it."

"I will." His look was one of total inspection. "I have a feeling you're a quick thinker, Mr. Kelly."

"Sometimes you have to be," I said.

He handed my .45 back, nodded again and this time he walked out ahead of me. He nodded to Rose too and I heard the door close behind him when I sat down to finish my hamburger. Rose couldn't finish hers at all. Her lower lip was trembling and she had to lock her fingers together to keep them from shaking.

I said, "Come on, kid, he was showing me a gun trick. All sound and no fury."

My tone was so complacent that she let out a nervous little giggle. It had all been so casual that she couldn't see an angle to hook her fears on and she finally unwound her fingers and waved her hands at me with a disgusted grimace. "Someday, Dog, I hope you'll tell me what this is all about."

"Someday," I said. "When do you see our boy again?"

"Tonight. He said he may call, so I did make an impression."

"Okay, the setup stays as is. You know how to reach me."

243

"Don't worry."

"I never worry when pros are involved. It's the amateurs who give you trouble."

"Thanks a lot."

"My pleasure. Give me a few minutes before you leave." I tossed a five-dollar bill on the table and got up.

Outside it was clouding up again and you could smell a mist in the air. A taxi stood by the curb, the engine turning over slowly. I got in, told him to take me to the Barrin plant where they were setting up the picture, had him wait in the parking lot with a twenty as a retainer and got out to find Lee.

The *Fruits of Labor* set was a self-contained community that looked like a hill of ants. Everything was in motion, but the seeming confusion was, in reality, controlled movement, totally organized, well planned and producing results.

I found Lee beside the wardrobe truck talking to a pair of reporters, let him finish, then said, "How's it going?"

He jumped when I spoke, faked a smile and ran his fingers through his hair. "Good. Fine. At least they got plenty to write about." His eyes crawled into mine when he made the last statement. I looked at him, knowing he had to ask it. "Dog . . . that business last night . . ." he let his words dwindle off.

I simply nodded.

"Why the hell did I bother asking you?"

"You kill or be killed, buddy. You should remember that from the old days."

"These aren't the old days. Shit."

"Forget it. They're checking me out now."

"Then what the hell are you doing here!"

"I'll come up smelling like roses."

"Dog . . ."

"Who's that bunch over there?" A crowd of about forty were standing in a knot sipping coffee from cardboard cups, watching the action with studied indifference.

"Extras. All locals. They're going to pick up some exterior shots in about an hour."

"Any trouble?"

Lee jerked a cigarette from a pack and lit it with a match that shook visibly. "Like from where?"

"Management."

He blew the smoke into the wind and shook his head. "That McMillan character rode herd on everybody about not interfering with production in the plant. Hell, he just likes to toss his weight around, that guy. Those cousins of yours are doing their little dance for the photographers, but that's all bullshit too. You know, I wish we'd never come to this damn place."

"Baloney. You're enjoying yourself. You're in solid."

"I was until you showed up. Now I keep waiting to hear the Klaxon go off and I'll start heading for the bomb shelter." He took a deep drag on the butt and flipped it off into the dirt next to the truck. "You see Sharon yet?"

"No."

"Damn it, Dog, she's worried sick about you."

"No reason to be."

"Quit giving me that crap. She knows more about you than you think she does."

"Nobody knows anything about me at all, old buddy."

This time his eyes had a funny glint in them. "You'll wake up one day. She's over in the production office if you want to see her. Your cousin Dennison turned over a room inside for us to use."

"Casting couch?"

"These days they do it anywhere." I turned my head and looked at him a moment. He smiled and this time it wasn't faked. "You're in love with her, aren't you?"

"Not until I tell her so myself," I said.

"You will, Dog. Then you'll run home to your kennel for your bone. I just hope the cupboard's not bare by that time."

"Go fuck yourself, fly-boy."

"Sure, Mother Hubbard. Buy me a dildo."

I walked away and didn't go in to see Sharon. I got back in the cab and told him where to go. Nobody followed us and we cruised for twenty minutes before we came to the house. It was almost done. We cruised some more, stopped and had a couple of beers and small talk before I had him drive me to see Lucy Longstreet again. Old Beth had found somebody who was willing to talk for a price and offer a piece of evidence for an even higher price. I gave her the amount plus something extra for her trouble and was about to call the deal off with Rose until I remembered that the bought stuff didn't always work out and decided to let it go ahead anyway.

I paid the driver off outside the police building because my car was still in the driveway and when I went inside Bennie Sachs gave me a courteous hello and invited me to sit down. The first thing he did was hand me my car keys.

"You sure you're done?"

"The lab's still checking dust samples. That drive around

the hotel was laid down with a composite from Maine and if there are any traces at all the lab'll find it. Impossible not to. Microscopic examinations are pretty thorough."

"All the better, Mr. Sachs. When I'm clear, I'm clear."

"I figure you will be."

Poker isn't my game, but I know how to keep the face. "Why?"

"We checked the rental company. They keep a record of their tire numbers. They weren't switched and the treads didn't match up either. Yours had a lot more wear on them. Same brand, though."

"Satisfied?"

"Almost."

"How about ballistics?"

"Not your gun, although I recognize the possibilities of a barrel switch. Not everybody carries a .45, and those barrels are easy to replace."

"Wouldn't that be going pretty far?"

"Not when somebody's a clever thinker, Mr. Kelly."

"Left-handed," I said, "but I'll take it for a compliment."

"It wasn't meant to be."

I got up and tossed the keys in my hand. "Well, good luck."

"Mr. Kelly . . ."

"Yeah?"

"Would you surmise . . . that any more trouble would be forthcoming?"

"There's always trouble, Mr. Sachs."

"I waved "so long" and went out to the car. I got in and tried to stick the key in the lock. It didn't work until I turned it upside down.

Chet Linden wasn't taking any chances. Somehow he had switched the whole car. Now when he had me killed all his tracks were covered. It was a real rabbit drive now. All the hunters were out and armed. It didn't make a damn bit of difference who got the bunny as long as the bunny was got. The old jack had the rabies and could kill off the whole town if he wasn't destroyed.

So run, rabbit, run!

SHEILA McMILLAN . . . REFLECTIONS
He knows. He knows more than he's supposed to know and I can't stop myself from thinking about him. He knew when he touched me what would happen, made sure of it, then let me do to him what I did and I came away feeling nice and good because there wasn't any fear left or memory

246

of pain with the horrible tightness inside my head that made my entire body tighten up into knots with the desire to scream and kick out in terrible vengeance from having been violated. The word was even distasteful now. Violated. When did I first hear it? I think it was when memory started without being remembered. No, that's a contradiction. It had to be earlier where it's dark and frightening with shadows that don't want to come to life and only appear in the occasional dream or when I feel their hands.

Even knowing that he knows is a quiet, comforting feeling. Others knew, but their awareness was always deceptive and instinctive responses were ugly enemies, the little creepy-crawlies that became sheer tortures.

Why couldn't they talk?

Why couldn't they be passive?

Why did they have to demand the male prerogative of penetration?

The shadows were far worse than the realities. They LURKED. Awful word because they really did LURK. They beat at you with huge clubs and forced and forced until the unbelievable pain turned a scream into a tiny whimper and why you lived at all was a mystery of life. You writhe, you drown, you run away into the black and hope they never turn the light on you at all, but somehow you know the clubs are there, upraised and ready to beat. Big, soft, sturdy clubs that take away everything you know you're going to want one day and all that is left is an inborn feeling of having been deprived and never knowing what you have been deprived of.

Sheila McMillan, wife of the greatest cocksman who ever lived. He told me so. Other women have told me so. Other men have confirmed the story. Sheila McMillan in love with a brawny, hairy-bellied cocksman who's in love with her and she can't give him any of that lovely stuff he wants unless she takes two of the never-remembers out of Dr. Elliot's small plastic bottle and it all happens when she's in never-never land.

You hate and vomit and go through the beautiful act with all the people who don't know. Except now they suspect. Or they are sure. Men are funny. If they can't get that they have to do something else, if they're really in love.

Why couldn't they talk?

Why couldn't they be passive?

For once I'd like to hurt. Now, that was a strange thought.

But why did he have to know? Dirty Dog.

I wished the bastard would come back.
There was a knock on the door.

I said, "How do you feel?"

"Lonely. I've been doing too much thinking."

"You're in the right place for it. I was conceived in that bed. They must have done a lot of thinking too before they decided to beget me."

"Unlikely. You probably were an accessory after the fact."

"I doubt it. Those days it was a time for thinking first. I prefer to believe I was planned. Bastardly or not, I was planned for."

She smiled, then suddenly changed the subject. "Was last night real?"

"You were there, Sheila."

"Somehow, it seems more like a dream." Her fingers toyed with the top of the sheet. "I have very odd dreams. My whole life is one terrible dream. Even when I'm awake I wonder if I'm *really* awake, because when I'm dreaming I think I'm awake and pinch my skin to see if I am or not and I believe I am." She turned and looked toward the open shutters that sagged inward on their hinges. "I wish I could be sure."

"You're awake, kid."

"I was thinking a long time before you got here."

"What about?"

"Everything. Nothing. Then everything again. Maybe you you can help me."

"Just ask."

"No. I won't do that," she told me. The covers moved as she took in her breath, held it, then let it out slowly. When she turned her head and looked at me again there was something different in her eyes. "You put me to bed."

"Somebody had to." I couldn't put my finger on what was different about her now. I picked a loose cigarette out of my pocket and lit it. "About last night . . ."

"There never was any last night," she said. "There's only from now on."

"I appreciate that, kitten. I covered all the exits except you."

"Would you have killed me too?"

"Nope. Women are for kissing, not killing."

"You're sexy," she said, changing the subject again.

"Hell, I'm tired and I'm dirty."

"Do you have a shower?"

248

"Sure, but all the hot water has run out."

"I understand cold water has a depressing effect on the male physiology."

"Somebody told you wrong. It's only some males and only some times. Right now I'm hard as a rock."

"Really?"

"No, I'm lying," I said, "but if I keep talking like this I sure as hell will be."

"You're mean."

"Certainly. I'm dirty too."

"So take a shower with me," she said.

The cigarette burned my finger and I squashed it out under my heel. It left a black smudge on the old wide pine planks. "Sorry, doll, I'm just a natural bastard, not the kind that makes himself into one."

"Don't fight with me, Dogeron. I told you I have been thinking. I don't want any more of those dreams."

"I'm not a doctor, either."

"They haven't been any help. Take your clothes off."

"No."

But there she was with me in the shower, slickery slick like Earle used to say, all soapy and turning around so I could swab her down a little better and when I was skiing all over her body with foam-filled fingers she laughed through the suds and said, "Could you really kiss me now, Dog?"

I kissed her, all right. A long, lovely, naked, tight-together kiss.

"You haven't got a hard-on," she accused me.

"I didn't think I needed one," I said.

"Really, you don't."

"Oh?"

"I bet you could do it soft."

"The hell I could. Look, kill that water and let's get dried off."

"Coward."

"Old," I said, nice and flat. "Men aren't padded with fat like you broads."

Her hands fluttered around me and age stopped being years and started being a long time ago. I said, "At ease, young lady."

"Pretty," she said. She turned the faucet off and stepped back to look at me. "You're larger than the ones in the British Museum."

"Thank you, sweetie." I threw a towel at her and stepped out of the shower. But I couldn't stop her. She ran her fingernails down my back and pushed me around while I was trying to swab myself off and there was her face looking up at me with delicious, wet lips and wild exuberant titties all poked out with hard round nipples asking to be eaten and something crazy in her eyes. This time when her hand touched me there was a tremor in her whole arm that made me want to explode right there. But I knew I had to play doctor or she'd never get the chance again.

Her fingers squeezed. "I try hard," I said.

"Try harder."

The timing had to be just right. "Where will I put it, kid?"

It was like somebody dropped ice water all over her, then that look came back again, some inner determination forcing it on.

You can hate the dentist. You can fear the dentist. Then your tooth aches and you go to the dentist. It isn't really so bad after all. You don't fear, you don't hate the dentist anymore. Or was it really that simple?

I said, "Didn't you ever take a shower with a guy before."

"Only Cross. Three times."

"What happened?" I tossed the towel aside and reached for the economy-sized can of deodorant. I sprayed it under my arms and under the crack of my ass until it got too cold to stand, then recapped it and sprayed myself with something that smelled pretty damned good. At least they never had it in Europe where the girls wore spinach under their arms. And never thought to bleach their pussies.

"You're nasty," she said.

Now I knew where I was going. "How long have you been married?"

"Too long."

"That's no answer." I had one pair of shorts left and was about to step into them.

"Don't put them on," Sheila asked me.

"Kid . . ."

"I *know*, Dog."

"What do you know?"

"That *you* know. About me. I can see it in your face."

"I'm trying to be professional about this, sugar."

"Uh-huh." And the smile was really real.

She let the towel drop and there was that beautiful naked body you read about with big, pushy breasts and a wildly triangular brunette snatch that hid the entrance to the root of evil with the slidy part skidding the way right into destruction's hollow.

250

"Am I nice?" she asked me.

"Tantalizing," I said.

"Get more descriptive."

I covered up my stupid hard-on with my shorts and pulled on a T-shirt. "Fuck you," I said.

"Why not?"

I looked at her then, and her entire body was a tingling, vibrating mass of muscular contortions and small undulations along the sides of her belly, but what she was telling me with her eyes was something entirely different and I took hold of her arm, led her into the bleak, dark bedroom where there was a big bed from a long time ago and whipped off my two pieces of clothing so only skin could touch skin and rolled across her so she could feel the initial slithery feel of bodies and held her close until her own mental anaesthesia could take hold and show in her eyes.

She didn't have to tell me. She was right when she said I *knew*. I let the hours become minutes and minutes become microseconds, and compacted everything she had taken away a long time ago and lived with so long into a beautiful night of nearly total exhaustion. I listened to the words and the details of her being raped again and again, felt the pain with her and hated the act with her and tasted her desire for the thing she held repugnant and when she called her husband's name at the height of orgasm without knowing what she was doing I knew she'd never have the dreams anymore.

Sheila looked at me, the moonlight crossing her face, emphasizing the wide, sleepy eyes. "Thank you, Dog," she said.

I had to grin at her. "You're not supposed to thank me, doll."

"May I offer you money?"

"If you want a kick in the ass."

"No, I wouldn't like that, but since all this was for me, I'd really like to give you something too."

"What's to give?"

"Make me a three-way woman, Dog."

"Hey, honey."

"Please? We've done everything else. One more . . . injection?"

"You're a hell of a patient," I said.

"You're a hell of a doctor," she told me. Then she assumed the classic, pornographic position and said, "Deep, Dog. This should be your favorite way if you live up to your name."

XXI

The sky burbled and burped and spit up a gentle shower of rain. Black clouds roiled overhead, deliberately holding back the sickness until they found the right ones to shower the contents of their entrails on. Waiting.

Waiting.

Everything was waiting. Somewhere.

Arnold bell was waiting. The Guido brothers were waiting. Chet Linden was waiting. The movie company was waiting. Cross McMillan was waiting. *Ferris 655* was waiting.

The seed that became a stalk that bore leaves that showed a flower became fruitful and I remembered Ferris. Six fifty-five was the drop number and only once did I meet the courier who had set it all up and that was back in 1948. His name was Weal and we used to refer to him as the Ferris Wheel because he was so damn devious he went around and around to keep from being tagged by anybody at all, taking his cut without asking questions, always delivering on schedule and never tried the shit the others did when they thought they had an advantage. I had to run him down because I didn't like any loose ends in the organization and besides, his damn anonymity was a challenge to me and they said I couldn't do it. So I did it anyway and finally saw the guy who terrorized the Nazi bigwigs who occupied Paris during the little time they were there and he saw me and all he did was give me that funny smile and walk away, head down, knowing I realized he really wasn't eighty years old, but maybe fifty or so and quick and strong enough still to be able to kill with hands or feet

252

and get away across the rooftops while the Gestapo were looking for an aged cripple.

How many years ago was that? Hell, now he *would* be an old man. Shit, the Ferris Wheel was still turning, but where and why and how? Especially why?

Then I knew why and I damn well had to make Ferris come out into the open. If he was cagy then, he'd be cagier now and with what was happening he was about to throw everything away. He'd figure it was still the old days and the old ways, but if things soured out the river would get it all and he'd kiss everything good-bye and go back to some little place some little somewhere, remembering all that went past and maybe smile because there was still enough left in him to almost carry out the last mission.

So think, baby, where would Ferris be? Where would the old wheel be hiding?

I thought, and I knew.

There wouldn't be a chance in hell of finding him because I knew where he was, and unless he tapped me on the shoulder or the long arm of improbable coincidence reached out, Ferris was buried in his natural cover.

Ferris, you bastard, I thought. You're going to make me smoke you out. Okay, old snake. I can do it. You're waiting to see if I can.

The sky laughed and spit down on me again.

Rain. And Teddy Guido was dead. Somebody had thrown a hand grenade through the window of his study and he was a little bag of garbage in a closed copper coffin on a shelf in Mario Danado's New Jersey mortuary. The services were slated for the day after tomorrow. The grenade would have gotten the entire family if they hadn't left the room a minute earlier. His brother was in South America shivering his insides out knowing his turn was coming next. I was on Chet's wipeout list as fast as he could get the men inside the perimeter and I told him to send the best and if they didn't make the hit I'd be on his back, like personally and with the old blade, so watch it, boy. All contacts were cut and it was time to flush the toilet. I was the bowel block that had to go down the drain. I told him I'd have to be surgically removed and he said he'd do that too, if necessary. I said to bring a big, long-handled spoon because he was going to need it.

I looked up at the house where my father fucked my mother and got me in the bargain and I said into the night, "Damn, Pop, I'm glad you fucked and didn't have intercourse. There's a difference, isn't there?"

Maybe the wind had a voice, but something answered me. "You're damn well told, son," it said.

I nodded and started on the last lap.

Down at the flag line a leering skeletal head with a black cloak was standing. It held all the armament.

Except the big one.

I had that.

They had the stockholders' meeting and I lost. I was holding a boxful of paper and elected to the board along with my cousins, but Cross McMillan was chairman and his boy was president with all the power going to the head of the table and only a few swing votes put it that way and it was enough. All I had was the dubious satisfaction of knowing Dennie and Alfred realized I was the one who had bought up all the crappy stock and the money I had spent was already down the drain. Sure, I owned Mondo Beach, but they had Grand Sita which stood smack square in the middle of all the action and it was theirs. Like theirs. The counselor could even prove it for them.

Time was running out and they damn well knew it.

Only I didn't know it.

We had dropped off the idiots and I sat across from Leyland Hunter, watching him play with his drink and he finally said, "You're gone, boy. I tried to tell you."

"Trying isn't good enough."

"You know McMillan can even stop the picture if he wants to?"

"Yup."

"What else do you know?"

"He won't."

"Why?"

"Cross wants me to fall, that's why."

"And you won't?"

"Hell, Counselor, I can't."

"Refuse to quit?"

"Why die before your time, old buddy?"

He put his glass down and looked at me across the table. "You're even worse than your old man."

"Inherited factors, Lawyer," I said.

"You have something on your mind."

I finished my drink. "Nothing I'll tell you."

"Why not?"

"You wouldn't believe it anyway."

"Why not?" he repeated.

"Once before you told me. I think I have the situation conned now."

"So con me."

"Shit," I said, "you're an old legal hound. How could I?"

"I think you can," he said. "What do you know?"

"As my erstwhile buddy put it, I have extrapolated."

"I see."

"The pig's ass you do," I said.

"So, as your lawyer, is there anything else you need of me?"

"To be sure, Counselor," I said. Damn, I was getting drunk and I couldn't afford to get slopped up. I reached in my pocket and dragged out an old envelope. I filled half of it with my own miserable penmanship, made Hunter sign it, then tossed him my two big bank books. "Is that adequate?" I asked him.

"You should have been a lawyer," he said. "If this were a dying man's statement it would stand up in any court. Holographs . . ."

"Consider me a dying man, mighty Hunter. What difference does a few days make?"

"Your choice, Dog."

"Of course. By the way," I added, "you screw that broad again?"

His smile was simple and sweet. "I took them both as mistresses until they can find somebody better. In fact I have even endowed them with a dowery."

"You're a dirty old man."

"I'm a sexy senior citizen, remember?"

"Will they?"

"A man of my age is thankful for all he can get and they seem to be grateful for all I can give them that they could not get otherwise. Funny enough, my clientele seems to think more of me now than before. Do you remember my receptionist . . ."

"Don't tell me you banged her!"

"No, but she caught me screwing the Polack and dropped her glasses and stepped on them." He got up grinning. "As a matter of fact, when I leer at her, certain physical, ah . . . er . . ."

"She comes."

"Precisely," he said.

"Sexy senior citizen hell," I told him. "You're a dirty old man."

"Isn't it nice?" Leyland said.

"I hope you miss me," I said.

"That I will, Dog, that I will. Just do me a favor "

"Anything, Counselor."

"You're not dead yet."

255

I repeated his words. "Isn't *that* nice. Barely a consolation, but a pretty thought nevertheless." I lit up a butt and sucked the smoke out of it. "When does Cross deplete Barrin?"

"The raid?"

"Yes, sir."

For the first time I saw him take out a silver cigar holder, select a long, thin cigar and snip the end off it. It was very studied and very new, like something a Polack broad might teach him. "Quickly," he said. "Maybe when all the publicity dies down. It's bound to come, you know."

"No, I don't know."

"What do you think you can do?"

The teeth in my grin were big and fat and I don't have any unfilled cavities. "Suppose I give him a little more publicity," I said.

"I don't like your tone of voice."

"Nobody does, Counselor. It's one of those things I keep in reserve."

"Trouble?"

"Absolutely. Or maybe not. Depends on circumstances."

"Which ones?"

"Everybody fucks, mighty Hunter."

"You're scaring me again."

"I intend to," I said. "Incidentally, the house is beautiful. Thanks."

My lawyer shrugged. "Your money."

"My Polacks too," I said. "Have fun."

They had rewritten the script to take advantage of the rain. The prognosis called for three solid days of downpour before the front moved out into the Atlantic, and a small army of slicker-clad figures were hustling between canvas-canopied areas protecting the cameras and sound booth to get ready for the next setup. The principals were all snug in a forty-foot trailer laughing over the clink of glasses while bit players, extras and those in the crowd scene were milling around under a carnival-sized tent.

A snow fence had been set up around the area and even in the rain with nothing special to watch, the curious from town were standing around, some with cameras ready to get shots of the cast when they came out of the trailer. A pair of prowl cars were drawn up to the curb and a half-dozen local cops were in idle conversation with friends outside the barricade.

It took me a half hour before I spotted Hobis and The Chopper. Somehow they had gotten hold of S. C. Cable

Production slickers and were policing the area with nail-pointed sticks. The old army game. Nobody bothered you as long as you were busy working. I told them to meet me beside the honey wagon in five minutes, circled the trailers and wardrobe truck and joined them there.

Hobis wasn't a bit happy. He cupped a cigarette, lit it and let the match sizzle out in a puddle at his feet. "Too damn quiet, Dog."

"That's good," I said.

"It ain't good at all. It's got a bad smell to it."

"Like how?"

He looked past me at the people around the fence and nodded. "Somebody's here. I can feel it."

"Do better than that."

"Faces. I never saw them before, but they're a type. They move different and they look different. Know what I mean?"

"I know what you mean."

"So somebody's here." He took another drag on the butt, pinched out the light and stuck the stub in his shirt pocket. "Maybe you know."

"I have an idea, but it's not part of your assignment. You two stay with Lee and Sharon."

The Chopper grunted and wiped the rain off his face with a finger. "Nobody's after *them*."

"I know. They want me."

"Maybe we ought to lay a cover around you then."

"Forget it. Let them spot you two and they'll play it cute. I'd sooner have a direct frontal attack when it comes."

"Crazy, man," The Chopper said. "You ought to know better. They know you too. Who the hell's gonna move in frontwise?"

"I think *they* will."

"Your funeral."

"Maybe theirs."

"At least we're paid in advance," Hobis told me. "Trouble is, I enjoy earning my pay. By the way, that your bust the other night? Like with the Guido bunch?"

I nodded.

"Neat." He gave me an approving look and grinned. "Couldn't do much better myself."

"Thanks. Now stay close to my buddies. The storm's just beginning to build up."

"Okay. If we make any of these characters we'll buzz you."

"Do that."

I waited until they were gone, then went back into the

257

rain and the wind that was teasing the earth into a muddy slop before it mustered its forces for the full-scale barrage that was waiting just behind the low scudding clouds. It was early afternoon and seemed like late dusk. At least everybody was miserable together.

Except Dick Lagen who sat in the back of an air-conditioned Cadillac and didn't seem a bit surprised when I slid beside him. "You're a hard man to locate, Dog."

"Not really."

"I've been here almost"—he checked his watch—"two hours."

"Waiting for me?"

"I knew you'd be curious."

He held out his pack of cigarettes. I took one and held it to the gold lighter he offered. I cranked the window down an inch and let the smoke drift out with the cold air. "You were wrong, buddy. I'm only interested in your methods. Something I can do for you?"

"In a few moments. I'm waiting for your . . . friend."

"My friends are few and far between."

"This one's rather special. As a matter of fact, here she comes now."

In the oversize slicker Sharon looked like some forlorn waif. She threw the hood back and droplets of water glistened on her hair. She laughed, tugged the door open and jumped in beside Dick before she saw me, then her face went through a small contortion of expressions before she smiled again.

"Hello, Dog."

"Hi, doll." I grinned at her and flipped the cigarette out the window. "I like you better in a miniskirt."

She shrugged out of the slicker, tugging the folders of papers from the folds, tossed them on the seat beside her and sat back with her dress halfway up her thighs. "Better?"

"Much."

Then she stared at the two of us a moment, frowned and brushed the rain away from the strands of hair that stuck to her face. "Am I interrupting a conference? When you sent for me . . ."

Dick Lagen patted her leg paternally and chuckled. "No conference. I expected to speak to both of you separately, but since you're both here . . ."

"What's on your mind, Dick?" I asked him.

"No need to be so abrupt, old boy. After all, I'm simply a reporter doing a job in the public interest, and if you've been following the papers, all this activity certainly is in the public interest. We have a reactivated Barrin Industries,

258

a motion picture being made on the premises, a new spirit coming alive in a town supposedly dead, and for those close to the scene, a specter of doom hovering over the new enterprise in the form of Mr. Cross McMillan. The splash, when it comes, will certainly be newsworthy."

"Only in the local papers, Dick."

"Ah, but we have you, Dog. The great unknown. That is, until now."

Sharon twisted in her seat, her face gone tight. "What does he mean, Dog?"

I shrugged.

Lagen said, "Shall I tell her, Mr. Kelly?"

"Why not? Just make sure you can document the answers." I turned and looked at him and whatever he saw on my face tightened him up like a bowstring. His tongue licked across lips suddenly gone dry, but he had pushed it thus far and he had to go the rest of the way. His eyes flicked toward the burly chauffeur standing under the umbrella fifty feet away talking to one of the local cops and the reassurance came back into his face with subtle relief.

"You may even be vain enough to document them yourself, Dog."

"I've been known to do that," I said.

"Dog . . ."

"At ease, baby, let the man talk."

"Thank you," Lagen said. I caught the tone. He thought he had the heavy bat and was up against a weak pitcher. He was rolling the bones with the odds all on his side and savoring the moment for all it was worth. "I mentioned before I was making inquiries about you, Mr. Kelly."

"Don't be so damn formal, Dick. Keep it Dog."

"Very well." He paused and handed me another cigarette. "Perhaps you wouldn't like the young lady to hear all this."

"If it's public information, why not?"

"Sharon?"

The worry was plain in her eyes, but I shrugged. "Go ahead," I said.

"May I refer to my notes?"

"By all means."

Lagen took out a small notebook, flipped open the cover and glanced at it. The whole damn thing was an act, but I couldn't care less. He said, "In 1946 you took your discharge in England, preferring to stay there rather than return to the States."

"True." I dragged on the butt and it tasted good. Sharon was watching me, her eyes shielded.

"You had a friend who was a mathematical, and a financial, genius."

"Quite true. Rollie had a flair for business."

"But no money."

"He was destitute at the time, to be precise."

"However," Lagen continued without interruption, "Roland Holland accepted a gratuity from *someone*"—I let him realize I accepted his accentuation with a smirk, "—and ran it up into a sizable fortune within a short time. Actually, he became an overnight millionaire."

"Legitimately," I said.

"Indubitably. However, he observed his obligations of unwritten partnership and transferred funds to his benefactor, who, in turn, used this wealth to go into business activities that were . . . shall we say, not quite legitimate."

"Why don't we lay it on the line and say it was crooked?" I said.

"Good. Crooked. His partner engaged in black market operations that gained him a gigantic independent fortune, but at the same time involved him with the most nefarious group of criminals Europe ever produced." Lagen looked at me, saw me sitting there blowing smoke rings at the cream-colored roof and sat back, satisfied that the play was all in his hands.

"There's an evolution to this," he continued. "Crime begets crime. Black marketing of medicines begets black marketing of cigarettes, then it's gun running and finally into the ultimate of all criminal activities, trafficking in drugs."

"You missed the ultimate," I said.

"Murder?"

"Call it killing and that's the ultimate," I told him.

"Ah."

"Don't be so smug. Off the record, do you deny these things?"

"On the record. No."

"Have you killed?"

I blew another smoke ring. "Why sure."

"You're awfully complacent."

It was too bad he couldn't read me at all. So I let him go on.

"The head of the biggest European criminal operation," he said. "And you came home. Death and destruction have followed in your wake."

"Shit, man," I said, "Stop waxing poetic. You're writing a column, remember?"

"No, it is yet to be written. I am simply gathering my facts together. Incidentally, how am I doing?"

"Beautifully," I said.

"There were incidents in New York, there were incidents here. . . . All checked with the police," Lagen said. "The handiwork of an expert."

"How about that?"

"Foresighted and clever," he mused. "But there is more to come. I am waiting for the final kill."

"Then you pounce?"

"With gusto," Lagen told me.

"Who does the killing?"

"They who are waiting for all those millions of dollars in a heroin shipment that you have, er . . . pirated?"

"You're off your rocker, columnist."

"Any rebuttal, Mr. Kelly?"

I finished the cigarette, wound the window down again and tossed the butt outside. The cop and his chauffeur looked back a second, then resumed their conversation.

"No rebuttal," I said. "I just want to hear your tag line."

Lagen smiled, a small enigmatic smile, looked at Sharon, then back to me and said, "Somehow she's a catalytic agent. When you're spoiled, I want to see you soured completely."

"Don't hold your breath."

"I may."

"What, for me to be killed?"

"Exactly. I know other things too."

"And you don't want me forewarned, therefore forearmed?"

"Naturally not."

"Spoken like a good reporter," I said. "Anything for a story."

"Do you blame me?"

I gave him another terrible smile and watched him draw up inside himself. I opened the door, got out and opened the door for Sharon. She grabbed her folder, snaked out into the rain and got behind me while I looked inside the big, black Cadillac and let him see all my teeth again.

"Naturally not," I said.

We waited there until he waved his chauffeur back in and drove away, the rain slashing down at us, then Sharon took my hand, drew me off toward the barricade where the spectators were still waiting and stood there beside me without saying anything at all.

Somebody blew a whistle. The extras came out from under the tent clutching their dinner buckets and paper bags. They all walked to the figure in the yellow slicker, got the directions, assembled themselves for the action shot, and when it came, walked toward the big gates of the Barrin Industries.

Sharon said, "Was all that true?"

I bobbed my head. "He even left the best parts out."

"You really are a criminal?"

"Of sorts."

"But you killed people?"

"Often, sugar."

"Yet after what you've started . . . these people here . . ."

"None of them will get hurt, kitten."

"He said something worse was going to happen."

"That's right."

"Dog . . ."

"Screw it, little blonde doll, I've lived my life. I tried to cut out and nobody will let me. So it's over. Don't let it rub off on you. I've outfoxed the cops on three continents and left my stupid little mark on society and there's nobody left to cry for me so what the fuck do I care, understand? It's almost over, but before that damn last chip goes on the table we're going to leave a clean house behind us."

"Dog . . . you said . . . *we are*."

"The royal plural, sugar. Forget it"

"I love you."

The way she said it hit me right in the pit of my stomach and every muscle in my body went tight. I looked down at her and saw the stillness in her face and knew what my father saw when he screwed my mother in that lonely room atop the building in Mondo Beach and for the first time I saw something else the rain had given me. It was in her face and the highlights came out beside the tiny smile and kaleidoscope images went past my mind without being recognized and I had to think hard to unwind enough to say, "Don't, kid."

It was like the first time I had seen her, with Raul bending over her giving the big pitch and she read him off so beautifully. She threw the rain away from her face and smiled. "I'm only a two-way woman, Dog, I've known men, I've gone down on them, I've had it backward, I've experimented in women . . . but I'm still a virgin. Isn't that terrible?"

"Get lost."

"Unh-uh. I've been waiting."

"Then wait for your guy. He may not be dead."

"I really don't care anymore."

"Then you'd better start because something decent's got to be left in this fucking world."

"Who's going to kill you, Dog?"

"Everybody," I said.

"Can I watch?"

I had held my pack of cigarettes in my hand too long. They were soaked and I tossed them into the mud. She was smiling and I smiled back.

"With pleasure," I said.

XXII

The rain had stopped, but the storm took over and it was wild outside. What had been rain was a slashing downpour, angling against the world like the creations of men were its enemy, trying to wash it down the drain so the earth could start over without all the needless ruination and I agreed with nature and went back outside to do what I had to do.

She met me in Tod's and I knew everything had gotten all screwed up when I sat down and said, "Hello, Rose."

Instead of answering she looked into her coffee cup and fiddled with a lone pretzel beside the saucer. "What happened?"

"You ask a lot," she finally said.

"I know. I pay for it, too."

There was no reason to push her. I let Tod bring me a beer, waited until he left and took the top off the glass, wiping the foam from my mouth with the back of my hand. "What happened?"

Her eyes finally crawled up into mine. "They really your family?"

"Only partly."

I reached out and grabbed her hand. "You hurt?"

"No."

"Everything work?"

"Oh, you got your pictures, if that's what you wanted. I couldn't believe people could be like that."

"What the hell happened to you, Rose?"

She sipped her coffee, took the cigarette I offered and let me light it for her. "You're all Barrins, right?"

I said Yes.

"Buddy . . ."

"Keep talking."

"He's a shit."

"I knew that a long time ago."

"Why didn't you tell me what kind of a shit he was?"

"I set up the escape route, kid."

"Thanks. Really thanks. I damn near didn't make it."

"Apparently you did though." I sat back and grinned at
her.

"Dammit, stop that smiling, Dog. Just because I'm a
total professional whore doesn't mean you have to smile at
me like that."

"It's because I like you, kiddo."

"Go ball yourself."

"Not right now."

When she looked up there were tears in her eyes and
they weren't new at all. "Lee's going to hate me," she said.

"Your fault."

"Dog . . . I'm not as tough as you."

"But you're as soft," I said.

"What good does that do?"

"Remember . . . I told you to marry my buddy . . . he
needs somebody like you?"

"Yes."

"Do it."

"Will he have me?"

"You must be out of your cotton-picking skull. He *needs*
you."

"But he doesn't need you anymore, does he?"

"The sky is empty, Rose. It's all over. Believe?"

"I believe." She put the cup down and tried hard to smile
until it finally worked. "You'll really let us alone?"

"I will."

"The bastard tried to kill me," she said. "I went all the
way with the bum and then he wanted to kill me. He never
got screwed like what I gave him and then some more plus,
but he got wound up so damn tight over something he was
going to wipe me out. You know, Dog, I'm a big broad and
I've been against these types before, but this guy is homicidal. If you hadn't set everything up, I would have been
over the terrace and a lump on the concrete."

"You're here now."

"I should say 'no thanks to you' . . . but it happened."

"Enjoy it?"

"The slob couldn't even get a normal erection."

"Help him?"

"All I could for the photos."

"Good."

"By the way . . . not like I never had pictures taken of me before, but what do you do with the negatives?"

"You can have them."

"I couldn't care less. Lee knows me."

"Then let's not leave any residue behind."

"I told him, Dog."

"What did he say?"

She smiled and opened her hands in a gesture of bewilderment. "They shot down the Red Baron too, that's what he said."

"He's been reading too many Peanuts cartoons," I told her.

"Is it over now?"

I nodded. "For you, yes. All over."

"Elliot has the films ready. I hope they help." She picked up her cup and sipped the last of her coffee. "I understand you're big D now."

"Big D?"

"Dead."

"How true," I told her.

"Somebody's being suckered in," Rose said. "Aren't they?"

"All the way, baby," I told her.

Sharon gave me a punch in the gut, hurt her hand and I kissed her knuckles for her. If she had hit me an inch higher it would have been a laugh, but she contacted the buckle of the gun belt and wiped the skin off her fingers in a fruitless gesture that made me smile at the femaleness inside her. "You're a dirty bastard," she said.

"Why does everybody call me that unless it's true?"

"I wish I had a gun!"

I gave her mine.

She didn't know how to hold it so she gave it back.

"All you can do is watch, baby," I said.

"You big fucking pig you!"

"Shut your mouth and kiss me."

She came at me like a tiger with a mouth so hot and wet, so damn demanding I had to grab her while we ate each other alive until it got so fierce we had to stand off and look at each other with that wild surprise in our eyes and I said, "Not like that, puss, not like that."

"Like that," she smiled.

The rain came down and slashed us apart again, but for a little bit we didn't even realize it.

266

Finally she licked the raindrops from her lips and crinkled her nose at me. "Things happen in strange ways, don't they, Dog?"

"Sometimes."

"Why did you make me wait so long before you told me about yourself?"

"I had things to do."

"There were times when I was pretty angry. I even told myself that maybe I'd be better off not having known you at all."

"Maybe you would at that."

"But then who would teach me all the things I have to learn yet?"

"There can't be that much left, puss."

She gave me a make-believe glare and almost threw another punch at me until she remembered her sore hand. "There's one thing."

"Loss of virginity is a natural function," I told her. "Nature provides the joy to soothe the pain and love to replace the regret of having lost the irretrievable."

"You don't have to be so philosophic about it. You forgot the fun part."

"Just keep it in mind."

A sudden burst of lightning turned the dusky day a dull blue and we waited for the clap of thunder. It came, echoed off into the distance and she reached for my hand. "What can I do to help?"

"Can you get to the personnel records of the movie company?"

Sharon nodded. "Of course."

"Good. I want you to run a check on everybody who hired on. Forget anyone under . . . say, seventy. Make a personal check of their social security cards and if any of them has a new-looking one, or one that looks like it might have been deliberately aged, note it down and check back with me. If they ask any questions, tell them it's because of your company insurance policy."

"Any special name?"

"This one won't be using his own."

"Can you tell me why?"

"No."

"Will this put you in any . . . danger?"

I shook my head. "It'll be worse if I don't locate him."

"All right. I'll try, Dog."

"You're a doll."

"I'm a virgin."

"Every broad is at one time or another. Don't sweat it."

She smiled a pixie smile and flicked some rain at me, then walked away toward the main buildings. Under the large tent somebody blew a whistle and the break was over, the crew streaming back to their stations, heads lowered against the slant of the rain. I chose my time, mixed with three of them, circled the spectator barrier and walked to my car. I had to wait a couple of minutes before I could edge out into traffic, but that was good too. Anybody tailing me would be caught in a real logjam and I knew where to cut out. When I reached the street I was looking for I cut to the right, wheeled it down the deserted strip and kept my eye on the rearview mirror. I made two more turns before I was sure, then I relaxed. Nobody was tailing me this time.

Elliot Embler handed me the envelope with the series of photos, took his money and thanked me for the cash bonus that topped it off. He had dismantled the equipment, put everything back in order and asked me about the negatives. I told him to hold on to them for ten days and, if I hadn't picked them up by then, burn them.

Fifteen minutes later I was at the Lodge and caught Leyland Hunter just before he was ready to leave for the city and gave him the extra set. When he finished looking them over carefully I said, "Your play now, Counselor. I believe the old man's will has been satisfied." He looked up at me with calculating eyes, but before he could speak I waved him off. "There were no stipulations concerning entrapment, buddy. Cousin Dennie walked square into this one on his own and if he wants, I can prod him a little to clear up a few other little unsolved mysteries people around here prefer to bury in the garbage pail of time."

"I doubt if that will be necessary, but I think it was all a sheer waste of energy. What have you gained?"

"My ten grand, for one thing."

"In stock certificates. I needn't tell you what their future values will be."

"How many times do I have to remind you that I'm an optimist?"

"So were the ones who died trying to fly before the Wright Brothers found the secret."

"Just get the papers ready."

"When do you plan to, er, confront them? It isn't really necessary, you know."

"Ah, but it is. And I want to go all the way with it. There's still Cousin Alfred."

"I see."

"Saturday night, Counselor?"

"Very well."

"You make the arrangements."

Hunter nodded, looked at me several seconds, then said, "Do you think you'll have time to enjoy your triumph, Dog?"

"I've lived this long," I told him. "Survival's a matter of being the fittest."

I took the old road out of town, deliberately circumnavigating the Barrin factory where the battery of Klieg lights set up for the night scenes glowed like a yellow umbrella over a normally darkened area. A generation ago it would have been a normal sight, the floods ringing the buildings making Barrin the bright heart of the city. Now it was almost like the last gasp of a dying fish.

Twice, I cut my lights before making turns, taking no chances on being followed. I had trailed too many cars myself under blackout conditions, guiding myself by the taillights ahead, completely out of sight of the lead car, and I didn't want it done to me. To double check I stopped twice too, waiting to see if anything went by me. Nothing did so I picked up the road leading out to Lucy Longstreet's retreat, picking out the landmarks through the metronome clicks of the windshield wipers.

When I reached it I eased into the driveway, cut the engine and went up and banged on the door. Nobody answered, so I waited a few seconds, knocked again and heard Lucy's raucous voice holler for me to come on in.

She was sitting by herself at a card table with a Scrabble game half finished, an empty coffee cup beside her, looking annoyed as hell. "Lose your partner?" I asked her.

"Temporarily. It ain't much fun playing alone, so sit down, Johnny." She reached her leg out under the table and kicked the chair out for me, squinted at me impatiently and said, "Let me get this word down and you can play too."

There was something about her that wasn't hanging right and when she picked four tiles out of the holder and laid them down it made a lousy job of Scrabble but a good piece of explanation. The word didn't fit, but it was clear enough. It spelled out *trap*.

And Lucy Longstreet had been around long enough to anticipate all the moves and when I was hurtling off the chair she was sliding for the floor as feet pounded through the doorway behind me. I had the .45 out and blasted the overhead light out with the first shot before a foot took the rod out of hand and sent it skittering across the room. But the odds weren't all that bad anymore. Anyone I touched was the enemy and they had to identify me personally. And the first one tripped over me into a ball of knuckles that put his teeth down his throat and left my fist slimy with blood. When he crashed into the wall I was rolling to the left, my arm sweeping out to yank the legs of another one out from under him. The gun in his hand blasted a swath of light into my face, hot, stinging powder etching a burn across my cheek. My hand grabbed the gun in his fingers, my other hand getting leverage on his elbow and I broke his wrist with a single twist and smashed the scream out of his throat when I backhanded the iron across his skull.

There just wasn't enough time. I saw the shadow looming above me and spotted the movement, so long-conditioned reflexes jerked my head aside and let padded metal ricochet off my temple in a blinding wave of pain and lights. I tried to move, but nothing worked at all and I knew that it was all over because the flickering glow of a cigarette lighter snapped on and there was enough peripheral vision left to see the outline of an automatic in it.

I knew I let out a weak curse when the crash came and all I could think of was that it was the silliest noise I ever heard a gun make and dying wasn't so bad after all if it could distort sounds like that and not even let you feel the agony of a bullet at all. No pain. Just a heavy, crushing weight that pressed down and down and down.

When the light went on I blinked the tears out of my eyes and through the ringing in my ears I heard Lucy Longstreet say, "You okay, kid?"

"Shit."

"Do that later. Right now get out from under that clown. He's dripping blood all over you."

I heaved up on my knees and felt the body roll off my back, got to my feet and looked at the mess on the floor. They were all alive and breathing, but pretty damn sick, especially the one Lucy had damn near brained with the old-fashioned lamp that used to be the centerpiece of her whorehouse parlor table.

I took a minute to catch my breath, then took a good look at the three of them. Two I had never seen before, but one was an old-time buddy. Now he had a broken wrist and one hell of a dent in his skull. Blackie Saunders, the wipeout boy from Trenton was going to have a hard time explaining all this to Chet Linden.

Chet was going to have an even harder time explaining this to me.

The cigar Lucy was trying to light had broken halfway

down its length and didn't want to take hold. She spat it out angrily and felt in her pocket for another one. When she got it fired she gave me a twisted grin. "Like the old days, kid. You know them?"

"I know where they came from. What happened?"

She gave a shrug as if it had been an everyday occurrence. "Came in about two hours ago. Scared the living crap out of Beth and the boys."

"What boys?"

"Old Stanley Cramer and Stoney. Beth had 'em out hustlin' for some dirt on your cousin. They come up with some goodies, too. He got to one of the girls who was scragged and she gave him a detailed letter."

"They all right?"

"Sure. Tied up out in the kitchen."

"Look, Lucy ... don't give it to me in episodes I haven't got ..."

"Relay, sonny. First tell me what we're gonna do with these buckos. If you want I still got contacts who'll . ."

"Forget it." I pushed past her and in five minutes I had all three of them wrapped up and gagged so tight they wouldn't be going anywhere unless I let them. I found my own rod, tucked it away, then pushed Lucy down into a chair. "Okay, Lucy, now all of it."

She nodded toward Blackie and puffed on the cigar. "That one liked to talk. He had a mad on for you, Doggie boy. Seems like they been in town checking out every one of your acquaintances and didn't have any luck until he heard old Juke telling Tod about seeing you and what a nice guy you was and how they had something to give you. Juke, he just rambled on and said they was coming here and then call you. Later, Stanley and Stoney came in, sent Juke somewhere on an errand and they followed the boys back."

"I didn't get any call."

"Not like they didn't try to get one through."

"I haven't been in any one place very long."

"That's what they figured too. So they decided to wait. Hell, after they put the others in the kitchen that one I busted over there even played some Scrabble with me. The dirty bastard used words that wasn't in the rules and made me play 'em. I should've really laid it on. You know what that lamp cost me?"

"Ten bucks."

"Yeah, but a dollar was a dollar then."

I threw her a disgusted smile and shook my head. "Let's get them out of the kitchen."

Beth's fright had turned to total indignation and she was all for throwing a pail of scalding water over the three of them. I talked her out of it and let her settle for kicking each one in the head and enjoying the muffled groans that seeped through the gags. Cramer and Stoney didn't want any part of them and had to have a few belts of Lucy's best Scotch before they could get the shake out of their hands. I had to prod Stoney into remembering where he put the letter he had and he finally dug it out of an old jacket that had been slung across the back of a chair.

It was nicely detailed, giving places, dates and two other names who might go along with the big squeeze if no recriminations were guaranteed. As for herself, she'd even appear in court if she had to. And I now had Cousin Alfred's ass in one hell of a sling.

When I finished reading I put the letter in my pocket. Both the men were watching me closely and I said, "Thanks. You all have something coming for this."

"We don't want anything, Mr. Kelly," Cramer told me. "Unless it's to see Barrin working full time."

"I wish I could promise you that, friend."

"You said you was going to try."

"All the way out. Trying doesn't mean it can be done though."

"But you're still gonna try?"

I nodded.

"Even with Cross McMillan on your back?"

"I wish that was all I had on my back. Those three inside are only the front-runners."

"But when Cross hears what . . ."

"Cross didn't send them," I said.

Their eyes met, then touched Lucy's. The old madam said, "It goes deeper?"

"You'd never believe, sugar. The funny part is"—I inclined my head toward the other room where the bloody three lay messing up Lucy's rug—"this end of the action doesn't bother me at all. It's that fucking McMillan who's got the power to hurt everybody and there's not a damn thing I can do about it. He's got the money, the control and enough hate for the Barrins to enjoy pulling everything down into a pile of rubbish."

"Piss on him," Lucy said.

"Try telling that to a city full of people with brand-new stars in their eyes."

"What'll we do with your pals inside?"

I felt a grin tug at my mouth and ease the tension from

272

my body. "Call Bennie Sachs to come collect them. All you know is that they broke in on you and did what they did. You have four reliable witnesses to go along with the story."

"What story?"

"Why, it's simple. Stanley here wiggled loose, untied Stoney and Beth and you overpowered the bums."

Cramer's voice was weak with surprise. "*Us?*"

"Sure," I said. "Those guys aren't going to deny it. Just do what I'm telling you."

Lucy had lived a long time. Her eyes had narrowed into the tired folds of fat and the pupils were little dark pinpoints reading my mind. I let her gauge me until she was satisfied, then she said, "Okay, Dog. That's the way it'll be."

I left Lucy making the call and Stanley Cramer walked me to the door. When I opened it he touched my arm. He was standing in the shadows and I couldn't see his face, but there was something odd in his voice. "Don't worry too much about that there Cross guy, Mr. Kelly."

"Why's that, Stan?"

"Because worrying don't leave time for nothing else to get done. You'll see."

"Glad to know there's another optimist left," I said.

The night lights around the factory made dull little halos in the rain. On the west side of the main buildings the trucks and trailers had been buttoned up, the only sound of life coming from inside the portable watchman's shack where a TV was blaring away and a couple of voices were loud in beery laughter.

My collar was turned up against the downpour that slashed at my back and I edged through the shadows to the rows of bushes that shielded the front of the building, got behind them and felt my way to the old service door that led inside. It squeaked open on seldom-used hinges, the noise echoing in the empty corridor. It had been a long time since I had come in this way and the place had been renovated since, so I stood there a minute until I was oriented, then picked my way through the darkened offices until I reached the foyer.

On the other side, in the area reserved for the S. C. Cable Productions office, I saw the deliciously familiar back of a beautiful little blonde poring over a ledger, one hand fingering a stack of printed cards. I crossed to the door, stood there enjoying the light glinting through the carelessly swept-back hair and said, "Hello, pretty girl."

Sharon jumped, knocked half the cards off the desk and swung around to look at me with her breath caught in her throat. "Dog! Damn, don't ever do that again." Then she saw my face and her eyes opened wide before she was able to speak again. "What happened to you?"

"Trouble. Nothing new. Nothing unexpected."

She got up and came into my arms, her fingers digging hard into my biceps. "Oh, Dog. Damn you, Dog!"

"At ease, doll. I'm all right." I pusher her away and tilted her head up with the palm of my hand. "A war's made up of battles, kid. I just won this one."

She let out a short laugh and wiped the tears out of her eyes. "And I don't suppose I get to know what happened, do I?"

"You suppose right." I pulled the door shut, locked it and checked to make sure the Venetian blinds were all shuttered tight. "You run down anything at all?"

"All I should tell you is up your bucket," she said.

"What about those Social Security cards?"

"Nothing." Sharon hooked her arm under mine and led me to the desk. "I doubled back on everybody they hired through Cable and not one thing looked phony. I'm no detective, but I know how to run personnel and everybody here is as square as a pair of Los Vegas dice."

The disappointment went through me like liquid tar and she sensed it. There was only that black, sticky feeling that kept you from going any place at all, holding you right in the target area like a staked-out goat waiting for the tiger to come get him.

"But I got another idea," she said.

I was so damned disgusted I almost didn't hear her. It finally sunk in and I turned my head to look at her.

"The factory is hiring too. I got the girl in their department to let me look at their records because I said we might need some character types in a hurry. There wasn't much time so I only ran down those who were around the sixty-five-year-old mark. Barrin doesn't hire over that age. Took a lot of phone calls to cross-check their identities, but I came up with three nobody could vouch for at all. Each had given local businesses as references, but two of those places said they had never worked there and the third one gave a business that didn't even exist at all."

"What business was that?"

She told me and the black, sticky feeling went away. "You have his address?"

Sharon picked up a card and handed it to me. "Nine-o-one Sherman. Know where it is?"

"Yeah," I said. "I know where it is."

"And don't tell me I can't go with you."

"No . . . I won't tell you that. You earned that much."

She stepped back and gave me a slant-eyed look. "You're agreeing a little too easily. I don't like that."

I could feel the tiredness in my voice. "It'll make you a perfect escape clause, kitten."

"What?"

"Never mind. You'll see what I mean."

I had played stickball on the street and fallen off the ice truck on the far corner. It was paved now, but then it had been hardpan, grooved by the iron-shod wheels of horse-drawn wagons and chain-driven Mack trucks. Once they had gaslights set between the curb and the sidewalks and we used to hang from the crossarms and scratch ourselves like apes to show off in front of the girls. It wasn't much brighter now, the dirty glass streetlamps barely illuminating their own bases. I eased down the pavement, pulled in at the shabby old frame building with the 901 painted on the second step of the porch, cut the motor and got out. Sharon followed me, saying nothing, then her hand slipped into mine and squeezed. Her fingernails bit into my skin and her palm was sweaty. I pushed the doorbell and waited.

Nobody answered. I pushed the button again. I tried the third time and was reaching for the doorknob when a voice came out of the blackness at one end of the porch and said, "What took you so long, Dog?"

"Ferris," I murmured softly. "You haven't got a very elaborate factory here, friend."

"But the product is highly refined, easily packaged, the demand enormous and the profit tremendous. Shall we go inside?"

He was old now, but the years had touched him lightly. If he shuffled in an elderly manner it was an artificial gesture and when he knew I realized it he smiled and let the cat in him take over. His hair was thin and gray, his clothes baggy and worn, but there was a muscular lankiness to his body that meant old habits didn't die easily and he had kept himself in shape even though it wasn't necessary any longer.

When I introduced Sharon he rubbed the back of his neck while he said hello, the old signal that meant he had to be satisfied with her status before he'd go any further. If I was in a squeeze and she was part of it, he was ready to pull the trigger on his own booby trap and he was alerting me to be ready to cut and run out of the line of fire.

I said, *"Bravo,* buddy," remembering the answer signal

275

and watched him relax. "She's part of my new team now," I explained.

"Sure," he told me. "Times have changed, but they really don't change at all. What's that French saying?"

"The more things change the more they remain the same," I said. "I thought you'd be dead by now, Ferris."

"Only the excitement died. I woke up one morning and decided the world was worth neither saving nor destroying. Even fine hatreds and the sheer love of pleasure become boring under the monotonous onslaught of time."

"Then why come back?"

Ferris eased himself down into a chair and when he leaned back the worn tweed jacket hiked up a little bit over the bulge of the guns he wore on either side of his hip. *A matched pair of German 9 mm. P-38s,* I remembered.

"A couple of reasons," he answered, his brown berrylike eyes looking at me closely. "First, I owed you one for taking that bullet instead of me on that last job in Berlin. The second was sheer curiosity. I wanted to see how an old retired pro would react when the big one was dumped in his lap."

"Don't shit me, Ferris." There was a cold snap in my voice I couldn't help.

He nodded, the berry eyes laughing at me. "You're still sharp, boy. You shouldn't have retired. Yep, there's another reason. The world is polluting itself to death. You can treat sewage, cap chimneys and go back to returnable bottles, but nobody stops the kind of pollution we were a part of. I thought maybe you could give it a try."

"When did you get interested in ecology?"

"The day a young man I knew and trained told me he was escorting a multimillion-dollar shipment of H to the States and smelled an intercept. We arranged a switch, but he wasn't careful enough and got himself killed in a restaurant in Marseilles."

"And I got tagged for the job."

"You were a natural for it, boy. I gave it all your earmarks, but since you got the name, I decided to give you the game and let you take it from there. I'm too damn old for the fun and games and money doesn't mean a thing to me anymore. You're still young enough to enjoy it all." He glanced at Sharon, still smiling with his eyes. "Unless you're *really* retired."

I could have shot the old bastard right then and there, but there still was some fun left in it and my face creased into a tight grin. "I'm retired, but let's say I'm called back

276

for a consultation. Just one other thing . . . how'd you find me?"

"You never bothered covering your tracks, son. Pretty stupid, wasn't it?"

"I never bothered thinking about it."

"You sure screwed everybody else up, though. The vultures took a while to locate you." He let out a little chuckle. "Some job you did on Bridey-the-Greek and Markham."

"I didn't kill them."

He chuckled again, his fingers rapping against the arm of the chair. "I know, but the others were all yours, weren't they?"

They was no use answering him. He knew the answers.

"Who's left, Dog?" He knew that answer too, but he wanted me to say it.

"Arnold Bell," I told him.

"And he's new, Dog. I hear tell he's even better than you were at your very best. He was paid in advance and is one of those crazy people who are dedicated to their jobs. You're his biggest challenge and after he kills you he'll be the king in his business. There will be other Turks and other Le Fleurs and they'll always be needing Arnold Bell to keep the raiders out of their empires. They laid everything on the line to have you wiped out because you are the biggest threat of them all. As long as you are alive they can never exist in security and safety. So the biggest gun of all comes out and the advantage is all his."

"You think he can nail me?" I asked him.

"Certainly. You know the mortality rate in this business. It's always the ones on the way up who knock off the ones on the way out."

"Then why bother setting me up?"

"An old man needs a glimpse of the past to refresh his memories, occasionally. At my age, that's all you have to live on. I'm just sorry I won't be there to see it happen. It should be a bloody mess. Maybe if you had run me down a little sooner I would have called the odds pretty even, but you've slowed up, buddy. The reflexes are still there, but the old computer doesn't send the messages out fast enough. They put old dogs to sleep, son. You're ready for the pound."

"Can I have one last bark?" I asked him.

Ferris nodded. "Maybe even a growl."

"Thanks a bunch. Where's the stuff?"

"In an old panel truck out back. Don't bother asking me how I got it through or how I'm going to get back. One

277

day they can read it all in my memoirs." He reached in his pocket, took out an ignition key and tossed it to me. "Like you used to say, it's your ball now, kid."

It nested in the shadows of the building, an old Dodge panel job with crumpled fenders and doors you had to wrench open. A tattered army blanket covered the holes in the seat cushions and there was no window on the driver's side. The ignition key unlocked the doors in the back and when I swung them open the sealed walnut coffin gave off a dull sheen in the light of my match. Sharon sucked in her breath with an audible gasp, her hands clasped tight around my arm. I pushed her loose, climbed inside and broke the seal on the lid. Her face was a pale white oval with brighter spots where her eyes were, watching me look in the satin-padded box.

"Dog . . ." Her voice was barely a whisper.

"The biggest corpse in the world, baby. There's enough heroin here to overdose every addict in New York." I shut the lid and climbed out of the truck.

"Dog . . ." she said again. "Heroin?"

"Big H."

"Yours?"

"All mine. Bundles of millions of dollars and it's all mine."

I didn't have to see her face to know the disgust was there. The loathing was there too when she asked, "What are you going to do with it?"

"Sell it, kid," I told her.

This time she didn't touch me. She took a small step away and became part of the shadows. Very calmly, she said, "I think I hate you, Dog."

"That's good, because you wouldn't understand the purchase price of the stuff."

"I understand, all right. I should have listened to you sooner. The world *would* be a lot better off without people like you."

"Then stick around and see it happen."

"I intend to, Dog. It's what you wanted me to do anyway, wasn't it?"

My guts knotted up inside me, but I had to get it out. "Yes." I looked around for Ferris, waiting to hear his sardonic little chuckle.

But Ferris had disappeared back into the past and had left me alone with his terrible present.

XXIII

You don't maintain a posture of dignity when you're staring
down the ugly muzzle of a .45 automatic. Not when you
know the history of the guy behind the blued steel and
thought that he had been eliminated hours ago. Not when
you're in a pair of striped shorts and nothing else, with
skinny legs that couldn't hold still and a lovely blonde
woman who had brand-new case-hardened eyes watching
you out of mild curiosity and total disdain.

I said, "Just one more time, friend, or Weller-Fabray
loses your services permanently. You know the new contact
number and you know where he's at."

"Please . . . Mr. Kelly, you know what will happen if I
tell you where . . ."

I grinned that same old nasty grin and he saw my hand
tighten around the gun butt. "I know what will happen if
you don't."

It wasn't much of a choice. If he told me, at least he had
an hour's head start.

So he told me and I coldcocked him for a long sleep with
the Colt.

I put the gun away and let my expression fade back
where it came from and went back to the truck with
Sharon. I looked at my watch. We still had another hour
before sunrise. It was the time of day when New York
City was in its postorgasmic trance, buried in its smog-
choked dreams, the hour between those going and those
coming. The rain was trying hard, but there would never
be enough of it to clean the stains from its steel-and-con-
crete skin. I turned the truck and cut across town to a gas
station where I had one phone call to make, filled the tank,

grabbed two coffees from the dispenser and got back in the cab again.

When Sharon took the steaming cup I handed her she said, "Would you really have killed him, Dog?"

I shoved the gear lever in low and let the clutch out. "He wouldn't have been the first."

"I didn't ask you that."

"He thought so," I told her.

A long time ago Freeport had been a lazy little village on Long Island, a short pleasure jaunt down the Sunrise Highway from the big zoo of Fun City. But that was a long time ago before progress had set in, with miscalculated planning and the population explosion to guide it. Now it was just another choked-up town with bumper-to-bumper parked cars walling it in, demanding to be called a suburb, struggling against the ebb and flow of traffic and charge accounts.

I found the street and I found the number of the pale yellow house that was the last on the block and coasted into the driveway with the lights off.

Off in the east the dull glow of a false dawn was backlighting the mist that shrouded the coastline. Inside the yellow house Chet Linden would be sleeping quietly, secure in the knowledge that the order was given, the order had been carried out, and the age of electronic engineering was the big wall no enemy could breech.

Sharon watched me while I breeched his ramparts with a pair of cute little gimmicks, bypassing the circuits in a way that would make him put knots on the heads of the so-called experts later on. She stood by quietly while I slid in the window, deactivated the secondary alarm on the door and she walked in with those steely eyes enjoying the moment . . . eyes of an animal lover waiting to see the bull kill the matador.

He woke up when he felt the cold end of the rod under his chin and heard me say. "Lights, honey."

The overhead fixture snapped on and Chet came awake with an incredible expression of hate at himself because he had failed and didn't bother to move toward the gun I snaked out from under his pillow and just lay still until I found the sawed-off bayonet beside his leg in arm's reach.

"You made a gross mistake, Chet. I told you to lay off. I even told you what would happen if you didn't."

He was watching the gun in my hand. He saw the hammer lying all the way back and the hole in the end looked as big as the tunnel to hell.

"You're sharp, Dog. What happened to Blackie and the others?"

"Guess."

"So you finally turned the corner," he stated.

"Get up and get dressed."

He looked over at Sharon.

"She's seen bare-assed guys before."

"I have to get dressed to get killed?"

"You always told me I had class."

"There's always the end of the line for people like us, isn't there?"

"Always."

"Sorry about that, Dog."

"Don't be sorry."

"Oh, not for me. For you. I hate to see you turn that corner." He kicked his feet out from under the covers and sat on the edge of the bed and looked at Sharon again. "And you're the one," he said. "Do you know about him . . . all about him?"

"I do now," Sharon said.

"I see." He let his eyes slide up to mine. "You destroy everybody, don't you?"

I shrugged.

But everybody has to fight for their lives. When you know there's only that last minute left you have to try whether you erupt into the violent exhaustion of death or try to think it through quietly, you try, and Chet elected to think.

"Can you stop him?" he asked Sharon.

"Everybody else has tried. Can you?"

He didn't cower and he didn't beg. He just got dressed and went ahead of us into his own living room and sat in his own chair so he could be comfortable when the boatman called for him to cross the river and wondered who the hell could be coming around at this time of night when the doorbell rang and I told Sharon to answer it.

The big guy came in alone like I had told him to do, saw me standing there with the .45 in my hand and never bothered making a play for his own piece that was hanging at the ready on his hip. He was all pro of the big team and didn't give a shit for anything at all, except he liked those pretty little explanations you could set down and study later and maybe qualify in the light of experience, wondering how the living hell you could make it all go when they turned the heat lamps on and turned the screws.

I said, "Outside," and took them to the truck. I let the big guy take a look at all the prospective bodies in the

281

shiny walnut coffin, then made him let Chet take a look too.

The big guy said, "What are you asking, Dog?"

"Only the keys to your car," I said.

The big guy handed me his keys. I looked at Chet and then back to the big guy. "He'll tell you one hell of a story," I said.

His calm, impassive Italian face looked at me with dark, faked-innocuous eyes. "I'd rather hear it from you."

"The ending is not yet, pal." I said. "It's never any good until you get to the ending."

"I know the one Dick Lagen is going to write. That newspaper syndicate had enough money to buy all the facts since the war ended and you began. They cleared everything through channels and there's no way out of the noose for you at all."

"Maybe you'd better talk to him," I said.

"He won't listen to me."

"But he'll sure as hell listen to me." I eased the hammer down on the .45 but kept my thumb on the hammer. "Or my GI tool here."

Until now I had never seen him really smile and I wished I hadn't. He looked at the blackness inside the truck, his teeth flashing white in the early dawn, "Should I save the coffin, Dog? My mother used to say 'waste not, want not.'"

"You do that, Vince," I told him. "Only don't save it for me."

The fucking rain never seemed to stop. It beat against the windshield and the one lazy wiper on my side barely brushed it away. Across the highway the early traffic was already crawling, tied up by a station wagon with a flat a mile back, impatient and angry, building up to a whole day mad.

Sharon didn't look at me at all, gazing idly out the window at the rows of cars, her hands limp with hopeless regret in her lap. When I took the cutoff to Linton, she glanced at me thoughtfully for a moment, as if she had made some kind of decision, then sucked in her breath, shook her head and turned away again.

But she couldn't keep it bottled up inside her, she had seen too much and the sense of it wasn't getting through. I knew by the way she was sitting there that she was trying to formulate her own answers, but they were coming out all wrong.

When it finally got to be too much it was like the words were being wrung out of her. "What is Dick Lagen going to write about you, Dog?"

"Does it matter?"

"Before . . . when you told me about . . . those other things, it didn't at all. Then when I saw the casket . . . was it *really* heroin?"

"Absolutely pure and totally uncut. Probably the biggest shipment that's gotten through in a long, long time." I kept my voice low and nice and even.

"And all yours. It was shipped to you?"

"That's right, but now it's been reconsigned."

"I won't let it happen, Dog."

"Let what happen?"

"That . . . policeman. He and that evil little man. The dirty bastards who push that stuff would never exist if they weren't protected somehow. I was a witness and I can identify them. I think Dick Lagen will be ready to listen to me."

Hell, let her think what she wanted. It was better for her this way.

"You'd need the evidence, baby. I don't think anybody's going to see that casket again. Lagen wouldn't try making unfounded accusations and nobody else is going to be offering the information."

Sharon let it settle in her mind, the gentle smile toying with the corners of her mouth saying it wasn't going to be like that at all. "What was your price, Dog?"

"You'd never believe me," I said.

"Yes . . . I really would." Her eyes were cold and direct again. "Was it in the millions?"

"More than that, kitten. Much more. Money couldn't even buy what I got for that hand-carved body box."

"What's worth more than money?"

"If you don't know now, you never will," I told her.

She still wouldn't take her eyes from me. They were like tiny drills augering into my flesh. "To you, Dog. What's worth more than money *to you?*"

"To come home. To be free." I was going to tell her something else, but caught it in time and just let it end there. I watched the road unwinding through the rain and suddenly felt the needlepoints of her eyes stop stabbing me. I looked at her quickly and her expression had changed, a small frown reflecting some annoying perplexity that tugged at her mind. She wet her mouth, clenching her lower lip between her teeth and I saw the tears rise in the corners of her eyes.

When I turned down the street where I had left my car in front of the house Ferris had used I saw the jam of cars up ahead, two with their blue lights winking in the morning light and a pair of fire engines standing in the middle of the road. A pall of dark haze was hanging over something by the curb, but the knot of curious people blocked it from view. They didn't block the shattered windows and crumpled porch on the houses opposite the area though.

I rolled down the window and called a couple of kids over to see what had happened. One had his school books bunched under his arm and looked kind of sick.

"Car blew up," he said. "That nutty little Jansen kid what's always stealing rides in cars saw the keys in that one and was gonna ride to school. It blew all apart when he started it. Gee, we tried to tell him and everything . . ."

Then I felt a little sick, too.

The other kid said abstractedly, "He just got outa reform school for the same thing."

I rolled the window up and sat there a moment.

"Dog . . .?"

"It was supposed to have been me," I said.

Her sob was a futile cry that caught in her throat.

"He's the last one out there. After him there won't be anymore."

"Who?" Sharon whispered.

"The worst one of all." I was all tight again. "Damn, there's so much more to do, too."

I dropped Sharon off outside the Barrin plant. She gave me a wistful little smile, pulled the collar up on her coat and walked through the rain toward the building. The S. C. Cable Productions trucks were still lined up on the west side, but all the activity had moved indoors and the canvas canopies were down except for the one over the area where a few of the crew were surrounding the coffee urns. I circled the complex twice before I spotted Hobis sitting in a parked car, stopped opposite him and waved him in beside me.

"Any action?" I asked.

"Just a little accident with a car downtown." He grinned at me, his lips tight over clenched teeth. "I sent The Chopper over to check it out. Either you're on the ball or your luck's running strong."

"What did he get?"

"It was that rented heap of yours, all right. Somebody used one of the new plastics with a heat-sensitized detonator wired to the exhaust. Easy to slap on and takes about five seconds to activate. A real pro job. I don't think the local cops even know how it happened yet. Sure tore that kid all to hell. What was the bit there?"

"He was trying to steal the car. I had left the keys in it."

Hobis shrugged and lit the stub of a cigar he took out of his pocket. "Scratch one potential con. Who did it?"

"Arnold Bell."

He nodded without looking up until he had the butt lit, then took a couple of deep drags on it. "Old Bell's diversifying. He used to specialize in that little .22 of his. Figure how he ran you down?"

"The city isn't all that big," I said.

"Uh-huh. But it still makes it a big job. You think he's working alone?"

"He didn't start off that way."

"Maybe he rang in some locals."

"Not Arnold Bell. The solo speed is the way he likes it. Now the big pot is all his if he makes the hit."

"As long as he was paid in advance," Hobis said.

I cut around the corner and headed back toward the factory again. Hobis's tone of voice had sounded a little strange and I looked at him, the question in my eyes.

Hobis said, "I called New York this morning. The whole European scene blew wide apart."

My hands went tight around the steering wheel. "How?"

"Some of Le Fleur's boys went after The Turk and threw a couple of slugs in his belly. The Turk thought he was dying and blew the whistle on the big man. The fuzz moved in and nailed all his records and put enough heat on some of the lower echelon so that they started talking too." He took another drag on the cigar and tossed the butt out the side window. "Would have made quite a package, only while he was being held in custody a twenty-year-old cousin of a guy Le Fleur had eliminated walked in with press credentials and popped his eyes out with a Luger. When the boiler blows, she really blows fast, doesn't she?"

"That gets the Guido brothers off the hook then."

"Kiddo," Hobis told me, "you've been away much too long. Over there they'd just call it quits and start over again when the storm dies down, but here you pay for mistakes or errors in judgment. It teaches others a lesson about being careful when they're using mob money to finance an operation." He let out a grunt that passed for a laugh and added, "You got something to say, haven't you?"

So I told him about the casket.

"To each his own," he said when I finished. "Where do we go from here?"

"Nothing changes. Just keep the plant covered."

"Your dough, buddy. Lousy action, but good pay."

I let him out beside the car he was working from, pulled

away behind a pair of trucks making sure nobody wa.
behind me and called Leyland Hunter from a gas station
on the outskirts of town.

It was Saturday morning and I was to meet with the
family at noon. Two hours later there was a special meeting of the new board of directors in the main office of the
building and I was expected to be in attendance.

They should have had flowers. There should have been
a funeral director present ushering in the guests with
hushed voice and a small bow. The butler tried his best, but
the enigmatic smile on his face belied the true nature of
the gathering. Something in his eyes ran a full sweep over
me like a radar scanning beacon without ever leaving my
face and I knew he had all the answers at his fingertips and
was going to enjoy the moment of truth when all the chips
were down. He said a pleasant good afternoon to Hunter
and me, took our coats and told us the others were waiting
in the library.

I looked at the pixie lawyer and showed the way with
my hand. "After you, Counselor. I prefer to make a dra-
matic entrance."

He turned that courtroom stare on me again. "One day
your entrance and exit will be simultaneous."

"Like getting into a car with a hot charge on it?"

"An excellent example. The day is coming closer all the
time."

"When it gets here, we'll worry about it."

He nodded, his face bland. "This could be *the* day, my
obstreperous friend. I have heard a certain nasty rumor."

"All rumors are nasty."

"Not like this one."

"Care to tell me about it?"

"I'm not given to promulgating rumors. If this one is
true, you'll know about it soon enough."

"Fine. Not . . . shall we?" I nodded toward the library
and followed him up to the big doors.

They were all there. The scene wasn't much different
from the first time, with one exception. Nobody was sitting
behind the big desk now. They were all grouped for mutual
protection at the far end of the room, drinks in hand, faked
joviality in their lowered voices, hostility seeping through
every pore, but with something hidden in their demeanor
that meant they had a time bomb ready to hand me and
if ever the picture of the old man on the wall was contemplating the gathering with absolute pleasure, it was this
moment. The painted eyes followed me with a challenging

dare that said I might jump the trap if I had been a real Barrin, but bastards didn't have a chance at all. The try had been good, but that's all it was . . . a try . . . and you don't *try* to leap the chasm; they make it or die at the bottom.

Nobody heard me when I said, "Fuck you, old man," then went over and sat on the edge of the desk while Hunter took his place behind it.

So far nobody had even said hello.

The lawyer didn't have to tell them. Dennie and Alfred simply nodded when Hunter took out the stock certificates and handed them to me, but the way they watched me was the same way the picture watched me and when Hunter said, "Ten thousand dollars' worth of nothing, Dog. All yours."

"It would have been the same had I not come back."

"Are you satisfied?"

I pushed the pretty green sheets back to him. "Hang on to them for me. And yes, I'm satisfied." I lit a cigarette and looked at my cousins who seemed to be enjoying their drinks. The only one who wasn't all the way happy was Marvin Gates and he seemed to be ashamed of himself for some reason or another. The booze had already taken hold and, whatever his problem was, it was disappearing in an alcoholic blur.

Alfred settled himself back into the big wing chair and made a mock toast at me with his glass. "At least we still have Grand Sita, Dog. Paid for now, of course. No outstanding mortgages, no debts. All free and clear with a standing offer to buy for quite a few cash millions of dollars."

"Good for you. I never wanted this place anyway."

"Ah, but the solvency of having it is an enjoyable experience."

"Fine."

"Our position here dictates the value of all the other properties. We can make Mondo Beach either worthless or of immense value. Of course, we have no intention of enhancing your section. Eventually it will erode into sand, grass and rubbish."

"Unless Barrin Industries takes a sudden turn for the better."

"And there's little chance of that, is there?" Dennie asked smugly.

"One never knows," I told him.

I heard Hunter's finger tap the desk for my attention. "They're well aware of the situation. Cross McMillan has bought a small piece of the estate here for an exorbitant price. Ergo, they are now free and clear and well situated for the years to come."

"Only until prices and taxes rise, Counselor."

"The same holds true for you."

"I didn't think they'd be that shrewd. What's the gimmick?"

Dennie came out of his chair sideways. He still reminded me of a snake slithering from its hole and if he had had a forked tongue he would have stuck it out and hissed. His smile was deadly as hell and he was tasting his big moment of satisfaction as he walked over to the desk and tossed a pair of black and white two-by-two photos in my lap.

His voice was maliciously soft when he said, "You're a dead man, Dog."

I looked at the pictures, clear, sharp, absolutely identifiable photos of Sheila McMillan and me all naked as hell in the big bed at the old beach house, positioned as pornographically as the best Swedish double-X rated jobs and when I showed them to Hunter I heard him grunt and tear them up.

"Oh, there are plenty of copies," Dennie said. "Cross McMillan has a set too. These went with the property sale. Now he has you earmarked for a grave. Unfortunately, since you are illegitimate, the burial site will remain unmarked. Something like your mother's."

When I hit him his whole face exploded into a shower of blood and teeth and before he was able to fall I caught him with a right to the ribs that make them crackle like broken sticks under my fist. Dennie's skull bounced off the wood, but he was still conscious when I hauled him up again and tore one ear off the side of his head and he tried to scream through his shattered mouth, but all that came out was a faint squeak before he fainted. I let him drop and turned around to the rest.

They weren't looking at me. The solitary ear, still bleeding from the shards of skin surrounding it took all their attention and I said, "My time bomb was better than yours."

Alfred got sick to his stomach.

Pam said something about getting a doctor, but the phone was on the desk and they had to pass me to get it. Nobody wanted to.

Then Marvin Gates said, "I took the pictures, Dog."

He thought he was going to die and wondered why I didn't bother killing him right then. I said, "Why, Marv?"

He gave me a mute shrug, waited a few second and fin-

288

ished his glass. "I'm a weak character. I talk too much, I give in too easily." He twirled the glass in his fingers, staring at it. "I don't give a damn what you do to me."

"Forget it," I said.

Veda got sick then too. She didn't heave. The vomit just dribbled out of her mouth. Very slowly her eyes rolled back in her head and she passed out, bubbling through her own lunch.

Marvin looked up from the empty glass, for a moment or two his eyes clear. "Cross is going to kill you, Dog. He has to. Everybody knows about you and his wife now."

I waved a thumb toward the family. "You get paid enough for the job, buddy?"

"My checking account has been fattened considerably by a cash gratuity. If I live, I can live the life of a fat, grubby worm. But independent."

"You'll live," I informed him. "Stay happy."

"Not knowing I helped kill you."

My face must have looked pretty weird because he seemed to draw back into his stupor again. "Don't wipe me off the list until you see me autopsied, my friend."

I heard Leyland Hunter gathering up the papers and stuffing them into his attaché case. He followed me outside and took his coat and hat from the butler in the foyer. Harvey looked at me with the same enigmatic smile and said, "I've already called the doctor, sir. I hear they can do wonders with detached extremities if the parts are rejoined in time."

When we were back in the car we drove two blocks before we stopped. Leyland Hunter decided the time had come for him to get sick too. When he finished, he wiped his mouth and watched a full minute before he said, "Where can you go now, Dog?"

That grin came back and I swung the wheel at the next corner. "Why, to see Cross McMillan, of course."

The little VW pulled out of a driveway a block farther on and stayed behind us another quarter mile before it turned off. It wasn't a killer's type of car, but I wondered why one just like it picked me up at the intersection just a short way from the plant. It hung back there, then it was gone again. The afternoon was gray and wet, almost like dusk, but nighttime was still a long way off.

Arnold Bell liked to work at night.

So did I.

XXIV

Five days. In that length of time all the interior and exterior shots of the Barrin complex would be completed and the *Fruits of Labor* cast and crew could go on to other locations and into their rented studios to wind up the intricate slot structure of the story with closed sets for the nudie scenes and galleries of exuberant spectators for the wide-open stuff. The story was all Barrin-oriented and the local facilities of Linton were enjoying a time of prosperity as if it had never happened before.

Publicity and public relations are terrible professional mind benders, and the smiling faces of the reborn never knew what was happening to them. Barrin Industries were alive again. They thought they knew that. Their talents were needed and they were there. The beehive was open. Suck the flowers, store the honey. The queen was laying her eggs, the drones were in attendance, and they didn't know the beekeeper was ready with the insecticide.

He didn't like the taste of the honey.

Someplace the stockholders were home all nestled snug in their beds and the little room was sprinkled with the men carrying the briefcases and folders of efficiency reports. The chair was held by the guy with the scar on his skull who had to kill me and he kept looking down the long table at me with a benign expression I couldn't quite comprehend, but he 'had the money to buy the kill if Arnold Bell missed, and even if it never happened, to pay for destruction piece by piece.

The Farnsworth Aviation report was brief. Barrin couldn't handle its projected output, but certain McMillan plants could.

And the raid was on.

Until the recess when the Farnsworth vice-president asked me over a cup of coffee if I had full title to a certain piece of arid desert land and I told him I did . . . acres and acres of it. In fact, quite a few square sections of the damn snake-infested place where the tourists took photographs.

Would I sell?

Conditionally, yes.

Leyland Hunter liked to have had a shit hemorrhage.

The picture of the old man was smiling more broadly now. I was taking the big run prior to leaping the chasm and he was waiting for me to fall in because I didn't quite get up enough speed. All the dirty slob wanted was for me to hit the side and carom down into total disaster knowing I almost made it. And almost isn't enough.

Pathos didn't become the old lawyer. Sympathy wasn't his bag at all, even when it came to me. He could purse his lips and remember the two broads in bed and even old Dubro, but legal sympathy he couldn't afford. He shook his head politely, took a bite of his tuna fish salad and said, "It isn't enough to save Barrin, Dog."

"What do they need?"

"A miracle," he suggested.

"Money won't do it?"

"Didn't a certain Roland Holland tell you the pros and cons of the great fiscal situation?"

"Somewhat, Mighty Hunter, but I'm no mathematician. Numbers come hard to me."

"Only your dick comes hard to you."

"Save the dirty talk for the dolls."

"Your land sale can keep Barrin alive for a month, and that's only because the public spotlight is on the scene. The minute it's off . . . good-bye."

"You sound depressed," I said.

"Naturally. I lived through an era. No, an epoch. I hate to see it destroyed. You opened the Pandora's box and let them all take a peek. They went for the bait and now the world collapses around them." He paused, looked at me intently, then asked, "How much are you worth in cash?"

"A few million left."

"Forget it, unless you feel like playing Santa Claus in a town of unbelieving kids. In one day they're all going to know and go home to broken dreams. I told you the worst thing to do was come back."

"Horseshit."

"You've lost, Dog." The way he said it was adamant.

This time I had to fake it. "Bullshit."

"No matter what animal drops it, the stuff is still feces," he told me. "I'll never know why you did it."

"All I wanted was to come home."

"You see what happened when you did?"

"Shit."

"What happened to the animals?"

"Look behind you."

Bennie Sachs hitched his gun belt up, nodded and took a seat beside my lawyer, but he didn't bother to even look at him. "We traced the car."

"I could have told you it was mine," I said.

"Plastics."

"Uh-huh. On the exhaust pipe. Heat sensor."

"Pretty smart, aren't you?"

"Right, friend."

"I had a call from New York."

"To be expected."

"I don't like you, Mr. Kelly."

"And I didn't ask for any admiration, either. What's your problem now?"

"Certain McMillan personnel are in town."

"Good for them."

"They're guards in his other plant. They seem to have a project in mind."

"Why haven't they hit me then? I haven't been hiding."

"That's what I can't figure out. Yet. But I will."

"Very nice, Officer. Just remember that you're here to protect your constituency."

"Go piss up a stick, Mr. Kelly."

I said, "I tried that once, but it all ran down on my hand."

When he left, Leyland said, "I didn't get that."

"I didn't either," I said. "Let's go back to the meeting. The raid ought to be about over."

The legal language sounded like a papal encyclical and it all boiled down to one thing. Cross McMillan owned Barrin Industries and Cross McMillan was committed to destroying Barrin Industries and there was no possible hope of keeping Barrin or Linton alive. The current contracts would be honored, but executed in other factories, leaving Barrin a shell without even a hermit crab to take occupancy.

Inside the building the machines were humming and the operators were smiling, but the crunch was on the way and the lunch buckets and thermos bottles would be just another nostalgic memory of days that almost were. How many times could a guy say *"shit!"* . . . so that it was an expletive like saying something when you bashed your finger with a hammer?

Screw the money. They all had their social security, their guaranteed pension, and if the government kept up its com-lib policies, they could get even more, except these weren't the ones to ask for it.

All they had was a hope and I smashed it.

There sure would be a lot of people at my funeral.

Everyone would be laughing.

I lit a cigarette and lounged back against the wall until he came out and when I saw him I said, "Hello, Cross. I hear you want to kill me."

He stopped, told the two with him to go on and pulled a cigar from his pocket, accepting my light. When he blew the smoke away he said, "Your semantics is lousy, Dog. I merely said I was going to have you killed."

"No guts, Cross?"

"Plenty, nithead, but why should I pay the big bill when I could have it done for me."

"Your tense stinks, if you want to play semantics. The shooters should be here now. Have trouble recruiting them?"

Cross smiled and I felt myself stiffen up. If they have to smile, I don't want any friendly overtones in the way a mouth twists because it means your back isn't clear like you thought it was and you made the biggest mistake of all. I had my hand on the .45 without taking it out of my jacket and nothing happened except McMillan smiled again and gave me a small pathetic look. "Come on outside," he said.

I let him get way ahead of me, and when the entrance was clear I followed him out and stood there in the big doorways of Barrin Industries with the man who had just destroyed it, looking out at all the smiling faces who thought the world had come home to roost and they had the lunch pails to collect the eggs in and I knew what I felt like . . . the stuff you put five pounds of in a two pound bag.

"I called them off," Cross said.

Hell, I didn't even pay any attention to him. I heard words and not intent. I took a drag on my butt, flipped it out into the rain and looked right past him when I asked, "Who?"

"The ones that were going to kill you."

"Balls."

"Got a cigarette?"

I shook one out of my pack, lit it for him and stepped back. His cigar was still smoldering on the step.

"They could have done it, you know," he stated.

"Maybe."

"I could pay for a lot of them."

"They'd get tired after a while. Expecially after I knocked off their gold mine."

"Not quite, Dog."

"Then let them go." I blew a stream of smoke in his face and he didn't even blink.

"I like to return favors, my canine compatriot."

"Talk sense."

"You get your life . . . because you gave me a wife."

"Buddy, you ain't no Ogden Nash. Stop rhyming."

He smiled again. His teeth showed too and his head flushed a little so I saw the scar across the bald spot where I had creamed him with the brick. But that was years ago and all I was interested in was the smile. "You'll live, Dog. But that's all. Absolutely all. You gave me back something I wanted all my fucking life . . . a wife I loved who could love me sexually. You knew she was frigid, didn't you?"

I couldn't figure where the hell he was driving in this weather. "I thought everybody knew it," I said. All I wanted was to put a permanent crease in his head and he didn't know how close he was coming to getting one.

"So they did," Cross smiled. He took another puff on the cigarette and reached in his pocket. He took out a fat manilla envelope folded carelessly in four sections and handed it to me. "Sheila loves me, Dog. I finally got really laid for the first time. Laid. Hell, that's not even the term. I got everything out of her I ever wanted and it took you to shake her out of whatever the hell was wrong with her." He sucked on the cigarette again and let it fall at his feet. "Care to tell me what it was?"

"No."

I wished all the guys standing out there in the rain would get the hell home.

"How many times did she go down on you, Dog?"

"Not too many."

Make your play, stupid. I haven't got time for games. It's getting dark.

"Fuck her a lot?"

"Enough to round out the evening."

"Was she good?"

294

"I had better. She was extremely prolific. Quite a comer."
Cross nodded.

He was very close to being shot and he still stood there watching the day grow darker and I couldn't see anybody around who could put me down. I was buried in the deep shadows with one hand on an army-style .45 with a round in the chamber, the hammer cocked and a clip in the handle. Two more full clips were in my pocket and it was going to be a ball when it started. Only nothing wanted to start.

"Sheila finally loved me, you prick. You gave her to me. She always loved me, now she loves me all the way." The rain suddenly came down in a slashing stream, driving into our faces and neither one of us could care less. "Funny," he continued, "having you do it. The doctors couldn't. The headshrinks couldn't. Nobody could. Then you came along and sexed the hell out of my wife and you did it. You gave me the thing I was never able to buy."

I just looked at him.

"Pretty silly, isn't it, but you damn well knew what you were doing, you bastard."

"Don't die for wrong words, Cross."

"Shut up, you silly bastard. I'm not afraid of you. Open that fucking envelope."

I unfolded the manila packet and thumbed the top back.

"You own all of Barrin, my dick-happy neighbor. My fucking almost-shareholder. I give you a worthless pile of brick, a damn pack of old men trying to extrude aluminum, a house full of horse's ass relatives, some contracts already assigned to my other companies, a dead city . . . and your life."

I threw my cigarette away and put the folder in my pocket. "Maybe I will bust your balls, friend."

"Don't try." Cross said. "You're in the shadows, but there are two of mine out there waiting too. They'll kill you before or after. Your choice."

Hell, I wasn't even worried about them. I let my hand fall away from my jacket. It was starting to get dark.

Cross McMillan stepped back into the light and looked at the big old-fashioned clock in the tower above him, then glanced back to me and smiled. I owned the biggest pile of garbage in the world because he owned all the access roads and the garbage pile could produce nothing. They were in Grand Sita drunk and hurting, but tomorrow they'd be sober and reconstructed while the living things came out of the garbage pile to devour me for having resurrected it to start with and the worst thing of all would be having to face the faces, the sad, deadened faces that had all the hope in the world there just a few days ago.

The voice behind me said, "You see, Dog, it doesn't always work out, does it?"

I looked at Sharon, but she still had those deadly eyes that said if she couldn't kill me, she'd be glad when somebody else did and I automatically reached out my hand and automatically she took it. My fingers ran around hers. She had taken off the ring that used to turn her finger green.

"He's dead," she said.

"Aren't we all?"

"Yes, we are, Dog."

The guy who walked in the light kept waving for those behind him to step on up and when I saw his face I said, "Hello, Stanley."

Stanley Cramer. From way back. There were four more with him.

"Mr. Kelly." He nodded toward Sharon. "Ma'am."

"Who's going to tell them, Stanley?" I asked him.

"Mr. Kelly . . . we all know. Sort of . . well, hell, kid, we've been back and forth before you was born, y'know?"

"Sure."

One by one they all stepped into the light so I could see their faces. Old men, but grinning old men and there was still youth there that read like the old motto, *DON'T TREAD ON ME!*, youth that wasn't fighting youth, but the youth of knowledge written into the crazy warped smiles and Stanley Cramer, elected the spokesman, said, "We kind of figured what you were looking for. Your cousins couldn't find it, but they weren't even sure it ever existed. We thought that package Jason gave old Pat was just a gag until you started the shakedown and we started thinking."

He held out a box big enough to put a pair of shoes in. "The papers are all in there. They'll tell you how it works. It ought to keep Barrin going a long, long time."

"What will, Stanley?"

There was a quiet murmur of laughter and he held out a shiny little ball about an inch around. It gleamed metallically in the dull light, a bluish silver with little rays of refracted yellow bouncing from it. Cramer laughed again and took his hand away.

The ball stayed right there.

He barely tipped it with his fingers and it came drifting toward me.

"The antigravity device," he explained. "Now we're in clover."

Someone farted.

It was Cross McMillan.

And then the old cypress pillar chipped right out between my head and Sharon's, leaving a tiny .22-sized hole in the wood so close it could have gotten either one of us an inch in either direction and nobody noticed but Sharon and me and I pulled her back inside leaving the chuckles of all the winners standing there in the rain and all I could think of was that word to say again.

XXV

"Dog."

She wasn't asking my name. She wasn't asking an explanation. She was just saying it. I pulled the overhead lights out and pushed her into the office where I could see the small crowd milling in the rain, still laughing, going toward their cars.

That shot didn't miss. That shot was as deliberate as hell.

Get rid of the crowd scene and come on in, it said. Arnold Bell is here to claim his inheritance. The killer of killers. Don't make me do it the easy way because they all have to know it was face to face and you were not nearly as good as I am. The price goes up, Dog. I get more for my kills than you ever did for yours. You can't lose me, you can't even find me. I pick the time and the place and maybe to make the job even more exciting, I take the little blonde along with you . . . and what would be better than telling the story of how you both went down pissing your pants and hurting like a son of a bitch with Arnold Bell laughing and able to spend his money at last. They'll pay me anywhere, even in Madrid. In Marseilles. In Istanbul. In Paris. Shit, they'll pay me anywhere, even in Moscow because you're out and I'm in. Pussycat, kiss the tiger's ass.

"Bend over, Tiger, the pussycat has big teeth."

"Dog . . . what did you say?"

"Nothing."

Her eyes had changed again. "Dog . . ."

"Look . . ."

"No. Please . . . Dog."

They were all gone outside and I snapped out the flood-

298

lights that illuminated the area. Someplace in the far reaches of the building a motor was humming.

"Was it true about Sheila?"

One of the slats in the Venetian blinds was crooked and I straightened it out. "Yes."

"Was she . . . good?"

"They're all good."

"You didn't . . ."

"I don't fuck broads because I love them, kitten. Shut up."

"They told me about . . . the ball. Before they showed it to you."

I looked at her. I was starting to burn now.

"I told them not to give it to you," she said.

"Thanks."

"Stanley laughed at me. He said I was only a . . . a . . . woman."

Hell, I had to laugh at that one. "You sure are, doll."

"A little while ago I wanted to see you dead."

"Somebody should have stepped on my mother's egg. Knock it off, kid."

"What are you going to do?"

"Get the hell out of here is what."

"I'm going with you."

The dark was so nice. It didn't show what I thought or felt and I could let my voice seep through my teeth with that same old whispery rasp that meant the game was in the last quarter and the outs still had a few minutes to beat the ins, only not many and if anybody got in the way they didn't have any chance at all.

"No dice, my lovely."

"Up your ass with a meat hook, man."

"What kind of language is that from a lady?"

"I'm no fucking lady, Dog. All I am is your broad."

I could see the whiteness of her hands in the darkness. "Don't lay it on me because your guy is dead. That's what you get for sending a fiancé to war, lady."

"How about that?"

"You're getting out."

The damn laugh she let out was soft and nasty and I felt her hand wrap around my arm and the heat from her body was a living, scented thing that spelled booby trap all the way and I still couldn't push her away because it didn't matter how I died anyway anymore.

"Where you go, I go," she said.

"I'll take you someplace you'll wish you hadn't gone to," I told her.

299

"Take me."

I ran my hand over her face, then down across her breasts and let it nestle in the beautiful V between her thighs. I could feel the furry outline under her clothes, the woman crevice and nearly the moist heat before I let my hand drift back up to her face again. "I will when I get there," I said.

We both liked the night, but this time it was on my side because I was letting myself be the hunted. I knew where I was and where I was going. The hunter didn't. He had to think, plot and plan, then act accordingly, knowing the trap might be there. Ever wary. Ever deadly. He knew all the tricks too. He could find me, he could find my car. He could put a bullet next to my temple to say he was waiting, always knowing the chance he was taking and somebody started laughing very low and I damn near looked to see who it was until I remembered it was me.

When *does* the fox outfox the fox?

She had parked her car in the main lot and some of the others were pulling out when I shoved her into the Ford and got behind the wheel. I pushed her down, slumped in the seat and got out into traffic and made the circuit behind the others who were all going to Tod's, and while I was making like I was looking for a parking place, backed into a driveway, turned around and swung back against traffic. I cut right into a deserted section, made a complete orbit, picked up the highway, headed toward New York, took the first intersection off and drove back into Linton on the old road.

It took a good hour and a half, but I finally found the right dirt road and turned the car into the area I was looking for and left the headlights on long enough for Sharon to see what I had to show her.

Leyland Hunter had hired a good crew. They had done a good job. Her old house was standing there sparkling white in the beam of my headlights with her old bicycle reconditioned and newly painted, leaning against the railing on the porch. A white envelope was tucked into the screen door and I knew what it was. I got out, walked around the car, opened the door and eased her off the seat.

She knew too, but she really wasn't sure until she opened the envelope and saw the key attached to the deed.

"Yours, little bleachie."

"Dog . . ." I could barely hear her.

"All reconditioned. Like when you left it."

"Why?"

300

"At least one of us has to have something to show for it all."

She tried to say something, but the tears stopped her. She put the key in the lock and turned the knob. The door opened silently. When she reached for the light switch it flicked on and I heard her breath catch in her throat.

"I guess the counselor asked questions," I said.

There was nothing pretentious about it. It was only an old-fashioned house so warm and comfortable you thought you could smell pies in the oven and hear kid voices from the yard while the older ones were slapping the cards down on the table with the women serving beer from pitchers and trading gossip in the kitchen. No place for women lib types at all. The paint smell still was there and the new carpet feel was underfoot and it was ready to be lived in if anybody wanted to live with all the nostalgia of a long time ago.

"It's lovely, Dog."

"You were lucky, honey. I wish I had had one like it."

"But you had the big house on the hill."

"Not me. I was a bastard."

"Is . . . upstairs . . . ?"

I shrugged. "Go look."

We went up the blue-carpeted stairs and when she opened the doors of each room she smiled and then she came to her own room. Where they had done their work only too well. Her eyes were wet and her mouth was wet and I had to leave her right then.

Outside it was totally dark and the target had to leave the congested area.

Very slowly, she turned around, looked at me a very long time and slid her jacket off. Just as slowly she unbuttoned her blouse and let it fall in a heap on the floor. She wasn't wearing a brassiere at all and her breasts were full, pouting, and the tips of them perked up into delicious little knots.

"No, honey," I said, and she hooked her fingers in her skirt so that it fell off too and all she had on was the little pair of bikini pants that lasted another few seconds before she was nakedly unashamed in front of me, her virginal pussy smiling with parted lips because it didn't know any better, the brown hair in its delicious isosceles making fun of the blonde above and she lay down on her own bed where she slept as a child, legs spread in total invitation, but looking at her hands a minute before asking the question.

"Who are you, Dog?"

"You know me."

301

"Nobody knows you, Dog. Not now. Maybe I know more than you think I do, but I want to hear you say it yourself."

"Why? You wouldn't believe me anyway."

"Take off your clothes."

"No."

"I want to see your dick."

"Damn it, stop that!"

"Let me see your dick." Her legs twitched and she smiled at me. My fingers started reaching for buttons and zippers.

"Damn it to hell . . ."

"Dog . . . don't fret. I couldn't help myself either."

My shirt and pants were gone and I had a hard-on I didn't deserve and she was lying there naked in the light with one hand stroking her belly down into the fuzz and I heard my ears ring and felt my stomach tighten and went over next to her where she could reach up and feel me.

"Sharon . . ."

She wet one finger and ran it between her legs. "Who are you, Dog?"

"Listen . . ."

"Start from the war. Tell me about Roland Holland."

I reached down past my fucking erection and picked up the .45 where I had dropped it and tossed it on the bed beside the pillow. It was an outlandish situation and I had to think and that was all I could do.

"Roland Holland," she insisted.

"A business genius," I said. "I gave him my savings and terminal leave pay to start up a company. I took out ten percent. He is legitimate."

She was still looking at one hand until she decided she wasn't wet enough, so touched her fingertip to her lips. "Ten percent of many millions is many millions."

"Smart, baby, now drop dead because I'm going to get dressed."

She squirmed around and pointed it right at me. "You said you were going to take me."

"Sharon . . ."

"That man in New York . . . Vince Tobano. He's a policeman."

"Damn it to hell, will you . . ."

"All you have to do is tell me. You turned me inside out to make me hate you. Why not just tell me?"

I wished my damn cock would go limp. The thing didn't have any kind of conscience at all. I picked up my pants, got a cigarette out of my pocket and lit it. Then sat on the end of the bed, my back toward her.

"They recruited me," I said.

"Who did?"

"The government. My cover was perfect. I was already rich. They made me a black marketeer, I got into the big stuff and when everything went bust it was never my fault but some sloppy operation on the other end. I was always in the rackets. Only the agency and a couple of individuals knew I was on the other side."

"In New York . . ."

"Doll, Vince Tobano is the straightest cop you ever met. The guy I shook the shit out of was Chet Linden who heads up the big D.C. splash. He was all bombed out thinking I'd blow the picture and when I handed them that casket I damn near browned out trying to keep the laugh in. Don't you know old Vince'll get a promotion out of the deal and that idiot Chet will get his ass eaten out by the old man in the Pentagon for letting it go that far? Hell, Chet wouldn't dare let his guys lay a gun on me or Vince'll take him apart. Or I might get teed off, which could even be worse. The fucking syndicate lost their millions in heroin, the mighty have tumbled, the Establishment is sucking their thumbs waiting to see how they can get back at us, knowing they never can, and . . ."

I looked down at my pants on the floor and she followed my eyes. One pocket where I had put the strange metallic ball was hanging up in the air.

"And I'd like to fuck you," I said.

"Why?"

"Because I love you."

"Then why haven't you?"

"You've been engaged. Now you said the guy was dead."

"Did you really have a moral obligation not to fuck me?"

"I prefer to think so."

"Sucker," she said.

I turned around and looked at her, one hand resting very lightly on her throat. "Don't say that."

"Tod almost told you."

"What?"

"There was a little girl who was ten years old when you went into the army and the only one who walked you to the railroad station. You said when you came back you'd marry her and you stopped in the dime store and bought her a green ring. She wore it for all the years until she thought the man she was waiting for was dead." She smiled,

303

dipped down into the pocket of her blouse and took the silly little ring out and put it back on her finger. "It must be awful having to wait for a virgin this long. I hope the going isn't too tough."

It was all too fast, too ridiculous and too true. It came back with the effect of a tidal wave, sweeping over me, washing out the old and planting the new. She was all beautiful and slippery and blonde and brunette at once with those crazy curving hills and sloped, wet banks like a rained-on race course that heaved and undulated with tiny muscular spasms aching to be relieved in a gigantic orgasm and I was there in her little room where she slept as a girl, in a room something like where my pop slept with my mother and now it was going to be all right, the factory, the old men, Linton, the coming home . . . it was going to be all right because they had given me that little ball of metal that would turn the world upside down.

And as I was rolling onto her I heard the voice say, "How pretty. How pretty."

But he shouldn't have said it the second time, enjoying the scene of naked flesh, part soft and part hard, wondering where to put the bullet, because wherever a .45 hits you it tears one hell of a hole and the .45 was right next to my hand and the first shot took his arm off and the second left no memory of Arnold Bell's face in anybody's mind because he had no face left to remember. His skin and bones were indented on the wall behind the headless body and tomorrow I'd have to get another crew out here to clean up and patch the hole and if I were lucky, the quarts of blood wouldn't flow through the cracks in the floor and ruin the ceiling downstairs.

"Now?" I asked her.

The two shots were still reverberating in her ears. She looked at the mess by the door and didn't get sick at all. She didn't hear me, but she knew what I said.

Sharon smiled and turned the old brass ring around so it looked like a cheap wedding band. "Shut up and fuck me," she said, "like a dog."